I0740580

Martha Walker Freer

The Married Life of Anne of Austria, Queen of France, Mother of Louis XIV.,

and Don Sebastian, King of Portugal. Historical Studies. Vol. 1

Martha Walker Freer

The Married Life of Anne of Austria, Queen of France, Mother of Louis XIV.,
and Don Sebastian, King of Portugal. Historical Studies. Vol. 1

ISBN/EAN: 9783337310141

Printed in Europe, USA, Canada, Australia, Japan

Cover: Foto ©Raphael Reischuk / pixelio.de

More available books at **www.hansebooks.com**

THE

MARRIED LIFE

OF

ANNE OF AUSTRIA,

QUEEN OF FRANCE, MOTHER OF LOUIS XIV.

AND

DON SEBASTIAN, KING OF PORTUGAL.

Historical Studies.

FROM NUMEROUS UNPUBLISHED SOURCES,

INCLUDING MS. DOCUMENTS IN THE BIBLIOTHÈQUE IMPÉRIALE, AND
THE ARCHIVES OF SPAIN AND PORTUGAL.

BY

MARTHA WALKER FREER,

Author of "The Life of Marguérite d'Angoulême, Queen of Navarre;" "The Life of
Jeanne d'Albret;" "The Court and Times of Henry III., King of France and
Poland;" "The Life of Henri Quatre," &c., &c.

IN TWO VOLUMES.—VOL. I.

SECOND EDITION.

LONDON:
TINSLEY BROTHERS, 18, CATHERINE ST., STRAND.
1865.

CONTENTS OF VOL. I.

MARRIED LIFE OF ANNE OF AUSTRIA.

CHAPTER I.

1612—1617.

ANNE OF AUSTRIA AND LOUIS XIII.

On the 18th of March, 1612, proclamation was made throughout Paris, of the betrothal of Louis XIII., by the grace of God King of France and Navarre, with the Infanta Marie Anne Mauricette, daughter of Philip III. King of Spain, and of Marguerite of Austria; also of Madame Elizabeth, eldest daughter of Henri Quatre and Marie de' Medici, sister of Louis XIII., with Don Philip Prince of the Asturias, eldest son of the Catholic King.

The year 1612, from the splendid festivities which ensued, was termed L'Année des Magnificences.

In celebration of the auspicious event of the marriages, a carousal was holden in the Place Royale during the first week in April; which was followed by a succession of brilliant fêtes, balls and banquet-ings at the Louvre, at Fontainebleau, and at St. Germain. The Spanish Ambassador, Duque de Pastraña, son of Ruy Gomez de Silva Prince of Eboly, the famous favourite of Philip II. late King of Spain, arrived in state at the Louvre, and saluted the youthful bride elect of the Prince of the Asturias; and throughout the festivities he gave her the honours due to the consort of the heir of Spain.* The Duke de Mayenne Charles de Lorraine Guise, was at the same time despatched to the court of Madrid, to compliment the young Infanta in the name of his master Louis XIII.; and to express the earnest desire of his Majesty to hasten her arrival in his realm.

By the signature of these marriage contracts, which bound the realms of France and Spain by double matrimonial alliance, the Regent Marie de' Medici and her reactionary faction reversed the policy of Henri Quatre; and pardoned the Spanish cabinet the calamities inflicted on the realm by the wars of the Holy League; and the perfidious intrigues and machinations which had finally compassed the assassination of a hero so dear to France.

In 1609 similar overtures for the marriage of the children of France and Spain had been summarily

---

* MS. Bibl. Imp. Colbert 500, vol. 110, p. 32. Mém. de Wicquefort. t. 1. p. 1.

rejected by Henri IV. Indeed, Henry testified an invincible aversion for such alliance; "as being a step impolitic, and likely totally to alienate the crowns; for, as the grandeur of France is the humiliation of Spain, no concord is possible. France can never forgive the woes, and political calamities inflicted during the past half century by the government of Spain."* The allies towards whom Henry inclined were the King of England, the German Protestant Princes, and the Dutch Republic. The secret aim of his policy was to humble the haughty princes of Hapsburg; to break the Spanish yoke from the neck of Europe; to curtail the dominions of Austria, by exciting to revolt and freedom her tributary kingdoms of Hungary and Bohemia; and by maintaining the rights of the Electors of the Germanic Empire, to choose and proclaim their Imperial Chief. Marie de' Medici, however, brought up in abject veneration for the Spanish monarchy; and actuated by intense distrust of the ministers and friends of her deceased husband, adopted, on her accession to the regency, a totally different policy. The vast preparations and edicts of Henri IV. for the campaign which his death interrupted, were cancelled. The alliance of

---

* Histoire de la Mère et du Fils, t. 1. This history was written by the Cardinal de Richelieu, and published during the cardinal's lifetime, under the name of Eudes de Mezeray, who was historiographer to the king.

England was for the moment abandoned; Sully was disgraced; Concini was created Marquis d'Ancre, and elevated to a place in the council; while the Holy See received assurances of the devotion of the Queen, and of her submission to the counsels, and interest of his Holiness. These measures were followed by civil disaffection: the Prince de Condé, the Duke de Bouillon, the Constable de Montmorency, and the Duke de Nevers, retired from court and intrenched themselves within their respective governments. "France," said they, "is now governed in Turkish fashion by that scoundrel and traitor the Florentine Concini; who sells by auction the honours of the realm, and dares to set his plebeian foot on the necks of the chivalrous captains of Henri Quatre." Duplessis Mornay, " the pope of the Calvinists," deemed this an opportunity not to be neglected: the Huguenot fortresses therefore soon bristled with arms; and Mornay, exulting already in the hope of success, defied the menaces of the Regent; and the more conciliatory overtures of his old adversary the secretary of state, Villeroy. The government of Queen Marie thus became isolated, and found support only from the Duke d'Epernon,* from Soissons, and other antagonists of

* Jean Louis Nogaret de la Valette, Duc d'Epernon, born in 1554. The Duke, a cadet of La Valette, was raised to his dignities by King Henri III., whose favourite he became. He married Marguerite de Foix Candale, a princess allied to the blood royal. The Duke d'Epernon

the late minister Sully; who, for power at court, were content to connive at the assumptions of Concini. At issue with the princes of the blood, and the more potent of the great vassals of the crown; with the Huguenots of the realm; and with the Protestant princes of Europe—the only policy which the Regent and her clique could oppose to combinations so hostile, was alliance offensive and defensive with Spain. The Grand-Duke of Tuscany,* uncle of the Queen, undertook to make the first overtures to obtain the renewal of the ancient alliance of the crowns. The Duke of Lerma,† prime minister of Philip III., graciously responded to the advance; and, a few months later, the double alliance between the children of France and Spain was proposed and accepted.

The Infanta Marie Anne Mauricette was born in the Escorial on the 22nd of September, 1601, five days before her future consort, Louis XIII. The Condésa de Altamira was her governess, and had trained her in habits of piety, and in courtly devoirs. Anne was a fair and bonny child, the darling of

died in 1646, at the age of 88. "Tout chez lui était splendeur et faste."

* Ferdinand 1st, Cardinal, Grand-Duke of Tuscany. His consort was Christine de Lorraine, daughter of Duke Charles III. of Lorraine, and of Claude de France, daughter of Henri II. and Catherine de' Medici.

† Don Francisco Rojos de Sandoval, Duke of Lerma, minister and favourite of Philip III., King of Spain.

the ceremonious court of Madrid, and of her father and her gentle mother, Marguerite.* She seems never to have been consigned to the dreary monotony of a royal nursery establishment, but appears to have always followed the queen her mother. At the masques and court revels, the dainty little Infanta often appeared *en scène*, drawn by two diminutive ponies in a golden car; or upborne, by tiny nymphs of her own age, in a mimic conch-shell. Anne early lost her virtuous mother, who died at Valladolid, after giving birth to a third daughter, the infanta Marguerite—a fatal event, preceded, as it was said, by the booming of the mystic Bell of Villela,† which was heard throughout the peninsula. Anne was eleven years old when she was betrothed to Louis XIII., and thus became the heroine of the splendid ambassage of the Duke de Mayenne. The Duke was received with enthusiasm by the Spanish court; which, perhaps, remembered that his father, and his uncle Henri, Duke de Guise, had proved themselves to be better subjects of Spain, than loyal to their own princes. On the 17th of July, 1612, Mayenne was presented to Philip III. by the Duke d'Uzéda. His Majesty, by a great stretch of con-

---

* Marguerite of Austria, daughter of Charles, Archduke of Grätzen, and niece of the Emperor Maximilian II.

† See History of Don Sebastian, King of Portugal, chap. 3.

descension, embraced the ambassador cordially, and presented to him the Prince of Asturias, who stood at his right, as the future husband of Madame Isabel of France. The marriage contract, which had been negotiated in Paris, was signed on the 22nd day of August, after final revision by the Spanish privy council. Philip gave his daughter a dowry of 500,000 gold crowns, with many sumptuous jewels. The money was to be paid to the representative of his Christian Majesty, on the day previous to the celebration of the marriage. In case the most serene Infanta became a widow, it was stipulated that she was to return to Spain in possession of her dowry, jewels, and wardrobe. The dower given by Louis XIII. was similar to that assigned from time immemorial to the queens-consort of France, and consisted of rich lands in Touraine and Le Pays Chartrain; the King also made gift absolutely to his future consort of all the jewels, and precious gauds and furniture, which she might accumulate during their union.* The pecuniary settlements being thus made to the satisfaction of King Philip, the Infanta was saluted, and treated as Queen of France; "a dignity which her Highness accepts with marvellous dignity and gravity." When Mayenne took leave of

---

* Leonard, Contrats et Traités de Paix, etc. MS. Archives de Simancas K. 22, quoted by Capefigue, Vie d'Anne d'Autriche.

her little Majesty, he requested that she would send some message to the King, her consort. " Give his Majesty assurance," promptly replied Doña Aña, " that I am very impatient to be with him." " Oh, Madame ! " interposed the Condésa de Altamira, " what will the King of France think when he is informed by M. le Duc that you are in such a hurry to be married ? Madame, I entreat you show more maidenly reserve ! " " Have you not always taught me to speak the truth, Madame ? I have spoken, and shall not retract," retorted the young Queen, pettishly.* She then gave the ambassador her hand to kiss, slowly tendering it, as the Duke believed, that he might observe and report its symmetry and delicate hue.

Three months previously, on the same day of the month, Pastraña had saluted Elizabeth, the child-bride of the Prince of Asturias, in the Louvre. Madame Elizabeth wore a surcoat and robe of carnation-coloured satin, a cross of diamonds, and a chain of pearls. " M. l'Ambassadeur," said she, as Pastraña bowed before her, " I thank the King your master for the honour which he has conferred upon me in giving me his favour; and I receive gladly from M. le Prince assurances of his affection. I

* Dreux du Radier, Vie d'Anne d'Autriche.

trust to render myself worthy of both the one and the other, as I ought."*

The bridegroom elect of Doña Aña, meantime, Louis, son of the great Henry, spent a wearisome youth in the Louvre, with few diversions and joys. The unhappy and premature death of Henri IV. not only exercised a fatal influence over the political destinies of France, but deprived his young son of judicious, and princely training. The miserable jealousies of the favourites and advisers of Marie de' Medici likewise, had debarred the boy-king of the example, and the counsels of his father's tried and wise friends. Instead of being inured to arms, and trained in gallant accomplishments, and taught the self-denial, and magnanimity becoming his kingly station, the unfortunate Louis was confined to a corner of the Louvre, the object at one time of his mother's indulgent weakness; at others, the victim of her caprice and passion. The young king was of a reserved and suspicious temper, sensitive to the slightest ridicule or neglect, having a memory retentive of petty affronts. His household was not selected with a view to correct the nervous shyness, and overbearing pride of his character. The fears of the Queen, and the ignoble precaution of her ser-

* Godefroy, L'Ordre et Cérémonies observées au Mariage de Philip IV. (then Prince of the Asturias) avec Madame Elizabeth, fille de Henri le Grand—Grand Cérémonial de France, pp. 70, et seq.

vants the marquis d'Ancre and his wife, induced her Majesty to choose young companions for her son of a class inferior to the usual *entourage* of princes. Such noble names as Rohan, Guise, Montmorency, Bouillon, and La Rochefoucault, were never heard amongst the playmates of Louis XIII. His chief friends were the three brothers de Luynes,* sons of a gentleman of Provence, of the town of Mornas; whose future marvellous fortunes rank amongst the most notable instances on record of dignities conferred by royal caprice. Louis nevertheless, showed aptitude for many boyish pastimes : he played well at tennis; showed keen relish for the pleasures of the chase, which, unfortunately, he was allowed only to indulge by hunting rabbits in the garden of the Tuileries. He passionately loved music, and learned to play on the spinet and guitar. He also amused himself by turning ivory, by drawing and colouring little pictures, and by snaring singing-birds. His Majesty's physician, Jean Hérouard, who was constantly in waiting in the royal apartment, kept a curious diary of the doings and sayings, and employ-

---

* The three brothers bore the names of Luynes, Brantès, and Cadenet. The eldest, Charles d'Albert de Luynes, was born in 1578. His godfather was Henri Quatre (Mercure de France, t. v.), which fact at once contradicts the stories current at court of the plebeian origin of the brothers. He was created Duke de Luynes and Constable of France; Brantès was created Duke de Luxembourg, on his marriage with the daughter of the Prince de Tingry ; Cadenet was created Duke de Chaulnes, on his marriage with the daughter and heiress of the Vidame d'Amiens, M. de Péquigny.

ments of his royal master; so minute as to become ludicrous, when the learned doctor condescended to chronicle the names of the viands served daily on the royal table; and the number of times his Majesty coughed and sneezed during the twenty-four hours! The boyhood of Louis XIII., however, is unveiled by these daily jottings; and the mystery solved, why the son of Henri IV. grew up to become the most timid, miserable, suspicious, and self-distrusting monarch who ever filled a throne, though possessing capacity, and some appreciation for things good, noble, and true.   Hérouard writes : *—

" *Monday, March* 10, 1611.— His Majesty this morning amused himself by composing doggrel verses, and gave some to make out to MM. de Termes, de Courtenvault, and de Montglât.   A young wild sow was fed in the royal kitchen by Bonnet, a water-carrier, who was killed by a fall.   The little sow lamented and fretted for her master, and at length refused to eat, and died of grief.   The King thereupon composed the following verse :—

> " Il y avait en ma cuisine
> Une petite marcassine
> Laquelle est morte de douleur
> D'avoir perdu son gouverneur ! "

* Journal du Roy Louis XIII., par M. Jehan Hérouard, son Premier Médecin.—MS. Bibl. Imp. Colbert, 2691.   6 vols. in fol.

" *Thursday, 20th.*—The King played at tennis; and then went to the room of Sieur de la Chapelle, his spinet-player.

" *March 28th, Good Friday.*—Heard a sermon at two o'clock; after dinner his Majesty entered his coach, and visited the Franciscan, and Feuillantine monasteries. He then went to the Tuileries, where he tasted a bunch of white grapes. He returned to the Louvre at a quarter to seven, and supped upon almond milk and milk gruel, eating the backs of two large soles. His Majesty said, 'I eat this fish because there is nothing else.'

" *June 4th.*—His Majesty dined at Ruel. At mid-day the King rode on horseback, and shot, with an arquebuse, a quantity of little birds. He then went to a joiner's, and made two little shrines of his own design, in which he suspended all the little birds.

" *November* 14th, *Friday.*—His Majesty commenced the day by study. As his lesson appeared to him long and difficult, he asked his preceptor, M. Fleurance, 'If I were to promise you a bishopric, pray would you shorten my lesson?' 'No, Sire.' Soon after M. de Bellegarde arrived. His Majesty gave him cordial welcome, and conducted him to the Queen.

" *November* 20th.—After supper his Majesty went to bed at nine o'clock. At eleven he suddenly rose on his knees, with eyes wide open, and, though asleep, called out loudly, ' Hé! jouez! jouez!' The day preceding he had been playing at billiards in the gallery of the Louvre, and afterwards at tennis.

" *December 22nd.*—His Majesty went to hunt * on the plain of St. Denis; he was suffering from tooth-ache, but would not confess it, for fear of losing his hunt. On his return his Majesty complained of ear-ache; and a plaster of ashes of palm-leaves, and vinegar was applied behind the ear. The inside of the mouth was fomented with a decoction of vinegar and rose-leaves, after which the pain subsided.

" *December 31st, Wednesday.*—The King confessed in the evening to le P. Cotton, his confessor and preacher in ordinary, in order to touch, on the Feast of the Circumcision, 330 sick in the great gallery of the Louvre."

The greater part of this Journal is still in manuscript. The zealous Hérouard continues, in similar fashion, to recite the smallest trivialities of the life

* " Le 8, Mercredi, 1614, le Roy pour la première fois va à la chasse. M. de Souvré aussi luy fait prendre une jupe de chasse fourrée de martes : la prend avec regret, disant que tout ceux qui le verront se moqueront de luy, qu'il est habillé en paysan. Il conteste jusqu'à une heure et demie ; enfin, il s'y résout et va voler le milan à la plaine de Grenelle, où il monte à cheval et prend le milan. Estant de retour, fait jeter le milan par la fenestre et luy donne la vie." . . . " Le 19, Dimanche, nourrit deux petits coqs, et pour les rendre courageux, leur donne du vin de clairet."

of his royal master, with a minuteness which defies transcription. The extract given, records some of the incidents of the daily life of Anne's royal bridegroom, the year before the solemnization of their nuptials.

This event took place in August of the following year, 1615. The courts of France and Spain put forth their utmost splendour to do honour to an occasion so august. The Duchess de Nevers Catherine de Lorraine, and the Duke de Guise, escorted Madame to Bordeaux, and from thence to St. Jean de Luz; where, on the banks of the Bidassoa, the brides were to meet the ambassadors appointed to attend, and present them to their future consorts. The King and the Queen Regent arrived at Bordeaux, and entered the city in a splendid barge, surrounded by a brilliant court, amidst the plaudits of the populace.* Their progress, however, had been dreary and perilous: the devastation of civil warfare had ruined the fertile south-western provinces; and the sight of the poverty-stricken inhabitants, and of their burned villages, was a sad and ominous spectacle for the eyes of the royal bridegroom. The King's progress was protected by the Marshal de Brissac and a division of artillery; for many strongholds of the Huguenots lay on the route between Paris and Bordeaux, and the

* Godefroy, Grand Cérém., t. 2, pp. 60-80.

joyous and brilliant cavaliers of Marie's court shrank from conflict with the rough bands of Saumur and La Rochelle, likely to oppose their advance. In the royal train were the Princesses de Condé * and Conty,† the Duchesses de Guise,‡ de Vendôme,§ and de Montbazon. Madame entered Bordeaux on the 17th of November; and their Majesties three days later, where they eagerly awaited the arrival of King Philip III. and his court at Fuentarabia.

About the beginning of November, 1615, King Philip, accompanied by his daughter, and by a swarm of courtiers, leisurely journeyed from Valladolid to Burgos, and took up his abode in the famed nunnery of Las Huelgas de Burgos. The marriage by proxy of King Louis and the Infanta was celebrated in the splendid cathedral of Burgos, on the 18th of the same month; the representative of his Christian Majesty being the Duke of Lerma. Two days before this solemnity, Anne made formal renunciation of her right of succession to the Spanish crown; and of the rich personalty and money of her deceased

* Charlotte Marguerite de Montmorency, daughter of Henri Constable de Montmorency.

† Louise Marguerite de Lorraine Guise, daughter of Henri Duc de Guise, slain at Blois, 1588.

‡ Henriette de Joyeuse, who had first espoused the Duke de Montpensier.

§ Françoise de Lorraine Mercœur. Her husband was the son of Henri IV. and Gabrielle d'Estrées.

mother, Queen Marguerite of Austria. "I, Doña Aña, Infanta of Spain, and, by the grace of God, Queen elect of France, being above the age of fifteen,—and therefore of competent years to understand the tenor and significance of the above articles—declare, that I hold myself content with the dowry assigned to me, which is larger than any other before given to an Infanta of Spain. To give greater weight to this my renunciation, I swear, with my right hand resting on the Holy Gospels contained in this missal by my side, to abide by the said renunciation; which I sign in the presence of my lord and father, and of my brothers, who have been pleased to assist at this solemnity." *

King Louis, meantime, despatched his favourite Luynes from Bordeaux to Burgos, to greet his consort, and to convey to her a letter.† The mission of this young cavalier first aroused the courtiers to the extraordinary favour with which he was regarded by the King. Luynes and his brothers Cadenet, and Brantés, were remarkable for their good looks and upright carriage; but they owed much of their *prestige* at court to their cool assurance, and their insensibility to the scornful

* MS. Archives de Simancas, A. No. 65, quoted by M. Capefigue.

† Tallemant, that cruel satirist, writes, " Le roi commença par son cocher Saint-Amour à témoigner de l'affection pour quelqu'un. Il voulut envoyer quelqu'un qui lui pût bien rapporter comme la princesse d'Espagne était faite. Il se servit pour cela du père de son cocher, comme si c'eut été pour voir des chevaux."—Hist. 79.

contempt with which they were often treated by the great lords of the court; and to the gibes current respecting their origin. Luynes bowed at the feet of Marie de' Medici, and of Concini, and humbly received their constant objurgations; while the King felt a grateful relief from restraint and shyness, in the society of his *parvenu* favourite. It was said at court, that at this period Luynes, Cadenet, and Brantés had only one court-habit amongst them; and that the Auvergnat brothers owed their favour to their skill in snaring magpies!* M. de Luynes nevertheless was welcomed at the proud Spanish court; he was caressed by King Philip, patronised by Lerma, and graciously received by his future royal mistress. Luynes presented the royal letter to her youthful Majesty enclosed in a portfolio of rose-coloured silk, embroidered in pearls with the ciphers L. and A. "Madame," wrote King Louis XIII., "it is not in my power, though my inclination prompts me, to receive you on your entry into my kingdom, to place in your hands my royal power, as I am inspired to do by the sincere affection which I bear you. I send to you, therefore, Luynes, one of my most trusted servants, to salute you in my name; and to assure you how eagerly you are here expected, and that I earnestly desire to tell you

Capefigue, Vie d'Anne d'Autriche.—MS. Simancas. B. 5.

so myself. I beg you, therefore, to receive with favour this said Luynes; and to believe all that he may say on behalf of your dearest friend and servant—LOUIS."

The young Queen smiled while perusing this note; destiny then doubtless appeared to her brilliant as fancy could suggest; and with child-like eagerness she dwelt on the pomps, the festivals, and the magnificences over which she had been selected to preside. Had the dark shadows which marred these splendours been even outlined in imagination, sad foreboding must have quenched her delight. The future, however, now appeared serene and halcyon. Anne therefore responded thus, in her own musical language, to the greeting so gallantly conveyed:—

"ANNE OF AUSTRIA TO LOUIS XIII.

"MONSEIGNEUR,—I have rejoiced much with Luynes on the good news which he has brought to me concerning the health of your Majesty, and the desire which you express to see me. I also wish myself there, where I can serve the Queen my mother, and yourself. Luynes has made me anxious to set out on my journey from the comforting assurances which he gives me. I kiss the hand of your Majesty, whom may God preserve, as I pray.—ANA." *

Capefigue, Vie d'Anne d'Autriche.—MS. Simancas, B. 5.

The Queen sent her lord a present of a superb rosary; also—what doubtless would be less welcome—a list of the ladies of her Spanish household, whom she wished might be permitted to continue their services in the Louvre. The Condésa de las Torres, Doña Luisa de Osorio, and Doña Marguerita de Cordova were the chief personages named on this list. Her confessor, Padre Francisco de Ribeyra, and her chaplain, Pedro de Castro, were likewise to form part of her Majesty's suite. Marie de' Medici acquiesced in these impolitic appointments. The King was thoughtless, and enjoyed his temporary emancipation from the monotony of the Louvre. Luynes and Concini were *parvenu* favourites—men who, at this period, being both uncertain of their position at court, would have retreated aghast at a proposal to thwart the wishes of the Catholic King.

Magnificent pavilions had been erected on the islet in the midst of the stream Bidassoa, for the repose of the two Princesses; and to enable them to receive a last finish to their elaborate toilettes before entering the state-barge which was to convey each to her newly-adopted country. The banks of the river were kept by squadrons of light horse, and by the royal body-guard, consisting of more than 500 men, under the command of the Marshal de Brissac. Companies of the King's gentlemen-at-arms, bearing their battle-axes, were stationed at intervals; while thousands of spectators gathered to witness the meeting of the courts. The scene was imposing and magnificent; and was surpassed only by the pompous reception given on the banks of the Bidassoa to Elizabeth de Valois, by her mother, Catherine de' Medici, and by her brother, Charles IX. Along the banks of the river, below the place of embarkation, magnificent pavilions and platforms rose, draped with white and yellow silk hangings, for the ladies of the courts of France and Spain not officially present at the ceremony. Anne quitted Burgos November the 20th, and after taking sorrowful leave of her father, commenced her journey towards Irun. She was attended by the Duquesa de Sessa, who had been especially appointed to present her to the ambassador of her royal husband Louis XIII., and to conduct the young Princess of France to Guada-laxara. In the suite of the young Queen were the Duque de Uzéda, son of the cardinal minister Lerma, the Dukes de Sessa, Maquéda, Infantado, the Count de Olivarez, and the Marquis de Montéléone, the newly appointed Spanish ambassador in Paris; besides a numerous suite of ladies, including those who were to follow her Majesty into France. Anne's journey was tedious and fatiguing; the roads were broken by heavy rains; and horses could with difficulty be

found for the transport of the prodigious cavalcade
of baggage waggons containing her Majesty's bridal
outfit, and rich effects. The baggage filled a hundred
chariots, each drawn by three horses; there were,
moreover, two hundred sumpter mules, laden with
velvet coffers richly emblazoned with the arms of
Spain. The passage of this convoy through the
streets of Bordeaux occupied nine hours, to the
wonderment and amusement of the loyal Bor-
delais. Anne passed the night of the 23rd of
November in the citadel of Irun. At dawn on the
morrow, the baggage crossed the Bidassoa; and at
mid-day a muster of the Spanish court was made,
and the cavaliers and ladies descended from the
rocky heights of Irun to the bank of the river. At
one o'clock the young Princess-elect of the Asturias
arrived, attended by the Duchess de Nevers, and the
Dukes de Guise, d'Elbœuf, and de Grammont, and the
Prince de Joinville. Amid loud acclamations, and
discharges of artillery, the Princess stepped into the
barge, and was rowed to the landing-place on l'Ile
des Faisans, and immediately entered a pavilion sur-
mounted by the white flag of Bourbon. Queen
Anne simultaneously stepped into her barge from
the opposite bank of the river, and likewise landed
and entered a pavilion crowned by the yellow flag
of Spain. The French nobles presently craved

audience of her Majesty; while the Spanish courtiers paid the same *devoirs* to Madame Elizabeth. The Duchess de Nevers and the Duke de Guise presented the French nobles of the suite to the Queen. Her youthful Majesty sat on a chair of state, attired in a robe of green satin embroidered with gold, having wide and pendent sleeves looped up with bouquets of diamonds. A small ruff of fine Flemish lace encircled Anne's delicate neck. Her fair hair fell in ringlets, and she wore a small coquettish hat of green satin, looped with strings of pearls, and adorned by a heron's plume. A fresh and blooming face greeted the eyes of the fastidious courtiers; and a complexion of dazzling brilliancy, said to be unrivalled in Europe. The Queen's eyes were blue and piercing, her brows were arched, her figure was *petite* and graceful, though somewhat spoiled by an enormous *pannier*. Behind the Queen stood the Duchess de Sessa, the Condésa de las Torres, and the chief hidalgos of her suite. The maidens, and women of the bedchamber, formed a half circle on each side of the royal chair, sitting in Moorish fashion on velvet cushions, and flirting their fans. The ceremony of salutation performed, her Majesty rose and quitted the pavilion. Madame Elizabeth did the same, and the Princesses exchanging a cordial kiss, moved slightly apart and conversed, while their attendants delivered to each other the long speeches prepared for the occasion. These over, the Duque de Uzéda approached Queen Anne, and kneeling, kissed her hand, which he placed in that of the Duke de Guise, who led her to the boat adorned by the French flag. Guise then repeated this ceremonial, and delivered Madame Elizabeth to the Duque de Uzéda. The Duchess de Nevers then took her place behind Queen Anne, and the Duchess de Sessa behind the young Princess of the Asturias; who could not refrain from weeping bitterly, in defiance of etiquette, on taking leave of her French suite. The barges then pushed off, amid a discharge of artillery, and the cheers of the spectators.[*]

Her Majesty reposed that night in the citadel of Bayonne, and early the following morning she departed for Bordeaux, where Louis anxiously awaited her. The royal residence in Bordeaux was the archiepiscopal palace. Anne was received in the great hall of the palace by the Queen Regent, attended by a numerous court. Marie embraced her daughter-in-law, and after conversing for a few seconds, led Anne into an inner apartment, where Louis XIII. waited, attended by de Luynes. Louis wore the mantle of his Order; his sword was girt at his side, and the rich collar of St. Esprit glittered on

---

[*] Godefroy. Grand Cérém. de France, t. 2, p. 70, et seq.

his breast. The King eagerly stepped forward and taking the hand of his bride, saluted her on the forehead. "Every one was amazed at the striking likeness subsisting between the royal pair. His Majesty frequently looked at his bride smiling; while her Majesty, notwithstanding that she seemed much oppressed with the weight and amplitude of her attire, could not help smiling very lovingly also." *
Louis continued to stand awkwardly gazing on the fair face of his bride, until, at a sign from Queen Marie, he timidly took her hand, and led her into the sheltering recess of a deep window; where the youthful pair conversed for upwards of half an hour, being presently joined by de Luynes. Anne next went through the ceremony of receiving the ladies of the French court, who were presented by the Duchess de Nevers: her Majesty then introduced her Spanish ladies to the King, and earnestly commended them to his favour. Louis, however, received their homage with frowning reserve; and turning to M. de Luynes, whispered some sneering observation on the stately salutation of the Condésa de las Torres, which appeared to convulse the favourite with suppressed laughter.

* Godefroy, Grand Cérém. de France, t. 2, p. 84.—Brief Narré de ce qui s'est passé à Bordeaux depuis le 21 de Novembre jusqu'au 29 du même mois.

The ceremony of the marriage was performed in the cathedral of Bordeaux on the Feast of St. Catherine. The Princess de Conty, and the Duchesses de Guise and de Vendôme bore the train of Anne's bridal robe of cloth of silver. The Queen wore a rich diadem of diamonds, the gift of her royal father; her hair was dressed *à la Française;* and the spectators applauded her girlish grace as she daintily rested on the arm of the Duke de Guise, who, with the Duke d'Elbœuf escorted her to the altar. The Regent was present at the ceremony, arrayed in mourning robes. The nuptial benediction was given by the Bishop of Saintes, as eldest suffragan bishop of the diocese, in the absence of the Cardinal Archbishop of Bordeaux. The royal pair left the cathedral at six in the evening, and were escorted to their abode by torchlight.

The court quitted Bordeaux about the 29th of November, and travelled to Tours, where their Majesties spent the winter months in seclusion. During this interval, the treaty of Loudun was signed by the Regent—an act which was important in every aspect —as it outwardly reconciled the *de facto* government with the ministers, and adherents of the policy of Henri Quatre. The treaty checked the almost boundless power of the Marquis d'Ancre by bring-

ing back to the Louvre the great peers of the realm;
it conciliated the Huguenot faction; and allayed the
frantic apprehensions raised by the matrimonial
alliances with Spain. The treaty was warmly promoted by M. de Luynes; who from thenceforth
ventured to wrestle against the hitherto omnipotent
influence of the Marquis d'Ancre, and his wife. To
Marie de' Medici the pacification was also welcome;
although Condé became installed thereby as President of the Council of State. She trusted by this
compact to find an antidote to Spanish ascendency
in her domestic circle; and to the influence exercised over her royal son by the charms of his
bride. The King on the whole was satisfied; as
his favourite declared himself content, though
piqued that peace had been negotiated and signed
without his own intervention. By the articles of
Loudun the Huguenot faith once more received dis-
tinct recognition from government; and Huguenot
members were declared eligible to sit in the Parliament of Paris. No foreigner was from thenceforth
to be naturalised in France, with a view to his in-
stalment in offices of state; Condé was to preside
over and to countersign the Privy Council edicts; and
all fiefs and properties confiscated for past rebellion
were to be restored to their former possessors. The
Marquis d'Ancre relinquished his government of

Normandy to M. de Longueville, and ceded the citadel of Amiens. Measures so popular were nevertheless distasteful to the young Queen; who was injudiciously exhorted by the Spanish ambassador, the Marquis de Monteléone, to exert her influence in opposition to Queen Marie, and to M. de Luynes, to procure their withdrawal. The position of the Infanta-queen, as Anne at this period was called, required prudence, the nicest counsel, and exquisite tact. A child still in age, mind, and manner, the young Queen ought to have been exhorted to avoid politics; and to shrink from participation in that wild and complex struggle of parties, which bewildered the strongest intellects. It was, however, the unhappy persuasion of the Queen that her mission was to revolutionise the policy of her adopted country; to introduce by force, or by persuasion Spanish maxims, Spanish habits, and Spanish policy—emphatically to serve her country by upholding the policy, the religion, and the dynasty of Spain against all assailants. Thoroughly imbued with the maxims and the instructions showered upon her by her father, King Philip, and by her brothers, before leaving Spain, Anne devoted herself, as far as her ability permitted, to carry out the advice secretly tendered to her by Monteléone; who had at this period free access to the palace.* Anne had been advised to flatter the Queen-mother; to conciliate the Marquis d'Ancre and his wife; to despise M. de Luynes; to win her husband the King, by tender submission and grace; but yet to show herself of inflexible resolve in all matters wherein the honour and interest of Spain were concerned. Thus, although she was exhorted to fidelity and secresy whenever state matters were imparted to her ear, her Majesty was desired to make exception to this rule in favour of Monteléone,† to whom she was to confide all matters, even of the most private and domestic nature. Anne therefore, soon became a puppet in the hands of Monteléone; while she fancied that she was fulfilling her duties as Queen consort, and asserting her independence, by her submission to counsels sanctioned by her royal father. The withering glance of Marie de' Medici, however, rested on her young daughter-in-law, whose girlish presumption she resolved to chastise. More fatal,

* The instructions given to Anne of Austria before she quitted Spain, still exist in their original draught at Simancas. The young Queen was exhorted to court the Queen-mother. It appears that Anne, young as she was, had already given tokens of ability for intrigue and dissimulation. The instructions contain this phase: " Avienterla que aunque no paresce sabe mucho, este mnger sabe mucho ! " It is there also laid down as an injunction by the Spanish Government, that information of the opinions and intended measures of the French Government were to be obtained by the Queen at any cost, or risk whatever.

† Don Hettore Piguatello, Duke of Monteléone, and Viceroy over Catalonia.

however, for the happiness of Anne of Austria, was the enmity of de Luynes; the favourite angrily resented the contempt of his young mistress, and loathed her condescensions. The mind of Louis XIII. must therefore be fortified against Anne's fascinations; the more especially, as the assiduous court paid by the Spanish ambassador to the Marquis d'Ancre, appeared to indicate the willingness of his Catholic Majesty to favour the usurping rule of Concini. The King spent his days in listless discontent, lounging about the apartments of his consort, and associating her in many of his boyish pastimes. Sometimes in petulant disgust at her Spanish *entourage*, Louis suddenly left her apartments and took refuge within his own; vowing, never again to visit the Queen until her grim duennas were banished from the palace.

Early in the year following her marriage, Anne had taken possession of apartments at the Louvre; while the Regent retired to the Luxembourg, a palace which owed its noble embellishments to her taste and munificence. "The household of our young Queen," wrote Montéléone, "is not yet named. Her apartments at the Louvre are suitable to her Majesty's dignity. The Countesses de Castro and de Torres (the latter is an angel, whose merits defy laudation), are lodged near to their mistress. The Infanta-queen is daily received with cordial delight by her subjects."[*] Notwithstanding the splendour of her outward position, Anne's affection reverted to Spain, to its peaceful palaces, reverent court, sunny climate, but, above all, she pined for the lively sympathy which there surrounded her. "Tell my father," writes she at this period, "that nothing but my beloved Spain can solace me." Amongst the grievances complained of by Anne to her father, was the diversity of counsel given by her French, and Spanish advisers. Marie de' Medici, through Madame d'Ancre sent word to her daughter commanding her to conform to French fashions in her dress: to sprinkle her fair hair with powder, and to lay aside her enormous hoop; also her Majesty intimated, that the French loved gay and sprightly women, apt of speech, and agile in the dance; and that no demeanour so offended them as solemn *hauteur*, and distant formality. Anne therefore only too readily arrayed herself in the most bewitching *modes à la Française*; and, yielding to the vivacity of her character, charmed the courtiers by her sallies; and by her eager participation in the pastimes of the court. The next mail that left for Madrid carried out a joint despatch from Madame de las Torres and from the ambassador, Montéléone, deploring the volatile disposition of their child-mistress; who, revelled in her French fripperies, and appeared to love that costume better than the decorous robes patronised in the land of her birth. The ambassador next comments on the quarrels of the royal pair, "who often disputed, like froward children, over their pastimes." He then proceeds to censure the undue influence exercised by Marie de' Medici over the King; especially complaining that the Queen-mother and M. de Luynes prevented his Majesty from demonstrating proper conjugal devotion towards his consort, by inspiring chimerical fears of the danger, which might be apprehended from the birth of offspring, at a period when his Majesty himself, had scarcely attained to manhood. "It is a grievous fact, that their Majesties live together as brother and sister," continues Montecléone. He then querulously continues to complain of,—

> "Cette Anne si belle,
> Qu'on vante si fort."

"The Infanta-queen continues in good health: it is very much to be desired, to render this Majesty all perfection, that we could correct certain irregularities of character; though every one ascribes her Majesty's unfortunate flightiness of manner to her youth. Her Majesty never speaks without jesting like a child; we cannot induce her to apply herself to serious matters; she forgets all counsels and instruction with incredible facility; and her petulance is such that we have neither leisure, nor courage to interfere. I must add that although we give continual attention to correct these defects, and to induce this young Queen to adopt manners more worthy of her descent and position, we are very careful not to disgust, or alienate her. We have now arranged that her Majesty's confessor shall visit and converse with her daily on matters private and domestic; but I dread the weariness and impatience which these interviews will finally, but too surely, inspire." * A fête occasionally enlivened the dull monotony of the court. The King gave a superb masked ball at the Louvre in the year 1616, during which their Majesties danced together. Anne performed a saraband with her royal consort, and was arrayed in great splendour.

The burdened spirit of Marie de' Medici, however, found little pleasure in the pageantries which charmed her daughter-in-law. Marie beheld her precious, but much abused, power passing away; and deep dejection oppressed her. The Pacification of Loudun had brought little intermission to her anxieties. Before the signature of that compact she had wrestled with the malcontents in distant

<hr>

* Capefigue, Vie d'Anne d'Autriche. — Archives de Simancas, A. 74.

provinces: now, all the old ministers of Henri Quatre, the Huguenot chieftains, the great lords of the realm who had abandoned Paris, rather than bow before the *parvenu* Concini,* swarmed in the saloons of the Louvre, and clamoured that every privilege granted at Loudun, should be conceded. Condé tyrannised over the council; defied the commands of their Majesties; and had compelled Concini, after despoiling him of his most prized governments, to retire from Paris, to the grief and consternation of Queen Marie, and the downfall of her authority. Louis apparently beheld these discords with composure, though in reality he was profoundly displeased. The Spanish ambassador, M. de Luynes, and the Papal nuncio, directed the King's attention to the league forming between MM. de Guise, de Bouillon, de Vendôme, and de Mayenne, under the banner of Condé to curtail the royal power; the which conspiracy had its origin alone in their jealousy of Concini. Marie, goaded to extremity, sought to extricate herself by commanding the arrest of Condé; which great event was effected by M. de Thémines in the Louvre, as the Prince quitted her Majesty's presence.† Orders were

---

* Concini had purchased in 1610, a few months after the death of Henri Quatre, the marquisate d'Ancre, for the sum of 130,000 livres.

† Histoire de la Mère et du Fils, année 1617.

then issued for the arrest of the colleagues of M. le
Prince; but MM. de Vendôme and de Mayenne, on
the first symptoms of agitation, fled from Paris; while
Bouillon received timely warning of the event at Cha-
renton, and escaped to Soissons. Riots ensued in
Paris on the arrest of Condé; the windows of the
Hôtel Concini were smashed; and a turbulent rabble
assaulted the Queen's palace of the Luxembourg, and
forcing an entrance therein, burned and destroyed
rich furniture to the value of 200,000 crowns. A
council of war was hastily formed, and measures
adopted to subdue the rebellion of the fugitive princes,
and to arrest their persons. Condé was transferred
to the Bastille by Thémines and Bassompierre;* the
former of whom received the bâton of Marshal for his
services on this occasion.

The young Queen, meantime, applauded the
resolution of the Regent; and during the tumult
following the arrest of Condé, remained calm, and
composed, and joyous, "as if, Sire, she had been
seated within your palace of Madrid!" By the
overthrow of Condé, Anne fancied that she descried
redemption for her Spanish ladies from heretic
threats; and the repression of the insolent assumptions of de Luynes. Marie herself was not, however,
deceived by the success of her hazardous experiment.

* Journal de ma Vie.

The sombre silence of her son; and the half-satirical
earnestness of his refusals to assume the conduct of
affairs, which she had on more than one occasion proposed to relinquish, filled her mind with foreboding. France trembled on the verge of a civil
war; names potent in the provinces, such as Longueville, Nevers, Guise, Mayenne, Vendôme, Bouillon,
La Rochefoucault, Soissons, had raised the standard
of revolt against a government guided by Concini,
the Florentine gambler.*   The Huguenots flew to
arms for the rescue of Condé: Sully, Villeroy, Bel-
lièvre, Duplessis-Mornay, Rohan, Lesdiguières, inscribed their honoured names at the foot of mani-
festoes calling upon the people to save the monarchy,
and the King.   Paris had risen to avenge the " perfidious " arrest of Condé, the hero of the hour; and
the Chamber beheld many of its members dissolve
in tears, as eloquent orators descanted on the woes
which afflicted the realm under the administration of
the widow of Henri Quatre.   Never had an ambitious
and artful favourite a more plausible, and popular
ground for the overthrow of an adversary.

The King, meantime, on his return from St. Ger-

---

* All kinds of evil suspicions were engendered by the queen's familiarity with Concini.   The Count de Lude one day being present when
one of Marie's ladies was sent to bring her majesty's veil, exclaimed,
sotto voce, " Un vaisseau qui est à l'ancre n'a pas besoin de voile." Which
piece of wit flew throughout Paris.—Tallemant ; Dreux du Radier.

mains, was seized with a fit of epilepsy, on All Saints'
Day, 1616. The Regent was performing her devo-
tions in the chapel of Feuillantine monastery, when
summoned in haste back to the Louvre. Concini and
his wife, during the panic, got possession of the little
Duke of Orleans, heir presumptive to the throne; and
ordered the Queen's guards to take possession of
the principal avenues of the palace, and to dislodge
therefrom the soldiers of Vitry's tried body-guard.
In a few hours Louis recovered his senses; and in
three days became convalescent. Queen Marie, in
conversing with Du Vair, keeper of the seals, imprudently asked him, what he thought of his Majesty's
sudden seizure? Du Vair said that he feared the
fit might return during the forthcoming spring;
which opinion, Marie, with her usual want of caution,
repeated to Héronard, first physician to Louis, who
confided her Majesty's observation to de Luynes.*
The latter immediately sought his royal master in
feigned consternation; and avowed his belief, that a
plot was in agitation to deprive his Majesty of life
by slow poison, at a banquet about to be offered to
the King by the Duke de Vendôme, at the instigation
of M. d'Ancre: †—" Sire," said the artful favourite,

* Bassompierre, Hist. de ma Vie. Histoire de la Mère et du Fils.
† Mém. Anecdotes, ou Galerie des Personnages de la Cour de France,
sous les Règnes de Henri IV. et Louis XIII

" MM. the Princes in alleged revolt are loyal to your Majesty; but the Queen your mother persecutes them, out of regard for M. le Maréchal d'Ancre. Sire, one unanimous wail of sorrow was heard throughout the provinces during your late illness!" The murmur of coming disaster, meanwhile, overwhelmed the unhappy Concini and his wife—at times he besought the latter to fly from the realm for the safety of their lives, their son, and their enormous wealth.* His late temporary exile, on the demand of the Princes, had filled his mind with dismay; while the premature death, at this season, of his only daughter, he regarded as a fatal omen. At times, Concini seemed to brave adversity; and proudly declared, that he would not abandon the Queen, but would test " how far the luck of an adventurer could go." The wily de Luynes did not fail to report to his royal master every alternation of his enemy's mood, whether of humility or arrogance. In a moment of despair, the Marquis confessed to Bassompierre that he possessed the enormous sum of six millions of gold crowns, " *sans parler de la bourse de ma femme*." Moreover, that he had recently offered to the Pope the sum of 600,000 livres for a life interest in the revenue of the duchy of Ferrara. " Sire," thereupon said de Luynes, " Concini is king of this

* Bassompierre, Journal de ma Vie.

realm ; he exercises absolute sway over this kingdom ; he defies your authority ; and wishes the ruin of the princes. He has possessed himself of the mind of the Queen your mother, whom he bends to his will ; besides influencing her heart towards Monsieur your brother, more than towards yourself. He is daily in the habit of consulting astrologers and wise men, on the probable duration of your life. Your council is devoted to him ; and when we ask for money for your Majesty's privy purse, none is forthcoming. His return from Normandy without your permission was, Sire, an unwarrantable audacity. As for her majesty the Queen-mother, you, Sire, may imagine how potent may become her power when the loyal rebellion of MM. les Princes is subdued. Will not her servants participate in this increased authority to the detriment, nay, to the probable subversion, of your prerogative ? " These words festered on the irritated mind of the King—already that jealousy of his only brother Gaston, from which such lamentable after-results flowed, rankled in the heart of Louis. "The three brothers de Luynes," wrote the ambassador Montcléone to Madrid, "are well intentioned cavaliers, but with little talent or genius ; nevertheless, the King is greatly attached to them. It is, however, well that your Majesty should be aware that there is now a deadly feud between the Marquis d'Ancre and this de Luynes; it is necessary for the Infanta-queen to exercise the greatest circumspection in her demeanour; but, as yet, she has not committed any error." Orders, thereupon arrived from Madrid to treat "the brothers" with distinction. Montéléone, when communicating to the ambitious favourite a flattering assurance of the good-will of the Catholic King, received in reply from de Luynes, the words accompanied by an expressive gesture. "I understand your Excellency; and at a suitable period you will perceive that I have accepted and profited by your message." * With subtle perfidy de Luynes, having thus encompassed his rival, brought the dark anger of the King to a climax by becoming the medium of communications between his Majesty and some of the revolted lords, who offered to return to court on the exile of Concini; protesting that, that personage alone, by his tyranny and exactions, had been the cause of their temporary defection. Vitry, captain of the body-guard, at length received commands to arrest the Marquis d'Ancre, and convey him to the Bastille. These orders were given second-hand to M. de Vitry; who himself graphically records his amazement on receiving such an important mandate from the lips of two inferior gentlemen of the wardrobe, and of one of

* Capefigue, Anne d'Autriche. p. 41.- MS. de Simancas, A. 74.

the gardeners of the Tuileries, high in the good graces of Louis, for his skill in trapping little birds.* Hatred of the unfortunate Marquis; fear of the powerful favourite; and the bribe of a promise of the vacant bâton of Marshal of France, induced Vitry to swear to keep the design secret from Queen Marie, and to accept the office—indeed, the future tenure of his post as chief captain of the guard compelled his acquiescence.

The measures of the conspirators were hastened by an act of sudden and ill-timed energy on the part of the Queen. Suspecting the machinations of Luynes, Marie, though she had several times affected to abdicate her authority, determined upon the exile of the favourite; and actually gave a mandate, without previously consulting the King, forbidding the brothers to present themselves at the Louvre, on the plea, "that they had concocted a plot to send the King from Paris," by which assertion her Majesty hoped to incite a *soulèvement* of the Parisian populace.† This fresh *tracasserie* completed the exasperation of the King. Hitherto his Majesty had resisted the sanguinary malevolence of his favourite; but now Louis gave permission that weapons might be used in case Concini opposed the mandate of arrest. Luynes therefore

* The name of this person was du Buisson.
† Journal de ma Vie, Bassompierre.

shaped his instructions to compass the end which he
had long meditated. The *guet-à-pens* planned by
one infamous man to compass the destruction of
another equally infamous, met with a successful result
on the morning of the 24th of April, 1617. The
Marquis d'Ancre was passing from the drawbridge
of the Louvre towards the wicket, leading into the
grand court, when Vitry, followed by twenty archers,
arrested him in the King's name. The marquis
turned sharply, and placing his hand on the hilt of
his sword, exclaimed, "*Moi? prisonnier!*" The
words were scarcely uttered when three pistols, fired
by Vitry, Duhallier, and de Perrans, were discharged
at the unfortunate man, who fell dead on the pave-
ment, at the feet of Vitry. Awful silence prevailed
for a few seconds. At length, Louis showed himself
at a window, attended by de Luynes, who raised
the sash; shouts arose of "*Vive le Roy! À bas le
tyran!*" The young King raised his hat, and ad-
vancing, exclaimed, addressing the conspirators :—
"*Grand' merci à vous! À présent je suis Roi!*"
Luynes then ordered the gates of the Louvre to be
closed, and the guards to be drawn out.* The body
of the unfortunate Concini was dragged by the hair
of the head to a porter's lodge at hand, and ignomi-

* Hist. des plus Illustres Favoris, Dupuy,— Elzévir, in-8vo. Journal
de ma Vie, Bassompierre.——Le Vassor, Hist. de Louis XIII.

niously cast upon a heap of straw. Vitry then entered the palace, and publicly received the royal thanks, having first excused himself on the execution done, on the plea, " that M. d'Ancre offered such resistance as to render his arrest impossible." The grand gallery of the Louvre, meantime, became crowded with courtiers, aghast at the catastrophe. Presently appeared Richelieu, bishop of Luçon, who stealthily approached to gather tidings for his mistress, Queen Marie. The King, Richelieu relates, was standing on a billiard-table, talking excitedly, and receiving the congratulations of his court.[*] A few hours after, Vitry was sent on a mission to arrest the Marquise d'Ancre. The unfortunate woman was ill in bed: she was roughly aroused, and conveyed to a prison-chamber in the Louvre; and, a few days subsequently, transported to the Bastille, after undergoing a severe interrogatory, and from thence, to that prison, in all ages of fatal omen, the Conciergerie. Marie de' Medici was next forbidden to leave her apartments; her regiment of guards was broken; and the Louvre committed to the safe keeping of the Marshal de Vitry. The body of the deceased marquis was wrapped in a cere-cloth, and buried at midnight in an obscure grave, under the organ gallery of the church of St. Germain l'Auxerrois. The

[*] " Ah, M. de Luçon," exclaimed the king, slyly, " me voilà enfin Roi ! "

populace however, on the morrow violated the grave; and tearing the body therefrom, dragged it through the streets of Paris, and after frightful mutilations, hung it by the feet from a gibbet. Three days after this assassination, an edict emanated from the royal pen, bestowing the immense confiscation of the property of the Marquis d'Ancre on M. de Luynes; together with the diamonds and *parures* of his wife—a collection so magnificent, as to equal, if not surpass, the contents of the jewel-caskets of the Queen-mother.[*]

M. de Luynes [†] had now scaled the perilous eminence of royal favour: he had attained to princely wealth; and needed only a suitable matrimonial alliance to confirm his fortunes; and to win, as he hoped, the favour of Queen Anne of Austria.

---

[*] Immense possessions in valuables fell also to the lot of the lucky favourite. In a cabinet in the apartment of the marquis a casket was found containing jewels to the amount of 200,000 francs. M. d'Ancre had had the precaution to invest large sums of money in foreign securities; these sums some of the sovereigns refused to pay over to M. de Luynes; others obeyed the wish of King Louis. The son of the marquis, however, eventually came into the possession of about 16,000 livres of annual revenue.

[†] A popular song of the period, sung about all the streets of the capital, spoke thus of de Luynes and his brothers—

> D'Enfer le chien à trois têtes
> Garde l'huis avec effroi ;
> En France trois grosses bêtes
> Gardent d'approcher le Roy !

CHAPTER II.

1617—1625.

ANNE OF AUSTRIA AND THE DUKE OF BUCKINGHAM.

THE catastrophe which had overthrown the reigning powers of the court did not at first affect the daily life of the young Queen. The King and de Luynes being both secretly uneasy at the success of their plot, sought solace by appealing to Anne's sympathy and co-operation. On the day of the death of the Marquis, Louis dined with his consort, and affected an ease and merriment which he was far from feeling. Numerous arrests followed the *coup d'état :* all the chief adherents of the Queen-mother were exiled, or lost office. As for Marie herself, she remained under guard in her apartments.* Louis sent a message to his mother, stating his intention to assume the conduct of affairs ; and praying her Majesty to absent herself for a period from Paris, by

---

* When she was informed of the assassination of Concini, Marie de' Medici exclaimed, "J'ai régné sept ans ; je n'attends plus qu'une couronne au Ciel !" Some one present uttered an ejaculation of pity for the fate of the marquis and his wife. Marie wrathfully replied, " Qu'on ne me parle plus de ces gens-là ; je les ai avertis du malheur où ils se sont précipités. Que ne suivoient-ils mes avis ? "

doing which she would enable him to prove himself, as always, her dutiful and devoted son. The greatest fear was manifested by de Luynes lest the Queen should obtain an interview with her son; and to keep the two apart was the anxious aim of this subtle plotter. Louis displayed unnatural indifference to the position of his mother; and suffered various plans for her safe custody to be discussed in his presence, the speakers permitting themselves the utmost latitude in censuring her demerits. At length it was resolved to send the Queen to Blois in a condition of semi-captivity. Marie sullenly acquiesced; but asked permission before her departure to see the King, and to take leave of the princesses, and ladies of the court. The interview was reluctantly granted by the King, or permitted by de Luynes. It was then resolved that the Queen's farewell should be made in the presence of the newly-appointed ministers; and that Marie should bind herself to say nothing to her son, but the words contained on a paper forwarded to her through the Bishop of Luçon. The conditions were hard on the fallen Queen; the new ministers were men whom she had mortally offended; and whom she had dismissed soon after her accession to power. The majority were the old ministers of Henri Quatre, who were cordially greeted by the people on their resumption of office. The King

entered his mother's apartment hand in hand with
M. de Luynes, and preceded by the two brothers of
the latter, Cadenet and Brantés; his Majesty was
also attended by Villeroy, Jeannin, Gesvres, Silléry
du Vair, and others.

The Queen approached, and made the speech
which she had promised to utter: it merely
stated her anxious desire for his Majesty's prosperity; and her sorrow at having incurred his displeasure. Marie then lowered her voice, and said
some beseeching words. The King, however, hastily
assured his mother of his affectionate care; but that
he was now King, and would suffer no colleague in
the government. His Majesty, making a low bow,
then took his leave. De Luynes next approached,
and kissed the Queen's robe; Marie spoke a few
words in a whisper; she then requested his intercession for the steward of her household, M. Barbin.
Before Luynes could reply, the voice of the King
was heard calling from the bottom of the staircase,
" Luynes! Luynes!" The latter then withdrew in
silence, and rejoined his royal master. The doors
of the Queen's apartments were then thrown open;
and during the whole afternoon she received the
farewell visits of the court.* Marie's self-command

* Récit véritable de tout ce qui s'est passé au Louvre, &c., Archives
Curieuses, t. 2, 2ème série.— Hist. de la Mère et du Fils, Richelieu.

was amazing; and it is asserted that throughout her bitter ordeal she never shed a tear. This firmness disquieted the coward heart of M. de Luynes; as he attributed her Majesty's composure to the fierceness of her wrath, and her craving for revenge, which swallowed up every minor feeling. This opinion, it is averred, induced him to sanction the persecution of Marie's servants which ensued; as he hoped to render a reconciliation impossible. Some of the ladies of the court wept at this parting interview. Marie coldly remarked: " Mesdames, weep not for me; it is long ago since I requested the King to relieve me from the burden of his affairs. If my actions have displeased the King, I feel also displeased with myself; nevertheless, I know that some day his Majesty will acknowledge that all that I have done has been just, and politic. As for the Marquis d'Ancre, I pray for his soul; I pray also that the King may be pardoned for the crime by which he was persuaded to remove him!" Marie shed a few tears on parting with her little son, Gaston Duke of Orleans, then in his ninth year; she also very affectionately kissed her daughters Mesdames Christine, and Marie Henriette. The young Queen does not seem to have paid her mother-

Le Vassor, Hist. du Règne de Louis XIII.—Vie de Marie de' Medici, Dreux du Radier.

in-law any visit of farewell; but as Queen Marie entered her coach to leave Paris in the evening, the King and Queen surveyed the cortège from a window of the palace, and both bowed their farewells. The streets of Paris were thronged with spectators, by whom the demeanour of the departing Queen was scanned with curious eye. No enthusiasm, no words of sympathy diminished the humiliation of Marie's exit from the capital, over which she had so long and imperiously reigned. Marie was attended by the officers of her household, including the Bishop of Luçon, who then filled the post of her Majesty's *secrétaire des commandements.*

The King and Queen left Paris immediately after the Queen-mother, and repaired to Vincennes. From thence edicts were issued, which displaced most of the public officers nominated during the regency. Barbin, the trusted servant of the Queen-mother, was consigned to the Bastille: and the trial of the unfortunate Marquise d'Ancre was commenced, and brought to a termination by a sentence of decapitation. This decree was executed on the 8th of July, 1617, the miserable and half-insane woman being condemned as a witch, and guilty of high treason in the sight of God and man.*

* *Histoire Tragique du Marquis d'Ancre et de sa Femme, Archives Curieuses,* t. 2, 2ème série. Bibl. Imp. MS. Dupuy. vol. 661, fol. 127.

The "poor little Cadet of Albert" was now the grandest gentleman of the realm ; and the owners of the most illustrious names in France bowed before the resplendency of his power. Endowed with the wealth of Concini, adored by the king, and the partner of his majesty's weekly raids on the "*pies grièches*" of the royal domains, de Luynes prospered. Grand alliances, however, were necessary to give permanent lustre to this splendour. While the miserable little son of the Marshal d'Ancre, who once bore the name of Conte de Peña, had become a beggar, charitably sheltered in the hôtel of the Count de Fiesque,—and who, a few hours after the cruel execution of his mother, had been compelled to execute a saraband with one of Anne's Spanish maidens for the diversion of her majesty,[*] —de Luynes availed himself of the wealth of which Concini had been despoiled to purchase a wife, whose rank might accord with the altitude of his fortune. Hercule de Rohan, Duke de Montbazon, Governor of Paris and l'Ile de France, had at this period an only daughter, Marie de Rohan, by his deceased wife, Madelaine de Laval Lenoncourt.

---

[*] Dreux du Radier, Vie de la Reine Anne d'Autriche.—Cayet, Chron. Septénaire. Tallemant des Réaux. Concini's son eventually became possessed of the foreign investments made by his parents, and inherited a patrimony of 2,000 pounds of annual revenue. He died without posterity, at Florence.

Mademoiselle de Montbazon, who had just completed seventeen years, was a charming and beautiful girl, gifted with extraordinary powers of intellect; but wilful, wayward, daring, proud of her princely lineage, and disposed to dispute the *pas* with any dame of the court. Marie possessed a witty and an audacious tongue; she loved splendour, and the gorgeous attire which set off her noble figure. She belonged to the band of the Queen's maids of honour; but hitherto the freedom of Mademoiselle de Montbazon's humour had debarred her from the favour of her royal mistress, whose rigid Spanish etiquette was severely shocked by the *abandon*, only however of manner, in which Marie indulged. This future famous favourite of Anne of Austria had been attached to the court for about eighteen months, without eliciting a single mark of regard from the young Queen, when M. de Luynes demanded her hand. The courtiers heard with incredulous bewilderment that the son of "*ce petit capitaine de Luynes*," the once indigent *protégé* of the Count de Lude, aspired to alliance with the princely Rohans, kinsmen of his Majesty Louis XIII. The Duke de Montbazon was a good-natured nobleman, benevolent in his condescensions, but renowned at court for his ludicrous and ignorant blunders, and for

his total want of discrimination. The duke's *bévues*
were so common, that he was declared to be the
hero of every laughable misadventure which diverted
the court. M. de Montbazon was completely ruled
by his high-spirited daughter; and as he revered
few things not present to his visual comprehension,
and finding that the *parvenu* de Luynes had attained
to a rank and splendour hitherto denied to the
blood of Rohan, he graciously consented to the
alliance when proposed to him by his sovereign.
The handsome person of the young favourite * had
favourably impressed Mademoiselle de Montbazon :—
"To hate M. de Luynes," says a contemporary, " it
was necessary not to have seen him ; for he had so
pleasant and affable an expression of countenance,
that many foes were thereby after an interview
converted into friends." The fortunate favourite,
moreover, was all-powerful to flatter, and propitiate the foibles of the haughty Marie. The
King promised to erect the estate of Maillé near to
Tours, purchased by de Luynes, into a *duché pairie*,
if this marriage was accomplished. Most of the high
offices filled by the Marquis d'Ancre were transferred
to de Luynes. Louis, moreover, promised to nominate

---

* "La douceur complaisante de son visage luy est comme une lettre
générale de créance pour toute sorte d'affaires ; et vers toutes sortes de
personnes."

the Duchess de Luynes, *surintendente de la maison de la Reine*, an office which conferred almost absolute power over the Queen's household; and to possess which, it is thought, greatly influenced the decision of Mademoiselle de Montbazon. De Luynes, in addition, bribed the good graces of his lady-love by magnificent gifts; and, as crowning tokens of his devotion, he obtained for her, previous to her marriage, the much-coveted *tabouret*, or a folding-seat in the presence of the Queen—a privilege which no princess of the house of Rohan, either married or single, had before enjoyed; and lastly, he laid at the feet of his mistress the magnificent diamonds of the unfortunate Marquise d'Ancre—a casket of which a queen might have been proud. The marriage took place in the month of August, 1617; and the King created his favourite, according to his promise, Duke de Luynes, and installed him as first minister of the crown. Louis also fulfilled his promise relative to the new Duchess de Luynes, who was appointed grandmistress of the palace, and chief lady of her Majesty's household.[*] A feminine revolt followed this appointment. Anne absolutely refused to

---

[*] " La femme de Luynes est une escervelée, qui n'a que dix-neuf ans, à laquelle son mari baille une governante pour la conduire ; et cependant M. de Luynes veut qui la maison de la reine passe sous sa disposition," &c.—Le Contadin Provençal,—Pamphlet contre M. le Duc de Luynes, Connétable de France.

accept the services of a princess, who, she said, was personally disagreeable to her. The Condesa de las Torres protested against the assumption by Madame de Luynes of power over the *camaréra mayor :* the good and virtuous Duchesse de Montmorency, first *dame du palais*, gave in her resignation, " as, being the widow of the late Constable de Montmorency, she could not retain a subordinate office in the royal household." The result of these squabbles was, that the King never visited his consort for six weeks. The Spanish Ambassador, moved by the distress of the Queen, thereupon sought audience of the Duke de Luynes, to be officially informed of the source of the *fracas.* Luynes replied that the King hated the Spanish ladies of his consort's household, especially Madame de las Torres, and the old Duchess of Villequieras, her majesty's former governess; but that this latter lady was so repugnant to the King that Louis had resolved never again to share her Majesty's apartment until after the departure cf the said duchess.* Montcléone faithfully reported the matter to Philip III., who, without further parley, recalled all the Spanish ladies, much to the distress and indignation of the Queen. Anne, meantime, had been so excited by the vexa-

* MS. Simancas, A. 75.—Capefigue, Vie d'Anne d'Autriche : the words of the despatch are " y que por no veria, dixava no dormir con la Reyna."

tious events of the year, that about the month of November she fell dangerously ill of low fever. The King showed much solicitude during the dangerous crisis of the malady, and frequently visited her sick-chamber. On learning the danger of her young mistress, the Duchess de Montmorency returned to the Louvre, and generously helped Madame de Luynes to discharge her functions at her Majesty's bedside; for etiquette required that a duchess should replace the *surintendente* during those intervals when leave of absence was requisite for repose and refreshment. Anne's recovery was tedious. The Ambassador Monteléone despatched weekly expresses to Madrid with news of her health. He prays Philip to send his daughter a quantity of oranges "similar to those your Majesty sent last year, which arrived as fresh as if just gathered from the tree." Monteléone proceeds to congratulate King Philip on the improved relations subsisting between the royal pair; and states, that the King evidently greatly admired his consort, who was growing up a beautiful and graceful woman; also, that the King often proudly alluded to the incomparable complexion of his wife, and remarked her abundant fair hair, "in which attractions she had not a rival in France."

Louis, about whom all these anxious speculations flowed, had now completed his eighteenth year; but the monarch who had just exiled his mother---who held the first prince of the blood a captive in the Bastille, and who had raised an obscure favourite to the altitude of a duke and minister in chief—is described by Bassompierre as "amusing himself by little games and devices, such as painting little pictures, singing, making little models with quills of the fountains at St. Germain, and by drumming—for his majesty was a skilful drummer." * " Bassompierre," said his Majesty, one day, " I must now begin to practise on the horn; some day I will waken the echoes in my forests!" "Sire," replied the skilful courtier, "I do not advise such exercise. Charles IX., it is said, ruptured a blood-vessel by blowing the horn!" "You are mistaken," promptly replied his Majesty; "the King only quarrelled with his mother, Catherine de' Medici, and kept her at Monceaux. Now, if the King had followed the good advice of M. de Retz, and had not returned to her, he would not have died at the early age which he did!" "From that period," remarks Bassompierre,†

* "Le Roy etait bon confiturier, bon jardinier : il fit mûrir des pois verts, qu'il envoya vendre au marché. On dit que Montauron les acheta bien cher, car c'étaient les premiers venus."--Tallemant. Vie de Louis XIII.

† Bassompierre, Journal de ma Vie.

" I took heed never to mention the Queen-mother in the presence of the king, finding that his fears had been excited respecting her."

Marie de' Medici, during this interval, wearied of the insults daily inflicted, fled from Blois, with the aid of her old friend Epernon; and had retired under his escort to Loches, where she threatened the realm with civil war.   On the 21st of February, 1619, the Queen escaped from the castle by a window 120 feet from the ground, by means of a rope-ladder sent to her by Epernon.*   Her two women followed, and her *chevalier d'honneur*, the Count de Brennes.   A coach was in waiting, in which her Majesty entered, and took the road towards Montrichard.   She was met outside the town of Blois by the Cardinal de la Valette, then Archbishop of Toulouse, with 300 gentlemen, who accompanied her to the fortress of Loches; where Marie was rapturously welcomed by Epernon, and afterwards received an oath of fidelity from the soldiers of the garrison.   The utmost panic seized the King and his ministers when they heard of this event.   Louis returned to Paris from St. Germain to hold council, at which it was determined to send le P. Berulle to negotiate; whose brain was thought to be a match for that of the subtle Richelieu, whom her Majesty, on arriving at

* Hist. de la Mère et le Fils, t. 2   Preux la Ruelle. : .

Loches, had summoned. Bentivoglio, who then filled the post of Nuncio at the court of France, caused this suggestion to be conveyed to the privy council. Although most of the great peers of France had returned to their duty on the downfall of Concini, yet the elements of revolt were not extinct in France. Moreover, the courts of Parliament throughout the realm had interceded for the Queen-mother, *la veuve de Henri IV.*, and had exhorted the King to be reconciled with her. At court she had many ardent partisans, such as Bassompierre, Guise, Bellegarde, and others. It was, therefore, now deemed by Luynes to be a politic and popular course to disarm her Majesty by negotiation, and to propose an inter-view of reconciliation with the King. The Cardinal de la Rochefoucault was despatched to offer to the Queen the government of Anjou, with the fortresses of Angers, Pont de Cé, and Chinon, provided that she consented to relinquish the government of Nor-mandy. The Prince of Piedmont, whose recent marriage with the Princess Christine without the consent or participation of the Queen-mother, had filled the measure of Marie's grievances,[*] now made reparation by visiting her Majesty at Angoulême.

---

[*] "Marier ma fille à un prince étranger sans m'avoir appelée, afin que ma honte soit manifeste à tous les roys et princes de la Chrestienté, et de toute la France," wrote Marie, indignantly, in the letter addressed to her son, and entitled "Plaintes de la Reyne-Mère au Roy son Fils."

The Duke de Montbazon also made the same pilgrimage on behalf of his son-in-law de Luynes; to express the earnest desire of the latter for reconciliation. Marie, by the counsel of Richelieu, accepted the proposals and overtures of her son, and promised to join the court at Tours. The young Queen, therefore, journeyed from Paris to Tours, where she made a sojourn of three months.* After the meeting and reconciliation between Louis and his mother, the King set out for the south of France, attended by his favourite, to restore the Catholic faith throughout Béarn; while Anne returned to Paris, having received a promise from Queen Marie to join her there, after she had visited her new government of Anjou, and the fortresses ceded in that province.

During the next two years the history of the young Queen presents few incidents worthy of record. Her great grief, and the chief topic of the Spanish Ambassador the Marquis de Mirabel, who had succeeded Montéléone in the Paris embassage, was the devotion manifested by the King for the young and brilliant Duchess de Luynes; who first moved the heart of Louis Treize, and taught his

* Anne wrote from Tours a pleasant little note to Madame de Montglat, who still resided at St. Germain, as preceptress to the sisters of the King. Her Majesty desired her love to the Princesses—"mais non pas à ma sœur de Verneuil, qui est une paresseuse."—MS. Bibl. Imp. F. fr. 3818.

Majesty some of the tender refinements of *la belle passion.* "The King," writes the Ambassador, "abounds in courtesies and attentions for the Duchess de Luynes: I have, nevertheless, good hope that the worst suspicions take rise only in the excited fancy of the Infanta-queen, and in the malicious tattlings of her women. The King, I believe, is too wise and virtuous to merit the imputation of criminal intrigue. Your Majesty should exhort the Queen to propitiate her husband, and to render herself agreeable and necessary to him by the thousand little coquetteries proper to enchain and entice volatile hearts." Anne was too haughty and resentful to profit by such counsel: she adopted with the Duchess de Luynes a distant and condescending demeanour; but towards the King her manner was grave, serious, and respectful. Louis, at this period, showed great consideration for his consort in public; nor was it until he fell again under the baneful influence of the Queen-mother that those miserable domestic *tracasseries* commenced which poisoned his existence. The Nuncio Bentivoglio mentions even, that, during the absence of the King from Paris in 1620—to subdue the menaced insurrection excited by the distrust of Marie de' Medici in the provinces recently confided to her— the young Queen, "to the joy of everybody," daily presided at the council of state. These days were the brightest and most prosperous of Anne's married life.

A shadow at this period was, nevertheless, cast over the content of the Queen by the anger which Louis displayed at the assiduities manifested towards her by the Dukes de Montmorency and de Bellegarde. M. de Luynes was even one day compelled to leave the circle at the peremptory command of his royal master, for having presumed to press to his lips a flower which had fallen from a bouquet worn by her Majesty. This boyish petulance, and his own neglect of her in private, angered the Queen; who now having attained to woman's estate, and being conscious of her charms, resented the querulous tyranny to which she was often subjected. The Duchess de Luynes meantime lived in the greatest harmony with her *parvenu* lord, spite of the prevalent rumours respecting her intimacy with her liege.* She espoused the interests of the Duke with that energy for which she was renowned: the palace under her sway was a model of order and discipline; nevertheless, she never at this period succeeded in gaining even the coldest approval from her royal mistress. Anne had a pungent tongue, and her memory was seldom at

---

* " La Duchesse de Luynes était très bien avec son mari."—Madame de Motteville, Mem., vol. i.

fault; the Queen, therefore, in her circle, often in the most *naïve* manner alluded to reminiscences which the superb minister would fain have forgotten. His four years of rule, however, had weakened his influence with the King, who could not endure the brightness of the light which he himself had kindled. The lips of Louis often turned white with passion as he beheld the homage exacted by De Luynes, "Le Roy Luynes," as he bitterly murmured.* Nevertheless, with strange inconsistency, in the year 1621, Louis conferred the sword of Constable of France on de Luynes, with the greatest pomp. The sword of the new Constable presented by his Majesty was valued at 30,000 crowns. The court was afterwards sumptuously entertained by the Constable at his Hôtel, the former abode of the Marquis d'Ancre; but which was then known by the familiar *sobriquet* of Hôtel des Trois Rois, as at the commencement of de Luynes' career his brothers lived with him. For each of these personages, Louis, with the most amazing recklessness, had created a *duché pairie*. Cadenet espoused the heiress of Pèquigny, and was made Duke de Chaulnes; Brantés made a still more illustrious alliance,

---

* One day Louis, riding by the Hôtel de Luynes, saw the English ambassador alight from his coach and enter the mansion. "Ah! il va à l'audience du Roi Luynes," bitterly exclaimed the King.

and married the heiress of Luxembourg, Charlotte Marguerite, only daughter of the Duke de Pincy Luxembourg, whose title he eventually bore.

The new Constable meantime followed his royal master to the siege of Montauban, one of the strongholds of the Huguenots; a place defended by the Marquis de la Force with incredible valour. The siege lasted three months, and terminated by the retreat of the royal army. The displeasure and distaste of the King for De Luynes increased during the progress of the siege operations; his arrogant independence sometimes excited his Majesty to frenzy. Bassompierre was made the confidant of Louis's dissatisfaction, very much to the dismay of that astute personage. "I will compel him, the base-born ingrate, to restore all that he has rifled; he desires to make himself King, but I shall counteract his plots! The poor adventurer!" sneered the petulant boy-King, "why, his relations once arrived by boat-loads, and not one of them had a silk robe to appear in my presence!" The disgust indulged by Louis at length attained such fervour, that he one day told the Constable in public that the Duke de Chevreuse was madly enamoured of Madame de Luynes; and therefore that he warned him to be on the watch. "But, sire," remonstrated the good-natured Bassompierre, "I have heard that it ranks as heinous sin to sow dissension between husband and wife." "May God please to grant me pardon," responded his Majesty, "but I have now such joy in spiting M. le Connétable, and in giving him annoyance!" Such being the sentiments of the King, expressed in semi-confidence to the most privileged amongst his courtiers, predictions abounded on the approaching overthrow of the Constable. The royal aversion was not lessened by the comments of Queen Marie; who now, having made peace with her son, had taken up her abode at the Luxembourg. On the raising of the siege of Montauban, fever raged in the camp; Luynes retired to Longueville, and there encamped, feeling indisposed. In the course of a few hours the dreaded pestilence seized him; his comfortless quarters and his perturbation of mind increased the severity of the attack, and death soon delivered the King from the man he now so utterly loathed. De Luynes died on the 21st of December, 1621, after an illness of a few hours' duration. His favour lasted five years. Few crimes mar his career: Luynes was weak and ostentatious; his greatest merit, perhaps, was that he had discerned the extraordinary genius of the Bishop of Luçon; and at the time of his death was negotiating with Richelieu to quit the service of Marie de' Medici for his own, offering, as a bribe, a seat in the privy council.

Luynes left a son and one daughter* by his consort. The King suffered the young duke to inherit his father's enormous wealth, under the guardianship of his mother. During the following year, 1622, Madame de Luynes married Claude de Lorraine, Duke de Chevreuse, son of Henri, Duke de Guise, killed at the States of Blois. The alliance was an illustrious one. M. de Chevreuse, however, was weak and incapable, and totally unable to guide or rule his witty and able wife. He was luxurious and indolent; and while enjoying the ease of the Hôtel Chevreuse, cared little for the intrigues of his consort, or for the success of her political enterprises.

Before her second marriage, the Duchess de Luynes incurred a temporary disgrace. The Queen, to the great joy of the nation, had been declared *enceinte*. Prayers were offered throughout the realms of France and Spain for a safe and prosperous term; and Anne was committed to the care of the Queen-mother, and ordered by her royal husband not to act in defiance of such authority. It happened that the Princess de Condé† suffered from temporary indisposition, and was compelled to keep her bed in her apartments at the Louvre. Anne

* Anne Marie de Luynes, who died a nun, at Maubuisson, in great odour of piety. The son of the Constable, Louis Charles Albert, Duc de Luynes, was born December 25, 1620, and died October, 1690.
† Charlotte Marguerite de Montmorency.

and a gay party of courtiers, including her widowed *surintendente* and Mademoiselle de Verneuil, went to visit the invalid. The evening was spent merrily, being enlivened by the wit, and the amusing adventures of the Marshal de Bassompierre, and the Duke de Bellegarde. At ten o'clock the Queen took leave of Madame de Condé. To arrive at her apartment, it was necessary to traverse the great gallery of the Louvre, at the end of which a magnificent canopy and throne stood, which on this evening was partly draped for a state reception on the morrow. On entering this apartment Madame de Luynes, and Mademoiselle de Verneuil took the Queen each by an arm, and proposed, in the exuberance of their mirth, that her Majesty should run with them a race down its length. Anne suffered herself to be persuaded by their importunity; unfortunately, her ladies suddenly releasing their hold as they approached the throne, the Queen fell on her face over a footstool. A few hours subsequently, a catastrophe occurred which dismayed the courtiers, and moved the King to one of those bursts of passion to which he was subject. With his own hand Louis wrote to the Duchess de Luynes, and to Mademoiselle de Verneuil, exiling them from the Louvre, and forbidding them to see the Queen to say farewell. The letters were delivered to the delinquents by the Queen-mother, who administered to each an angry reprimand, and dismissed the ladies, weeping bitterly.* The Duchess de Montmorency† was thereupon promoted to the office of *surintendente,* which she retained for many years, conciliating every one by her gentle and winning deportment.

The return of the Queen-mother to Paris had been attended with many annoyances to the Queen, her daughter-in-law. After the death of the Constable de Luynes, Marie again beheld herself supreme over the court, ruling almost as imperiously as before the overthrow of the Marquis d'Ancre, and her subsequent exile. Distrustful of his own powers and judgment, Louis again sought refuge in his mother's more enterprising and resolute character; while Marie relied on the hidden support, and sage counsels of her chancellor, Richelieu, bishop of Luçon. The power and disaffection of the great nobles still menaced the royal authority. Condé had been released from the Bastille by de Luynes, to counterbalance, as he hoped, the renewed influence of the Queen-mother, after her reconciliation with her son at Tours. The prince was esteemed to be one of the wisest and most prudent of men: his military

---

* Journal de ma Vie, Bassompierre.—Année 1622.

† Laurence de Clermont, the third wife of the Constable Henri Duc de Montmorency.—See Freer's Last Decade of a Glorious Reign, for the history of the Duchess, and of her persecutions, vol. 2, p. 17.

talents were not great; but his name, his alliances,
and his relationship with many of the great Huguenot nobles, added to the guileful cunning of his
character, had gained him reputation. For the first
six months after the death of de Luynes, Condé
filled the vacant place of royal Mentor; and during
this interval Marie lived in intimate union with
Queen Anne, their majesties usually appearing in
public together, and amiably patronizing the Princess
de Condé. The young Duke of Orleans at this
period became a daily visitor at the *lever* of the
Queen his sister-in-law. Gaston was a beautiful
forward boy of fourteen, idolized by his mother for
his sprightly wit, and for his apparent devotion
to herself. The brothers, in character, were entirely opposite. Louis XIII. resembled his father,
Henri IV., in his contempt of soft luxury; and in
his readiness to submit to temporary privation.
Monsieur, on the contrary, was fastidious, luxury-
loving, and pleasure-seeking. His raiment was
perfumed, and made of the most costly fabrics;
rings glittered on his white fingers; and his fair long
hair was adjusted to perfection. The dancing of the
young prince was pronounced to be exquisite; his
voice was melodious; he excelled in the composition
of charades, and *jeux d'esprit*; and he aimed at a
lisping precision of speech, which ere long became a

fashion at court. Beneath this effeminate exterior, nevertheless, the heroic spirit of his ancestors of Albret slumbered. Monsieur showed an early predilection for arms; his fencing was admirable; he was an expert archer; and rode on horseback with an ease and grace which always excited the envy of the King.* Monsieur's inclination for magnificence and costly ornamentation pervaded all his pursuits. While his brother contented himself with snaring magpies and small birds, Gaston, at this period, having just attained his majority, and therefore becoming master of his patrimony, set up a hunting establishment on a grand scale at his château of Montargis; where he built kennels and stables, which, a few years subsequently, were razed to the ground, when the Duke capriciously transferred his stud to Villers Coterets, a huntinglodge in the forest of Soissons. The Duke at this period divided his leisure, when in Paris, between the Louvre and the Luxembourg; spending hours at the latter place with his royal mother in the studio of the *maestro*, Rubens, whom Marie de' Medici had lured from Antwerp to embellish her

* Un gentil mot du Sieur de Pluvinel était—Que le Roy à pied est Roy de ses sujets; mais qu'à cheval il est Roy des Rois—voulant montrer combien est excellente en cette art sa majesté.—Le Portrait du Roy Louis XIII., par le Sieur de Bellemavre au Sieur de Méroncourt à Venise. Paris, 1618.

palace by his immortal pencil. When at the Louvre, Gaston entertained his fair sister-in-law and her ladies; and once more made the saloons echo, as in olden times, with merry laughter, and witty repartee. Soon the greatest solace of the fair young Queen was the society of so fascinating a cavalier as her brother-in-law; who, moreover, with lazy good nature, adjusted many a little dispute arising between Anne and the Queen-mother, which might have acquired unsought-for importance, if submitted to the arbitration of Louis Treize. Prominent amongst the grievances between Anne and her imperious mother-in-law, was the fact that Marie proposed that the state receptions of the Louvre should be transferred to her saloons; and, through Richelieu, she even succeeded in convincing her royal son that such arrangement would obviate many evils to be anticipated from the youth, and inexperience of his consort. Anne replied, that such tutelage was unbecoming her proud position as reigning Queen of France, and Infanta of the Spains. Her Majesty, therefore, firmly declined to be present at the Luxembourg whenever the court paid its homage to the "august Marie de' Medici." This resolution was supported by the counsel of the Duchess de Chevreuse,* who, after her marriage, had again ap-

* Marie de Rohan, widow of the deceased Constable de Luynes. She

peared at court as chief lady of honour in waiting, and wiser perchance for her brief eclipse. Marie also complained, that Anne, when addressing her by letter, terminated with the words *"votre affectionée fille,"* instead of by the formula, in imitation of that adopted by the King, of *"votre très humble et obéissante fille."* The Queen bore with meekness the coldness of the Queen-mother, and the anger of the King, who was again enslaved by his mother; for at this period Richelieu still acted in subordination to the directions of Marie de' Medici. Marie, and her chancellor continually depreciated the intellect, and *savoir vivre* of Queen Anne, so apprehensive were they of a rival in Louis' confidence. " Nevertheless," says an enthusiastic contemporary, " Anne is truly pious; her heart is noble, her constancy great, her self-control eminent: she unhappily remembers injuries; but she is easily persuaded by commendation, and by affectionate appeal." The intercourse between Anne and Monsieur was not over-pleasing to Louis XIII.; that sombre nature ever construed friendship for another, into depreciation of himself. Anne, unhappily for her future peace,

married the Duke de Chevreuse in 1622. " C'était le second des MM. de Guise, et le mieux fait de tous les quatre : le Cardinal était plus beau, mais M. de Chevreuse était l'homme de la meilleure mine qu'on pouvait voir ; il avait de l'esprit passablement."—Tallemant, t. 2, p. 38.

had adopted the maxims of the famous Marquise de Sablé — at this period in the meridian of her celebrity, but who, nevertheless, was one of the most selfish and heartless of the "brilliant women," the glory of the Parisian saloons of the 17th and 18th centuries. "I am persuaded," said Madame de Sablé, "that men without criminality may feel and demonstrate the tenderest sentiments for the lady of their heart, and fancy. I maintain that the desire of pleasing women inspires the grandest and noblest actions; and that it imparts wit, liberality, and countless virtues. Women, being the gems and ornaments of the world, are created to become the recipients of such homage; they may therefore accept, and ought to encourage adoration and service; which, however, they need repay only by innocent condescensions." Such a code was repugnant to the jealous temper of the King; isolated, and living at the Louvre, as her sister-in-law the Queen of Spain, lived in the seclusion of El Escorial, Anne might have ruled Louis XIII. and France; but the frolics of the court, and the *etourderies* of the Queen offended the King's susceptibilities, which became further aggrieved by the ironical expostulations with which Anne met his remonstrances. "The admiration shown for me by MM. les Ducs de Montmorency and de Bellegarde, is only a just tribute to the attractions of their queen!"* exclaimed Anne, proudly. Louis also tartly reprimanded his consort for permitting the assiduities of Monsieur; inasmuch as her coquetting and ridicule, he said, rendered the Duke more averse than ever to offer suitable *devoirs* to his betrothed wife Marie de Bourbon Montpensier; an alliance approved, and desired by the Queen-mother, and by himself. Mademoiselle de Montpensier being the richest heiress in France, it had been deemed imperative by Henri IV. that the succession to so many duchies should neither lapse to a subject; nor be possessed by a foreign prince. Henriette, Duchess de Joyeuse, in her own right, and dowager of Montpensier, had taken for her second husband the Duke de Guise; her daughter, therefore, was receiving her education with her half brothers and sisters of Lorraine. The little heiress was plain, pale, and insipid, *triste* in humour, small, slightly deformed in person, totally unable to comprehend, and even feeling frightened at the brilliant sallies of her affianced lord. The Queen disparaged her future sister-in-law,

* " Le Duc de Montmorency était très assidu auprès d'Anne d'Autriche ; il fit même le passioné. Louis en parut alarmé : et les amis du Duc lui conseillèrent de s'absenter de la cour. Marie de' Medici se chargeant de convaincre son fils que ce bruit injurieux à la jeune reine n'était qu'une imposture des ennemis de Montmorency."—Anquetil, Tallemant. Madame de Motteville allows that the Duke permitted himself great liberty towards the Queen, under the cloak of what was termed " la galanterie espagnole."

and did all she could to render Monsieur indifferent; "because," argued her Majesty, "if the future Madame brings her husband children, I shall fall in public esteem, and suffer deeper political insignificance." Nevertheless, on the hint of her royal consort, whose wrath subdued even Anne's assurance, her Majesty attempted to persuade the young Duke to seek the society of his affianced.

The Queen-mother and her policy, meantime, continued to be in the ascendant. The death of the Cardinal de Retz, and of the Keeper of the Seals Du Vic, creatures of the late Constable de Luynes, enabled Marie to extend her patronage. The sword of Constable was given to Lesdiguières on his abjuration of the Calvinist faith; and the Marquis de Vieuville, an old adherent of the Queen's, received the seals. The Chancellor de Sillery was banished from the court; and, at the urgent demand of the Queen-mother, Richelieu was admitted a member of the privy council. Marie had demanded a cardinal's hat for her *protégé* after the signature of the peace of Angers. De Luynes promised the interest of the French government with the Holy See; but as the King manifested displeasure at the elevation of Richelieu, whom he was wont to designate "an officious meddler," a private letter was addressed to his Holiness to neutralise the effect of the public demand.

Richelieu discovered the intrigue through the celebrated Capuchin, Father Joseph de Tremblay,* and
meekly informed his patroness. Upon this Marie
promptly proposed a marriage between M. Combalet,
nephew of de Luynes, with Mademoiselle de Pont de
Courlay,† the niece of Richelieu, and thus won the true
support of de Luynes. All persons, therefore, being,
as the Queen hoped, propitiated, a second application
had been made to his Holiness. During the interval
the Constable de Luynes died. Louis, therefore,
advised by Condé of this fresh application, again
dispatched a message through Corsini, the papal
nuncio, to the effect "that he should not feel
aggrieved if his Holiness deemed it advisable, and
found excuses, to refuse this request." Again the
royal duplicity was discovered by Richelieu, and
confided to the Queen-mother. Marie entered her
son's cabinet in a passion of resentment : she drew
the most disastrous picture of the condition of
France ; and her eulogy of "the humble prelate

---

* François Leclerc de Tremblay, born in Paris, Nov. 4th, 1577, son of
Jean Leclerc de Tremblay, French Ambassador at Venice, chancellor of
the Duke d'Alençon, brother of Henry III., and of Marie de la Fayette,
daughter of Claude de la Fayette, Sieur de St. Romain. He took the
habit of St. Francis, February 2, 1599, and entered the monastery of the
Great Franciscans, Rue St. Honoré.

† Marie Madeleine de Vignerot, daughter of René de Vignerot,
Seigneur de Pont de Courlay, and of Françoise du' Plessis-Richelieu,
sister of the Cardinal. Marie de' Medici presented the bride with a
dowry of 200,000 livres, and a *parure* of diamonds worth 12,000 crowns.

whose wisdom and learning were to avert ruin from the realm," bewildered the King. Louis confessed his want of appreciation of Richelieu's merit; but consented to dispatch an express to Rome, to contradict "the error of the nuncio," who had misunderstood the royal observation; and to ask for the prompt elevation of M. de Luçon. The much-coveted hat was bestowed upon Richelieu by Pope Gregory XV., September 1622. The astute Richelieu had no sooner received the insignia of his cardinalate from the hand of his sovereign, at Lyons, than he prostrated himself at the feet of Marie de' Medici: " Gracious Majesty! this purple, which I owe to your Majesty, will be ever before my eyes as a symbol of the solemn vow which I have made, and now renew, to shed every drop of my blood, if necessary, in your service!" The joy of Marie was intense: the mother of the King—mother, and trusted ally of Monsieur heir-presumptive — the mistress of Richelieu, and able to command at will that glorious intellect and unrivalled daring—Marie might well consider her newly-recovered power, steadfast and immoveable!

The rule of the Cardinal de Richelieu commenced. His first process of government was to exhibit to the timid and suspicious Louis the volcano beneath his throne; and to direct his startled gaze on the swarm of malcontents which stung, and ravaged his fair heritage and prerogatives. Richelieu displayed terrible pictures : the revolt and arrogance of the great peers, whose ambition shook the throne; the treason of the Huguenots of the realm—their tenure of fortified places by treaty; their alliances with foreign powers; and their insolent demand for separate political and synodical action. He then changed the scene to the domestic disquietudes of the court—the towering ambition of Marie de' Medici, the Cardinal observed, no *faithful* minister of Louis XIII. might ignore; the levity and Spanish inclinations of the reigning Queen; the ambition and frivolity of the heir-presumptive, whose vanity might betray him into the toils of unprincipled men ! Every one 'of these bristling thorns pierced the heart of the King. The Cardinal's system with Marie de' Medici was, to bemoan the suspicions and illiberality of the King his royal master; his headstrong will and lack of filial deference; the cunning of Condé; the insecurity of her Majesty's position; and the high promise of Monsieur. For a season this course of tactics succeeded with Marie de' Medici; but the Queen required the Cardinal's deeds to accord with his words; and his actions to follow, or at any rate to assimilate with his predictions—a consequence overlooked, in his astuteness, by Richelieu.

The court was divided by the new law-giver into two camps—his friends, and his enemies. For the former no caresses and privileges were deemed too high a boon: for the latter, mendacity could not sufficiently blacken their motives and character; or persecution and ruin too thoroughly overthrow their prospects. The meek humility of Richelieu's manner towards his household dependants; the deferential homage which, at the commencing of his power, he paid to the high personages of the court; and the triple velvet with which he encased the potent hand so terrible in its blows, enabled the first years of his ministry—his initiation in office—to glide away with but little notice, and no opposition.

The method which Richelieu is recorded to have taken in order to propitiate and to gain the favour of Anne of Austria is so extraordinary, and opposed to his intercourse with his royal patron during the following decade of years, that it is difficult to believe a fact, which is related and affirmed by trustworthy historians, and chroniclers of the period. It is asserted that Richelieu attempted to strengthen his position by commencing an intrigue with the wife of his sovereign. There is no doubt that the isolated position of the young and fascinating Queen, estranged from her royal husband partly through his strange caprices, and exactions, and badly counselled by her friend and *confidente* Madame de Chevreuse, offered a tempting lure to the vicious, and unscrupulous. Richelieu hated Monsieur the heir-presumptive, with bitter hatred—at first, for some rude words of sarcasm, the more galling as falling from boyish lips; and because he descried in the disposition of the Duke a fretfulness which convinced him that so restless, and volatile a spirit never would retain its subjection to the will of any minister. Richelieu's admiration was calmly accepted, it is said, by Anne, as a homage rendered to her charms; and as incense offered by the first minister to the political personage which she never ceased from aspiring to become. "The Queen," says Anne's ardent friend and apologist, Madame de Motteville, " confessed to me that in her youth she never could comprehend that what is called *l'honnête galanterie* could be blameable, any more than the liberty enjoyed by Spanish ladies of the court of Madrid; who, living like nuns in the palace, and never speaking of men but in the presence of the King or Queen of Spain, yet boast of their conquests; and discourse upon them as facts calculated rather to enhance their reputation, than to defame it." Anne related to Madame de Motteville, in days when the memory of the sore trials of her youth had almost faded from the mind of the mother of Louis XIV., that one day Richelieu was craving her friendship, and assistance with an air too gallant and animated, and with words of passionate admiration, and that she, who detested him, was preparing to answer in contemptuous anger, when the door opened, and the King appeared.   Anne added, that she never after reverted to the subject, fearing to do the Cardinal too much honour by appearing to remember his presumption; "but I did myself infinite injury with the King my consort; for the bad offices of M. le Cardinal increased our misunderstandings."*   Richelieu, it might be imagined, would have been the last man to involve himself in the meshes of a perilous intrigue: but it is asserted, that the Cardinal, at this period, was consumed with a frantic admiration for his young mistress; and that Anne, whose heart remained untouched, amused herself by ridiculing and spurning this foible. But for certain suspicious incidents which occurred between the pair, years after this event, and when the Cardinal's passion was supposed to be extinct, the episode would seem too improbable to challenge

---

* "Le Cardinal haïssait Monsieur : et craignant, vu le peu de santé que le Roi avait, qu'il ne parvint à la couronne, il fit dessein de gagner la Reine. Pour parvenir à son but, il la mit sans qu'elle sût d'où cela venait fort mal avec le Roi et avec la Reine-mère, jusque-là qu'elle était fort maltraitée de l'un et de l'autre. Après il lui fit dire, par Madame de Fargis, dame d'atours, que si elle vouloit, il le tireroit bientôt de la misère dans laquelle elle vivoit."—Tallemant, t. 2, p. 282.

belief. The evil influences of Madame de Chevreuse were fast dissipating the decorous reserve of Anne's manners; and vitiating her mind. Anne had learned to love her and to trust her, as the forlorn cling to the one bright, and genial object which cheers their existence. Marie de Rohan was now devoted to the Queen. Anne's enemies were her foes; and the beautiful, strong-minded woman would have given her life, as she eventually sacrificed fortune, for the sake of her royal mistress. Intrigue, unhappily, occupied the mind of the Duchess; and, incorrigible in her vanity, Marie succeeded too well in diverting the melancholy of the Queen by the recital of her forbidden diversions. When condoled with by her intimates on the indolence, and pompous emptiness of the Duke her husband, Madame de Chevreuse replied promptly, "*Je m'en endommage!*" Subsequent to this period Madame de Chevreuse engaged in a correspondence with the handsome Earl of Holland, then Lord Rich, who had visited France in 1622, to negotiate for the Rochellois; and who returned in 1624 as one of the ambassadors sent to confer on the marriage of Henriette Marie de France, with Charles, Prince of Wales. In their correspondence these persons naturally wrote much concerning the leading personages of their respective courts, and Anne of Austria, and George Villiers, Duke of Buckingham, the favourite of James I. of England, often afforded a theme for the writers. The magnificence of Villiers, his beauty of person and chivalrous character, is believed, even at this period, to have made a deep impression on the fancy of the Queen. Buckingham, also, she was told, was joined to a partner uncongenial, and incapable of appreciating his rare powers. Anne believed this hero-worship to be blameless,—the great ocean separated her from Buckingham, — besides, it invested the correspondence of Madame de Chevreuse with a personal interest. The Queen, therefore, imagined that she might fearlessly accept the messages of her admirer; and reciprocate *la belle galanterie*, without dread of the spies, and the reprimands of the Louvre.

While Anne was thus indulging in soft blandishments, she, with her imprudent *confidente*, ventured upon all kinds of malicious *minauderies* towards the Cardinal. They dared to jest with, and ridicule his professions; and to devise *des puits d'amour*, into which they devoutly hoped he might fall. One day the flippant Duchess told his Eminence that her Majesty would be charmed, she thought, to see a churchman arrayed in cloth of silver,—*gris de lin !* Still further, these thoughtless women are said to have indulged their mirth. The Count de Brienne

is the relater of the anecdote, which he thus retails :*
"The Queen and her *confidente* were at this time mad
with fun and frolic. One day, when they were conversing together, and could talk and laugh at nothing,
save at the expense of the amorous Cardinal, Madame
de Chevreuse said, 'He is, I assure you, passionately
smitten, and I know of nothing which he would not
do to please your Majesty. Shall I send him here some
evening, dressed *en baladin*, to dance a saraband?
Shall I? Would your Majesty like it?' 'What folly!'
replied the Queen : nevertheless, Anne was young,
she was a woman, she was full of spirit and fun, and
the idea diverted her. The great minister, although
he had in hand all the politics of Europe, could
not defend his heart from the assaults of love. He
accepted the singular *rendezvous* proposed by the
Duchess—for already he believed himself secure of
conquest. Boccan, who played admirably on the
violin, was summoned. Secrecy was impressed upon
him, but when are such secrets kept? Richelieu
appeared clad in pantaloons of green velvet : at his
garters hung silver bells, on his hands were cas-
tanets, and he danced the saraband, which Boccan
played. The Queen and her favourite, attended by

* Mém. de Brienne, t. 1, p. 274. "On rioit à gorge déployée ; et qui
pouvait s'en empêcher, puisque après cinquante ans j'en ris encore moi-
même ?" asks the Count de Brienne, when he ends his story.

Vautier and by Beringhen, remained concealed behind a screen, through which the gestures and movements of the dancer were seen!"

The Cardinal speedily detected the *escapades* of which he had become the victim, and resented the insult; at any rate, his project of captivating the mind of the giddy young Queen had failed. "She rejected," he complained, "his friendship, his paternal care; and, in the haughtiness of her Austrian blood, despised his counsels." If Richelieu failed, as recorded by de Brienne and other chroniclers, to obtain power over the mind of Anne of Austria, it is certain that the minister discerned a waywardness in her character, which convinced him of the necessity of compassing her subjugation by rougher, and more arbitrary measures. Fate did not long withhold from the unscrupulous minister the power which he coveted.

The treaty with England, by which a daughter of Henri IV. was given to Charles I., was finally signed in Paris, March 13, 1625, after the death of James I.; who had previously subscribed the marriage contract of his heir, with Henriette Marie. The Earls of Carlisle and Holland were the ambassadors sent by Charles to sign, on his behalf, the articles and the private arrangements agreed to between the courts; and to be present at the marriage ceremony, which took place, May 11th, 1625, on a platform of state raised before the portal of Notre Dame. Madame de Chevreuse had been the great promoter of the alliance, being won over to English interests by Lord Holland, "who had," says Bishop Hacket, "an amorous temper and a wise head; and could court it as smoothly as any man with the French ladies." Marie de' Medici also sanctioned her daughter's marriage with a heretic prince; and entered into the views of Richelieu; who desired, with politic foresight, to wrest from the Huguenots of the realm their great ally, by uniting the crowns in matrimonial alliance. The young Queen at first declared herself inimical to the alliance, on account of her sister the Infanta Marguerite, whom she held to have been betrayed, and deserted by King Charles. Persuaded by Madame de Chevreuse, Anne, swayed by a multitude of motives, at length cordially congratulated her sister-in-law, whose society, nevertheless, she seems to have seldom sought; and declared herself "so truly French as to prefer* the alliance of Charles with Henriette, rather than that with her own sister Madame l'Infante,* for whom she had other views!" King James, before his decease, had issued a command to the Duke of Buckingham, "to get the English fleet in order, to bring

* The Infanta Marguerite espoused the Emperor Ferdinand III.

over our dearly belovd daughter, the princess Henrietta:" a mandate confirmed by the new sovereign, who was even more infatuated than his father, with the superb favourite. Great was the sensation at the French court when it was announced that the Duke, the dispenser of the revenues of three potent realms, was about to shine in Paris. Many a heart throbbed in expectation of the visit; and amongst those whose anticipations were perhaps the keenest, was the fair Queen of France, and her companion, Madame de Chevreuse.

At this period Anne possessed as little influence in the state as her friend—perhaps, indeed, a less degree of power—because Madame de Chevreuse lavished wit, beauty, and wealth to win adherents; and was fettered by no scruples.

The King seldom saw his consort in private. He was often absent from Paris on short military campaigns; and when resident at the Louvre, Anne was too petulant and resentful to submit to his *brusquerie;* or too impatient to devote herself to the task of soothing his melancholy, or of sharing the dreary conversation, and still more dreary musical entertainment of two guitars, and a violin, which often whiled away the evenings in his Majesty's apartments. Louis had nothing to say to a young and beautiful woman; he loved to sit in silent abstraction, and disliked the presence of ladies. His praises of Richelieu incensed the Queen; as did also his habitual abuse of Spain, and the dynasty of Hapsburg, whose overthrow, he was wont to declare, it was the high mission of France to accomplish. This indifference between the royal couple enabled Richelieu to insert .the wedge of a still more entire disunion : the minister and the Queen-mother inspired the mind of Louis with distrust of his wife ; and Anne did nothing to kindle love, or to command respect.

The Duke de Chevreuse had been appointed as the proxy of King Charles to wed Henriette ; he was also, with the duchess his wife, chosen to conduct Queen Henriette to Dover, to meet her newly espoused lord. The duke's wealth and splendid jewels, was the public reason assigned for the distinction conferred upon him ; for Madame de Chevreuse possessed, by the bequest of her first husband, the diamonds of the unfortunate Marquise d'Ancre. One evening Lord Holland visited the Duke de Chevreuse unexpectedly, and found him, with his consort, dressed for a masque at the Louvre ; " but never did I before behold such jewels, and never again expect to see such profusion adorning the persons of subjects ! " * The duchess coveted the am-

* Thomson's Life of George Villiers, Duke of Buckingham.

bassage to the court of England, not so much to display her diamonds, as the lustre of her eyes before the admiring gaze of Lord Holland; a fact, which she scrupled not to confess. The marriage ceremony of the Princess Marie Henriette remained a memorable pageant to Queen Anne of Austria; as on this occasion only, during the reign of her consort, did she publicly enjoy the magnificence and *appareil* of her position as Queen-consort. At this ceremony, nevertheless, she was compelled to yield precedence to Marie de' Medici.* The charming bride, Princess Henriette, won, by her grace and amiability, the praise of the English ambassadors. "My lord," wrote Lord Holland to the Duke of Buckingham, "I protest that she is a lovely, and sweet young creature. Her growth is not great, but they all swear that her sister, the Princess of Piedmont (Madame Christine), was not taller than she is at her age." † In most of his despatches Holland mentions Anne of Austria; so that the imagination of Buckingham, by the time he arrived in France, fired by dwelling on the beauty, the wrongs, and the isolation of the Queen, was ready to assign evil significance to every kindly overture

* Godefroy, Grand Cérém. de France, t. 2. Mercure de France, ann. 1625. "Après suivait la reine de France très superbement vêtue d'une robe de toile d'argent en broderie ; menée et conduite par ses deux écuyers."

† Thomson's **Life of the Duke of Buckingham.**

tendered by her Majesty. Rumours of the superb
retinue appointed to attend the Duke of Buckingham,
excited curiosity, and interest in Paris. It was ironically said "that King Louis must vacate his Louvre,
to afford space for the Duke and his suite!" On
the 24th of May, Buckingham entered Paris; his
suite consisted of seven hundred persons! He was
accompanied by the Marquis of Hamilton, by his
brother-in-law the Earl of Denbigh, and by six
gentlemen, sons of noble families. His equipages
consisted of three coaches lavishly gilt and adorned,
drawn each by eight horses. Buckingham was also
attended by a band of musicians; and by his staff
of Thames watermen—twenty-two in number—clad
in rich liveries. For his personal attire, Buckingham
made elaborate preparation; "for, my lord, they are
here so fine, so curious, and so magnificent, that
your Excellency will be much pleased," had been the
report of Gerbier, steward of the Duke's household,
sent by his master to purchase paintings, and
goldsmiths' work in France. "For his body, my
lord had twenty-seven suits embroidered and laced
with silk and silver plushes; besides one satten uncut
velvet suit, set all over, both suit and cloak, with
diamonds, the value whereof is thought to be about
10,000 pounds. He has, moreover, a feather made
with great diamonds; a sword-girdle, hat-band, and

spurs, all studded with diamonds ; and another rich suit of purple satten embroidered with fine pearls." * The noble, and handsome face of Buckingham beamed with delight, when, after making his obeisance to the King and the Queen-mother in the great hall of the Louvre, he inclined before the fair young sovereign, whose attractions had so stimulated his vanity, and presumption. The jealous and carping spirit of the French cavaliers found no rallying point as they beheld the personal gifts of Villiers, and the kingly carriage " of the handsomest-bodied man of England." The polish of his address, which Clarendon lauds as " sweet and accostable," and his generosity and magnificence, were noted with admiration. Nevertheless, the pomp affected by the Duke kindled the ire of his entertainers;† and his gifts, which were at first accepted with gratitude, offended by their prodigality.

The impression made on the Duke by the charms of Anne of Austria increased his infatuation ; while Anne herself imprudently gave him every opportunity of access to her presence. Madame de Chevreuse continued to be the arch-temptress, and

* Bassompierre. Mém. d'un Favory du Duc d'Orléans : écrit par M. de Bois d'Annemets—l'heureux Favory. Thomson's Life of the Duke of Buckingham. Cabala MS., 312.

† The Duke was hospitably entertained by the Duke de Chevreuse at his hotel, Rue St. Thomas du Louvre.

persuaded her royal mistress, at the suggestion, it is said, of Lord Holland, that to flatter and encourage the passion of the Duke would tend to the glory of France; inasmuch as the Queen, reigning over the heart of Buckingham, would govern the counsels of King Charles. Nevertheless, the Queen admitted the reality of Buckingham's attentions with reluctance. Madame de Motteville asserts, that no treason to her husband and King entered the imagination of Anne of Austria. The Duke was handsome, and the pearl of European chivalry; and, by the extraordinary familiarity in which he lived with King Charles, was admitted by other monarchs to intimate freedoms. Proud, therefore, of her conquest—and glad, perhaps, to exhibit before her husband's eyes the homage which her charms excited in the bosom of the most fastidious of cavaliers—Anne acted on the evil counsel of Madame de Chevreuse, forgetting her queenly rank. "The Duke of Buckingham," relates Madame de Motteville,* whose mother, at this period, held the office of bed-chamber woman to Anne of Austria, "had the audacity to attack her Majesty's heart. He was tall, well-made, handsome, noble, spirited,

* Mém. de Madame de Motteville, t. 1. Madame de Motteville was not an eye-witness of the facts she records, as she had not then permanently entered into the service of the Queen. She records the reminiscences and confessions of Anne of Austria. It was in the year 1640 that Madame de Motteville became resident bed-chamber woman to the Queen.

magnificent, liberal, and the favourite of a great king. He had the spending of all his master's treasure, with the loan of all the crown jewels of England to adorn his person. Is it marvellous, therefore, that, possessed of so many amiable qualities, his aim was high? or that he indulged in noble, but dangerous and blameable, desires? If the happiness was his of persuading those around that his homage was not importunate, we must presume that his aspirations were received, as the Divinities of old were said to accept the offerings of mortals—that is to say, that their devotees remained in ignorance whether their homage was acceptable, or the reverse. The Queen made no secret of these events; but has without reserve confessed to me that in her youth (though the illusion is now dissipated) she did not comprehend that what is termed *l'honnête galanterie* could be wrong, when no pledges were given or accepted." The experiment was a dangerous one, as Anne was not long in discovering; for the penetrating eye of Richelieu comprehended the insolence of the aspirations cherished by Buckingham. He beheld with mingled satisfaction, and perhaps jealousy, the condescensions of the Queen; for he perceived that no artifice could more certainly serve him to neutralise Anne's enmity, and to annul her influence, than to arouse the jealous ire of Louis XIII. as to his consort's inclination for the

Duke personally; and her relations with him as the ambassador of the English king. Moreover, a scene of levity in the gardens of the Louvre, most disgraceful in Anne's position as Queen of France, came to the ears of the minister; and which, years afterwards, was related in detail by Madame de Chevreuse to the famous coadjutor, Cardinal de Retz, and is recorded by him, doubtless with much profligate exaggeration, in the original edition of his Memoirs.

The homage and adulations of all the ladies of the capital seem well-nigh to have turned the ill-poised mind of the Duke of Buckingham. The beautiful Madame de Chevreuse divided her condescensions between himself and her old lover Lord Holland; the Duchess de Guise regaled him by sumptuous banquets and masques; the Queen-mother did the honours of her Luxembourg to so privileged a guest; Madame de Sablé held receptions in his honour, in which the wit and learning of the capital were arrayed for his delectation; and the brothers de Luynes, Dukes de Chaulnes, and de Luxembourg, placed their establishments at his disposal. Condé held festivals at Chantilly in his honour; the new constable Duke de Lesdiguières, and his plebeian but hearty consort Marie Mignot, welcomed the splendid ambassador and his suite. Anne of Austria was gracious; his majesty King Louis, smiled grimly on the genial representative of his brother-in-law; and Queen Henriette Marie left nothing to be desired in her anxiety to propitiate the favourite, who ruled the court of England. No wonder that Buckingham, amid these fair and witty dames, forgot his "silly Kate;" * and was in no haste to exchange the revels of the Louvre, for those of Whitehall. His sojourn in Paris, however, did not exceed eight days. The royal bride then left the Louvre, *en route* for Calais, where she was to embark for England. The queens Marie, and Anne, were to accompany Henriette, and to say farewell at Calais. Richelieu remained in Paris; while the King, after taking leave of his sister, repaired to Fontainebleau, where the court was to assemble on returning from Calais.

On the second day of June, 1625, a magnificent cavalcade quitted the Louvre and defiled through the gates of Paris, on the high road towards Amiens. The royal suite comprised the Duke and Duchess de Chevreuse, Mesdames de Launay, de Boissière, de Guercheville, and de St. George; the Dukes de Bellegarde, de la Force, and d'Elbœuf; and the Duke of Buckingham and his colleagues, Lords Carlisle and Holland. At Amiens the royal progress was arrested

---

* The name given to the Duchess of Buckingham in their correspondence by King Charles and her husband.

by the sudden indisposition of Marie de' Medici.
The court therefore, halted for the space of a few
days, that the Queen-mother might be able to resume
her journey to Calais. Marie lodged in the episcopal
palace; Anne of Austria in a house with a large
garden attached, on the banks of the Somme. Buckingham, meantime, acted the despairing and distracted lover, at the prospect of his approaching
separation from the young Queen, "that fairest and
sweetest of sovereigns;" and to put the mildest
construction on Anne's conduct, it must have been
volatile and giddy to a degree, which might warrant
most injurious inferences. There seems to be little
doubt but that her heart and fancy were touched
by the devotion of Buckingham; who talked in exalted strains of the political wonders which he would
achieve for France, as a tribute to her charms. The
life of the Queen had been hitherto so joyless and
uncongenial, that probably the very glow of her
gratitude at the Duke's homage, may have incited
him to bolder enterprise. Festivals, meantime, diver-
sified the sojourn of the court at Amiens. The bap-
tism of the eldest son of the Duke de Chaulnes *
was celebrated by a fête given at the citadel. The

---

* Honoré d'Albert, Seigneur de Cadenet, created Duke de Chaulnes
on his marriage with Charlotte d'Ailly, Countess de Chaulnes and de
Péquiny. The King gave him the government of Picardy.

sponsors of the young heir were the three queens, Marie, Anne, and Henriette, and Monsieur. Buckingham on this occasion appeared in magnificence truly regal, " portant le plus bel habillement, et mieux assorti que se verra jamais !" He wore the collars and badges of four Orders—the Garter, the St. Esprit, the Golden Fleece, and the Order of St. George. His hat was adorned with a heron's plume blazing with diamonds, and fastened by a cluster of five of the largest diamonds belonging to the British crown. A ball followed the banquet, which was opened by Buckingham and the Queen, Monsieur dancing with his sister, Queen Henriette. Madame de Chevreuse followed, led by Lord Holland ; and the Duke de Chaulnes danced with the young Duchess d'Elbœuf.* The next day Monsieur gave a sumptuous entertainment. At the conclusion of the banquet, Buckingham and the English ambassadors escorted Queen Anne to her abode. In the garden on the banks of the Somme, in the soft June moonlight, another suspicious interview between the Queen and the Duke of Buckingham ensued ; which produced a disastrous impression even on her Majesty's truest friends, who felt how ungenerously the Duke had compromised their royal mistress. It appears that the Queen, attended by

---

* Catherine Henriette de Bourbon, daughter of Henri Quatre and Gabrielle d'Estrées. The Duchess died June 20, 1663.

the Duchess de Chevreuse, by her lady-in-waiting, Madame du Vernet, and by her equerry, M. de Putange, and accompanied by the Duke of Buckingham, and by Lord Holland, strolled into the garden at dusk hour. The Duke led the Queen; Madame de Chevreuse was escorted by Holland; and Madame du Vernet by M. de Putange. It was the duty of this last named person never to lose sight of his royal mistress, but to be always ready to perform any slight service which she might require. Nothing at first occurred to disturb the serenity of the promenaders: the Queen and her cavalier, with the other personages of the suite, reposed for some time on chairs by the river side, enjoying the refreshing breeze. Anne at length rose, and was led by the Duke into an alley shaded on one side by lofty elms, and on the other, closed by a tall trellis covered with creeping plants. Instead of following the Queen, Madame de Chevreuse and her cavalier turned into another sombre walk; while M. de Putange and his companion discreetly remained seated where they were, not wishing to intrude on the conversation of such illustrious personages—the more so, as Putange declared that he supposed M. de Buckingham had some message to impart to her Majesty before his departure, which was fixed for the following day. In a few minutes the voice of the

Queen was heard summoning her equerry. Madame de Vernet and Putange hastened to join their royal mistress, whom they found agitated and discomposed; while Buckingham, with his hand grasping the hilt of his sword, leaned defiantly against the trellis. Anne began to reprimand her lady and her equerry for having quitted her; but when respectfully asked the cause of her alarm, her Majesty replied in confusion, "that its cause was, surprise at finding herself alone with M. l'Ambassadeur." "The Duke of Buckingham," relates La Porte,* an equerry who was in attendance on the Queen at Amiens, "finding himself alone with her Majesty, and favoured by the gathering obscurity, took the insolent liberty of attempting to kiss the Queen, who immediately cried out, so that aid quickly arrived. Putange, equerry in waiting, was not far away; and doubtless the consequences might have been perilous had not Putange permitted the said Duke to retire. Everybody in the garden soon gathered on the spot; then everybody fled, and

* La Porte, who was confidentially trusted by the Queen, and who was then an inmate of her abode in Amiens, gives the following relation of the adventure :—"Après s'être bien promenée la reine se reposa quelque temps, et toutes les dames aussi ; puis elle se levait et dans le tournement d'une allée où les dames ne la suivirent pas, sitôt le duc de Buckingham se voyant seul avec elle à la faveur de l'obscurité qui commençait à chasser la lumière, s'émancipa fort insolemment jusqu'à vouloir caresser la reine, qui en même temps fit un cri auquel tout le monde accourut."—Mém. Particuliers de La Porte : Genève. 1756.

it was resolved to suppress all mention of the matter." *

"Chance," says the methodical Madame de Motteville, the *confidente* of Anne's more sober years, "having led her Majesty with the Duke of Buckingham into a walk concealed by a tall trellis or palisade, the Queen, surprised at finding herself alone, and doubtless importuned and frightened by some too passionate expressions from the Duke, cried out aloud, and calling her equerry, blamed him for having neglected to follow her. By this cry her Majesty demonstrated her wisdom and virtue, preferring unsullied innocence and self-respect, rather than to yield to the prompting of fear which possessed her, lest her cry of distress, coming to the ears of the King, might cost her much sorrow. If on this occasion," continues Anne's warm apologist, "her Majesty betrayed that her heart was susceptible of some tenderness for the man who adored her, it must be owned that her love for virtuous purity, and propriety prevailed."† The following day, Buckingham quitted Amiens with Queen Henrietta. Marie and Anne escorted the bride for a distance of one league on her road, for the Queen-mother continued too unwell to

* Ibid., Mém. de La Porte.

† Mém. de Motteville, tome I. The Duke de la Rochefoucauld also relates the incident, which created unspeakable consternation and comment. He says, " Que la reine fut contrainte d'appeler ses femmes."

make the entire journey to Calais, and King Charles was beginning to be impatient, and to wonder at the delay of his bride. "The Queen did me the honour to confide to me," says Madame de Motteville, "that when the Duke of Buckingham presented himself to say a last farewell, and to kiss her robe, she was sitting on the front seat of her coach, with the Princess de Conty by her side; and that the said Duke hid his face behind the curtain, as if to speak a few words in private, but in reality to conceal his tears, which were falling plentifully. The Princess de Conty then said that she could answer to the King for the virtue of the Queen; though she could not speak so positively of the hardness of her heart, as the tears of the Duke evidently affected her spirits." Enough had, however, been done, and said, to render very bitter the future life of Anne of Austria; and to fill the mind of Louis XIII. with suspicion. From the period of the advent of Richelieu to power, the young Queen was always attended by his shadow, in the person of a household spy and informer; but who the person then was thus employed by his Eminence, does not clearly appear, though probably it was Madame de Vernet.*

* Nicolette d'Albert, youngest sister of the Constable de Luynes: she espoused M. Vernet, a person of low origin, dancing-master to the pages of the Duke de Montmorency. Mademoiselle d'Albert, previous to her

The Duke of Orleans, and all the chief noblemen in attendance at Amiens, accompanied Queen Henrietta to Boulogne, leaving their Majesties with a very limited suit. Tempestuous winds, however, unfortunately prevented the embarkation of the Queen of England. The English fleet lay at anchor in Boulogne roads, having landed the Duchess of Buckingham, the Countess of Denbigh, and the Marchioness of Hamilton, who had been despatched by King Charles to pay homage to their royal mistress. The delay lasted for more than a week; during which Anne frequently corresponded with Madame de Chevreuse, and sent her letters by La Porte. "I came and I returned," says the latter; "I carried letters to Madame de Chevreuse, and returned with her replies, which appeared to be of the utmost consequence, because Queen Anne ordered M. le Duc de Chaulnes to take care that the gates of Amiens were never closed, so that I might not be delayed at any hour, even in the night."[*] Anne at the time when she issued so unusual an order, little dreamed of the construction likely to be attached thereto. A prey to the wildest grief at quitting

marriage, had greatly compromised her reputation. She was handsome and sprightly, and through her brother's influence was appointed dame d'atours to the Queen; while her husband was made Governor of Calais. She subsequently married Henri de la Marck Duc de Bouillon, through the favour of Richelieu.

[*] Mém. Particuliers de M. de La Porte.

France, Buckingham determined to bid one more distracted adieu "to the fairest vision which had ever gladdened his sight." An express from his master King Charles, served as an excuse for his sudden return to Amiens with La Porte, accompanied by Lord Holland; under pretext that he was ordered to consult the Queen-mother on some matter, as he said, relative to the reception in London of Cardinal de Berulle, and of Henrietta's unwelcome suit of ecclesiastics. Madame de Chevreuse, meantime, despatched private letters to Anne of Austria, warning her of Buckingham's audacious intentions; and counselling her not to admit him to her presence. Buckingham's consort also sent a humble missive to Anne, accompanied by an elegant fan of feathers, adorned with the portraits of Charles I., and of her husband. While the Duke proceeded to audience of Queen Marie, La Porte sought the abode of the young Queen, and was admitted to her ante-room. Anne was in bed, having recently been bled; she took the letters from La Porte with an indifferent air, and exclaimed, after perusing them, hearing of the arrival of the Duke, "They are indeed come back, these cavaliers; I thought that we were delivered finally from the society of 'ces Messieurs'!" Anne, therefore, being forewarned, had leisure to deny admittance to the Duke had she been wisely inclined.   Having rapidly despatched his business with the Queen-mother, Buckingham hurried to Anne's abode.

The Queen was jesting with Madame de la Boissière on the Duke's return, when he abruptly entered the apartment. Without observing the preliminary salutations prescribed by royal etiquette to those persons admitted to such audience, the Duke rushed forwards, and dropped on his knees by the Queen's pillow. So great apparently was Anne's surprise, that she remained silent for some moments; and then turned an appealing look, half laughing, half weeping, at the grim matron her lady of honour, who stood in the *ruelle* of the bed. "'Monseigneur,' said Madame de la Launay, indignantly, 'it is not our custom to act as you are now doing!' 'Madame, I am not a Frenchman; neither am I bound by your laws!' So saying," relates Madame de Motteville, "he addressed the Queen, uttering aloud tender declarations. Her Majesty replied by complaining of his audacity, but without perhaps showing as much anger as she ought; but still commanding the said Duke, in severe tones, to rise, and retire from her presence."* "When I returned to her Majesty to receive her orders for the morrow,"

* Mém. de Motteville, t. 1.

nevertheless, relates La Porte, " I found both my English lords, who were staying much later than etiquette admitted. Madame de la Launay, the lady in-waiting, never left her Majesty's side; neither would she permit any of the attendant women, and officers of the chamber to depart, until these gentlemen had taken their leave."* Buckingham again obtained audience of Anne on the following day; and then took his final departure for Boulogne.

The young Queen of England sailed on the 22nd of June,† much to the delight of King Charles, and of his goodly company of lords and ladies, who had been waiting the arrival of the beautiful bride since the beginning of the month. " Queen Henrietta—so it is alleged—was detained by her mother's illness; but if all be true that is reported, they can have made no great haste, having to march to Boulogne instead of Calais, with a little army of 4000 at least; whereof, the Duke de Chevreuse and his followers make up 300, besides 60 that belong to his kitchen."

On the same day the French court set out for Fontainebleau, where Louis XIII. waited. Anne

---

* La Porte, Mém. Particuliers. These memoirs are included in the Collection Petitot.

† Mém. d'un Favory de Monseigneur le Duc de Orléans. " C'étoit une chose admirable de voir se superbe appareil (de vaisseaux Anglais); on ne se la peut représenter qu'on ne s'imagine de voir une grande ville flottante ayant plusieurs clochers."

trembled, as she anticipated the effect which the report of the festivities at Amiens might have produced on the mind of her stern consort. "The King," relates La Porte, the most faithful of all Anne's adherents, "testified the strongest jealousy at all these proceedings; and believed the malignant interpretation put upon them by her Majesty's enemies. The Queen-mother, however, tried to disabuse her son's mind; and told him that it was nothing, for that if the Queen had desired to do evil it was impossible, she having had so many around her. This reason, though incontestable, did not extinguish the jealousy of the King, as he proceeded to demonstrate." On the 20th of July, just five days after the arrival of Anne of Austria at Fontainebleau, Louis sent his confessor, le P. Seguéran, to intimate to Madame de Vernet, his will that she should resign her office of *dame d'atours* to the Queen his consort, and retire from court. The same dismissal was given to M. de Putange, and to the Queen's first physician, Ribéra,* who both departed from the palace on the same day. The Chevalier du Jars, another officer of the Queen's household, whom her Majesty had just sent to England with letters for Madame de Chevreuse, and one whom she especially favoured,

---

* The reason of the disgrace of Anne's Spanish physician has never been ascertained. Ribéra was not permitted to remain in France.

was likewise dismissed. La Porte was also included in the sentence; his zeal for the Queen's service being well known. On the 21st of July, therefore, Seguéran again made his ominous appearance at her Majesty's *lever*. "The King, Madame, desires that you will still dismiss another servant of your household of the name of La Porte." "The Queen looked at me very sorrowfully; and then desired the reverend father to say to his Majesty, that she begged him to name at once all those persons whom he would not permit her to retain, that the affair might be ended." These proceedings greatly increased the discord between the royal pair.* Louis addressed the sharpest of written rebukes to his thoughtless consort: and even threatened her with divorce. "Teatino! so early a visit as this to my lady Queen bodes no good. Alas! the signs are evil!" had been the exclamation of Doña Estephania, Anne's Spanish tirewoman and nurse, when she had admitted Father Seguéran to the presence of her royal mistress.

Anne remained at Fontainebleau in a condition of great depression and solitude for upwards of two months. She seems to have offered no excuses to her royal husband; while her resentment

---

* Anne sharply observed one day to her royal consort, "Qu'elle n'avait pu empêcher que le Duc de Boukingham n'eût de l'estime, et même de l'amour d'elle!" an observation which greatly incensed the King.

against Richelieu glowed fiercely. Anne, in her wrath, accused the Cardinal of seeking to sow dissension between the King and herself, to procure her divorce, so that Louis might marry Richelieu's niece, *la Veuve Combalet*—a pretty but shrewish woman, who, during her uncle's despotic reign, shared his influence, and became the divinity of the politic Parisians. Richelieu made several attempts to conciliate her Majesty, and to intercede for her restoration to the good graces of her husband. Anne repulsed every overture; but drew forth her weapons of retaliation and, " offered the astute Cardinal war to the death." It might have been supposed that the chagrin and anxiety which Anne had endured would have taught her prudence; instead of which, her correspondence multiplied with Madame de Chevreuse, who still remained in England, and with the newly-arrived Spanish Ambassador, the Marquis de Mirabel. She manifested interest in all the proceedings of the Duke of Buckingham; and once, when some alleged act of the Duke's was accidentally discussed in her presence, she coolly contradicted the report, saying, "*je viens de recevoir de ses lettres !*" In England, also, the Duke's enthusiasm for Anne of Austria was not tempered by prudential considerations; or by delicacy for the feelings and honour of a great monarch, the brother of his own royal mistress, Queen Henrietta. He wore Anne's portrait; toasted her at the Whitehall banquets; displayed her likeness in most of the chambers of his princely mansions, disregardful of the feelings of his own "silly Kate,"—all which aberrations were duly chronicled by the French ambassador in London; and transmitted for the perusal of the Cardinal minister, and to become the source of endless gloomy ponderings in the mind of King Louis.

CHAPTER III.

1626.

ANNE OF AUSTRIA AND THE CONSPIRACY OF THE PRINCE DE CHALAIS.

THE marriage of Madame Henriette over, the excitement of the court subsided; and the daily incidents of the palace were varied only by the dissensions and reconciliations of Marie de' Medici, and her minister. These violent spirits differed, clamoured, threatened each other with annihilation, wept, and embraced. The successful issue of Richelieu's policy in the affair of the strongholds of the Valteline, which France refused to deliver up to the Holy See, pending the settlement of the question relative to the disputed possession of these places, raised the reputation of his Eminence to high repute. The important concessions, moreover, which Richelieu wrested from some of the chief Huguenots of the realm; and his firm attitude in upholding the majesty and dignity of the crown, delighted the King, whose aspirations were despotic, though he lacked firmness to enforce his will. In the deportment of the Cardinal there was a novel ingredient which astonished and awed the swarm of unruly courtiers, who had rendered the regency of the Queen-mother one vast cabal. Richelieu jested with the merry, wept with the melancholy, granted favours to the unfortunate; looked downcast under verbal obloquy, and even seemed anxious to turn away wrath by the magic of a soft answer: great, therefore, had been the individual surprises of certain railers, malcontents, and caballers, to find themselves suddenly transported to the Bastille by virtue of a privy-council warrant; or seized in the night, and conveyed under escort to some distant château, all under the hand and seal of the gracious churchman, who dominated at the Louvre. Le Père Joseph,* or *l'Eminence Grise*, as was the *sobriquet* of the able tool of Richelieu—so clever, indeed, that doubt arises whether the Cardinal was not the puppet, and Le Père Joseph the motive power in the relation between these astute men—also, was fast rising into a personage of importance; being treated with deference by the ministers whom it had pleased Richelieu to retain at their posts.

Over the life of Anne of Austria, however, the darkest blight had fallen. Her lord, King Louis, suffered her indeed to live under the sheltering roof

* Joseph Leclerc de Tremblay, Capucin.

of his royal Louvre; but he permitted her there
to exist only as a political and social nullity, to
whom the most ordinary amusements of her rank
and station were denied—a Queen, who had to ask
permission to quit the precincts of the palace; who
could confer no favour; and whose splendour, even
on public occasions, was surpassed by that of the
Queen-mother, to whom she had to yield precedence.
The proud spirit of the Queen rebelled against these
restrictions; over the heart of her husband her
beauty exercised no spell; to him her vivacity was re-
pellant; while the very sound of her rich and sonorous
language reminded Louis of a foe.   No rival, nevertheless, dominated over the heart of the boy-king;
the wanton beauties of the late reign never attracted
a glance from the sad eyes of Louis XIII.; indeed,
flippancy of manner was punished by exclusion from
the Louvre—a rigour which was for some time un-
sparingly exercised after the scandals of Henrietta's
marriage festivities.   Anne's most happy time was
spent in seclusion at St. Germain, where she often
craved permission to sojourn, followed by a few ladies,
in order to superintend the formation of the gardens
planned by Henri Quatre.   The Queen passionately
loved flowers;[*] and a similarity of taste often

---

[*] Anne had a great aversion to roses, and fainted on inhaling their
perfume.

brought into her society her young and brilliant
brother-in-law, Monsieur. Impetuous in all things,
Anne gave herself up to the pleasure of his society;
and discarded in favour of Monsieur most of the
etiquettes which then hedged in a queen of France,
even from familiarity with her husband's brother.
She was heard to address Monsieur in public as
mon frère; she permitted him to kiss her hands;
to enter her presence unannounced; she sent him
letters, which she asserted related only to botany, a
science in which the young Duke was an adept. In
short, with girlish coquetry Anne was preparing for
herself a more cruel ordeal than any she had yet
undergone.

Gaston, Duke of Orleans, had now attained his
eighteenth year. Heir-presumptive to a throne—the
occupier of which was childless, and pronounced
by the most learned physicians of the realm to be in
a condition of health, from epileptic fits and other
maladies, from which fatal results might ensue at any
period—Monsieur was a personage to be revered
and conciliated.

Fondly beloved from his youth upwards by his
mother, and indulged by her without reason, the
young Duke, until after the exile of Queen Marie,
set discipline at defiance. The late King had
nominated M. de Brèves as the governor of his son

Gaston—a statesman of enlightenment, who had added to the glory of the reign of Henri Quatre by his able diplomacy at foreign courts. His attachment to Marie de' Medici rendering him suspected, de Brèves was dismissed by the Constable de Luynes, who gave the office to his own early patron, the Count de Lude. M. de Lude was too wealthy and influential a nobleman to give that abject obedience to the royal commands expected from him; and therefore, soon resigned his post to the Marshal d'Ornano, who forthwith entered on his functions, and prospered. Monsieur, on the completion of his education, became the centre of a knot of idle, insolent, and mischievous young cavaliers; who, living on their wits, and by the sufferance of certain potent dames of the court, sought to kindle the ambition of their royal master; and to urge him into endless schemes opposed to the government of the King, all tending to their own aggrandisement. The leaders amongst these gentlemen were MM. de Puylaurens, de Chalais, de la Valette, de Bois d'Annemets, the Duke de Vendôme and the Grand Prior his brother, the young Count de Lude, M. de Marcheville, the Count de Louvigny, and MM. de Coigneux and de la Rivière, and others.* These unruly spirits professed reve-

* The Count de Soissons and the Duke de Bellegarde inscribed themselves of the faction of Monsieur. The princes of Vendôme were the sons of Henri Quatre by Gabrielle d'Estrées.

rential devotion for the Queens, Anne and Marie; they sympathised with the former; and to mark such feeling attended assiduously the *levers* of the Spanish ambassador. The Cardinal de Richelieu they abhorred and ridiculed; while they crooned over his Majesty, and predicted his early death, and the consequent elevation of their own royal master. Instead of checking this licence of word and deed, Ornano encouraged such, being convinced likewise, that Gaston would ultimately become King of France. It might seem difficult for these mischief-makers to find grievances for Monsieur, who was young, flattered, indulged, and surfeited with luxury and wealth; nevertheless, two wrongs by which he was afflicted were discovered, discussed, and unfolded. The first grievance was, the alliance contracted for the Duke with Marie de Montpensier; the which, barred him from the free choice of a consort; deprived him of the influence accruing from a foreign alliance; and rendered him for ever subject in purse and dignity to his brother the King. The betrothal of the Duke to Mademoiselle de Montpensier was the subject of much factious discussion. The King, the Queen-mother, and Richelieu, promoted it as a matter of sound policy, and of honourable fulfilment of a pledge given by the late king. The Prince and Princess de Condé naturally gave no encouragement to a marriage, which would probably remove Condé from his proud position of the third personage in the realm. A portion of the house of Guise-Lorraine jealously deprecated the elevation of its head, by the marriage of the step-daughter of M. de Guise with the heir-presumptive. Gaston himself spoke spitefully of his pale *fiancée;* and imprudently declared, that, like M. de Buckingham, he would vow allegiance only to his sister-in-law, Queen Anne. The young Count de Soissons opposed the alliance, on the ground that Mademoiselle de Montpensier had been promised to himself by Marie de' Medici, during her regency, in lieu of her own daughter Madame Henriette, should the alliance of the latter with the heir of the English crown be accomplished. The sentiments of the young princess were in favour of alliance with Monsieur; and probably no person was more astonished than Marie de Montpensier herself to hear a union discussed, which from childhood she had deemed to be her destiny. Anne very imprudently suffered her wishes and opinions on the alliance to transpire; which declaration was met on the part of the King by an absolute command to Monsieur to fulfil his engagement. The Queen-mother at the same time reiterated this order; though it is believed that she now secretly encouraged the Duke in his aversion for his betrothed. The faltering health of King Louis rendered Monsieur a grand card in the hands of skilful diplomatists. Spain wished to maintain the French alliance. Anne of Austria, childless, and probably soon likely to become a widow, pleased the young prince, and was said to be herself influenced by his fascinations. The question, therefore, arose in the subtle brain of the Queen-mother, whether sound policy, and a due regard to her own interest did not direct that Gaston d'Orléans, on succeeding to his brother's crown, should also take to wife the widow of his predecessor? It is asserted, and on very strong evidence, that the young Queen likewise pondered deeply on this question; and eventually signified to Mirabel, and to others, her willingness, in case of widowhood, to follow the example of Queen Anne de Bretagne, who twice wore the matrimonial crown of France.* There can be no doubt that at this period the alliance between Monsieur and the Queens, to overthrow the power of Richelieu, was projected. Marie de' Medici fiercely resented the independence of Richelieu, and hated his system of centralization and repression; and to procure his

* Consort of Charles VIII., and subsequently of Louis XII., by whom the queen had two daughters—Claude, heiress of Bretagne, who married Francis I., King of France; and Renée, married to Duke Ercole I., of Ferrara.

disgrace, or removal from the ministry, was the first necessary step towards his overthrow. Whether Anne contemplated the dilemma into which her resentment was plunging her is doubtful; the Queen throughout her chequered career was ever ready to plot, and to dissemble; but the consequences of her intrigues never seemed to have aroused her solicitude.

Madame de Chevreuse, meantime, that arch and daring spirit, so full of resource and constancy, had not yet returned to France; but, alarmed at the wrath of her sovereign, the Duchess had wisely remained at Brussels, on a visit to the Archduchess Infanta Isabel. By some means, not on record, though probably by a letter from the Queen, the Duchess was put *au courant* with the proposed intrigue; and entered into it with ardour, and with her accustomed audacity. Through Madame de Chevreuse, therefore, Anne caused a notification to be made to the Marshal d'Ornano, the ex-governor, but bosom friend of Monsieur, " that it would gratify her much if he could find means to prevent the marriage of M. d'Orléans with Marie de Bourbon-Montpensier."* " I acted thus, because I believed that this marriage, favoured by the Queen-mother, was against my interests; because, if the future

* Mém. de Motteville. t. i. p. 27.

Madame bore children, and I had none, she would be more highly considered than myself,"[*] is Anne's own declaration. Amongst the most devoted admirers of Madame de Chevreuse was Henri de Talleyrand, Prince de Chalais,[†] master of the wardrobe to the King, and first gentleman to Monsieur, in whose train he always appeared. Chalais, therefore, betrayed by the dazzling charms of this syren, and too happy to supplant Lord Holland in her favour, prepared to obey her behests.

D'Ornano, meanwhile, having declared himself a devoted adherent of Queen Anne, did all he could to disgust the Duke of Orleans with his bride-elect. "If you, Monseigneur, espouse a subject of the King your brother, you will yourself fall into greater subjection to his authority. Your fortune and lands will ever remain in his Majesty's power; and if at any future period you stand in need of foreign support, or help, to not one potentate of Europe can you appeal!"[‡]

* Mém. de Motteville, t. i. p. 27.

† Henri de Talleyrand-Périgord, Prince de Chalais, grandson of the famous Marshal Blaise de Montluc. He was master of the wardrobe to the King, and one of the lords in waiting on Monsieur. Chalais had married Jeanne de Castille, daughter of the financier Jeannin de Castille, and widow of the Count de Chancy. "Madame de Chalais est une belle personne. Elle s'aime tellement qu'elle s'évanouit si elle vient seulement à souhaiter quelque chose qu'elle ne puisse avoir."

‡ Mém. d'un Favori de Monseigneur le Duc d'Orléans. M. de Bois d'Annemets was the favourite, and the writer of the memoirs; which therefore possess the value of having been written by an eye-witness of the events which they record.

The foreign alliance to which, it is supposed, d'Ornano hinted, was the union of Monsieur with the Infanta Marguerite, sister of Anne, once the betrothed of King Charles I. of England, and eventually the consort of the Emperor Ferdinand III. This alliance—failing one with Anne of Austria in the event of the death of the King—was highly approved by Monsieur; being, as he said, altogether more august and profitable, if less wealthy than a marriage with Mademoiselle de Montpensier.

This grievance of his compulsory marriage being well engrafted on the willing mind of Gaston d'Orléans, the Marshal d'Ornano next commented on his shameful exclusion from the privy council; a disgrace inflicted by the *parvenu* minister, whose dismissal was necessary to vindicate the honour of Monsieur. The Duke declared that this slight was keenly felt by himself; and that he was determined to have redress, or to withdraw from court. At the beginning of Easter week, 1626, the King left Paris for Fontainebleau, accompanied by Monsieur, and by the Queen-mother. Anne likewise received a command to follow; and as her Majesty loved very much "*à respirer l'air des bois*," she journeyed thither with pleasure. The day following the arrival of the court at Fontainebleau, Monsieur opened his battery by informing King Louis "that it was a reproach and

shame to him, that being his Majesty's brother, he
had no share, or influence, in affairs of state." A
sharp discussion ensued, during which Monsieur took
the opportunity peremptorily to decline the hand of
Marie de Montpensier; adding, "that the neglect
which he experienced convinced him of the wisdom
of the opinion expressed by his friends, that a foreign
alliance was requisite for his honour and prosperity."*
Louis replied soothingly, "that he would consider
the request, and make answer in a few days."
Richelieu, meantime, had his attention riveted on
the malcontents; and soon he discovered the simmer-
ings of their resentment, and fathomed the sullen
passiveness of Anne of Austria. From her Majesty
the eyes of his Eminence took survey of the position
of the Duchess de Chevreuse in Brussels, " *cette femme
qui faisoit plus de mal que personne :*" and with his
habitual discernment, Richelieu divined that some
plot, hostile to the existing order of affairs in France,
was in agitation. Monsieur, meantime, stormed, and
despatched d'Ornano, the bearer of his complaints, to
the villa of the Cardinal at Fleury ; where the prudent
prelate had deemed himself safer than to abide at
Fontainebleau. The Marshal obtained audience of

* Mém. d'un Favori.—Vie du Père Joseph, Capucin nommé au car-
dinalat, contenant l'Histoire Anecdote du Cardinal de Richelieu. A. St
Jean de Maurienne, chez Gaspard Butler. 1704.

the minister, who received Monsieur's message without surprise, and declared himself "the humble servant of M. d'Orléans." During a promenade made by d'Ornano and the minister in the gardens of the latter, the Marshal was seized with cramp in the leg and a trembling of the limbs;* ailments, which afterwards were declared to be sympathetic with the ire which surged in the heart of his Eminence. The following day—as five days had elapsed since the Duke petitioned the King—Monsieur sought audience of his mother, and announced his resolve to leave Fontainebleau; adding menaces concerning his intended destination. Marie, alarmed, soothed her son, and promised, that as on the morrow a privy council was to sit, his wishes should be gratified. From this point it is difficult to follow the Queen-mother in her dubious course; whether or no Richelieu temporarily resumed his old power over her mind by his concessions relative to Monsieur, it is certain that the acts of Marie de' Medici again corresponded, for some interval, with the policy of the minister. A secret council was holden the same evening, in the apartments of the Queen-mother, at which the King, the Cardinal, and the Chancellor d'Aligre were

* " Il luy arriva un accident digne de remarque, ayont été saisy, en se promenant dans le jardin du Cardinal, d'un tremblement si furieux dans une jambe et une cuisse, qu'il pensa tomber de son haut."—Mém. d'un Favori.—Archives Curieuses, t. 3.

present. It was resolved to gratify Monsieur, but to arrest so pernicious a counsellor as the Marshal d'Ornano. The introduction of the Duke as a privy councillor was effected on the morrow, after an angry tirade from the Marshal; who claimed, but was refused, the privilege of entering the council chamber with his late pupil, and standing behind his chair, as the secretaries of state attended his Majesty. The same night d'Ornano was arrested in the *Chambre Ovale*, and conveyed to the chamber which had been used as a temporary prison for the unfortunate Marshal de Biron, also made a prisoner at Fontainebleau. The tumult in the palace was great; and Puylaurens, one of the *mignons* of Monsieur, rushed to the chamber of the Duke, crying out in consternation that M. d'Ornano was arrested! The Duke sprang from his bed in frantic passion, and was hastily arraying himself, when an equerry entered and summoned him to the presence of the King.

Gaston found the King surrounded by the chief noblemen present at Fontainebleau, and looking cool and unmoved, as he might have been if discussing the odds of a game of tennis. In the apartment was the Queen-mother, *en robe de chambre*; also the Cardinal. Louis opened the conference by calmly saying, "that to his very great regret he had been compelled to order the arrest of the Marshal d'Ornano, who had treacherously attempted to create brawls between his brother, and himself." The eyes of Monsieur sparkled with fury. "Your Majesty has been grossly deceived: nobody can judge of the innocence of M. d'Ornano better than myself! Never has he given me advice counter to your Majesty's service. The authors of this evil deed are abominable and wicked; and never will I pardon them until I have reduced them to dust under my feet." The Cardinal here interposed, and gravely demanded whether Monseigneur referred in such language to his Majesty's ministers? "I speak of, and refer to the accusers of M. d'Ornano. See, Messieurs, whether you will dare to be amongst their number!" replied Monsieur. The King here assured Monsieur of his affection, saying, "that he regarded him as a son and an only brother, and would soon make clear to him *les tromperies* de M. le Maréchal. "The very thing I beseech your Majesty to do," responded Gaston undauntedly, "as I pray you to give me back my friend promptly, when you are assured of his innocence." Monsieur then abruptly left the room.* A silence of some moments ensued. Richelieu then proposed the further arrest of MM. de Masargues and Dangeant, the brother-in-law, and

* MS. Bibl. Imp. Beth. 9162. fol. 18.

the secretary of the prisoner; also, that Madame la
Maréchale d'Ornano should be arrested, and conducted outside the gates of Paris, and there discharged from custody.*   His Majesty gave assent to
these measures; and then dismissed the high personages present, complaining of fatigue. The next day
d'Ornano was conveyed to the fortress of Vincennes
under a strong guard, and confined in its most un-
wholesome chamber, which admitted a pestilential
malaria from the moat beneath.† The friends of the
Marshal asserted that he was a victim to the King's
indecision respecting Monsieur; for that when the
Duke was emancipated from the control of his tutors,
his Majesty had commanded Ornano to repress the
ardour of Gaston's suit to Mademoiselle de Montpensier. The rage of Monsieur was not assuaged
when he learned the departure of the Marshal for
Vincennes; and the young cavaliers of his suite assiduously inflamed his wrath, especially Chalais, and M.
de Louvigny. The Duke one day suddenly encountered the Chancellor d'Aligre, and haughtily asked
him, whether he was one of those who had counselled
the iniquitous arrest of M. d'Ornano? Surprised by
the excitement of the Duke's manner, the Chancellor

* " Madame d'Ornano fut menée par un enseigne des gardes nommé
Fouguerolles à Gentilly."—Mém. d'un Favori du Duc d'Orléans.
    † Ibid.

stammered "that he was as much astonished as his royal highness, and had nothing to do with the affair;" an answer which was punished by immediate dismissal from office.* The Duke put the same abrupt question to Richelieu, who boldly responded, "that he was not intending to make the same answer as M. le Chancelier; who, as well as himself, had advised the King to effect that arrest, after hearing his Majesty's statements."

As moderation and apparent disinterestedness were assumed by Richelieu at the commencement of his power, he immediately petitioned the King to suffer him to withdraw to his house at Fleury; as he found that he had irrevocably offended Monsieur. Without waiting for the royal reply, which Louis never gave but with hesitation, his Eminence ordered his coach and quitted Fontainebleau.†

This "flight," as it was termed by Monsieur and the turbulent spirits around him, raised the confidence of the conspirators in their insane projects; and confirmed them in a criminal design they harboured, to rid themselves of the obnoxious minister by taking his life. The Count de Soissons promised

* Bassompierre, Journal de ma Vie, ann. 1626. "Les dames de la cour," writes the gallant Marshal, "étoient fort mêlées dans ces intrigues; les unes en haine de la maison de Guise, qu'elles voyoient agrandir par la prochaine alliance de Monsieur; les autres en haine de Mademoiselle de Montpensier; et les autres pour l'intérêt du mariage de Monsieur."

† Journal de ma Vie, Bassompierre.

his co-operation, after exacting a solemn declaration from Monsieur, that he relinquished all pretensions to the hand of Marie de Montpensier. The Duke de Vendôme, and the Grand Prior, his brother, flocked to the standard of Monsieur on this supposed triumph of his policy; while frequent communications passed between Chalais and Madame de Chevreuse. These letters were submitted to Monsieur, who showed them to Queen Anne. Madame de Chevreuse, meantime, maintained the closest relations with the Marquis de Lainez, an attaché of the Spanish legation at Brussels. The assassination of Richelieu was daringly discussed by these plotters; a deed to be followed by the emancipation of M. d'Orléans, the liberation of the Queen from her matrimonial bondage, and possibly by the compulsory abdication of Louis XIII. in favour of his brother. As a step to the accomplishment of this great project, Chalais advised that M. le Grand-Prieur,* "*qui était très redoutable et habile, ayant sur tous part en l'esprit de Monsieur,*" should without delay repair to Havre, and win over his uncle the Duc de Villars, governor of that important port, to the cause of Gaston. Up to this point

* Alexandre de Vendôme, Prior of St. John's, youngest son of Henri IV. and Gabrielle d'Estrées, Chevalier de Vendôme. "M. le Grand-Prieur professait une inimitié publique contre Richelieu, qu'il accusait de détourner les grâces que le Roi voulait verser sur sa maison ; il se vantait d'être le seul Mardochée qui ne fléchissait par le genou devant ce superbe Aman."

all had prospered in safety and secrecy: the retirement of Richelieu from court, however, moved the impatient spirit of the hostile clique; and it was determined to forestall the slow progress of any negotiation with Spain, by striking an immediate blow at the life of the Cardinal. Nine of Monsieur's most intimate friends held council three days after the arrest of Ornano, and decided the matter under the presidency of the Duke; these persons were Chalais, Soissons, the Marquis de la Valette,* Puylaurens, Bois d'Annemets, Louvigny, Marsillac, Vendôme, and St. Géry. The scheme of the assassins was simple in its atrocity: it was planned to send six inferior officers of the household of Monsieur to Fleury, the country house of Richelieu, where the latter was residing alone and comparatively unattended, at three o'clock in the morning of the day but one following. These personages were to rouse the household of his Eminence by clamorous shouts; when admittance was obtained, which was to be demanded in the name of M. d'Orléans, who, they were to state, was on his road to breakfast at Fleury, they were to pick a quarrel with the servants, draw their swords, and to assassinate the Cardinal in the mêlée.† The Duke

* Son of the Duc d'Epernon, and husband of Gabrielle de Balzac-Verneuil, daughter of Henri IV. and Madame de Verneuil.

† Bassompierre.—Mém. d'un Favori de M. le Duc d'Orléans.—Mém. Anecdotes, &c., Louis XIII., t. 1.—Le Vassor, Hist. de Louis XIII.

was then to put himself at the head of the malcontents, and act as circumstances might dictate. His seditious challenge was to be for the Church, the liberty of the princes of the blood, the annihilation of the Huguenots, the alliance with Spain, and the rights of the Queen. When all was prepared, and nothing but the actual blow of the assassin seemed needed to effect the longed-for emancipation, Chalais failed his accomplices. He possessed a friend, one M. de Valencey, who had appeared to relish the designs of the confederates when a word of disaffection had been accidentally dropped in his presence; but who had never actually declared himself. To this personage Chalais had the weakness to confide the plot on the eve of its execution. "How, monsieur," exclaimed Valencey, in generous indignation, " so audacious and abominable a plot is projected by the King's servants, to slay another and a cherished servant of his Majesty, and you do not hasten to denounce the vile conspiracy! You will at once do so, monsieur; or take the consequences of my own immediate revelation of the treachery!" In vain Chalais entreated for silence; but Valencey insisted that he should at once accompany him to Fleury, and warn M. le Cardinal: "Do it, Monsieur, in your own words; give your own explanation—make the best of it; but go I must to his Eminence alone, or in your company."

Chalais in despair obeyed; and the two repaired to Fleury and obtained audience of the Cardinal. Richelieu listened to the story with an aspect of pitying compassion; and feigned to believe the repeated assertions of Chalais that he had always hated the foul plot, and had resolved to denounce it. His apparent belief, and gentle deprecation, with the tears he plentifully shed on this occasion, quite reassured the indiscreet young cavalier; who hastened from Fleury back to Fontainebleau, hoping to prevent the departure of Monsieur's band of bravoes. Valencey meantime, after receiving the cordial thanks of the Cardinal, was directed by him to seek instant audience of the King and Queen-mother, and to unfold the plot. It was between eleven and midnight when Valencey reached Fontainebleau; but access was readily obtained to their Majesties by the pass furnished by Richelieu. Marie's consternation was intense; while Louis summoned du Hallier and M. de Vitry, and commanded them to repair to Fleury, taking thirty archers and thirty horse soldiers to guard the Cardinal, whose meekness in remaining at his house after being warned of his peril deeply affected their Majesties.[*] This detachment met Richelieu at dawn on his

---

[*] Bassompierre, Journal de ma Vie, ann. 1626. Bassompierre was in waiting at Fontainebleau while the events occurred which he relates.

way to Fontainebleau. The duke's assassins had arrived during the night at Fleury, knocked up the household as had been arranged, with every aggravation of insolence, and violence. The doors of the mansion, however, to their surprise, flew open on their mandate. The retainers of Richelieu bowed obsequiously before the *avant-coureurs* of so august a person as Monseigneur; while the Cardinal in person expressed his sense of the honour done him, "so much so, that he placed the château at the command of the leader of the company, and intended himself to set out and escort his royal highness to Fleury." While Monsieur's envoys were meditating on the purport of these words, the clever Cardinal gave them the slip, and stepping into his coach, which he had caused to be prepared, he set out for Fontainebleau. Gaston was just rising when Richelieu arrived: the Cardinal proceeded straight to the apartment of the young prince, and mildly reproached him for not giving him warning of the honour he intended to confer by his visit; ending, by placing Fleury at his command. Taking Monsieur's shirt from the trembling hands of M. de Chalais, the Cardinal courteously handed it to the astonished young prince, and took his leave.* The incident was then suffered

* Mém. de Richelieu.—Bassompierre.—The duke, to conceal his design, and to account for an early departure from the palace on the morning fixed

to drop.   Queen Anne and Monsieur were filled with amazement at the failure of their enterprise, not knowing from what quarter the Cardinal had obtained his information.   Chalais kept his own counsel, until the truth was forced from him a few weeks later by the address of Madame de Chevreuse. The intrigue, however, received only a check from the unexpected *dénouement* at Fleury.   The design of the Cardinal's assassination was still the topic of the correspondence of the conspirators; amongst whom M. de Chalais, despite of his recent treachery, became the recognised organ of approach to the ear of the Duke of Orleans.*

Richelieu, however, held a clue.   Had Chalais promptly avowed his breach of faith, the subtle intriguers might have been less confident and more cautious.   The first step in the counterplot was skilful: his Eminence overwhelmed Chalais with attentions; and as an eminent mark of confidence, announced his intention to take up his abode at the house of the latter at Maison Rouge, when the court removed to Blois.   He then blandly requested as a personal favour from the King, that Madame de Che-

for the execution of the plot, had organised a hunting expedition. "Monsieur," said Richelieu significantly, on taking leave, " vous ne vous êtes pas levé assez matin ; vous ne trouverez plus la bête au gite ! "

* Chalais promit d'être fidèle à l'avenir, et leur donnait cette libre reconnoissance de sa faute, qu'il leur faisoit pour marque de sincérité."

vreuse might return to court, as he desired to merit the favour, and approbation of Queen Anne. M. de Vendôme, at the intercession of the Cardinal, was reassured, and bidden by his Majesty to bring back his brother and join the court at Blois, when their grievances should be redressed. M. de Soissons received an unexpected communication from M. le Cardinal, conveying the information that his Majesty confided to him the peace of the capital during his absence in the provinces; and directing the Count on no pretext to quit Paris.*

As soon as the Cardinal was settled at Maison Rouge, he summoned his friend the formidable Capuchin Père Joseph, and relating all that had recently occurred, asked for aid to thread the labyrinth.† "It is at Brussels that we must search out the intrigue: give me a sure man, and I will answer for the result!" exclaimed Père Joseph. The Cardinal acquiesced: selecting the young Count de Rochefort, one of his pages, and a Rohan by birth, he sent him to Père Joseph, with orders to obey the Capuchin in all matters. Rochefort was conducted to the Capuchin monastery, Rue St. Honoré, and was there taught to imitate the deportment, and the rule

* Bassompierre; ibid. Vie du Prince de Chalais, Henri de Talleyrand. Galérie des Personnages Illustres de la Cour de France.

† Vie du Père Joseph. Mémoires d'un Favori de Monsieur. Archives Curieuses.

of the fathers. When the travesty was perfect, Père Joseph sent him on foot to Brussels, wearing the habit of a Capuchin monk, and furnished with a letter to the superior of the Order in Brussels, who had promised further introductions. Rochefort was the cousin of Madame de Chevreuse; he was gifted with the energy and spirit of his race. By the assumption of sanctity, and by the secret influence of Richelieu, the young Capuchin soon procured an introduction to Marquis de Lainez. To this nobleman he pretended to confide his discontent with his calling, and his hatred of France; adding, that his desire would be to enter a monastery in Spain. So cleverly did he at length insinuate himself into the confidence of Lainez, that the latter undertook to procure him permission to drink the mineral waters at Forges; which Rochefort stated, was a boon necessary for his health, though unattainable, on account of the dislike with which he was regarded by the Provincial of the Order in France. The pass was obtained at the request of the Archduke; and Rochefort prepared to return to France, triumphant in the possession of a packet of papers, which Lainez, as he anticipated, had affectionately requested him to convey thither, and deliver to a personage who would await him at Forges. A courier from the Cardinal met Rochefort half way between Brussels and Forges, to whom he delivered the important packet. Richelieu had copies made on the spot of the contents of the packet, which was then resealed and given again to Rochefort. The latter continued his journey, and arriving at Forges found a person who gave the name and address of La Pierre, advocate, Rue Perdue, Place Maubert, Paris; who, exhibiting a letter from Lainez, demanded the papers. This person was followed by the Cardinal's spies to Paris, and was traced with his papers to the house of the Prince de Chalais. On his return home, an agent of police arrested La Pierre under pretext of robbery; his person was then searched, and the packet being missing, was at once known to have been left in the possession of M. de Chalais. The copied papers seized were then examined by the Cardinal; who found, amongst other documents, a long letter without signature, addressed to Chalais, in which not only was his own assassination spoken of as *un fait accompli*, but the writer went on to discuss casualties which might attend the death, or deposition " of the most august person of the realm." * This event accomplished, the marriage of Anne of Austria with King Gaston was assumed as a future fact which had received her Majesty's own assent, and that of the Queen-mother; and which,

* Vie du Père Joseph Leclerc de Tremblay.

when communicated to Philip IV., King of Spain, had also obtained his Catholic Majesty's approbation. Mention was made also, of a letter, written by Anne to her brother, in which she had intimated her consent to, and approbation of all the designs of the conspirators; and moreover, that she had despatched a special courier to Madrid, to convey this epistle to King Philip. Furnished with such a detail of this "infernal project," Richelieu triumphed—for the most august heads of France must incline reverently before the power won by this knowledge. The letters written by Chalais in return were intercepted; and by these the Cardinal came by the further information, that the Spanish cabinet agreed to the design of the conspirators; but declined to take a part in the plot until some notable success had been attained. The intercepted correspondence was at once laid before the King by his minister. With a cry of anguish, the unhappy King read, and bewailed the cruel destiny which arrayed against him his nearest kinsmen. He insisted, nevertheless, on the immediate arrest of all concerned in the plot. Richelieu combated this desire; he wished to envelope the plotters, and to allow them no avenue of escape, before the final blow was struck. Towards his wife the bitterest resentment rankled in the heart of Louis, never more to be effaced. The apologists of Anne of Austria aver that the Cardinal enveloped her in this conspiracy, which in reality was aimed only at his own overthrow, on purpose to neutralise her power; and to render the criminal wife, the helpless foe. They aver that no one but the King and Richelieu saw the letter addressed to Chalais, which was afterwards said to be destroyed; and they deny that Anne ever wrote to her brother in approval of the plot as directed against the person, and the throne of Louis XIII.* It is not, however, denied that Anne consented to espouse Gaston d'Orleans; and was looking forward to the death of her husband as a fact of speedy accomplishment. The archives of Simancas furnish proof positive of her assent; and of her knowledge of the negotiation then proceeding for her future union with M. d'Orleans. Moreover, the arrests and sentences which by and by followed, smiting some of the noblest princes of the land, must have moved the nation with strong indignation, if inflicted to vindicate a cruel fraud; at the instigation likewise, of a minister new to the people, and

---

* No apologies which have since been made for Anne of Austria can efface the undoubted fact that Louis XIII. believed her to be guilty; besides, why was the Queen subjected to persecution and surveillance, if no evidence attested her connivance in the projects of Chalais, and other conspirators?

whose power was not then cemented by public confidence, or awe.

On the 6th of June the court removed to Blois, the Cardinal still remaining at Maison Rouge. On the 12th the Duke de Vendôme and his brother the Grand Prior arrived : and on the night of the 14th of the same month, the princes were both arrested in their beds by Du Hallier captain of the body-guard, and committed close prisoners to the castle of Amboise. The reason assigned by his Majesty for the arrest of his illegitimate brothers was, that they excited the people to hatred of his government, and to contempt of his person ; besides traitorously assuming an attitude hostile to M. de Richelieu.* Meantime, Madame de Chevreuse returned to France, and joined her royal mistress at Blois, resuming her empire over the mind of the Queen ; and more than her past influence with M. de Chalais. Monsieur also arrived at Blois, fearing not to stand over the mine he was preparing to explode. Here the expediency of gaining over some of the principal governors of provinces and important frontier towns, was suggested to Monsieur, by Bois

* Relation de tout ce qui s'est passé à l'emprisonnement de M. le Duc de Vendôme, et M. le Grand Prieur son Frère, au Château de Blois.— Archives Curieuses, t. 3, 2ème série.

d'Annemets, and Chalais. A certain Abbé d'Aubasine presented himself at Blois to pay his respects to
the King; and happening to state in confidence to
Chalais that the Duc d'Epernon, Governor of the
Angoumois, and of the Pays des Trois Evêchés, was
disaffected, and a partisan of Monsieur, it was determined that his royal highness should write to the
duke, and make certain propositions. Chalais had
some difficulty in persuading the duke to this step;
as Monsieur always showed an intense aversion to
attach his signature to any document. In this
instance he suffered himself to be overpersuaded;
and whilst he was engaged in the concoction of the
epistle, M. de Marcheville suddenly entered the
apartment. Monsieur being startled in the very act
of doing violence to his inclination, turned pale,
and seizing the paper, stuffed it into the pocket of
his *hauts de chausses*. This Marcheville, though one
of the *mignons*, had carefully avoided giving countenance to the designs of the malcontents; and feigned
to be ignorant that his royal master had secrets.[*]
The sudden resignation of M. de Marcheville on the
following day; and leave of absence being solicited
by another of the duke's chamberlains, M. d'Audilly,

* Mém. d'un Favori de M. le Duc d'Orléans.—Archives Curieuses,
t. 3.

might have warned Gaston, and his friends, that
prudence, and caution were advisable. Chalais,
however, continued to repair in the dead of the
night to the chamber of Monsieur; and there,
amongst other evil counsels, he induced the infatuated Prince to follow up his letter to the Duc
d'Epernon by another to M. de la Valette, the
duke's son and his lieutenant at Metz; on whom
Gaston was told that he had claims, as Madame
de la Valette was the illegitimate daughter of Henri
Quatre.   The Duc d'Epernon, grateful, perhaps,
for the clemency shown by Louis after the troubles
excited by the flight of Marie de' Medici from Blois,
sent Monsieur's letter straight to the King.   The
young Marquis de la Valette, a few days later,
also replied through M. de Louvigny, "that he
was the humble servant of Monsieur, and would be
happy to serve him: nevertheless, in an affair of
such importance as to deliver up to his royal highness his Majesty's fortress of Metz, he must first
consult his father and chief, Monsieur le Duc d'Epernon."* Richelieu, at this juncture, having secured his
proofs of the treasonable negotiations pending; and
having skilfully assembled his foes at Blois, presented

---

* Relation de tout ce qui s'est passé au Procès de Chalais, 1626.
Aubéry, Mém. pour servir à l'Histoire du Cardinal-Duc de Richelieu,
t. 1. Cologne, 1667.

himself before the King, and denounced the traitors. He also informed his Majesty that the Count de Soissons had insolently prepared measures to accomplish the abduction of Mademoiselle de Montpensier, who was living in Paris at the Hôtel Guise ; and that M. d'Orleans and Queen Anne were privy to the intended outrage. Louis became violently agitated ; but after poring some time over the documents submitted by his minister, he ordered the latter to proceed with the utmost rigour to unmask the traitors, and to confound their devices ; pledging his royal word to be guided by the counsels of his Eminence. Richelieu then advised his master to proceed forthwith to the city of Nantes—a visit already jotted down in the royal programme of travel before the return of Louis to the capital. He next despatched Rochefort to Paris, the bearer of an order commanding Madame de Guise and her daughter Mademoiselle de Montpensier, to give his Majesty rendezvous at Nantes—thus defeating any enterprise contemplated by the Count de Soissons. Monsieur and his friends now commenced to feel the prickings of distrust : private warnings harassed them ; in which it was reported that Goulas, the duke's secretary, and MM. de Marcheville and d'Andilly had been observed stealthily creeping from the abode of

M. le Cardinal. Moreover, their friends in Brussels seemed to lose heart at the enterprise; while the Marquis de Mirabel maintained an ominous silence respecting Richelieu, and mentioned even the word "submission." The Queen, likewise, was observed to weep in secret, and that little intercourse existed between the Queen-mother and Anne; while the King studiously avoided, as far as possible, any acknowledgment of the fact that the partner of his throne inhabited Blois. A further augury of coming evil was descried in the visit paid by the Prince de Condé to the Cardinal at Limours—an honour never before conferred.

The court, meantime, commenced its progress, and made temporary sojourn at Tours, Saumur, and Amiens. At Saumur a quarrel happened between M. de Louvigny and the Count de Candale. Chalais, who was of the party, took the side of Candale; when M. de Louvigny, beside himself with rage, reproached Chalais with his treasonable intelligence in the presence of the Duc d'Elbœuf. Louvigny having thus committed himself, sought audience of the King on the morrow, and confessed the overture which he had made to M. d'Epernon and his son, on behalf of Monsieur. Louis listened coldly; dismissed Louvigny, but commanded his arrest before the lapse of

three hours. Under the searching scrutiny of
Richelieu, Louvigny confirmed his previous confession,
and owned to be privy to the plot for the assassination of his Eminence; moreover adding, that Chalais
meditated the death of the King, which he intended
to accomplish when, as master of the wardrobe, he
adjusted his Majesty's ruff, by scratching him slightly
on the neck with a poisoned pin. A warrant thereupon was at once despatched for the arrest of M. de
Chalais, who was seized and carried to Nantes, as he
was stepping on board the barge in which Monsieur
was travelling, at a place just below Amiens. The
Cardinal now held every clue to the projects of
his enemies. Chalais lay in prison; Madame de
Chevreuse and her royal mistress trembled as the
dark tribulation approached. Marie de' Medici, who
had been accused in some of the papers intercepted,
of approving the marriage of the supposed widow of
Louis XIII. with Monsieur, and anxious to vindicate
herself in the opinion of her son, was nervously com-
plaisant; Mademoiselle de Montpensier, smitten with
awe at finding herself involved in a state plot, was
humble and obedient. Ornano, and the two brothers
de Vendôme lay in prison; Condé, that irascible and
touchy personage, so haughtily patronising, had been
compelled, lest he should be suspected of collusion in

the plot, to seek the good will of his Eminence at Limours; and even to sooth any probable irritation by speaking of an alliance as possible, between the heir of the Condés and *la petite* Clémence de Maillé Brezé, niece of Richelieu.* As for Monsieur, it was the policy of Richelieu to unmask and to humble him; but to cast him prostrate at the royal feet eventually on easy terms. Expiation by death, by torture, by banishment, by humiliations unparalleled, was nevertheless to be exacted from the miserable tools, and dupes of his royal highness's ambition, and duplicity. Above all, Anne of Austria was for evermore to be reduced to a position of abject dependence on the King and his minister; and discredited to a degree that her favour or disfavour became alike indifferent; while the fact that her Majesty was the eldest daughter of Spain, then considered to be the most potent monarchy of the universe, increased rather than diminished the triumph of the Cardinal. Monsieur, therefore, during the journey between Tours and Nantes, was scolded, cajoled, caressed, and

---

* Nicole du Plessis de Richelieu, sister of the Cardinal de Richelieu, married Urban Marquis de Brezé, subsequently Marshal of France. She had two children, the Princess de Condé, and Armand de Brezé, Duke de Fronsac, co-heir of the Cardinal with his cousin de Pontcourlay, also nephew of the Cardinal. Madame de Brezé died insane. For many years previous to her death she laboured under the delusion that she was made of glass, and shrieked if approached.

frightened. He was mysteriously exhorted, both by the Cardinal and the Queen-mother, to be on his guard; that the gentlemen of his household were in bad odour with the King; and that some political catastrophe was at hand. M. de Coigneux, who though in favour with his royal highness, had not participated in the cabal, was chosen by Louis as his medium of communication with his brother; while the Cardinal prepared more potent seduction for the weak brain of Monsieur from the lips of his trusty Capuchin, Père Joseph, who was summoned to Nantes by express.

A commission, composed of the new Lord Keeper Marillac, of the presidents Cussé and De Bry, and of the King's private secretary Beauclerc, of Fouquet, Machault, and De Criqueville, Masters of Requests, and of six members of the Parliament of Bretagne, was empowered to try the unhappy Chalais; and to investigate the alleged plot to its most secret ramifications.[*] Monsieur, though outwardly free, was warned by the Queen-mother not to venture without the city, under pain of arrest. Madame

* Relation de tout ce qui s'est passé au Procès de Chalais.—Aubéry, Mém. pour servir à l'Histoire du Cardinal-Duc de Richelieu, t. 1. The proceeding of the Cardinal caused great murmurings. Chalais, it was asserted, ought to have been tried before a Parliament of the realm, and not by a tribunal of judges nominated by his accusers. The act of the minister was stigmatised as " un procédé inique." " Les amis du cardinal répondirent qu'il avait pris ce biais pour ménager l'honneur des familles."

de Chevreuse, likewise, perceived herself to be under *surveillance ;* while the young Queen cowered under the displeasure of her lord, and while weeping over her forlorn condition, was repeatedly heard to utter the undignified wail, "that M. le Cardinal wanted to send her back to Spain, in order to marry the King to *la veuve Combalet."* Richelieu, meantime, proceeded to unravel the plot, with the utmost parade of moderation, and attention to the forms of ancient procedure; it was the first essay of the power of the minister; and a foretaste of the judicial arrangements by special commission which eventually made every disloyal heart quake. Certain members of the commission were appointed to interrogate the Duke of Orleans. Monsieur was previously admonished to make candid, and ample revelations ; while Père Joseph "assured Monsieur that if he confessed everything demanded from him, that he should receive a pardon, and even a recompense." Letters were first shown to the young Prince from the envoys of France at certain small German courts ; and also one from the ambassador in Vienna, warning the King that a conspiracy existed, and that its details were not unknown to Monsieur, to her Majesty the Queen consort, and to certain personages mentioned : its objects being first, to assassinate the Cardinal de

Richelieu, and subsequently to dethrone the King for incapacity, mental and physical; and to marry Queen Anne, to the Duke of Orleans. The plot was to be supported by the influence of the Duke of Buckingham over the English cabinet. Monsieur shuddered at his peril, and clung to the protection of Richelieu as his refuge in the terrible investigations pending. The morning of the 11th of August, therefore, found Monsieur ready and fluent; he made and signed a declaration, of which the following is an abstract:—1stly: That it was true M. le Comte de Soissons was in his confidence, and diligently reported to him affairs brought before the privy council; 2ndly: That Chalais was employed as their amanuensis and messenger; that it was true the latter had advised him to slay M. le Cardinal, to seize the fortress of Havre, and to demand for M. de Cœuvres the government of Pont de l'Arche, which strong fort they coveted in order to protect their flight from Paris to Havre; that Chalais had counselled him to propitiate, and to enter into secret relations with the Huguenot chieftains; that the said Chalais had instructed, and recommended one Louvigny to journey to Metz to invite and gain over the Marquis de la Valette to his (Monsieur's) interests; 3rdly: That M. de Chalais had told, and sworn to him (Monsieur) that the King had encamped 10,000 men in the vicinity of Nantes, in order, as Chalais concluded, to compel him to retire to Nancy, or to Brussels."* This cowardly avowal formed the nucleus of the charge of treason against M. de Chalais. The letters of the Duchess de Chevreuse,† of the Duke d'Epernon, and of M. de la Valette were given in as evidence; also certain letters which had been intercepted, from Joannés valet to M. de Chalais, addressed to Martin, his brother. Lastly: Richelieu and le Père Joseph produced their charge against Monsieur, Queen Anne, and Madame de Chevreuse, by show‑ ing copies of the letter brought into France by M. de Rochefort, addressed to Chalais, with the replies returned by that miserable young cavalier. On the same day, the 11th of August, the Commis‑ sioners met in the refectory of the monastery of the Franciscans at Nantes; and proceeded to the dis‑ charge of their preliminary duties, previous to com‑ manding the presence of the criminal before their tribunal. Chalais during this interval had remained in a condition of pitiable despair. Madame de Chevreuse

* Relation de tout ce qui s'est passé au Procès de M. de Chalais.— Vie du P. Joseph de Tremblay. Le Vassor, Hist. de Louis XIII.

† These letters were found in a casket at Maison Rouge, the country house of Chalais ; they were chiefly love epistles—" Mais il se trouva des choses peu respectueuses pour Louis XIII., que ces amants railloient sur sa froideur, et sur ses autres défauts naturels."– Galerie des Personnages Illustres de la Cour de France, t. 1. Lyon, 1806.

alone, with noble generosity, sought to soothe his trouble; and addressed to the poor captive a comforting note, which she caused to be sewed within the plait of a starched ruff sent to Chalais, by his request, to wear when he appeared before his judges. Such was the panic occasioned by the sudden arrests, and the mysteriousness of the hidden causes of inquiry, that the agent employed by Madame de Chevreuse proved a traitor, and carried her note to the Cardinal; who caused the writing to be copied, and produced it on the following day against the Duchess.

It was determined by the High Court to issue orders of arrest against the Duchess de Chevreuse, the Count de Soissons, the Duc d'Epernon, and his son, l'Abbé Aubasine, M. de Louvigny, and certain *mignons* of Monsieur—to wit, MM. de Bois d'Annemets, Puylaurens, St. Géry, Marsillac, le Meilleraye, and de Mouay, — nevertheless, that such warrants should first be authenticated by the sign-manual of the King.* Triumphant in the possession of these documents † Richelieu laid them before the King at a council specially summoned on the

---

* Relation de tout ce qui s'est passé au Procès de M. de Chalais.— Aubéry. Mém. pour servir à l'Histoire du Cardinal de Richelieu, t. 1.— Mém. d'un Favori de M. le Duc d'Orléans.

† " Richelieu assura le Nonce Spada que Chalais avait engagé Gaston à des éclats qui auroient dû devenir très préjudiciables à la paix du royaume, comme de quitter la cour, de se retirer à La Rochelle, et de

morrow. Louis desired to hear some of the witnesses; the council was therefore adjourned till after dinner of the same day. Invitations were issued to the Presidents Cussé and de Bry to attend; and before this assemblage Louis resolved, by the advice of his minister, to summon Queen Anne and Madame de Chevreuse. The Duke de Bellegarde, Louvigny, the Duke d'Elbœuf, le Père Joseph, the Count de Rochefort, and the Marquis d'Effiat were first heard. The intercepted correspondence was read over by the secretary Beauclerc, in the presence of his Majesty, who reclined in a *fauteuil* with a gloomy scowl upon his countenance. Marie de' Medici presently entered, and seated herself by Richelieu; in so doing her Majesty whispered a word in his ear, which his Eminence noticed by a slight inclination of the head. At the command of the King the folding doors opposite were opened, and Anne of Austria appeared on the threshold, unattended, save by an usher and by one half-scared lady. Anne dismissed her attendant; and then advanced, and took a seat at the bottom of the table indicated by the Cardinal, as the King neither rose, nor took the smallest notice of her presence. The interrogatory which followed unfortunately never

soulever les Huguenots."—Galerie des Personnages Illustres de la Cour de France.

transpired; that it was severe and uncompromising, the tears shed by the Queen, and its after effect on her health and temper testify. Anne seems steadily to have denied the allegations against her; unfortunately, however, her Majesty had previously given peremptory contradiction to undoubted facts well known to her royal husband and to his minister, from terror at the consequences of her indiscretion. The letter written by Madame de Chevreuse to Chalais, and placed in the Queen's hands, must have taxed her fortitude; for there now remains little doubt that Anne had tampered in the schemes of these foolish plotters to a degree which for ever bereft her of the regard of her husband; who emphatically affirmed his belief in her culpability. When questioned concerning her speculations on the King's intended deposition, and her design to espouse Monsieur, Anne replied, " that she should have gained thereby too small a stake to render it even probable that she had blackened her conscience by the imagination of such a crime!" * " Her Majesty thereupon, with tears, bitterly upbraided the Queen-mother for the persecu-

* " Le Roy fit venir la Reine au conseil, où il lui reprocha qu'elle avoit conspiré contre sa vie pour avoir un autre mari. La Reine, à qui l'innocence donna des forces, outrée de douleur de cette accusation, lui parla avec fermeté, et lui dit, à ce que j'ai sçu par elle-même, qu'elle auroit trop peu gagné au change pour vouloir se noircir d'un crime pour un petit intérêt."—Motteville, t. i., p. 28. Madame de Motteville always believes the statements offered to her by Anne of Austria with implicit faith, deeming her Majesty immaculate.

tions and indignities heaped upon her since her arrival in France." No minute of this council was preserved. Anne's reply, relative to M. d'Orléans, alone, of all her answers to the various charges, was suffered to transpire.

When the Queen retired, Madame de Chevreuse was summoned before the Council. The Duchess entered, sustained by a consciousness of wit, beauty, and of aptness of speech, and retort. She was subjected by the King himself to a long and humiliating inter-rogatory; and dismissed, placed under the *surveillance* of the captain of the body-guard. M. de Louvigny was next introduced, to make further revelations relative to the malignity of the treason of M. de Chalais. The latter, besides his avowed intent to kill Richelieu, and to depose the King, was accused of regicidal designs by de Louvigny; who, a few weeks previously, was considered to be the intimate friend of the unhappy prisoner. Chalais, who was master of the wardrobe, meditated the murder of the King, according to the statement of Louvigny, by steeping the shirts worn by his Majesty in a subtle poison; intending to accelerate the action of the venom, by scratching the King on the nape of the neck with a poisoned pin, while adjusting his ruff. "This Chalais," says the Abbé d'Artigny,[*]

---

[*] Hist. du Critique et de la Littérature, t. 6, p. 219.

" was of a temper so malicious and spiteful, that when he was attiring his Majesty he made faces behind the King's back; also, when in prison, he could not hold himself from speaking evil things of the King; and even to offend him deeply, by letters which he presumed to write. Louis XIII. could not refrain, therefore, from one day exclaiming, 'This man has truly a malignant, and churlish temper!'"

On the 18th of August, Chalais was led before his judges, after having been subjected to three searching interrogatories. His condemnation was unanimously voted; the prisoner appealing against his sentence, and denying the charges alleged. The decree condemned Chalais to decapitation, after suffering the torture of *les brodequins*, and to the pains of degradation, and the confiscation of his estates. No sooner was the unfortunate man conducted back to his prison, than he was again beset by the emissaries of Richelieu, seeking, by any promises, to extort confession; and especially, to wring from the unwilling lips of the prisoner full details respecting the *liaison* existing between Anne of Austria and her brother-in-law. For long Chalais resolutely insisted on the innocence of the Queen; stating, although it was true, that for a period of seventeen days the death of the King and his minister had been discussed—yet, that after the arrest of MM. de Vendôme, and after

the failure of the conspiracy to kill Richelieu at
Fleury, he had tampered with the conspirators, at
the command only of the minister, to discover their
progress and designs. Vanquished at length by the
subtle Père Joseph,* Chalais made other avowals : he
stated that Queen Anne, Monsieur, and Madame de
Chevreuse, were implicated in the conspiracy; that
the Queen-mother herself was so far committed, that
she had acknowledged if the King died, a wise
policy would direct the acceptance by Monsieur of
the hand of his brother's richly dowered widow, on
assuming the crown of France: that the death of the
Cardinal de Richelieu had been decided upon, to
be accomplished as opportunity occurred; that it
was a fact that the Queen had communicated the
details of the conspiracy to her kindred in Spain,
and had received the approbation of Philip IV. her
brother. Transported with his success, the wily
Capuchin entered his patron's presence, and tendered the admissions which placed the highest
personages of the realm at the mercy of the
Cardinal. Richelieu, it is said, repaired privately
the same night to the dungeon of the prisoner, and
promised him life, and ultimate pardon, provided

* " Le Capucin l'assura, de la part du Cardinal, que s'il avouait tout ce
qu'on lui demanderoit, il aurait sa grâce ; et sur la parole d'un religieux
dont la réputation n'avoit point été attaquée, cet accusé declara plus qu'il
ne savoit pour certain des mécontents." – Vie du Père Joseph, Capucin.

that he would repeat his confession in the hearing of his guards; or reveal every incident in a private interview with the King.

The Duke of Orleans, during these proceedings, maintained a most undignified attitude: avoided by the courtiers—uncertain whether he would long be tolerated by the King; clinging to the wily Capuchin Joseph; and creeping warily to the apartments of the Queen-mother, who scarcely dared speak to her son, to learn the attitude of affairs. The young cavaliers of his suite fled from Nantes. Puylaurens and Bois d'Annemets alone mustered courage to face the storm. Le Coigneux, meantime, ascertained that Monsieur could free himself from the effects of his misconduct, only by consenting to immediate marriage with Mademoiselle de Mont-pensier. The Duke thereupon, ventured to propose stipulations, one of which was, the pardon of M. de Chalais; but was met by the crushing inti-mation that the criminal had made confession, and had deeply implicated both Monsieur and Queen Anne; and therefore, that the Duke must accept with gratitude the will of the King, or take the consequences. Monsieur then alleged certain rea-sons, which would prevent his immediate espou-sals; nevertheless, on the morrow he suddenly visited Marie de' Medici, and assented to his marriage, provided that the Marshal d'Ornano and Chalais were liberated; and that certain pecuniary concessions * were granted—all which negotiations he committed to her care, and to that of M. le Coigneux. The Duke's submission was well timed: the irritated spirit of Louis XIII. brooked not trifling; and his Majesty conceived that his honour demanded that the immediate union of his brother to Marie de Montpensier, should stifle and refute the reports current respecting Monsieur's *liaison* with Anne of Austria. Certain reforms were likewise commenced in the household of the Duke, on the authority of the King: three of his chamberlains were summarily dismissed; and the Duc de Bellegarde was placed at the head of his establishment.† Louis, meanwhile, offered to his brother oblivion of the past, on condition of his marriage with Marie de Montpensier: ‡ upon that event, his Majesty proposed to put Monsieur into possession of his appanage, the duchies de Chartres and d'Orléans and the county of Blois; to settle upon him lands to the amount of 100,000 livres annually; with a

* Mém. d'un Favori de M. le Duc d'Orléans.

† Journal de ma Vie.—Bassompierre, ann. 1626.

‡ Richelieu, it is said, caused Monsieur's horoscope to be drawn before his marriage, to ascertain whether his royal highness, or his posterity, were likely to succeed to the crown of France. The answer of the oracle was " Imperium non gustabit in æternum."

nett revenue of 760,000 livres for the expenses of
his household.* Le Père Joseph undertook to
render Monsieur satisfied with this munificent offer:
a few arguments, a little deprecation, and the transparent assurance "that after Monsieur's reconciliation with the King, he would be in a better condition to intercede for the prisoner, and the rest
of the accused," prevailed. The ceremony of the
affiancing was performed August 20th, in the apartment of the Queen-mother, by the Cardinal de
Richelieu; and the pair were married at midnight.
The ceremony was performed with the pomp befit-
ting the occasion, and the publicity which King
Louis desired. The marriage contract was signed
at five p.m. on a table standing on a platform of
state. The King sat under a canopy, supported by
the Queen-mother; opposite, sat Queen Anne, with
an aspect pale and discomposed, having on her right
the young bride. At the table stood Richelieu, at
the head of a numerous assemblage of bishops. The
apartment was filled with a brilliant court, including
Bellegarde, d'Elbœuf, Bassompierre, Marsillac, the
Duchesses de Rohan, d'Halluin, de Guise, de Bellegarde, and others. The King had commanded
that no order of precedence should be observed;
and that the ladies should take place in the vicinity

* Mém. d'un Favori de M. le Duc d'Orléans.—Vie du Père Joseph.

of the *haut dais,* as they arrived. A scramble for precedence, nevertheless, occurred between the Duchesses d'Halluin and de Rohan—the latter lady being the strongminded and resolute daughter of the Duke de Sully—during which, the illustrious ladies so far forgot decorum as to pinch each other in their efforts not to lose the *terrain*, that each declared the other wished to usurp.* " The royal pair were affianced, and at midnight espoused. Never was there before seen so sad a ceremony. Madame was dressed in a robe of white satin, adorned with her own superb pearls, and with those belonging to the Queen. We had neither violins, nor music of any kind. Monsieur had not even a new habit. Furniture was borrowed to decorate the bridal chamber. Few private persons have been married with such scanty pomp. The King came to the *coucher* of Monsieur, and handed him his shirt; and the Queen-mother was present at the toilette of Madame. When every one had retired, a laughable incident occurred. A little lap-dog was accidentally shut up in the chamber of the newly-married pair; which obliged Madame de Guise, who occupied an adjacent apartment, to rise and hunt the miserable

---

* Bénédiction Nuptiale de Monseigneur le Duc d'Orléans, Frère de Louis XIII., et de Marie de Montpensier.—Godefroy, Grand Cérém. de France, t. 2.

animal, whose yelps added to the ridicule of this fine marriage."*

The marriage concluded,† Monsieur ventured to insist on the hopes inspired by M. le Cardinal, that mercy might be shown to the accused. Chalais also loudly claimed the immunity so perfidiously promised by the Cardinal, on condition of his confession. The sentence pronounced on the unfortunate young man was, nevertheless, confirmed by the King; who mitigated only the rigour of the penalty, by forbidding that torture should be employed before execution. His Majesty was pleased, moreover, to annul the attainder of that branch of the house of Talleyrand from which Chalais sprang.‡ The sentence was appointed to be carried out three days after the celebration of Monsieur's marriage; meantime, the fate of the minor delinquents was pronounced. Madame de Chevreuse received sentence of banishment from court; and was conducted by an exempt of the royal guards to her husband's castle of Dampierre; where she was

---

* Mém. d'un Favori de M. le Duc d'Orléans.

† "Chalais apprit ce mariage par le bruit de canon. Il ne dit mot, et attend tristement le sort que cet évènement lui annonce. On l'avoit mis en cachot."—Galerie des Personnages Illustres, t. 4.

‡ Relation de tout ce qui s'est passé au Procès de M. de Chalais.— Aubéry, t. 1. One chronicler, an eye-witness of the execution, states that Chalais said on the scaffold:—"Ce n'est pas sur l'espérance qu'on m'a donné de ma grâce que j'ai avoué, mais parceque la conviction était entière."

consigned to strict *surveillance*. The King for some days insisted on her imprisonment in the Bastille; and was deterred only from this severity by the intercession of Richelieu, who was a great admirer of the spirited Duchess; and by the entreaties of M. de Chevreuse, who undertook to answer for her submission. "The Duchess was transported with fury," writes Richelieu; "she went so far as to assert that we knew her not, when we concluded that she had only wit, coquetry, and vanity: nevertheless, she would soon show us that she was good for something else; for there was nothing that she would not suffer to be avenged, and no indignity to which she would not joyfully submit to compass such."* Before her departure for Dampierre the Duchess had petitioned to be allowed to retire to England, where her beauty and vivacity had rendered her popular.† Madame de Chevreuse, however, who hated the melancholy solitudes of Dampierre, continued to agitate so effectually, that, after an interval of six months, she obtained permission to visit her husband's kindred of Lorraine, at Nancy. The Count de Soissons, advised of the accusations

---

Cousin, Vie de Madame de Chevreuse.— Mém. du Cardinal de Richelieu, t. 3.

† "Madame de Chevreuse fit confesser (aux dames Anglaises) que toutes leurs beautés n'étoient rien au prix de la sienne."— Mém. d'un Favori de M. le Duc d'Orléans.

preferred against him, propitiated the wrath of his royal master by resigning his post as governor of Paris, and by quitting the realm, a self-condemned exile : the warrant of arrest was thereupon cancelled. The post of governor of Bretagne was taken from the Duc de Vendôme, who continued for some time a captive at Vincennes. Condé also bowed before the policy of the Cardinal; and did not venture to present himself for a long period at court for his supposed connivance in the plot at Fleury. Sundry minor awards were allotted to the inferior agents of the conspiracy ; fines, imprisonments, and banishments warned the *valetaille* of the great lords that the formidable ruler of France took cognizance also of their derelictions, as well as of the more heinous offences of their masters.

The most illustrious offender still remained to be visited with a public manifestation of royal wrath. The condition of the young Queen was pitiable. The King refused to hold communication with her ; and she was forbidden to see the Duchess de Chevreuse, or to converse with M. d'Orléans. Marie de' Medici, sheltered only by Richelieu from the indignation of her son for her semi-adherence to the intrigues under investigation, dared not afford even a semblance of protection or countenance to the Queen.

On the 27th of August an order was issued, signed by Louis, and countersigned by his minister, forbidding *entrée* to the Queen's saloons and cabinets to the noblemen and gentlemen in waiting, or to the courtiers of the Louvre, unless they paid their respects to her Majesty in the King's presence; and entered her apartments, and departed therefrom in his suite. A restriction more humiliating, and subversive of the courtly splendours and deference enjoyed by her predecessors queens of France, could not have been inflicted. Anne likewise received the imperious commands of her royal husband never to grant a private audience without first advertising Queen Marie, or the Cardinal; and naming the personage whom she was about to receive, and the object of the interview.* Correspondence with Madame de Chevreuse was strictly forbidden; as also with Madame de la Valette. The severity of this punishment, however, did not subdue the proud heart of the Queen. Neglected by her husband, she persistently turned for sympathy towards her own kindred of Spain, whose counsels aggravated her position; for the King her brother, never effec-

* Mém. de la Rochefoucauld, t. 1.—Dreux du Radier, Vie d'Anne d'Autriche.—Motteville, t. 1.—The latter insists that the " persecutions " which the Queen experienced were not inflicted for any fault of her own, " Mais les premiers marques de l'affection du Cardinal de Richelieu furent les persecutions qu'il lui fit."—Griffet, Hist. de Louis XIII., t. 1.

tually interfered to ameliorate her position ; or to intercede in her behalf.

The Duke of Orleans continued to make unceasing efforts to procure a commutation of the sentence pronounced on Chalais, but to no purpose. Early on the morning following his brother's marriage, the King quitted Nantes for Paris, being preceded by the Queens, Anne and Marie. It was thought that his Majesty's sudden journey was to avoid further solicitations on the part of Monsieur. The Duke, nevertheless, continued his intercession ; and implored the Cardinal to stay the execution, until he could rejoin the King his brother. His Eminence replied, "that he had no power to grant the request of his Royal Highness." The same answer Richelieu returned to the mother* of the unfortunate Chalais ; who, on her knees, implored mercy for her misguided son on the plea, that Chalais had previously saved the Cardinal's life, by confessing the plot to assassinate him, at his château de Fleury. It must, nevertheless, be owned that Louis acted with clemency towards the guilty contrivers of a plot so aggravated ; for to assert that such existed only in the scheming imagination of the Cardinal de Richelieu, is utterly to disregard the evidence

* Françoise de Montluc, daughter of Blaise de Montluc, Marshal of France.

which has descended to these days. That many
documents were suppressed, as damaging to the
honour of the crown, and to the reputation of
Queen Anne, is not surprising; neither can it
excite wonder that King Louis commanded that no
minutes of the privy council before which his Queen
was arraigned, should be preserved and registered.
" She wished for my death, and coveted another
husband during my lifetime! " was often the bitter
remark of Louis XIII. when any one pleaded the
cause of the Queen; and such remained his Majesty's
settled conviction on his death-bed. The Duke of
Orleans, the Count de Soissons, the Duke d'Epernon
and M. de la Valette, the Duchess de Chevreuse, and
her potent kindred of Rohan, were not likely to
have accepted the odium of such a conspiracy without protest, if, in fact, the whole affair had been a
device, trumped up by Richelieu to rivet his power.
Philip IV. of Spain remained silent; and never
denied, through his ambassador or otherwise, the reception of the letter stated to have been written by
the Queen. The Archduchess-Infanta Isabel, moreover, never repudiated the assertion that the intrigue
was discussed and matured in Brussels, her own
capital; which so good, and conscientious a princess
would have done if possible, in aid of her niece Queen
Anne, oppressed under so grave a charge of domestic,

and state treason. The fact, however, which seems amply to prove the truth of the conspiracy, and of the charges respecting the Queen, is, that three years later, Anne, of her own accord, proposed a renewed discussion of the policy of her alliance with M. d'Orléans, after the then expected death of Louis XIII. The health of the King was precarious; and the result of his repeated attacks of illness so uncertain under the rude medical treatment of the day, that the expectation of his death repeatedly acted as a snare, to lure the malcontents to premature revelation of their designs.

M. de Chalais suffered on the twenty-sixth day of August.[*] Before his execution he made recantation of all his avowals; and adhered only to the statement, "that for seventeen days only, before his interview with M. le Cardinal at Fleury, he had meditated the death of the Cardinal; and the deposition of Louis XIII." The interference of his friends, however, served to prolong his agony. In the hope that the prayers of M. d'Orléans might

---

[*] Relation du Procès de Chalais.—Aubéry, Mém. pour servir à l'Histoire du Cardinal de Richelieu. t. 1. "Il n'a rien dit à tout cela [son arrêt], qu'il résignait son âme à Dieu, et son corps au Roy. Chalais est mort dans la plus grande résolution qui ait jamais été veue. Il a dit dans la chapelle : 'Ne suis-je pas bien malheureux d'avoir desservy le meilleur prince qui soit au monde ?'"—Deux Lettres touchant la Mort de M. de Chalais, de Nantes, ce 26 Aoust 1626, à 7 heures de soir.—Aubéry, t. 1.

eventually prevail, and therefore that the gain of a few days might be life to Chalais, they bribed and carried off the public executioner of Nantes. The morning appointed for the execution dawned, and no headsman appeared. By order of the Cardinal, the execution was delayed until six in the evening, when two prisoners under condemnation of death taken from the common jail, undertook to perform the task, on receiving a pardon for their services. These unskilful executioners mangled the poor prisoner in the most shocking manner; and succeeded in despatching him only after thirty-five strokes of the axe.* The body of the unfortunate Chalais was given to his mother; who caused it to be interred before the high altar of the Church of the Franciscans of Nantes.

When all was over, M. de Louvigny, the original denouncer of Chalais, was arrested and committed to close prison at the suit of Monsieur, for having accused the latter falsely, maliciously, and disloyally; attributing to the brother of the King, high crimes

---

* " On a tirez deux hommes destinez au gibets des prisons de cette ville, dont l'un à fait l'exécuteur, et l'autre lui à assisté pour lui servir. Mais ça a été avec si peu d'adresse, que, outre les deux premiers coups d'une épée de Suisse, qu'on a achetée sur le champ, il lui en a donné trente-quatre d'une doloire dont se servent les tonneliers ; et a été contraint de le retourner de l'autre côté pour l'achever de couper, le patient criant jusqu'au vingtième coup—' Jesus, Maria, et Regina Cœli !' "— Extrait de Deux Lettres touchant la Mort de M. de Chalais. Aubéry, Mém. pour servir à l'Histoire de M. le Cardinal de Richelieu.

which had no foundation ; and which, for the honour
of the crown, needed to be atoned for, and retracted.
Having pardoned Monsieur for his late, and principal
share in the conspiracy for which Chalais suffered,
Louis XIII. and his minister required justification
for their clemency ; and a plausible, statement which
might clear the reputation of the heir-presumptive
of France.

CHAPTER IV.

1626—1630.

ANNE OF AUSTRIA AND MARIE DE' MEDICI.

On her arrival in Paris, Anne earnestly petitioned
to be allowed to retire to St. Germain. She was
afflicted with a constant nervous tremor; and suffered at intervals from such prostration of strength
as to create serious alarm. The mental anxiety
which she had undergone had shaken her health;
and in her solitude and depression, Anne lamented her separation from Madame de Chevreuse.
Peril and disgrace, however, unfortunately brought
not to the Queen's mind a juster appreciation of
the responsibilities, and dignity of her position.
She took no step, on her return to the Louvre, to
reconcile herself with her husband; she treated
Richelieu in public with negligent indifference; and
made no attempt to conceal the greatness of her
indignation against Marie de' Medici, for "the shameful abandonment" which she had experienced at

Nantes.　Festivities were rare events at the Louvre; and the recent ordinance, forbidding *entrée* to the Queen's cabinets and saloon to the gentlemen of the court, had condemned Anne to virtual solitude.　The Queen was surrounded by domestic spies, who made reports to Richelieu; for the latter watched with jealous vigilance her correspondence in England, and Spain.　Aware of this *surveillance*, the Queen nevertheless, continued to correspond with the Duchess de Chevreuse, with her kindred in Spain, with the Infanta at Brussels, with the Queen of England, and even with the Duke of Buckingham, through the instrumentality of Gerbier, steward of the household to Buckingham; who yet lingered in France, under pretext of collecting works of art for the decoration of his master's palaces.　King Charles and his ministers were at this period specially odious to Louis: the feuds of the French attendants of Queen Henrietta Maria, and the indiscreet zeal of the priests, had necessitated their banishment from England.　London was provoked almost to a tumult by the doings of these personages; and by the unhappy influence which Madame de St. Georges exercised over the quick temper of her royal mistress.*　From this lady,

---

* Galerie des Personnages Illustres de la Cour de France, t. 4. Charles had given his wife four ladies of honour—the Duchess of Buckingham, the Marchioness of Hamilton, and the Countesses of Denbigh and Carlisle, with whom the French ladies were perpetually at feud.

who was the daughter of the King's old *gouvernante*, Madame de Montglât, Louis heard of the extravagant, and indecorous manner in which Buckingham raved of the Queen of France; and of the Duke's indiscreet comments on Anne's unfortunate destiny as a wife. Lord Montague was despatched by Charles to explain the step which he had found himself compelled to sanction, relative to the expulsion from England of Henrietta's French attendants.* Louis, however, being apprized by Madame de St. Georges, that the ambassador carried letters from Buckingham to the Queen, and to the Duchess de Chevreuse, Montague received, on his arrival in Paris, an order to leave the realm without audience; or being permitted to deliver his despatches. Bassompierre was appointed, a few days subsequently, as ambassador extraordinary to the court of Great Britain ; deputed to mediate, on behalf of the Queen-mother and King Louis, between Charles and his Queen ; and to insist on the plenary execution of the marriage contract which granted to Henrietta the full, and public exercise of her faith.

The office of first *dame d'atours*, vacant by the

* " Les dames et les autres étrangères reçoivent ordre de se préparer à retourner en France dans vingt-quatre heures.—Le Roi les va voir à l'hôtel Sommerset, leur déclare sa volonté, et leur fait quelques présents. On les embarque au plutôt. Henriette, désolée, écrit en France."—Personnages Illustres, t. 4.

banishment of Madame de Chevreuse, was given by the Cardinal to Madame de Fargis, the wife of de Fargis,* late French ambassador at Madrid. Anne objected violently to the appointment; but, after a few months of sullen protest, ended by taking Madame de Fargis into favour; and by yielding absurd compliance to her counsels. Madame de Fargis was the daughter of M. de la Rochepot, the old and faithful servant of Henri Quatre, and his ambassador for many years at the court of Madrid. So flighty and ill regulated, was the conduct of Madeleine de Silly, that at an early age she had been confided by her father to the care of his old friend the Countess de St. Paul, a rigid Huguenot, as became the representative of the elder line of Caumont de la Force; and whose hôtel in Paris, seems to have served as a kind of penitentiary for unruly damsels of rank. The discipline of the Hôtel de St. Paul proved of no avail. Mademoiselle de Silly so compromised her reputation with the Count de Cramail and others, that she was compelled to seek the shelter of a convent. "One might have imagined," says a contemporary, "that this lightsome lady was beautiful: not at all; her face was marked by small-pox; but she was agreeable, witty, lively,

* Charles d'Angennes, Seigneur de Fargis. He was ambassador in Spain from the year 1620 to 1624.

gallant, and a most charming companion." Mademoiselle de Silly, however, declined to take vows; and remained at her convent, the Carmelites of the Faubourg St. Jacques—often scandalizing the community, but winning toleration by her incomparable temper, and fun — until the death of her father, and of her eldest and only sister, the Countess de Retz.* Madeleine, now sole heiress of her late father, thereupon took leave of her friends the Carmelites, under pretext that her health forbade her to follow the severity of their rule. Her old levity returned in full vigour, on mingling again with the world; she appeared at the assemblies of the Hôtel Rambouillet, and there captivated M. de Fargis d'Angennes, cousin-german of the Marquis de Rambouillet, her host. Wit, humour, and joyous *abandon* were more to a d'Angennes than morality, or *bienséance*. Madeleine de Silly became the wife of M. de Fargis, who had just been appointed ambassador to Madrid, and accompanied him to Spain. Her sojourn there lasted four years; and great had been the admiration excited by the graceful, and lively ambassadress. Madame de Fargis, however, rejoiced in her husband's recall from his mission; for

* Françoise de Silly, wife of Philippe Emmanuel de Gondy, Général des Galères, subsequently priest of the Order de l'Oratoire. He died in 1662.

The gloomy and decorous court of Philip IV. wearied, and taxed too severely her powers of self-control. She had scarcely arrived in Paris when the post of lady of the bedchamber to Queen Anne fell at the disposal of Richelieu. Madame de Fargis instantly solicited the appointment through the Cardinal de Berulle, who was confessor, and director of the Carmelites of the Faubourg St. Jacques; and whose friendship she had won during her seclusion with the nuns. Berulle introduced the fair petitioner to the potent minister;* who found the wit of Madame de Fargis so much to his taste, and was so satisfied with her apparent devotion to his interests, and by her promises to rule the Queen and her household in subservience to his will, that Richelieu decided upon the appointment. Madame de Fargis accordingly, in defiance of the repugnance manifested by the Queen, entered upon her functions, which virtually gave her the privileges of the first lady of the household, as Anne at this period had no *dames du palais*. Madame de la Flotte † was at the same time appointed by the Cardinal as governess of

* " Le Cardinal (de Richelieu) donne des rendez-vous à Madame de Fargis chez le Cardinal de Berulle, à Fontainebleau et ailleurs, de peur de faire trop d'éclat si c'était chez lui-même ; et aussi à cause que Berulle passoit pour un béat."—Tallemant, t. 2.

† Catherine Le Voyer de Lignerolles, wife of René du Bellay, Seigneur de la Flotte Hauterive ; her daughter, Renée du Bellay, was the mother of Marie de Hautefort.

Queen Marie's maids of honour; and about this period she introduced her grand-daughter, the celebrated Marie de Hautefort, at the Luxembourg. The merit of Mademoiselle de Hautefort was discerned by Marie; who presented her to the notice of Louis XIII., as a damsel of " singular virtue and probity."

Madame de Chevreuse, meantime, had been busily engaged on the work of proving to the Cardinal de Richelieu "that she was not the friendless, and incompetent personage he took her to be." Intent on vengeance, few could have more skilfully combined the elements of dissension ; or have fostered so cleverly the prevailing discord between the powers of Europe. In France discontent was rife : the crown was gradually, but firmly resuming its ancient grants of privileges to the great barons of the realm, which had been so cruelly misused; the King aimed at being in future the sole fountain of honour, and dispenser of grace. The haughty lords, who were paramount over the provinces of the kingdom, saw themselves displaced for trivial misdemeanours ; and their governments given to new men, creatures of the minister, and dependent upon the bounty of the King for their position, and revenue. The Huguenots rebelled under the strong hand of Richelieu ; the Rohans beheld their pretensions to the

once Protestant principality of Béarn, so long a
menace to the descendants of Henri IV., derided.
Duplessis-Mornay wrote in vain, and found his threats
futile; and Lesdiguières, wise in his day, secured
the fortunes of his house by renouncing Calvinism.
The strongholds wrested from Henri IV. by his
restless subjects of the reformed faith, Richelieu now
redemanded; and announced that, that focus of sedition La Rochelle, and its adjacent territory, must
submit to the universal ascendancy of the crown, by
the expulsion of its heretic municipality: and of its
defenders, de Rohan, and his brothers of Soubise.
The frantic cries of the French Protestants, thus
menaced by a minister armed with irresponsible
power, echoed in the English council; and the Duke
de Rohan sent his brothers de Soubise, to implore the
aid of Charles I. and the favourable auspices of
Buckingham. A mandate of extermination for the
great Huguenot citadel had already gone forth;
the engineers, and the surveyors of the Cardinal
encircled La Rochelle; and by the command of his
Eminence were engaged in fortifying the island of
Ré, which had been captured by M. de St. Luc,
after the Huguenots had suffered a naval defeat from
the ships under M. de Montmorency. The influence
of the Duchess de Chevreuse was yet alive in England. Lord Holland was devoted to her; Bucking-

ham conciliated her favour for the sake of, and as a means of access to Anne of Austria; and King Charles admired her sprightliness, and extolled her personal charms. She was, moreover, a near kinswoman of the "great Rohans." Marie de Rohan Chevreuse, therefore, whose relatives might kindle civil war throughout Bretagne, and the south of France, felt that her enmity could make itself felt, even when her foe was the omnipotent Cardinal ruler of France. Spain, already passively inimical, was ready to take up arms on the slightest provocation. The restraint in which her ambassador lived in Paris; the grievances of the young Queen Anne; the unfriendly distance maintained by King Louis towards his wife's kinsmen; and the earnest desire manifested by Philip IV. to disturb the *entente* between the crowns of France and England, apparently riveted by the marriage of a French princess with Charles I. rendered the Spanish minister accessible to negotiation. The question concerning the succession to the duchy of Mantua, moreover, opened a multitude of grievances, and heartburnings. The new duke was one of Louis' most potent princes, Charles de Gonzague de Cleves, Duc de Nevers. The Emperor Ferdinand II. opposed his investiture; and, in concert with the Spanish Viceroy of Milan, and the Duke of Savoy, invaded the duchy and its dependency of

Montferrato. Nevers appealed to Louis XIII., and besought his intervention; a prayer, to which the politic Richelieu gave little heed, pending his warlike designs on the Rochellois. In the Duke of Lorraine, Madame de Chevreuse found a ready and willing ally,* Charles IV. had espoused his cousin Nicole, eldest daughter of Duke Henry of Lorraine and Marguerite de Gonzague, and heiress of the duchy. The duke was a vacillating, unsteady man; a slave to feminine charms and wiles; and indifferent to his consort, whose attachment he repaid by attempts, after their marriage, to set aside her claims on the duchy, and to assert those of his father the Count de Vaudemont, as the nearest male heir of the late duke his father-in-law.† Charles received Madame de Chevreuse with distinction; he assigned for her use the beautiful palace of Blamont; and abetted her intrigues to bring about a coalition of the Powers against France. The campaign was to be inaugurated by the succour of La Rochelle. The Duke always inclined to the alliance of Austria, rather than

---

* " Elle éblouit, séduisit, entraîna l'impétueux et aventureux Charles IV."—Cousin, Vie de Madame de Chevreuse.

† Henry Duke of Lorraine had two daughters, co-heiresses, Nicole and Claude. Nicole married Charles IV., her cousin, eldest son of the Count de Vaudemont, third brother of the duke her father. Claude married François, younger brother of Charles IV., and their posterity continued the ducal line of Lorraine. Claude was the mother of the famous Duke Charles V. of Lorraine, who never possessed his duchy, then confiscated by the French. He became the brother-in-law of the Emperor Leopold.

to that of France. Richelieu had demanded several of Charles' frontier strongholds ; and, unable to cope against so potent a pleader, he had sought safety under the protection of the Emperor. The design of the confederates, after the relief of La Rochelle by the British fleet, was, that the Duke of Buckingham should disembark, and accept a command in the late beleaguered city ; that the Duke of Savoy should then invade Provence ; that the Duke de Rohan, at the head of the Calvinist armies, should raise Languedoc ; while the Duke de Lorraine made his way through Champagne to the very gates of the capital,—such having been the proposed campaign, and dream of all the traitorous subjects of France from the days of the great Constable de Bourbon. To execute the plan of the conspiracy it was necessary that the English fleet should take the initiative ; and by the succour of La Rochelle, and the destruction of Richelieu's famous forts on the island of Ré, enable the French dissidents in the south to take heart enough to listen to the subtle promptings of Philip IV. and his minister, the Count-duke de Olivarez. As Philip II., the zealous champion of the popedom, had tampered with the allegiance of the heretic Henri de Navarre, in his war with his orthodox sovereign King Henry III., and promised aid to the Huguenots ; so now, Philip IV. was ready to become the ally of the Rohans, provided that the realm suffered calamity enough to destroy its competition with the monarchy of Spain. It appears that the Queen was kept constantly informed of the progress of this negotiation : unadmonished by her recent narrow escape, and by the clemency which she had received at the hands of the King her consort, and of the minister whom she pursued with such reckless hate, Anne ventured still to cabal. Such was the Queen's hardihood, and so perfect were her powers of dissimulation and silent endurance, that no past danger ever seems to have been sufficiently remembered to act as a warning for the future. Her very helplessness, beauty, and affability, won devoted attachment ; so that no princess ever possessed adherents more faithful, and determined. Under a silent and submissive demeanour strong passions agitated the spirit of the Queen : her haughtiness of character invested her with self-control ; while her passive, but determined enmity rendered her a foe to be dreaded even by Richelieu.

The young Duchess of Orleans, during the course of these events, gave birth to a daughter at the Louvre, May 29th ; and died a few days afterwards, surviving her marriage with Monsieur scarcely ten months.* To propitiate Monsieur, and to make

* Bassompierre, Journal de ma Vie.--" En ce temps Madame accoucha

him loyally oblivious of the vexations he had experienced at Nantes, Madame received enthusiastic welcome at the Louvre; and was invested with privileges derogatory to the prerogatives of the Queen-consort. The duchess was dispensed from the obligation of visiting the saloon of the Queen daily; neither was she expected to present herself three times in the week at her Majesty's *lever*, as had been the invariable etiquette of the court of France. At the public receptions of the Louvre, Marie de' Medici, and Madame gathered around them a *coterie* of the most brilliant personages of the court; while Anne sat in her chair of state comparatively abandoned, being timidly addressed by Monsieur, and saluted with ceremonious politeness by the King. Madame does not appear to have been deeply lamented; her infant daughter,* heiress of her immense wealth, was confided to the care of Marie de' Medici, who had her brought up at the Tuileries, under Madame de St. Georges.† The fancy of Monsieur soon became fascinated by the radiant loveliness of a fair young princess of Gonzague-Nevers, daughter

d'une fille, contre l'attente et desir de leurs Majestés et de Monsieur, qui eussent plutôt demandé un fils; et elle, étant demeurée malade de sa couche, mourut peu de temps après."—Mém. de Mademoiselle de Montpensier, t. i. Madame, and Queen Anne had lived in much mutual coolness, and dislike. " Madame se regardoit comme la future reine," and exacted obsequious homage.

  * Anne Louise Marie d'Orléans, la Grande Mademoiselle.

  † Jeanne de Harlay, Marquise de St. Georges.

of the Duke of Mantua, a *débutante* at court, and to whom he commenced to offer ardent suit.

Bassompierre, meanwhile, had returned from London, having partially succeeded in mediating between Charles, and his consort. Henrietta, however, still mourning her early friends, and believing herself lost in a land of heretics, where her priests were pelted in the streets by the London populace, and her faith derided, implored the Queen her mother to permit her to visit France—" But, Madame, this happiness, if you grant it to me, can only be obtained by permitting M. de Buckingham to become my escort to your court." The Duke of Buckingham also confided to Bassompierre his longing desire to return to Paris; and charged the ambassador to sound the Cardinal on the subject, and to hint that great achievements in diplomacy, very advantageous to France, might be obtained by their personal conference.* Bassompierre performed his mission, and stated the Duke's wish, which was met on the part of Louis XIII. by an indignant refusal.†   Anne also

* " Je lui fis entendre qu'on ne le recevrait pas, et envoyai Montague en toute diligence vers lui."—Bassompierre, Journal. " Buckingham pretend se servir de l'occasion des brouilleries qu'il cause lui-même, afin de voir la Reine Anne d'Autriche, dont il se declarait l'amant."—Mém. du Duc de Rohan.

† " Puisqu'on refuse de me recevoir en France comme un ambassadeur qui veut porter le paix, j'y entrerai malgré les François, en général d'armée qui porte la guerre!" retorted the Duke of Buckingham.—Mém. du Duc de Rohan.

privately requested Bassompierre to write to M. de Buckingham to put off his visit; and to state in her name, that such would be very displeasing to her.* The disappointment of Buckingham hurried him into the folly of lending a favourable ear to the solicitations of the Rochellois, whose interests were supported in England by M. de Soubise. He moreover, entered into a close correspondence with Madame de Chevreuse; and selected as the medium of his communications with the Duchess, Walter Montague, second son of the first Earl of Manchester, who was about to travel in France. Richelieu, however, was too wary to be so surprised; or to suffer the enemies of France to complete their coalition ere he struck the blow which should subjugate his master's rebellious subjects of the reformed faith. Moreover, Monsieur was again sullen and unmanageable, although honours, privileges, and wealth were heaped upon him with a lavish hand. For some inscrutable reason of her own, Marie de' Medici opposed the desire of Monsieur to espouse for his second wife the Princess Marie de Gonzague, of whom he continued madly enamoured. The Cardinal, whose policy it was to humour his royal patroness in all possible ways, save in those matters which might have operated for his own downfall, supported her Majesty in this refusal; and

* " La Reine me commanda d'écrire au Duc. pour lui faire savoir que sa venue ne lui sera pas agréable."—Bassompierre.

gained over the King to show similar disapprobation. Monsieur threatened, stormed—but was finally propitiated for an interval, by the promise of a military command.*   Without waiting, therefore, for his foes to perfect their design, Louis XIII. invested La Rochelle; and appointed his brother as general-in-chief of his armies, nominating Bassompierre, and M. de Schomberg, as his aides-de-camp, and counsellors.   This concession, however, was extorted from the King, who jealously watched the career of Monsieur: and was conceded only, on news of the sailing of Buckingham, and the fleet from Portsmouth, during a sharp attack of his old malady, which prevented Louis from leaving the Château de Villeroy, whither he had arrived from Paris *en route* for the camp.

Buckingham meanwhile set sail, at the beginning of July, 1627, with a fleet of fifty men-of-war, and of sixty smaller vessels, and an army of 7,000 men.†　Charles declared to his council that his reasons for invading France were threefold — 1st, that King Louis had declined to grant a passage through France to some English levies under Count Mansfield; 2ndly, that the French fleet had made prizes

* Bassompierre, Journal de ma Vie; Tallemant, Vie du Duc d'Orléans; Le Vassor, Histoire du Règne de Louis XIII.

† Hume, Reign of Charles I.; Siège de La Rochelle, Archives Curieuses, t. 3, deuxième séries.

of some small coasting vessels hovering about La
Rochelle; and lastly, because the Huguenots were
oppressed, and in danger of losing all their strongholds, La Rochelle being already besieged. The Duke
of Buckingham was more candidly explicit on the
causes, and motives of the war. "In spite of all the
power and might of France, I will see her fair Queen
again!" exclaimed he publicly, at a farewell banquet
at Whitehall. The Duke's galley was adorned with
a yellow and black banner, the colours of Anne of
Austria; and her cipher was everywhere displayed.*
The chief cabin on board was dedicated to her
charms: it was draped with yellow silk damask;
at one end was a life-size picture of the Queen,
shrouded by superb curtains of cloth of gold, before
which golden candelabra were placed, holding lighted
tapers of white wax.† The madness and infatuation
of this conduct admit of no palliation; the prosperity
of the Duke's career must have induced insanity;
and have rendered him cruelly forgetful of the position of Anne of Austria, and of the disgrace which
his insensate ambition had already inflicted. So unexpectedly was the expedition decided upon that the
municipality of La Rochelle were not even apprised

* Tallemant des Réaux; Le Cardinal de Richelieu.

† "Cette chambre était fort dorée: le plancher était couvert de tapis
de Perse, et il y avait une espèce d'autel où était le portrait de la Reine,
avec plusieurs flambeaux allumés."

of the sailing of the fleet when Buckingham appeared before the town : the people therefore refused to admit their intending allies, before due inquiry had been made as to the object of the landing of so formidable a force.*   Buckingham thus repulsed, attacked the island of Ré, and began to batter the great fort of St. Martin, which was defended by the brave M. de Toiras with admirable valour. The cannonade, however, was suspended for a few days, by order of the Duke ; who, being probably assailed with misgivings as to the motive of the war, and perhaps a little disheartened by his reception by the Rochellois, abated in much of his boasted vigour. Richelieu immediately ordered the despatch of 6000 men under Schomberg, to Ré, who encamped on the island, and rendered essential assistance to Toiras ; while Monsieur diligently pushed the siege by land. The Duke of Buckingham was profuse in his civilities to any French gentleman who visited his fleet. M. Saint Surin, a distant kinsman of Richelieu, especially recommended himself to the Duke's favour ; and the latter one day introduced him into the chamber on board the galley where the picture of

* The Rochellois, who had received no previous hints of this expedition, refused to admit the English succours into their town, on pretence that they could not take such a material resolution without the concurrence of the other Protestants, with whom they were associated ; but in reality they were afraid of their allies, suspecting that Soubise and Blancas had agreed to betray the place into the hands of the English.—Hume.

Anne of Austria hung. Buckingham boldly avowed his admiration for the Queen, and his desire to visit Paris; bitterly complaining of the uncourteous refusal of the prayer, which he had preferred through Bassompierre. He ended by requesting M. Saint Surin to communicate again his desire to the Cardinal; engaging, if his Christian Majesty consented to receive him in the capacity of ambassador from his Britannic Majesty, that he would presently take pretext to retire from before La Rochelle, and leave the city to its fate. St. Surin undertook the mission; but repented his officiousness when he found himself arrested after his interview with the minister, and about to be consigned to the Bastille " for presumptuous and traitorous communication with the enemy; " a fate from which his kinship to Richelieu delivered him.*   Meanwhile the garrison of Fort St. Martin was reinforced by the unforeseen and gallant descent of Schomberg. The blockade, also, being loosely maintained, the beleaguered garrison obtained abundance of provision. On the 20th of October Buckingham landed his troops, and again attacked the fort ; he was repulsed with immense slaughter, and his soldiers driven into the sea by the troops under Schomberg. Retreat became inevitable ; and the embarkation of the soldiers

* Tallemant, Vie du Cardinal de Richelieu.

under such disastrous circumstances was attended
with further loss of life. The Duke rejoined his
fleet, having lost more than half of his land forces,
and immediately set sail for England.[*]

The vigilance of the Cardinal was rewarded in
another quarter by an important capture. Walter
Montague,[†] as has before been related, had been
charged with the perilous office of carrying the correspondence, and the replies returned by the English
court to Madame de Chevreuse. Through his spies
Richelieu learned that suspicious circumstances were
attached to the frequent journeys to and from Nancy
made by the young Englishman ; and that the letters
he was known to carry, were probably of more momentous import, than effusions sent by the English
admirers of the Duchess. A warrant was thereupon
issued for the detention of Montague, which was
delivered for execution to the Marquis de Borbonne,
who arrested him on the frontiers of Lorraine, and
conveyed him a prisoner to the neighbouring castle
of Coissy.[‡] His papers were seized and despatched
to Paris. The fact of the arrest of Montague was

* Siège de La Rochelle, Archives Curieuses; Hume, Reign of Charles I.;
Bassompierre, Journal de ma Vie.

† Walter, second son of the first Earl of Manchester, a Roman Catholic,
and subsequently abbot of St. Martin de Pontoise. Montague possessed
much influence in the councils of France under Marie de' Medici and
Anne of Austria. He died, 1670, at the abbey of St. Martin, and was
interred in the church of l'Hôpital des Incurables, Paris.

‡ La Porte, Mém. p. 304.

communicated to the Queen, as her Majesty was supping in public. Anne turned deadly pale, and pushed the dishes from before her as they were presented; then rising, at the conclusion of the repast, she retired to her private apartments. Her distress and consternation appear to have been extreme; it was possible that Montague's papers might again fatally compromise her position—at any rate, she dreaded lest the examination of the prisoner would reveal her own guilty knowledge of the design forming, for the invasion of France. Her perturbation was increased by the arrival, a few hours later, of a note from Madame de Chevreuse, written in wild alarm, apprising her Majesty of the arrest of Montague; but professing total ignorance as to the nature of the despatches, and letters of which he was the bearer.

Anne spent the night, and part of the following day weeping in her oratory, alone with Madame de Fargis, devising means for communicating with Montague, in order to discover what the confiscated papers contained. The sympathy of Madame de Fargis at this juncture, elicited the Queen's entire confidence: with all her wilful perversity, and dissimulation, there was, at any crisis, a touching helplessness, and grief in Anne's aspect, which usually proved irresistible in evoking the best energies of her adherents.   Her friends felt themselves honoured by the outward abandonment, on the part of their royal mistress, of the distance imposed by her rank; by her *naïve* appeals to their sympathy; and by her admissions that, abandoned by their help, she esteemed herself lost.   Through the Cardinal de Berulle, Madame de Fargis discovered that the prisoner Montague was to be immediately escorted to the Bastille; and that certain regiments of the royal guards, were already selected to proceed to Coissy on the morrow.   In one of these regiments the Queen suddenly remembered that her faithful La Porte had been drafted as a soldier after his dismissal from her service, on the return of the court from Amiens.   Her Majesty, therefore, applied to M. Lavaux, who was intimate with La Porte, and the father of one of her dressers, to bring the latter to the Louvre at midnight, when she would confer with him secretly in her oratory.   To such clandestine, and undignified interviews Anne was driven, to hide the miserable intrigues, from which she could not refrain.

Anne seems always to have taken the opportunity to cabal when her adopted country was in straits, and needed loyal devotion.   At this period France was menaced abroad by the arms of England, Spain, Savoy, and Lorraine—the Emperor Ferdinand defied her power; and in spite of earnest expostulations, was proceeding to ruin, and dethrone the French prince, whom the rights of primogeniture had placed on the ducal throne of Mantua. At home civil war menaced the realm; the Huguenots were utterly disaffected and malcontent; and the heir presumptive to the throne threatened to league with rebels, against whom he had accepted a command. Monsieur had suddenly retired from the camp before La Rochelle on the arrival there of the King. He stated in excuse, that Louis had promised him the command in chief, which engagement was annulled by the royal presence; moreover, that the continued opposition made to his marriage with Marie de Gonzague convinced him that "their Majesties never had his welfare and happiness at heart." At court the Queen-mother was involved in violent dissensions with the Cardinal minister, respecting the Lord Keeper Marillac, whom Richelieu wished to supersede in the ministry in favour of the more able de Châteauneuf. Such was the position of affairs when Queen Anne joined in the correspondence of the Duchess de Chevreuse with the foes of France. This incident in the troubled career of the Queen, would probably have escaped record, but for the pen of La Porte. It does not appear that, at this period, any correspondence injurious to

Anne fell into the hands of the King. Richelieu probably did suspect, and acted on his suspicion; but proof of Anne's misdemeanour failed him; and it was ever the policy of the Cardinal, "never to accuse, without he could likewise stab." "The news of the arrestation of my lord Montague threw the Queen into a strange fright," records La Porte:* "she dreaded lest her name might be compromised by the papers taken from Montague; which, if such a fact had been laid before the King, with whom she was not then on good terms, his Majesty might ill-treat her and send her back to Spain, as he would most assuredly have done. This fear so greatly disquieted her Majesty, that she could neither eat, nor sleep. She was in this quandary when her Majesty suddenly remembered that I was a soldier of one of the regiments chosen for the escort of my lord. She, therefore, enquired of Lavaux where I could be found; he looked me up, and conducted me at midnight to the Queen's chamber, after every person had retired. Her Majesty explained to me her trouble; adding, that having no person whom she could trust, she had sent for me, believing that I should serve her with devotion. She said, that on the report which I was to bring her, depended her worldly salvation, and honour.

* Page 301 et seq., Mémoires, La Porte, Pettitot, vol. 54.

The Queen then explained her desire; and directed me to take the opportunity when I was on guard near to the person of the said prisoner Montague, to ask him whether in the papers taken from him her Majesty was named? Also, if it should happen, as it was certain to befal, that when in the Bastille he should be subjected to severe interrogatories, and pressed to reveal all the accomplices in the intended league, I was to pray, and admonish earnestly the said my lord, not to name her Majesty. I succeeded in informing Montague of the distress of the Queen; and he replied, ' That her Majesty might rest tranquil; for that he believed she was not named directly, or indirectly, in any of the letters, and despatches taken from him;' also, he assured me I might tell the Queen, ' that he would rather die than reveal, or say anything that could injure her!' When I delivered this reply, the Queen actually trembled for joy!" writes La Porte. Anne escaped this time with the fright. The young " my lord " was subjected to no examination of consequence in the Bastille, and was simply detained there until the peace with England, concluded in 1629; when, out of deference to the clamour of the Duke of Lorraine, " the ambassador accredited to his court," was conducted under escort to the frontiers of the duchy, and there released.

The Rochellois, meantime, were comforted in their

adversity, and desertion by the entry into their harbour of a fast sailing vessel, bringing a letter from Charles I., assuring the citizens of his continued support: and that he was preparing a fleet, and armament which would at once insure the concession of their liberties. Delays, however, arose, of which the French government knew how to profit. Throughout the winter of 1627, and the first months of the following year, the siege was carried on with wonderful vigour. The king remained in camp until the 9th of February, 1628; when, feeling indisposed, he returned to Paris, leaving Richelieu sole commander-in-chief, with the power of life and death over every person engaged in the siege.* Aware that the Rochellois could never be subdued while their city was open to the approach of an English fleet, Richelieu commenced that wonderful work, the mole and fortification which close the harbour of La Rochelle. Two French engineers, Louis Metezeau, a townsman of Dreux, and Jean Tiriot, were the designers of the work, which was carried on under the inspection of the Cardinal; whose courage, and perseverance were sustained by his able counsellor

---

* Bassompierre, Journal de ma Vie; Siège de La Rochelle, Archives Curieuses. Aubéry, Mém. pour servir à l'Histoire de M. le Cardinal de Richelieu. " Le Roi donna ordre exprès au Duc d'Angoulême et aux Maréchaux de Bassompierre et de Schomberg, d'obéir au Cardinal comme à sa propre personne."—Richard, Vie du Père Joseph.

the Capuchin father, Joseph de Tremblay. The Cardinal lived in a lone house known as Le Pont de la Pierre, situated a stone's cast from the beach. There the Cardinal and "his shadow" worked, plotted, pondered, and sustained each other during the blockade: they sketched imaginary schemes for the glory, and the political government of France, which, impossible as these designs then appeared, the matchless genius of these two men realised under the fostering growth of King Louis' inaptitude for affairs of state; his ever wavering health; and the suspicions which poisoned his existence.

Long and angry debates ensued meanwhile, in the English Parliament relative to Buckingham's policy; * which retarded the sailing of the promised succours, and enabled the French engineers to continue their works, the aim of which mystified the British cabinet. The fate of the rebel city was rendered more desperate by the assassination of Buckingham; who fell by the knife of one Felton, August 24th, 1628, after granting audience to Soubise, and other French gentlemen at Portsmouth, as he was again about to embark to relieve Rochelle.† The

* It has been asserted that Anne of Austria was compelled by the King and by Richelieu to exert her influence over Buckingham, for the welfare of her country, by writing a letter to the Duke, in which she commanded him not to set sail before a period which she indicated.

† Hume : Thomson's Life of George Villiers. Duke of Buckingham; Le Vassor. Hist. de Louis XIII.; Rapin. History of the Reign of Charles I.

assassin had served in the former expedition to Ré, and had felt himself aggrieved, because the captain of his ship having fallen during the memorable embarkation from that island, the Duke declined to promote him to the vacant post. The news of the death of Buckingham was received with satisfaction in France. The Queen refused for long to believe that the gallant, handsome favourite had fallen. " No!" exclaimed Anne, " it is impossible! I have just received letters from the Duke."* When convinced of his death, her dejection was great; and for some time her Majesty seemed to find solace only, in the correspondence of Queen Henrietta. The latter, however, had hated the presuming favourite, whom she accused of attempting to degrade her to the forlorn position of her sister-in-law; and who had suggested the banishment of her French ladies, to avenge his own exclusion from the Louvre. The command of the English fleet was conferred on the Earl of Lindsay; who, on the 25th of September, appeared off La Rochelle with a fleet of seventy-two vessels, and attacked Richelieu's new fortifica-

---

* Buckingham often spoke of his conquests over royal ladies in terms highly irreverential. Madame de Chevreuse told the celebrated coadjutor archbishop of Paris, De Retz, that the Duke said to her one day, " J'ai aimé trois reines, et j'ai été obligé de les gourmer (to cuff them) toutes trois." " De vivre avec la reine (Anne d'Autriche) d'une manière un peu galante et rude, à deux faces, de l'humeur dont je connois la reine," said Madame de Chevreuse.

tions, but failed to destroy them; or to open the
harbour. The inhabitants, meantime, were reduced
to the last extremities of famine; on the repulse of
their allies, their despair and sufferings compelled
them to open negotiations with their incensed
sovereign, and his minister. These overtures were
made October 23rd. On the 30th the city surrendered, and was punished by the total abrogation
of its charters and privileges; besides the imposition
of a fine to an immense amount, to defray the cost
of the fortifications and siege works. On the 1st of
November, All Saints' Day, the victorious Richelieu
celebrated mass at the high altar of the late heretic
cathedral dedicated to Ste. Marguerite, after the
solemn reconsecration of the church by the Archbishop of Bordeaux. The same day Louis XIII.
made his state entry into the revolted city. Thus,
after seven successful revolts against the royal authority in the space of 100 years, the factious Rochellois
were totally subdued; their fortifications levelled;
their privileges annulled; and their harbour effectually barred against the approach of any fleet but
that of their liege sovereign. The English fleet
under Lord Lindsay made sail after the surrender of
La Rochelle, and safely put into port in Portsmouth
harbour. The ignoble termination of this expedition
occasioned stormy, and even tumultuous debates in

the English Chambers. Peace, however, was eventually concluded with France in September of the following year, 1629 : the articles of the marriage treaty of Henriette Marie were confirmed again ; England abandoned the Huguenots of France to their fate ; an amnesty was to be granted for all concerned in the late transactions ; and Madame de Chevreuse was to be recalled from banishment, and suffered to reside in the château of Dampierre.*

The submission of La Rochelle was followed by an expedition undertaken by the King in person to compel the Spaniards to raise the siege of Casale ; which was invested by Don Gonzalez de Cordova. The Emperor persisted in his refusal to grant investiture of the duchy of Mantua to Charles de Gonzagues ; and demanded that the territory should be relinquished to him as lord paramount, until the rights of the various claimants were examined, and adjusted. Duke Charles implored the succour of the King ; and the policy of Richelieu being now favourable to the old tactics of Sully and Henri Quatre, the Duke's prayer was conceded. The reduction of the remaining Huguenot strongholds of the South the minister postponed to the more propitious season,

* The charms of the Duchess de Chevreuse had much power over Richelieu. Madame de Motteville says, " que ce ministre, malgré la rigueur qu'il avait eue pour elle, ne l'avait jamais haïe ; et que sa beauté avait eu des charmes pour lui."—Motteville. p. 62, t. i.

when both Spain and Austria, humbled by the victorious arms of France, as he had predetermined, should thereby be compelled to abandon these rebellious vassals to the mercy of the government. The King, accompanied by Richelieu, quitted Paris February 4, 1629, for his Italian expedition. He was attended by the Dukes de Longueville, d'Elbœuf, de Schomberg; the Marshals de Bassompierre, de Crequi, and other noblemen. The army, flushed with its recent success before La Rochelle, was obedient and enthusiastic; and regarded the relief of the fortress of Casale, and the expulsion of the Spaniards and Savoyards from Montferrat, as a very inferior achievement. The prospect of a war with Spain was a bitter accession of grievance to the Queen; and at this period her stolen interviews became so frequent with the Spanish ambassador the Marquis de Mirabel, as to give great umbrage to the King. One day before the departure of Richelieu from Paris, he paid a visit of formal courtesy to Queen Anne, to say farewell. As the visit of the minister had not been previously announced, he found Mirabel closeted with her Majesty; the other person only present being Madame de Fargis. The Cardinal advanced, and after inclining profoundly before the Queen, addressed Mirabel with his usual bland cordiality of tone. "Monsieur l'Ambassadeur," said he, "his Christian Majesty desired me, on the first opportunity, to express to you his regret and astonishment at the haste which the Emperor has shown in sending his armies into the Milanese, and against Duke Charles of Mantua, an old subject of France!" "The Emperor might certainly have shown more prudence if he had waited for the termination of our negotiations with your Eminence. His Imperial Majesty doubtless believed that the affair would drag on here with endless tedium, as it has so often happened; he therefore deemed it politic to urge on a *dénouement* by arms!" responded Mirabel, sarcastically. Richelieu showed that he was piqued at this reply; and to turn the conversation he addressed the Queen on some indifferent matter. Anne, however, rose, and taking the hand of Mirabel interposed, saying, "M. l'Ambassadeur, do not excite yourself. I, who have at heart the interests of Spain in equal degree with those of France, cannot approve of the precipitancy shown by the Emperor in sending his armies as a menace to our frontiers. I will myself write to the King my brother, on the subject." * It had been often better for the Queen if she had remembered the celebrated axiom of Richelieu :— "If words are the first power in the world, silence is the second!" When this conversation was repeated

* Capefigue, Vie d'Anne d'Autriche—Archives de Simancas. § 471. MS. quoted by M. Capefigue.

by Richelieu to the King, he was greatly offended that the Queen had declared "that she had the interest of Spain as much at heart as that of France," and personally administered a sharp rebuke; forbidding her Majesty during his absence to see the Spanish ambassador, who had alone disobeyed the recent ordinance prohibiting *entrée* to the Queen's private saloons, to the gentlemen of the court.

During the absence of the King, Anne withdrew to St. Germain, attended by her household; while Marie de' Medici, installed in the Louvre, represented the absent majesty of France, and held all court receptions. Occasionally Anne ventured to trespass upon the strict injunctions which she had received to avoid the capital, by paying private visits to the Val de Grâce, a convent which she had recently founded. Even this privilege of retreat Anne had managed to abuse, by granting secret audiences in the convent to Mirabel, and to other personages who presumed not to present themselves at the Louvre. Richelieu's spies, however, soon detected the subterfuge; and it was several times reported to the minister that M. de Mirabel had been seen to leave his coach in an obscure street adjacent to the Faubourg St. Jacques, and proceed on foot to the Val de Grâce, where he was admitted; and after an interval of several hours, was observed in the same furtive manner, to return to his coach.* The mystery so foolishly maintained by the Queen in her intercourse with her own family, and her pertinacity in refusing to impart the purport of any of her frequent communications; added to the well-known facts, that she was in correspondence with Madame de Chevreuse, and occasionally so with Monsieur, afforded ground for the suspicion that she was disloyal to her husband's crown. Her preference for everything Spanish; and the favour which she showed to persons who spoke her native tongue, such as Mesdames Bertaut and de Fargis, and the daughter of the former, afterwards the celebrated Madame de Motteville, perpetuated the notion, of which Anne unreasonably complained, that she was still in heart an alien from France. It was moreover suspected, and all but proved, that at this period Anne reported to Mirabel any decision of the privy council affecting her brother's affairs which accidentally came to her knowledge; on any hasty, and inconsiderate word which dropped in her presence from the lips of the King or his minister, concerning their Catholic Majesties.† In the abbess of the Val de Grâce, Luisa de

---

* Journal de Cardinal de Richelieu, qu'il a fait durant le grand orage de la cour, ez années 1630 à 1644. Tiré des Mémoires qu'il a écrit de sa main.—Amsterdam, 1664.

† Philip IV. and Elizabeth de Bourbon, eldest daughter of Henri Quatre and Marie de' Medici.

Milley, Anne found a companion and firm friend. The brother of the abbess was a subject of Spain, being a native of Franche Comté, and governor of Besançon. Luisa de Milley had been educated in the Carmelite convent of Avila: all her aspirations were therefore Spanish; and as many of her connections resided in Spain, this *liaison* afforded the Queen an easy, and invaluable mode of communication with her own country.

"The Queen," writes Madame de Motteville, "being still young, but desirous of providing for her eternal salvation before all things, had selected the convent of the Val de Grâce as a place of retreat, where she could always retire, and taste that peace which is to be found only at the footstool of God." Anne, in 1621, bought the Hôtel de Valois, for the sum of 36,000 livres; the old building was partially demolished, July, 1623, and the remaining apartments adapted to conventual purposes, after the Queen had selected a suite of rooms for her own occupation. Anne built a superb private oratory, the altar of which was decorated with a painting and a crucifix, gifts of Philip IV. of Spain. The community of Val Profond, a small convent situated about nine miles from Bièvre, was chosen to inhabit her Majesty's new foundation; but why these ladies were so favoured does not appear. The nuns, with their abbess, La Mère d'Arbouze, were installed at the Val de Grâce in the early part of the year 1623. The community was of the Benedictine order; and their abbess appears to have been renowned for saintly austerity, as she was transferred during the following year to the convent of La Charité; there to enforce discipline, and the rule of St. Benedict, which had fallen into disuse, to the great scandal of the neighbourhood. Luisa de Milley, abbess of St. Etienne, was then chosen by the Queen as the head of her house, and assumed rule at Val de Grâce about the year 1625. Anne immediately established relations of the closest confidence with the new abbess, who sympathised deeply in her Majesty's distresses. The abbess was subsequently accused of having sanctioned public prayer in her chapel, for the downfall of the Cardinal minister; and of all the other enemies of the very Christian, and persecuted Queen of France. La Mère Luisa and her nuns looked upon Anne as an immaculate saint, whose prayers and patronage brought the blessing of Heaven on their house: they faithfully kept her secrets, and performed her bidding, even when such involved imminent risk to themselves. No betrayal, or hostile witness ever confronted the Queen from the Val de Grâce; and the glorious, and magnificent house which hereafter rose on the foundation of the humble convent of La Mère Luisa, was dedicated by Anne of Austria as much in memory of the devoted fidelity which she had there experienced, as a lofty monument of her joy, and thanksgiving for the birth of Louis XIV. The other personages, besides the Abbess Luisa and Mesdames de Chevreuse and de Fargis, at this period in the confidence of Queen Anne, were her physician, Vaultier, and her apothecary, Michel Danse. Vaultier had been for some time high in the favour of Marie de' Medici, who had taken measures to bespeak for him a cardinal's hat. He subsequently passed from the service of Marie into that of her daughter-in-law, Queen Anne; and became an ardent, but injudicious servant of the latter, entering into all the petty cabals, which the ladies and women of Anne's household raised against the minister. Amongst her humbler servants were La Porte, Lavaux, his wife and daughter, a dresser named Catherine, and her nurse, Doña Estafania, who wisely shut her ears against insinuations and scandals, and consequently, lived a life of tranquillity.

The Duke of Orleans, meantime, fled from the kingdom to Nancy; so intense was his resentment at the persistent opposition manifested by his mother and the King, at his suit to the Princess Marie de Gonzague. Marie de' Medici, during the Italian

campaign, dominated in Paris, living for the moment
on amicable terms with Richelieu's beloved niece,
Madame de Combalet, who was about to shine at
the Palais Cardinal, as Duchess d'Aiguillon.   A
glorious campaign, which terminated by the successful action of the Pas de Susa; and the relief and
cession of Casale to the French, rejoiced the court
and nation.   The King, after installing the Marshals
de Crequi and de Bassompierre over the captured
territory, received the thanks of the Duke of Mantua,
and returned to France to carry on the campaign
in the South for the total reduction of the Huguenot
power.   The exploits of "l'Armée de Valence"
were as signal as those of the division in possession
of Montferrat.   Town after town, with but few
exceptions, submitted to the royal power, and was
graciously pardoned for past treasons, though deprived of treasured charters and religious exemp-
tions.   Languedoc submitted: the Duke de Rohan
laid down arms, and accepted articles signed at
Alais, in which it was stipulated that the fortifications of the great Huguenot strongholds of Nimes,
Castres, d'Usez, and Montauban, should be demolished.   The Huguenots were compelled to make
restoration of Church lands and benefices seized,
or appropriated by them from the commencement
of the civil wars in 1561; all churches were dedicated

afresh, and the orthodox service re-established. The Cardinal refused to receive the petitions of the ministers of the churches; he declared that he knew no distinction between the religion of any of his Majesty's subjects; that all should participate in the paternal regard of the government; and no person, or sect be distinguished, except for loyalty, and devotion to the glorious race of Bourbon.

Louis XIII., leaving his minister at Montauban, arrived at Fontainebleau at the beginning of May 1629, where the Queens had repaired to offer their congratulations. Marie received her son as a hero descended from Mount Olympus; but the pouting lips of Anne of Austria had no smiles for Louis. Her ironical salutations, and allusion to his victories over Spain and the Empire justly provoked his anger; while her dejection, the absence of splendour in her attire, and the readiness with which she yielded her precedence, and prerogative to Marie de' Medici, excited the King's distrust. Anne ever thus let the opportunity slip to establish ascendency over the mind of Louis. While the Cardinal dictated peace at Montauban, she should have seized the moment to propitiate her consort; who found the *exigeant* humours of the Queen-mother hard to endure. Until the return of Richelieu, Louis found recreation in the chase. He also derived relaxation from his musical instruments; and in setting verses to dreary tunes of his own composition. The King also found amusement in carving wooden shrines with his under secretary, M. de Noyers, who excelled in that art. Richelieu at length returned to receive the congratulations of his royal master on his diplomatic victories in the South. The reception of his Eminence by Marie de' Medici, however, was stormy and ominous. Richelieu, during his sojourn in the South, had taken no counsel of the Queen-mother respecting his compact with Rohan and his followers; he had even severely reprimanded Marie for her arbitrary detention at Vincennes of the Princess Marie de Gonzague; and had sent an order for the release of the young princess, at the solicitation of Monsieur, and of her cousin-german the Duke de Longueville. Moreover, he had blamed the conduct of Marie in other matters relative to the Duke of Orleans; who, while pretending to respond to the overtures of the King to return from his self-inflicted exile, had stipulated that he should not be required to visit his Majesty, until time had allayed the acrimony of his feelings in having been so cruelly thwarted in his matrimonial designs. The Duke had therefore sullenly retired to the capital of his appanage, Orleans. Richelieu had recourse to his usual remedy to defeat the anger of the Queen-mother: he pretended to be overwhelmed with dismay, and prepared to quit Fontainebleau, "as he perceived that his fate was sealed, and her Majesty's displeasure irrevocable." His subtle Eminence next commanded his niece, De Combalet, to resign her office in Marie's household; and his cousin, De Meilleraye, to tender his bâton of chamberlain. The King, alarmed at these preparations, flew to his mother and besought her to pardon a delinquent so submissive. Marie, unable to resist the entreaties of her King and son; and moved by the meek deportment of a minister whose power as she well knew, might, if he chose to exert it, prove irresistible, consented to a truce.* The winter of 1629-30, therefore, passed in stormy altercations and reconciliations; the ill-regulated temper of Queen Marie relieving itself by vilifying the Cardinal in public; and by accusing him to the King as a liar, a deceiver, and an ingrate. "We shall see M. le Cardinal ere long, pack up his

---

* Journal de ma Vie, Bassompierre, année 1629. Aubery, Mém. pour l'Histoire du Cardinal de Richelieu. The Queen-mother, when she first saw the Cardinal after his return, asked after his health. "Je me porte mieux que beaucoup de gens qui sont ici ne voudroient!" replied Richelieu. Marie, surprised, then turned the conversation by a jest on the Cardinal de Berulle. "Je voudrois bien," interposed Richelieu, "être aussi avant dans vos bonnes grâces, comme est celui dont vous vous moquez." En quittant Marie de' Medici, Richelieu alla chez le Roi, et lui demanda permission de se retirer du ministère.

baggage and decamp, or I shall quit the court!" M. Bonnevil, first *valet de chambre* to her Majesty, represented that M. le Cardinal seemed greatly depressed at the report of the depreciating things she was constantly heard to utter. "M. le Cardinal," replied Marie de' Medici, "is elastic, and able to adapt himself to any *rôle*; one minute his spirits are joyous, the next he seems to be half dead: rising from a poor little pitiful abbé, see how grandly he plays the part of Eminence, and prime minister! He treats me, his benefactress, with a more bitter hate than he gave to M. de Luynes; and he pretends to exclude me, the mother of his King, from power! Ah! M. le Cardinal weeps his crocodile tears at pleasure!" In such fashion did this violent woman agitate the court. During the winter season of 1629 the cabal was formed that nearly overturned the power of Richelieu: and which was defeated only by his own extraordinary sagacity, and by the weakness of Louis XIII. Marie was the soul of the cabal: her Majesty gathered round her, in support of her cause, and the downfall of the insolent prelate, the Princess de Conti Marguerite Louise de Lorraine - Guise, the old friend of Henri Quatre, who was still frivolous, coquettish, flighty, and fascinating—"*la première dame qui a appris à sa majesté Anne d'Autriche d'être coquette* "—the Duke de Guise, Condé, Monsieur, the Duchess d'Elbœuf; Marillac, whose dismissal from office had been resolved at the Palais Cardinal; the Duchess de Lesdiguières, the Marshal de Bassompierre, Mesdames de Fargis and de Chevreuse, Vaultier, the Count de Soissons—in short, all the influential malcontents of the realm. The Queens, moreover, sought reconciliation; which was presently demonstrated to the world by the frequent appearance of Anne at the Luxembourg; and by Marie's presence in the saloons of the Louvre. The Cardinal took matters quietly; he armed a legion of spies, domestic and public, who followed his foes to their most private retirement; and the result of their investigations, he jotted down in that amusing Journal of Events, in which he records, apparently with *naïve* surprise, the agencies employed for his overthrow.

Early in the year 1630, however, the note of warfare again resounded. Spain refused to ratify the concession made by Don Gonsalez de Cordova, Viceroy of Milan, and agreed to by the Duke of Savoy; and her armies, under the famous Marquis de Spinola, marched to invest the fortress of Casale, which was still garrisoned by French troops under the Marshal de Crequi; while Count Colalto besieged Mantua. Richelieu was prepared for a campaign, which he had foreseen: the triumph of the Emperor over his revolted Bohemian subjects—who had thrown off their allegiance and elected for their King the Protestant brother-in-law of King Charles of England, the Elector Palatine had inspired his Imperial Majesty with the notion that his army was invincible; and would soon sweep Montferrat of her Gallic invaders. The gallant veterans of Susa and of La Rochelle, and of many a hard contested siege in the South, rose again to arms at the call of their King; and Louis soon saw himself at the head of a fine army, every soldier of which longed to fly to the rescue of his countrymen, beleaguered by the hated Spaniards, in Casale. For the moment political feuds were forgotten; and every class in the realm acquiesced in the wise, and able mandates of the minister. The King insisted on assuming the conduct of the war; an enthusiasm, nevertheless, partly kindled by the warlike counsels of Richelieu, who descried less danger in being followed to the camp by the King, than in leaving Louis exposed to the hostile influences of the Louvre. His Majesty quitted Paris and arrived at Lyons, accompanied by the Queens,* about the 3rd of April: from thence Louis proceeded to

* Marie de' Medici was offered, but refused, the regency of the realm during the King's absence, in order to follow her son, and more effectually subvert the influence of Richelieu.

join the camp at Grenoble, after making a short
sojourn in the district of the Lyonnais. Richelieu,
meantime, had been negotiating with the Duke of
Savoy; overtures which resulted in nothing, and
which were terminated by the sudden advance of
part of the royal army to besiege Pignerol. His
Eminence, however, quitted the camp, and journeyed
to meet the King at Grenoble, attended by Giulio
Mazarin—afterwards the famous Cardinal of that
name—who had been sent by the Pope on a secret
mission to negotiate an armistice between the Powers.
From Grenoble Richelieu travelled to Lyons to salute
the Queen-mother; and to test his favour in the
capricious esteem of Marie. He found her Majesty
more hostile than ever, and surrounded by his hottest
foes, such as Beringhen, Vaultier, and others, and
especially the Lord Keeper Marillac. In noting this
last fact, Richelieu, in his Journal, adds the significant line,

"Qui amat periculum, peribit in illo." *

On the occasion of this visit, Mazarin first bent the
knee before Anne of Austria, being presented to
her by Richelieu, with the following insolent words

---

* Journal du Cardinal de Richelieu, qu'il a fait durant le grand orage
de la cour ès années 1630 jusques à 1631. " La Reine dit à Bullion qu'elle
attendoit son temps, auquel le Roy ouvriroit les yeux et les oreilles ; et
qu'elle mourrait plutôt que de voir le Cardinal. Vaultier a aussi dit, que
la Reine espéroit que Dieu la vengeroit."

—"Madame, I present to you the Sieur Giulio Mazarin; your Majesty will doubtless approve of this sagacious personage; as he, an agent of his Holiness, bears, as you perceive, a strong resemblance to the late Duke of Buckingham." * Anne blushed, and unfurled her fan to cover her confusion.

Chambéry, meantime, capitulated to the royal arms during the sojourn of the Cardinal at Lyons, much to the secret triumph of Louis. The campaign in Savoy prospered; place after place surrendered, as during the previous invasion of the duchy by Henri Quatre. The health of the King, however, gave way before the excitement, and fatigue to which he was exposed. He fell ill at St. Jean de Maurienne; from which place his Majesty, at the earnest entreaty of his physicians, returned to Lyons, leaving the further conduct of the war to Richelieu, Schomberg, Crequi, and Bassompierre. Louis' disorder was bilious fever, of very aggravated description. The weakness and depression of the King increased: and Marie de' Medici beheld her son restored, as she hoped, to her maternal influence. Melancholy, irritable at the slightest proposal to discuss or transact state affairs; anxious alone for conference with his confessor, the venerable Père Souffran; and lured only to momentary

* Tallemant, Vie du Cardinal de Richelieu, Hist. 66.

forgetfulness of his misery by the blue eyes of Marie
de Hautefort, Louis was ready to agree to any stipu-
lation, or concession rather than debate a point.*
The hopes of Richelieu's enemies therefore revived :
the cabal rallied ; and letters of counsel, and entreaty
poured upon the Queens, that they should now exert
their united powers of persuasion to exact from the
King a *lettre de cachet* forbidding the return of
Richelieu to court; and decreeing his banishment
from the realm. Anne entered with eagerness into
the conspiracy; and constantly discussed its details
with the Queen-mother, and with Vaultier, and those
interested in the downfall of the minister. The
principal persons in the secret were the Princess
de Conty, the Lord Keeper Marillac, the Duchesses
d'Elbœuf † and d'Ornano, ‡ the Duchess de Lesdiguières, Madame de Fargis, Bassompierre, and the
Duc de Guise and his consort Henriette, heiress of
the house of Joyeuse. The Duke of Orleans was
also consulted; and an active correspondence was
again imprudently instituted between the young
Queen and Monsieur. The Spanish ambassador,

* Vittorio Siri, Mém. Recondite, t. 3.—Bassompierre.

† Henriette Catherine, légitimée de France, daughter of Henri IV.
and Gabrielle d'Estrées.

‡ Renée de Lorraine, daughter of the Duke de Mayenne, chief of the
League. Her husband, the Duke d'Ornano, was a prince of the house
of Sforza Santa Fiore.

likewise, seems to have advised Anne to enter again on the perilous course of intrigue, which had already entailed such degradation on the royal dignity. As the King's malady increased, the spirit of the caballers became sanguine; and they proceeded to discuss not only the removal of Richelieu from office, but whether his high misdemeanors did not merit retribution. Monsieur counselled the arrest of his Eminence, in which opinion he seems to have consulted the wishes of Marie de' Medici; others proposed, that he should be assassinated in camp; another proposal was, that the person of his Eminence should be made over to the Spanish government, to be transported to one of Philip's colonies of the New World! Madame de Fargis, meantime, was employed by the Queen to write epistles, and to convey messages. Anne's animosity against the Cardinal is described as unsurpassed by that of his most bitter political opponent. By the advice, it is said, of Madame de Fargis, prompted by Mirabel the Spanish ambassador, Anne was reckless enough to consent again to the discussion of the policy of her marriage with Monsieur, in case of the speedy decease of Louis.* Madame de Fargis, at any rate, was a party to this correspondence; as there is no

* Dreux du Radier, Vie de la Reine Anne d'Autriche; Siri, Mém. Recondite; Aubéry, Mém. du Cardinal de Richelieu.

doubt that the project was again submitted to Monsieur, with the assent and full knowledge of Anne of Austria. The prospect of being deprived of the queenly diadem of France had inexpressible bitterness for Anne of Austria; who certainly had no reason to review either with pleasure, or with triumph the events of her married life. In this interval she had suffered as a princess and a wife; her husband had openly showed alienation and dislike—wrongs, she had attempted to avenge by culpable intrigues, which had heaped upon her disgrace, and privations. The crown matrimonial of France, however, seems to have borne a superlative charm for all the princesses of Hapsburg; and they clung to its glittering honours amid contumely and neglect. Eleanor of Austria, Elizabeth of Austria, Anne of Austria, Marie Theresa of Austria, and Marie Antoinette of Austria, were women, all distinguished for personal, and mental charms; but their married life was fraught with domestic, and political misfortune; and they failed personally to adapt themselves, either to the sovereigns their respective husbands, or to the manners and traditions of the land of their adoption. In the case of Anne of Austria, absolute dislike existed between Louis XIII. and herself, in addition to the absence of personal sympathies, and pursuits. The Queen had many undoubted grievances to suffer from the frigid, imperious, and vacillating temper of her consort; and from his almost ludicrous dread of dictation, to which, however, no man could have been more subject. She saw her personal charms despised,* and her society avoided; her pecuniary means were curtailed from dread of the power which the command of money would have given her to intrigue, with foreign courts. To avenge herself for her privations and want of influence, Anne had recklessly sullied her royal dignity; her adventures with Buckingham resounded throughout Europe; and her connivance in the conspiracy of Chalais had greatly redounded to her discredit; while it must be confessed that few husbands could have pardoned the treachery, and indelicacy of her overtures to Monsieur, in case of her own widowhood, and his accession to the throne of France.

The precarious condition of Louis' health renewed Anne's political anxieties. On the 30th of the month of September, 1630, the disease presented so unfavourable an aspect, that his Majesty's physicians gave up their hope of saving his life. An abscess had formed on the liver; the sufferings of Louis

---

* " Elle avoit les mains parfaites, et ne les regardoit pas sans une secrète complaisance."—Monville, Vie de Mignart, who painted the portrait of the Queen in 1659.

were intense, and his strength rapidly failed. Marie de' Medici never left the bedside of the King, except when he was engaged with Souffran, his confessor.* During the intervals of his relief from pain, Marie extorted from the King a solemn promise, or, as is stated by some contemporaries, his oath, that in case of his recovery he would dismiss Richelieu. Anne also showed herself assiduous in the sick chamber. On the 1st of October the physicians informed the King that his recovery was hopeless. Louis received the tidings with resignation, and requested the sacraments of the Church. Mass was celebrated by the Cardinal de Lyons, in the presence of the Queens;† at the end of the service Louis caused himself to be raised on his couch, and addressing those present, said,—"I grieve that I am too weak to speak to you all—I can only ask you to pardon any wrong that I have committed. I wish the same prayer to be made to all my subjects. Le Père Souffran will tell you all that I would add, if strength permitted me."‡ He then

* Récit du Maladie du Roy à la ville de Lyons, par le Rév. P. Souffran, son Confesseur ordinaire. Lyons, Vermonet, 1630.—Le Vassor, Hist. de Louis XIII.

† "Monsieur le Cardinal de Lyons dit la messe dans la chambre, et le communia."

‡ "Ces paroles attendrirent si fort le cœur de ceux qui étoient présents, que tous, la Reine, messieurs les Cardinaux, et autres officiers de sa maison, se jettant à genoux, pleurants et sanglottants, crièrent : 'C'est à nous, Sire, de vous demander pardon. Pardonnez-nous, Sire !'"

beckoned to the Queen to approach his bed; when he bade Anne farewell, and embraced her. All persons then retired, leaving the King with his surgeons, and his confessor. The Queens betook themselves, as it was said, to prayer; Marie de' Medici especially professing to be overwhelmed with grief and consternation.

On this day Bassompierre returned from a special mission to Monsieur at Orleans, and obtained immediate audience of the Queens, Anne and Marie. The Marshal brought messages from Monsieur to his mother, referring to the measures which he considered advisable in case of the demise of Louis, and of his own accession. Amongst other directions Marie was instructed to command the arrest of the Cardinal minister; who was known to be on his road from the camp to Lyons—a journey which he had undertaken after receiving certain intelligence of the precarious condition of the King. What message Bassompierre was intrusted with, to Queen Anne never transpired; Monsieur had a salutary remembrance of the peril incurred in the affair of Chalais, and seems to have coldly responded to her Majesty's overtures. Indeed Anne had lost much in his regard and esteem, by her late

—Récit du Père Souffran. " Ego testis oculatus et auritus," testifies the reverend Jesuit.

pertinacious opposition to his union with Marie de Gonzague.   Richelieu, meantime, had been warned of the intrigues concocting against his power, and perhaps against his life, by the zeal of M. de St. Simon ;* a gentleman, whom he had a little time previously recommended for service in the royal household, on the displacement of personages which occurred after the execution of Chalais. This St. Simon had quietly insinuated himself in the good graces of Louis, by his modest demeanour and apparent indifference to politics. "On my arrival in Paris from my English ambassage," writes Bassompierre, in 1627—"I found that Barradas† had been dismissed, and that his place [in the King's chamber] was given to a young boy of pitiful aspect, and still more sorry wit, of the name of St. Simon." "You have heard that Barradas has been dismissed," writes the poet Malherbe, December, 19, 1627 ; "we have in his place a Sieur de St. Simon. The King presented him on Wednesday last to the Queen his

* Claude Duc de St. Simon, born 1606 ; married Diane de Budos, by whom he had one daughter, married to the Duc de Brissac ; for his second wife, M. de St. Simon espoused, Charlotte de l'Aubespine, who was the mother of the celebrated Duc de St. Simon.

† A young cavalier of Burgundy, who succeeded to brief favour after the death of De Luynes, whose lineage appears to have been almost unknown. The reason of his disgrace is thus recounted by Malherbe : " Un jour le Roi par caresse, lui jeta quelques gouttes d'eau de fleur d'orange au visage dans la chambre de la Reine. Barradas se mit dans une telle colère, qu'il sauta sur les mains du Roi, lui arracha le petit pot où étoit l'eau, et le lui lança aux pieds."

mother: he is a young boy of eighteen." The King
first showed favour to St. Simon because the latter
brought him accurate news of the hunts holden on
the royal domain; and he was also a good rider, and
was careful of his Majesty's horses. St. Simon, who
possessed the shrewd discrimination which distinguished his celebrated son, perceiving that his fortune
rested neither in the hands of the Queens, nor even
in the favour of his royal master, attached himself to
Richelieu; and served the minister by the accuracy
of his reports, and the vigilance of his warnings.
From the latter, therefore, Richelieu received report
of the activity of the cabal plotting his overthrow;
and immediately set out to neutralize, and confront
the danger. Orders had been issued by Marie de'
Medici to refuse entrance into the King's chamber
to M. le Cardinal. On Richelieu's arrival in Lyons,
however, one of those miraculous revivals had occurred in the condition of the King, which had so
often destroyed the projects of Monsieur, and his
clique. Louis peremptorily asked to see his minister,
of whose presence in Lyons he was apprised by St.
Simon, and by his confessor Souffran.* The unexpected turn in the King's malady caused great
affright and consternation; and a conference was
holden in the chamber of Marie de' Medici to decide

* Récit du Père Souffran.

on the steps to be adopted. The Queen-mother dwelt on the solemn promise made her by the King to dismiss his minister—Louis having stipulated only, that peace might first be re-established in Germany : also between France, and the Empire by the concession of the rights of the Duke of Mantua. The Marshal de Marillac, nevertheless, advised that the death of the minister should now be compassed, and offered to strike the blow ; his brother, the Lord Keeper, counselled the Cardinal's immediate exile to his diocese of Luçon ; Bassompierre his arrest and imprisonment in the Bastile ; the Queen-mother declared herself in favour of a sentence of banishment ; an award stated to be likewise approved by the Duke of Orleans. Anne demanded the exile of the minister whom she denounced as the great obstacle to a cordial understanding between the courts of France and Spain.* This conference was scarcely over before all its details were fully known to Richelieu ; and afterwards, in the coming period of his unquestioned power, he is said to have retaliated on the wily plotters their own award on himself. The same evening the King passed through another

* Bassompierre : " On rapporte qu'il y eut une grande assemblée à ce sujet, chez Madame de Fargis ; et que le Cardinal entendit tout au moyen d'une sarbacane, et que chacun subit plus tard le traitement qu'il voulait faire éprouver au ministre."—Notice sur Richelieu ; Mém. de Richelieu, depuis 1610 jusqu'à 1620.

dangerous crisis of his malady; and for some hours all again was agitation, and panic. Believing that his end approached, Louis sent his confessor, Souffran, to his consort, to ask in his name pardon for all the trials, and possible provocations of her married life. "But this august princess," records the venerable father, "took to weeping and shrieking[*] in such frantic emotion, when I opened my mission, and seemed on the point of fainting, so that I could not conclude all that I wished to impart to her Majesty. Prayers were diligently offered for the King's re-covery night and day; and the Holy Sacrament was exposed on the altars of all the churches in Lyons." Anne's hysterical tears doubtless, flowed from extreme suspense, and from the agony of fear which assailed her at the presence of the minister; being conscious of the equivocal character of her correspondence with M. d'Orleans. The same evening, and during a paroxysm of the King's disorder, when all persons present round his Majesty's couch believed that respiration so laboured must soon cease, Richelieu sent for Bassompierre, who was colonel of the Swiss guards, and humbly requested him to bring over the officers of that regiment to his service; so that in

---

[*] "Cette princesse jeta de si hauts cris, et espandit tant de larmes, quand je lui dis cela, qu'elle pensa s'évanouir ; et je ne pus parachever ce que je voulois dire."—Récit du Rév. Père Souffran.

the event of the King's death he might reckon on a faithful military escort to the frontier.* The Cardinal wept, and assumed his most beseeching demeanour. Bassompierre, as indeed it was his duty to do, listened with gravity : and replied, that his oath of fealty forbade him to divert the services of the royal guards, even for a temporary purpose ; but that M. le Cardinal, in the event which he anticipated, must submit himself to Queen Marie de' Medici, who, he was informed, would assume the direction of affairs until the arrival of the new king from Orleans.† Richelieu dismissed the Marshal with a little salutation full of resignation : and prepared himself for the coming event. His niece, Madame de Combalet, quitted Lyons during the night, taking with her many valuable effects appertaining to her uncle ; while the Cardinal himself made rapid preparation for flight. Everyone avoided the fallen minister excepting the newly married Duchess de Bouillon, sister of the late Constable de Luynes, who offered to Richelieu the shelter of her husband's stronghold of Sédan. At six o'clock on the following morning the bells of all the churches of the town rang jubilant peals ; the altars

---

* Préface des éditeurs de la première édition des Mémoires de Bassompierre. Cologne, 1665.

† Bassompierre is said to have hinted to the Cardinal that he might obtain his desire by prompt application to M. de Villeroi, Governor of Lyons, through M. de Châteauneuf, cousin-german to Villeroi, and the Cardinal's devoted adherent.

were adorned, and the gorgeous aisles of St. Jean de Lyons at mid-day echoed to the notes of "Te Deum Laudamus"—the night of suspense was passed; and Louis le Juste was restored to his people! The breaking of another internal tumour had brought the King to the verge of the tomb; but Louis slowly revived from the deep syncope of exhaustion, feeble but free from pain, and comforted by the favourable verdict of his physicians, who now answered for the life of their royal patient. The court at Lyons fell again at the feet of Richelieu; the Queens nursed their wrath; and took comfort in the solemn pledge which they had extorted. A dreadful misgiving, however, seized the young Queen, that possibly the Cardinal was in possession of the secret of her correspondence with Monsieur, which knowledge he might impart to the King. The recovery of Louis was marvellously rapid; on the 14th of October he removed for change of air to the Château de Bellecour,† near to Roanne, and soon continued his journey to Paris. Marie meantime, had been laid up for a few days at Lyons with a swelled knee, and did not accompany her son to Bellecour. Louis

---

* Récit du Rév. P. Souffran, who terminates his interesting narrative with the wish that the King's unexpected recovery "serve à l'amendement de cette cour, qui est maintenant pleine de bonne volonté : mais connoissant son inconstance je crains que, *venient filii usque ad partum, et non est virtus pariendi.*"

† "Maison de Madame de Chaponay."—Bassompierre.

had urgently prayed his mother to hide their determination to dispense with the Cardinal's services,
until after the arrival of the court in Paris.   The
King piqued himself on his powers of dissimulation;
and was even proud to be compared in crafty address
to Charles IX.   Richelieu, under pretext of state
business, remained with the Queens, and even attended them to Paris, travelling in the same boat; so
important did the Cardinal deem it to prevent further
communications between Anne, and the Duke of
Orleans.   The personage who at this period played
the part of spy in the household of the young Queen
does not appear; probably the Cardinal's agent was
Madame de la Flotte Hauterive, a lady who, by dint
of solicitation, and by the bright eyes of her grand-
daughter, Marie de Hautefort, had recently succeeded
in obtaining her nomination as *gouvernante* of Queen
Anne's maids of honour.*   Madame de la Flotte
originally had visited Paris to sue in person a cause
pending before the Parliament of Paris; and which
involved the whole of her little patrimony.   She
waited upon the powerful minister, authorised by a
passport to his presence from Madame de Combalet,
and accompanied by her grand-daughter.   The
acute powers of observation, and of resolve possessed
by his petitioner were not lost on the Cardinal; the

* "Un emploi au-dessous d'elle," says Tallemant des Réaux.

charming face, and dignity of demeanour of the young girl, her companion, confirmed Richelieu's prepossession. The widow quitted the presence of his Eminence flattered, and moved by strange ambitious anticipations. The suit was in the course of a few days decided in her favour; and Mademoiselle de Hautefort was presented by Madame de Combalet to the Princesse de Conty; who, captivated by her lovely face, took her that same evening in her coach to the fashionable promenade, Le Cours de la Reine, and introduced her to the Queen-mother. Marie de Hautefort was subsequently enrolled amongst Marie's maids, and was lodged in the Luxembourg : while her grandmother, who was still handsome, entered the service of the politic minister; and was eventually placed by him in the Louvre in the important, though subordinate office of governess of the maids of honour, of her Majesty Queen Anne.

On the arrival of the Queens in Paris,* the hostile cabal eagerly greeted their Majesties, who returned triumphant in the possession of the King's promise to

* " Marie de' Medici descendit au convent des Carmélites du Faubourg St. Jacques, avant d'aller au Luxembourg. On crut que la perte du ministre fut encore concertée là, entre les deux reines, et Marillac, Garde des Sceaux. Les apologistes de ces princesses soutiennent qu'on ne s'occupa que de dévotion chez les Carmélites ; et que les deux reines, entrées dans le monastère, n'eut pas un long entretien avec Marillac," etc., etc.—Galerie des Personnages Illustres de la Cour de France, pendant les règnes de Henri IV. et de Louis XIII., t. 4.

exile his minister. The peace, meantime, upon which Louis had based his assent, was on the eve of accomplishment. The French envoys, le Père Joseph and M. de Brulart, wrung from the fears of the Emperor a recognition of the rights of the Duke de Nevers to the ducal throne of Mantua. On the 13th of October, 1630, the treaty was signed between his Imperial Majesty Ferdinand II. and the King of France in the town of Ratisbon. Casale was ceded to the Duke of Mantua, and was to be evacuated by the Spanish garrison ; and the King engaged no longer to oppose the election of the Imperial prince as King of the Romans; or to sanction the designs of Gustavus Adolphus King of Sweden, who, in alliance with the deposed Elector Palatine King of Bohemia, and other Protestant princes of Germany, threatened the empire with sanguinary warfare. The reluctance of the King to disgrace his minister, nevertheless, was manifest : in the course of a few weeks, Richelieu's ascendency had been confirmed ; and the bewilderment of the King amid the accumulations of state business accruing on the termination of the war, was painfully conspicuous. The Queen-mother, meantime, continued to besiege the King with reproaches, for his tardy fulfilment of his solemn promise. In vain Louis sought to pacify his mother ; and to persuade her even into a temporary reconciliation with the

Cardinal. He explained the urgency of his affairs, the dearth of able statesmen, his own fears and presentiments; and finally, implored her to pardon Richelieu, to accept a seat in the council of state, and to act in conjunction with a prelate so shrewd, faithful, and competent to exalt the nation, and to maintain the royal prerogatives. Marie responded to her son's appeal by a rude negative: "Either M. le Cardinal leaves the court, or I abandon your Majesty. What! you hesitate to give this just satisfaction to your mother, and prefer an insolent churchman, who will finally drive your people to revolt, as he has already rendered your court a desert?"* The young Queen added her entreaties, and besought her husband to conciliate the Princes, to give due preponderance to the Queen his mother, and to reconcile himself sincerely with the king her brother, and with M. d'Orléans, - all which might be achieved by the disgrace of M. le Cardinal. Richelieu, meantime, conducted himself with consummate prudence. He

* Journal de M. le Cardinal-Duc de Richelieu. The Cardinal relat.s with considerable complacency all the violent speeches made by the Queen-mother. One day she exclaimed to Bullion, secretary of state, " Je me donnerois plutôt au diable, que je ne me vengeasse!" Another day, Marie, conversing with a Jesuit of the court, le Père Chrysostom, said that she hated the Cardinal, "pour l'état qu'il avoit mis la France." The Jesuit replied, "que tout le monde estimait le contraire." "Le peuple est une bête; il ne faut pas prendre garde de ce qu'il dit," replied her Majesty angrily. "Elle dit au roi que j'étais un grand menteur; et que je lui avais fait signer des papiers pour d'autres."—Journal de Richelieu.

sent his niece from Paris, and commanded that his most valuable effects in the Palais Cardinal should be packed; while he constantly alluded in public to his probable departure, and dismissal from office; and made parade of recommending certain persons, whose abilities, he thought, might serve the state, to the various chiefs over departments of the government. Daily he presented himself in the antechamber of Marie de' Medici, and of Anne of Austria. The doors of the Luxembourg Palace were closed against him: the young Queen, however—moved perhaps by her dread of what the Cardinal might betray—granted him occasional audience. The meek deportment of his minister touched the King—most vividly, perhaps, when Richelieu presented himself in the royal closet laden with state papers, despatches, minutes from the provinces, reports from the disaffected districts of the realm, ecclesiastical edicts, and summaries of the doings of those encroaching personages, MM. de la Cour du Parlement; all of which he now made parade of laying before his royal master for perusal, and signature. Louis yawned, and irritably pushed aside the obnoxious documents. On one of these occasions he beckoned to his new favourite St. Simon, who was occupied in the antechamber in finishing off a trifling toy, put together by the King. Louis rose from his chair, and, followed by St. Simon, approached the window. " Let us stay here in peace awhile," said his Majesty listlessly, *" et puis ennuyons-nous, ennuyons-nous, ennuyons-nous !"** Fresh political complications menaced the newly-signed peace of Ratisbon, raised by the clever Richelieu, and his clever agent the Capuchin Joseph. The spirit of Louis died within him at the bare contemplation of the diplomacy and intrigue impending; and to vanquish which, as Richelieu made his Majesty clearly understand, his own services, or those of Marie de' Medici and her son d'Orléans, were indispensable. On the 9th day of November, therefore, his Majesty paid an early visit to the Luxembourg, to explain to the Queen-mother his political necessities, his personal wishes, and, above all, to intimate his determination respecting his minister. He found the Queen more irate than ever against the Cardinal; and incensed at his dissensions with the Lord-Keeper Marillac, which betokened the prompt dismissal of that functionary. She declared Richelieu to be an unprincipled trickster, the hollowness of whose apparent devotion to herself she could no longer doubt. Louis listened to her Majesty's tirades in sullen silence, utterly confounded by Marie's passion and vehemence. " This said Cardinal, lies in word and deed. Has he not written to our son d'Orléans, that if he will abandon our interests, his political

* Tallemant des Réaux, Hist. de Louis XIII.

grievances shall be redressed ?   Has he not written
to Messieurs de Vendôme that we desire their eternal
captivity ?   M. le Prince, also, has been informed by
this mendacious slanderer, that our enmity is the
cause of his continued exile."*   Whilst their Majesties were thus in high altercation, Richelieu arrived at
the Luxembourg.   His opportune visit had doubtless
been concerted with the King ; who had commanded
him to make every submission requisite to pacify
Queen Marie.   The ushers on duty had refused,
as usual, to pass his Eminence on to the royal cabinet.
The Cardinal, however, went to the chapel ; and from
thence boldly traversed the private corridor which led
to the Queen's apartments, and thus gained access to
the room in which Marie and her son were conferring.†   The Cardinal rapped at the door, which
was opened by the King, who took the hand of
his minister, and presented him to Queen Marie.
" Madame, you were speaking of me, your humble
servant, who deprecates your anger and prays for
pardon."   Marie, with a gesture of disdain, turned
from the Cardinal, who had fallen on his knees at her

* Journal de Richelieu sur les orages de la cour, ès années 1630—1641.
" Que dites-vous là, Madame ?   La colère vous emporte trop loin," exclaimed the King.   " Vous m'affligez si sensiblement que je ne me re-
mettrai jamais du chagrin que vous me causez."— Galerie des Personnages Illustres de la Cour de France, t. 1.

† Bassompierre, Journal de ma Vie.   Louis is said by Bassompierre
to have exclaimed with dismay, on seeing his minister, " Le voici !"

feet. "Behold, mon fils, this wicked and false traitor! His intention is to take your crown, and give it to M. le Comte de Soissons, when the latter shall have espoused la Veuve Combalet! Are you unnatural and undutiful enough to prefer such a varlet to your mother? Sire, spurn from you this destroyer of your domestic concord, the bitter foe of your mother, your wife, and your brother!" As the Queen-mother had now worked herself into an extremity of passion, Louis retired; but made a sign to the Cardinal to remain.* Richelieu again tried to deprecate the wrath of his once confiding patroness; but Marie drove him from her presence with reproaches, and by protestations of never-ending enmity. The same evening Louis again sought his mother, and found her in conference with the Princesse de Conty,† a determined opponent of Richelieu's policy. A second parley ensued; in which the King was so moved by the tears and entreaties of his mother, that he again solemnly renewed his promise to dismiss Richelieu. His Majesty then retired, announcing his intention to depart for Versailles; from which palace a letter of dismissal, and exile should be addressed to the minister.

* Galerie des Personnages Illustres, etc. etc. : Histoire du Cardinal de Richelieu ; Aubéry ; Le Vassor, Histoire de Louis XIII.; Leti, Teatro Gallico, t. 1, in 4to; Dreux du Radier, Vie de Marie de' Medici.

† Louise-Marguerite de Lorraine-Guise. After the death of the Prince de Conty, in 1614, she is supposed to have made a secret marriage with Bassompierre.

Meantime panic prevailed amongst the friends and adherents of Richelieu.   That much-enduring lady, Madame de Combalet, again received notice to pack up her effects, and await the final resolution of her uncle, who contemplated a retreat to Pontoise, and from thence to Havre de Grâce. The following day the King made fresh efforts to subdue the obduracy of the Queen-mother.   He prayed her to consent that the presidency of the council might at least remain with the minister for six weeks longer.   " My affairs absolutely demand this concession. In fact, Madame, I have commanded my generals in Italy to hazard a battle if Casale is not surrendered, as stipulated by the peace of Ratisbon." Marie wept, but made no sign of relenting.   " Madame," resumed his Majesty, eloquent in the defence of a minister, who monopolized all the toils of government, " Madame, I entreat that, at least for this period, you will speak more condescendingly to M. le Cardinal ; in truth, he is indispensable to me ; you are too prejudiced, too violent. M. le Cardinal serves me faithfully.   I shall never recover from the grief and chagrin which you occasion me !" Marie, however, refused to listen to her son's expostulations ; and peremptorily insisted on the departure of the minister. " Mon fils," said her Majesty, " either the Cardinal or I myself leave Paris within the next few hours. Choose, mon fils, between a mother who loves you, and a traitor who betrays you and yours!" Madame de Combalet at this instant, chancing to send by one of her Majesty's ladies a petition to make a farewell visit, Marie declined to grant the audience. Louis, therefore, again took leave of his mother, despairing to move her purpose. At the Louvre he entered his chamber, and, throwing himself on a couch, remained some time in meditation. "St. Simon," at length exclaimed his Majesty with a sigh, "St. Simon, did you ever hear, or witness before such a scene? My mother is implacable." "Sire, I confess I thought myself in another world on hearing your Majesty so thwarted! Nevertheless, you are our master; it is for you alone to decide!"* Louis rose: the shadow of wrathful suspicion fell, which so often darkened his youthful features; and his lips trembled with passion. "I am master, as you say; who shall presume to judge between me and my faithful minister? I will show them all that I am master!" The King again fell into taciturn silence. St. Simon had heard enough, however, to encourage him to send word to the Cardinal de la Valette, to counsel Riche-

* Galerie des Personnages Illustres, t. 4. The Duc de St. Simon, in his Memoirs, relates : "Il est souvent arrivé à mon père d'être réveillé en sursaut en pleine nuit par un valet de chambre qui tiroit son rideau, une bougie à la main, ayant derrière lui le Cardinal de Richelieu, qui s'asseyoit sur le lit, en prenant la bougie, s'écriant quelquefois qu'il étoit perdu, et venoit au conseil et aux secours de mon père, sur des avis qu'on lui avoit donnés, ou sur les prises qu'il avoit eues avec le Roi."—Mém. t. 1, chap. iii.

lieu to avoid too precipitate a departure, as matters might still be adjusted. The King quitted Paris early on the following morning, St. Martin's Day, 11th of November, 1630, attended by St. Simon, Beringhen, the Marquis de Mortemar, the Dukes de Montmorency, and de Créqui, and other officers of his household. Marie de' Medici on the preceding evening had announced her intention to attend her son to Versailles. It was the Queen's habit to take a cup of broth in the morning before she left her bed, and to sleep afterwards for an hour: her Majesty, therefore, failed to rise in time to accompany the King. At 10 o'clock Richelieu, being apprized of the departure of the King, determined again to wait upon Marie. "Monsieur," said he to Bassompierre in the guard-room of the Luxembourg, "you will not long be troubled to salute, or present arms to a disgraced and unfortunate man like myself!" The Marshal made courteous reply; and attended Richelieu, cap in hand, to the door of the chamber where Marie and Anne were closeted together in earnest conference.

St. Simon, meantime, mindful of the benefits conferred upon him by his patron, ventured again to rouse Louis from his depression by interceding for Richelieu, whose crime, he said, was "in having dared to repress the treasonable enterprises of the Queens

and of M. d'Orléans; the latter wishing to usurp
the royal power, if his projects had not even a
wider scope, as was asserted by M. de Chalais."
" Your Majesty's glory and reputation are involved
in not weakly sacrificing to feminine vengeance a
minister so loyal, and able!" St. Simon then
affirmed that M. de Richelieu was in possession of
an important secret: the disclosure of which depended on his remaining in power, as its betrayal
would all probability prove fatal to a private personage. Louis listened with eager interest; so much so,
that St. Simon despatched an express to the Cardinal
de la Valette, advising his Eminence to set out without delay with Richelieu, for Versailles; but carefully
to prevent his intention from transpiring.*   This
transporting intelligence greeted Richelieu on his return from the Luxembourg, where he had been again
vainly to plead for reconciliation at the feet of Marie
de' Medici, and of Anne of Austria. Some inkling
of the King's vacillation, and of a probable turn of
fortune in the minister's favour, actuated some of the
more prudent members of the court. Richelieu found

* " Je ne m'arrêterai point à la fameuse Journée des Dupes," writes
the Duc de St. Simon, " où mon père eut le sort du Cardinal Richelieu
entre les mains, parceque je l'ai trouvée dans —— (Siri.), toute telle
que mon père me l'a racontée."—Tome i., chap. iii. The name of the
historian quoted by St. Simon cannot be deciphered in the MS. of his
Mémoires. Vittorio Siri, however (Mem. Recondite), states that he received every detail of La Journée des Dupes from the lips of M. de St.
Simon.

his hôtel crowded with personages assembled to offer him respectful condolence. Amongst these personages was M. de Châteauneuf, then the friend of Richelieu, and Lord-Keeper elect after the fall of M. de Marillac, an event resolved upon by the Cardinal. Châteauneuf presented to the Cardinal a letter from the Duchesse de Chevreuse; who had been temporarily won over to the side of Richelieu by his patronage of Châteauneuf, with whom she was in confidential correspondence. M. le Jais, and the Cardinal de la Valette, MM. de Meilleraye and de Brezé, likewise joined the assemblage.* The news from Versailles soon brought Richelieu *tête-à-tête* with Louis XIII., who shed tears, and threw himself on the neck of the Cardinal. Louis then heard with indignation the history of the intrigues at Lyons; the detail of Queen Anne's correspondence with Monsieur, when he (the King) was supposed to be lying on the eve of dissolution; of the *empressement* shown by Marie de' Medici to act for her son d'Orléans; and of the orders transmitted by Monsieur from Orleans, through M. de Bassompierre. "The King then exposed to M. le Cardinal all the

* Galerie des Personnages Illustres de la Cour de France, sous les règnes de Henri IV. et Louis XIII., t. 4. p. 114, *et seq.* " Le bagage du Cardinal était déjà en chemin sous l'escorte de quelques soldats, et ses mulets allèrent jusqu'à trente-cinq lieues au-delà de Paris, sans entrer dans aucune ville de peur qu'ils ne fussent arrêtés, et que le peuple ne s'avisât de piller le trésor qu'ils portèrent."

diabolical things attributed to him by the Queen mother, with all the artifices by which she hoped to persuade her son to remove him from the conduct of affairs." "M. le Cardinal," exclaimed Louis, "the Queen my mother, is instigated by a few turbulent spirits to persecute you. I will, however, control such! It suffices, Monseigneur, I am content with your services. Stay with me! I give you my royal word to protect you against their cabals." Louis then, with that mingled majesty and decision, which on rare occasions he could assume, gave his hand to his minister, and leading him into an adjacent gallery, where the gentlemen waited, presented him to the assembled court.*

In Paris, the coterie of Queen Marie continued jubilant over her supposed triumph. On the evening of the 11th, their Majesties held a reception, which was attended by many of Richelieu's friends; who, ignorant of the revolution in their patron's favour, thought it politic to conciliate the power supposed to be in the ascendant. These persons received no signs of recognition from their Majesties. The following day, November 12th, the news of the great counter-plot at Versailles burst upon the

---

* "Les Ducs de Montmorency et Créqui, avertis sous mains par St. Simon, vont à Versailles: mais Bassompierre fut une des plus grandes dupes de cette fameuse journée."

astonished courtiers, and convulsed the Queen-mother with despair, and indignation. The first intimation was the arrival of an order of arrest issued by the King, and countersigned by Richelieu, against the Lord-Keeper Marillac; who was at once seized, and conveyed under a strong guard to a house which he possessed in Lorraine. The seals were given to M. de Châteauneuf, a personage who was the confidential friend and ally of the exiled Duchesse de Chevreuse. The King despatched the secretary of state de Brienne, to inform the Queen-mother of Richelieu's re-establishment in office; and to pray her Majesty's consent, and approval. On the 20th, Louis removed to St. Germain, and summoned the Queen his consort, and Madame de Fargis, to meet him there. Anne obeyed in trembling uncertainty. M. d'Orléans also received a similar order, which he obeyed, as he thought it expedient to make friends with the Cardinal; especially, as he knew from trusty sources, that Richelieu had been informed of the matrimonial overtures which had been again hazarded by the young Queen. Monsieur therefore paid a visit in great state to Richelieu, attended by twelve gentlemen, and promised him favour and reconciliation. "Thus," says a contemporary, "the great day of St. Martin des Dupes passed without effect whatever; Queen Marie, compelled to tolerate

the Cardinal, refused a conference, or any token of
amity whatever. ' *Je prendrai mon temps; je le
trouverai, et feray ce que je veux! Dieu ne paye
pas toutes les semaines, mais enfin il paye!*' said her
Majesty." On the 29th of November, the Queen and
her son met. Louis greeted his mother shyly, but
respectfully; and asked as a favour, that she would
continue to give him the benefit of her presence at
the council; and to aid his minister Richelieu by her
great experience. Marie wrathfully replied, " that
she would never voluntarily see M. le Cardinal; that
she would rather die than assist him with her counsels!" Another day at St. Germain, M. de Nogent,
one of the gentlemen of Queen Anne's chamber, but
a secret partisan of Richelieu, suddenly entered the
saloon of his mistress, and found Anne in tearful conference with the Queen-mother, the Marquis de
Mirabel the Spanish ambassador, and with her physician Vaultier. When Nogent entered he overheard
the young Queen exclaim, " Ah, what beautiful and
consolatory sentences one finds in the Psalms of
David! My spirit revives when I read such words
as ' Qui seminat in lachrymis, in exultatione metet.' "*
Nogent immediately reported what he had heard to
the Cardinal, who was at St. Germain. The *entente*
between the Queens again renewed Richelieu's

* Journal du Cardinal de Richelieu.

terrors. " Bonnevil, about the 12th of December, informed the King and M. le Cardinal that he believed there was a cabal offensive and defensive formed by the two Queens and Monsieur; the object of which was to ruin his Eminence by the diabolical lies, and testimony of Madame de Fargis, and others," is the record entered by the pen of Richelieu, in his Diary of the exciting events of this crisis in his history.

Marie at length showed signs of relenting, fearing that hostilities might terminate by her total exclusion from affairs of state. On Christmas day, she intimated to the King her willingness to meet Richelieu in council, provided that the members met in the apartments of the young Queen; as, wrote she, " I cannot yet resolve to receive M. de Richelieu at the Luxembourg."* To humour the exacting spirit of Marie de' Medici, Louis had hitherto assembled the privy council in an apartment of the Luxembourg. Further conditions were attempted by Marie: she demanded the pardon of Marillac; a promise of protection for her own partisans; also an assurance that Monsieur should

* " Parceque le dit Cardinal avoit trop de temps à être chez elle en attendant le conseil qu'on ne tiendroit pas toujours dès lors que le Roi seroit entré; ce qu'elle ne vouloit pas, pour l'aversion qu'elle avoit contre luy; et la peine que ce luy étoit de le souffrir, et encore rien qui luy appartient."

not be permitted to marry without her permission.
All these conditions were peremptorily declined, as
the Queen-mother continued to demonstrate a spirit
essentially hostile. Monsieur met the minister in
the court of the Louvre, and responded to his obeisance by turning his back on Richelieu. Marie also
made a *razzia* in her household, and dismissed
en masse every person related to the minister, or
supposed to be favourable to his policy: moreover
she sent to demand from Richelieu his key of office
as superintendent of her household; * and commanded him to restore to her the Hôtel du Petit
Luxembourg,—a gift which she had made him in the
palmy days of his favour.

* Marie aggravated this extreme mark of displeasure by sending as her
messenger a simple *valet de chambre*, with a verbal message!

CHAPTER V.

1630—1631.

ANNE OF AUSTRIA AND MADEMOISELLE DE HAUTEFORT.

MADAME DE FARGIS, meanwhile, continued to assail the Cardinal de Richelieu, to upbraid him for his ingratitude, and to flay his reputation by her sarcasm. According to Richelieu, she was accessory to all the peril and annoyances which he experienced; exasperating her mistress, Queen Anne, against him; and proving herself the steady ally of M. Vaultier, and the agent of the exiled princes in their attempts to convulse the court. Meantime, it was said that the *liaison* which Madame de Fargis retained with the Count de Cramail, and with Beringhen, first *valet de chambre* to the King, was open to grave suspicion; so much so, as to render her removal from the household of the Queen advisable. The King, moreover, could not endure the presence of a personage who had acted in accord with his consort throughout her late negotiations with Monsieur: his Majesty, therefore, listened greedily to the defamatory stories in circulation, and thereupon resolved

on the dismissal of de Fargis.* At the same time,
Richelieu resolved to forbid the frequent interviews holden between Anne, and the Spanish ambassador. Boutillier was therefore despatched to
Mirabel to deliver a formal order from the King,
forbidding the Marquis from *entrée* to the Louvre,
except on state festivals;† also, it was intimated that
for the future, when the ambassador wished for
audience of Queen Anne, such privilege was to be
solicited in the prescribed way, notice being given
to her Majesty's chamberlain three days previously.
The abbess of Val de Grâce, moreover, received a
notice not to admit persons within her convent
during the abode there of Queen Anne; and to
forward to the minister a list of all applicants for
audience. The ambassador, in a state of extreme
irritation, sought an immediate interview with King
Louis, to ask reparation for so notable an affront.
The King coolly replied, " M. l'Ambassadeur, you
are cognisant of the intrigues afloat at my court,
which deprive me of tranquillity. You ought not,

* The Queen-mother seems also to have acquiesced in the propriety of
this dismissal : " La reine-mère vint au conseil où l'on résolu la liberté
de M. de Vendôme, et l'eloignement de Madame de Fargis."—*Journal de
Richelieu.*

† " On résolut, aussi, de mander au Marquis de Mirabel que le roy
désiroit qu'il vescut en France comme les ambassadeurs de France font en
Espagne : et qu'il ne vînt plus au Louvre sans audience, et ne pensât plus
n'y sa femme d'avoir libre entrée, laquelle ils avaient usurpée jusques à
présent."—*Ibid.*

by your frequent audience of her Majesty, to have provoked comment; or to have seemed to sanction and encourage such disorders. It is not my intention to revoke my mandate. I will thank you to inform me, whether the King your master, would have suffered for a single day at his court, the cabals, and disquietudes which for years have convulsed mine?" * Richelieu then added, that M. de Barrault, his Majesty's ambassador in Spain, was compelled to adhere to the recognised etiquette in his visits to her Catholic Majesty, sister of King Louis; and that during the last four months he had never failed to present himself twice in the week to salute her Catholic Majesty, and had not been admitted to audience. Intelligence of these proceedings reached the ear of Anne, who now passed most of her time at the Luxembourg, in the society of the Queen-mother, and was often many days without seeing her husband. Mirabel paid a furtive visit the following day, to the Val de Grâce, whilst Anne was attending mass in the convent chapel; and succeeded in obtaining brief audience of her Majesty, who was attended by de Fargis, as she quitted the convent. On the 27th, Anne sent for M. Boutillier, under secretary of state. The interview is thus related by the pungent pen of

* Journal du Cardinal de Richelieu.

Richelieu, in his Diary: *—"The Queen sent for M. Boutillier to say, that she was informed that some persons were rendering bad offices to Madame de Fargis, and that it was intended to dismiss her; that she had, therefore, sent for him to say to me that the greatest pleasure that I could do her was to prevent this; that until now she had been the victim of oppression; but she desired that I should know she would no longer endure such ignominious treatment; and that she was not so miserable and insignificant a personage as not to be able some day to resent her wrongs."† Boutillier replied, that he had received no official intimation that the exile of Madame de Fargis was resolved upon. The Queen retorted—"I know it from trustworthy sources: let it suffice." Monsieur, also, visited Richelieu to intercede for Madame de Fargis, at the request of the Queen, who was "stirred with marvellous anger at the insult about to be offered to her." Intercession, however, proved useless: Louis and his minister were resolved upon the exile of the frivolous and intriguing woman, whose counsels led her mistress astray. Richelieu was, doubtless, moved to

---

* Journal du Cardinal de Richelieu.—"Mécontentement de la Reyne Régnante contre M. le Cardinal." Richelieu always speaks of himself in the third person.

† "La petite Lavaux a dit au cardinal que la colère de la reine avoit été jusqu'au point de dire : Je ne luy pardonnerai jamais—non jamais!"—Ibid.

this decision by pique at the conduct of de Fargis; who had obtained her nomination to the royal household by professions of devotion to his interests. "On the 30th of December," writes Richelieu, "la Fargis received an order to leave the court, in the most considerate and favourable manner possible, as she was to ask for permission to resign. The Queen testified great indignation against the Cardinal. She said several times, in the presence of Madame d'Angoulême, and of Madame la Princesse, 'that, as for the order which had been given to the ambassador of Spain, it was for the King of Spain her brother, to resent and avenge it, as would be seen; but the exile of Madame de Fargis was her affair; and that all concerned in it might be assured that she would never relax in her displeasure.' Moreover," continues Richelieu, "the fury of the Queen was unappeasable, for she exclaimed, in the presence of little Lavaux, 'No, never will I pardon M. le Cardinal.'"

"*January 3, 1631.*—The Queen went to visit the Queen-mother, where she remained a long time; on her return, her eyes were red and swelled. She bitterly complained of the indignities to which she was subjected, especially that his Majesty threatened to dismiss her apothecary, Michel Danse: the said Michel Danse having observed to her Majesty, that he knew why M. le Cardinal wished to dismiss him—it was, to have opportunity to poison her, so that the King might espouse Madame de Combalet! The Queen responded again with a menace, adding —'*No es mas tiempo de habler con el Cardenal, pero bien de hazer!*'

"*January* 5.—The Spanish ambassador waited on M. le Cardinal to notify that her Majesty had applied to him to intercede for her apothecary: the said Cardinal responded* 'that he would mention the request to the King, who was master and lord.'

"*January* 6.—M. de Chaulnes visited the Cardinal with the King. After his Majesty had departed, the said de Chaulnes informed the Cardinal that his sister, Madame de Bouillon,† met the Queen at the Carmelite Convent, and that her Majesty made bitter comment on her position and treatment; upon which the said Dame de Bouillon replied, 'that perhaps it was her Majesty's own fault, by living on bad terms with the King, and with those persons in whom his Majesty confided.' Her Majesty replied, with warmth, 'No! M. le Cardinal wishes to divorce me from the King, my lord, and send me back to Spain.' ‡ The same

<hr>

Journal du Cardinal de Richelieu ès Orages de la Cour, &c. &c.

† Sister of the brothers De Luynes. The Duchess, when Madame de Vernet, had been dismissed for her share in the disorders of the court when at Amiens. She had subsequently married the Duke de Bouillon.

‡ "La Reine a encore tenu ce même langage à M. de Chaulnes (Honoré de Luynes) le 2 Janvier, 1631, à ce qu'il dit à M. le Cardinal."

day, M. le Cardinal de la Valette went to pay his respects to her Majesty, and while in discourse he gently observed that her Majesty should not so bitterly resent the past; neither ought she to threaten so unreservedly. The Queen replied, 'I fear nothing: they have done the worst against me that they can. I know what my conduct in future shall be, and they have no power to prevent me. I repeat, I have nothing to fear! I need patience only—and time will do the rest.' The Queen then paused, and glancing uneasily at the Cardinal de la Valette, hastily added—"I perceive that, perhaps, I talk too much: I will say no more.'

" *January 7.*—The King has had intelligence that the Spanish ambassador has been all this afternoon shut up with the Queen at Val de Grâce; also, that la Fargis was lodging with le Père de Gondy, close at hand; and that a person named Bordier has been going between the said ambassador, the Queen, and la Fargis, in defiance of the strict orders given by his Majesty, that the said ambassador should not see the Queen without leave. The ambassador quitted Val de Grâce at dusk hour; and whilst he was there, his coach waited in an adjacent street.

"The King desiring, this same evening, to go to the play, her Majesty refused to accompany him; and

simulated faintness in order to be able to excuse
herself.

"*January* 8.—The King expressed again the same
desire, and sent to ask the Queen his wife, to accompany him to see a comedy: her Majesty refused to
go, although M. de Bonnevil * gravely represented
the matter.

"The Cardinal de la Valette informed the Cardinal that on a certain day the two Queens, as they
retired from the court circle, said (alluding to his
Eminence), '*Nous avons bien à faire de luy donner
plaisir tandis qu'il nous procure du déplaisir, et de
la peine!*'

"*January* 20.—The prioress of Val de Grâce
sent secretly to inform M. le Cardinal par le R.
de P. (*sic*), that Montagu,† in disguise, had talked
at the grate with the Queen; also, that many persons whom they did not know, now spoke there to
her Majesty; and that the last time that she visited
the convent a letter was given to her at the grate,
which her Majesty read and then burned: the writer
was supposed to be Madame de Fargis." ‡

This entertaining Journal, written by the Cardinal,

* One of the four secretaries of state, and often sent by the King to
expostulate with Queen Anne.

† Walter Montague, then a monk of St. Martin de Pontoise, and
greatly in the confidence of the Queens.

‡ Journal du Cardinal de Richelieu.

reveals the irritating *espionnage* exercised over the words and actions of the young Queen. Anne's puerile plots to displace the powerful minister recoiled upon herself, and covered her with obloquy. Her position at the court of France, over which her predecessors had ruled so imperiously, was humiliating to a great princess. Her personal liberty even was fettered; and St. Germain, the Luxembourg, and the Val de Grâce, were the only places which she had permission to visit at pleasure. The court assembled in the splendid saloons of the minister; and while Queen Anne moped in a corner of the Louvre, Madame de Combalet received the homage of the great ladies of the capital. In defiance of the orders of the minister, Madame de Fargis lingered in Paris; from whence, however, she made precipitate retreat to Jouarre on learning that a packet of letters, which she had formerly written to some person in Lorraine,* had been seized on the person of one M. de Senelle, ex-apothecary to the King; whom she had sent to Nancy to recover possession of these papers, which she now deemed it expedient to destroy. At Jouarre, de Fargis had an interview with the Duchess de Chevreuse. Marie apparently greeted the fugitive with sympathy, and listened to her plaints against the Cardinal; with

* Probably to Madame de Chevreuse.

whom, however, the Duchess was now reconciled through her friend the Lord Keeper de Châteauneuf. From Jouarre, de Fargis travelled to Nancy; and from thence she was imprudent enough to despatch letters to the young Queen and to other high personages, repeating her slanderous accusations against the minister. Scarcely had her messenger passed the frontier of Lorraine, than Richelieu's emissaries seized and despoiled him of his despatches, which were at once transmitted to Paris.

"Amongst these papers," writes the Cardinal,[*] "were found letters addressed to the Queen, and others for M. le Comte de Cramail, Mademoiselle du Tillet, and the Marquise de Sourdis. These letters contained mention of high crimes; and discussed advantages to be derived from the death of the Cardinal. They also made allusion to the death of the King; and mentioned the old project of marrying the Queen to Monsieur. They stated that the Queen-mother opposed the marriage of Monsieur with a princess of Mantua to please the Queen, as his Majesty's health was apparently greatly on the decline. They testified to intimate correspondence

* Journal de Richelieu. "Ces lettres parlaient de la mort du Roi advenant, de faire épouser la reine à Monsieur. Elle écrit au Comte de Cramail qu'elle envoyait des mémoires à la reine contre le Cardinal. Les lettres tésmoignent un véritable amour entre elle et le Comte de Cramail."

between the writer, the Queen-consort, and Monsieur; and gave advice to the said Queen Anne to do her utmost against the Cardinal. De Fargis, also, wrote to M. de Cramail, to get up petitions against the Cardinal, and to forward them to the Queen. De Fargis, moreover, said to M. de Cramail ' that she would send the necessary tokens to the individual indicated; but it would be requisite that this man should be especially faithful, as she herself was.' All these said letters were shown, and identified to be in the handwriting of de Fargis, by the persons to whom they were addressed."

The Duchess de Chevreuse, meantime, paid a brief visit of a few days to Paris, and was permitted to see the Queen without restriction; which concession diminished the acrimony of Anne's resentment. Her Majesty sent the duchess to the hôtel of the minister to intercede for de Fargis; and, likewise, she persuaded Monsieur, who was then staying at the Luxembourg with Queen Marie, to speak to the King on the same subject. Louis silenced Monsieur's loquacity; adding, bitterly, " that in a few hours her Majesty would be made aware of the justice of the proceedings against a personage every way so contemptible, and unworthy." The Cardinal replied, "that the exile of the said Dame de Fargis being approved even by the Marquis de Mirabel, and ordered by his Majesty Louis XIII., he could in no way interfere."* The day but one following, as Anne was preparing to depart for the Val de Grâce, to grant a stolen interview to Mirabel, Boutillier, under-secretary of state, appeared to demand audience of the Queen on behalf of the Cardinal de Richelieu, the Lord Keeper de Châteauneuf, and the ministers of state de Schomberg and d'Effiat, who presented themselves at the portal of Anne's audience chamber, before her Majesty could command herself sufficiently to reply to their message. Anne's usual placid demeanour faltered somewhat, as she took her seat, and prepared to listen to the communication about to be made in such formal state. Richelieu then blandly informed her Majesty of the arrest of Senelle, and of another envoy of the Countess de Fargis; and laid the letters captured from these persons on the table, for Anne's inspection—"which we did," relates his Eminence, "with all possible respect." The Queen then identified the writing and letters of de Fargis; but said much against the said de Fargis, for the wicked thoughts that she suggested respecting the marriage between Monsieur and herself, in case of the demise of his

---

* " Le Marquis de Mirabel dit à Bonnevil, quoique piqué de la défense d'entrer au Louvre, qu'il eût voulu qu'on eût ôté Madame de Fargis il y a longtemps."—Journal de Richelieu.

Majesty. She said "that she had conceived such an aversion for the person of Monsieur, that she did not think that she could ever be brought to consent to such an alliance." The Cardinal then drew her Majesty's attention to a paragraph in one of the letters of Madame de Fargis to the Count de Cramail, in which she exhorted the latter, "to forward as many petitions as possible to the Queen against Richelieu." "Madame," observed the Cardinal, "truth is everywhere to be obtained. I pray you, therefore, do not seek so far for grievances against me; but if your Majesty has aught to complain of, tell me my fault." "Monseigneur, I must be very malicious to say anything against you, not having cause." * The audience terminated with a ceremonious farewell; previous to which Richelieu apprised the Queen that the Marquise de Senécé had been appointed by the King to replace Madame de Fargis as first lady of the palace. Anne received the communication in silence: but after the departure of the minister her tears flowed; and she hurriedly retired to her oratory, and appeared no more in public during the day.

The court, meantime, continued to be a very focus of intrigue: pleasure and festivities were no longer

* Journal de Richelieu. " Elle répondit, qu'elle serait bien méchante de dire quelque chose contre lui : n'en ayant aucun sujet."

sought by the courtiers, but were replaced by the evil excitements of petty plotting, scandal, and slander. Each man and woman of the court was attached to one or other of the hostile parties; and either rallied round Marie de' Medici at the Luxembourg, Anne of Austria at the Louvre, Monsieur at the Hôtel d'Orléans, or Richelieu at the Palais Cardinal. Jealousy, suspicions, and a lawless excitement relative to the issue of the political feuds prevailing, quenched the wit, the gaiety, and the magnificence of the courtiers. In these days of cabal, frivolous stories acquired a disastrous degree of importance; a depreciatory whisper sufficed to blast a promising career, and to inscribe a name on the terrible black list of the Cardinal. The spirit of Marie de' Medici quailed at the contest before her; and yet she rejected with disdain the overtures of the minister, while weeping in the solitude of her palace at the obloquy which had befallen her; and at the fatal omens * which she descried of approaching calamity. The Duke of Orleans, who was watched with gloomy suspicion by King Louis, one day courted the smiles and friendship of

* "Il arriva, comme la reyne se couche à minuit, une grosse et grande bougie qui dure jusqu'à neuf ou dix heures du matin, s'éteignit sur les quatre heures du matin. La reyne envoya querir le dit Censure pour lui demander si cela ne signifioit qu'elle dût perdre?" "On dit que la reine a diverses prophécies, qui lui disent que dans la fin de 1631 elle sera aussi heureuse et grande que jamais!"—Journal de Richelieu.

Richelieu; and on the next furiously declaimed against his power, and vowed to support his mother to the death. Reassured by the sympathy of her younger son, Marie, during January of the year 1631, took the fatal resolve of making one more effort to dislodge Richelieu. Stories were circulated by her Majesty's command, depreciating the honour and fame of the minister; ludicrous incidents were invented, and industriously detailed to undermine his influence, in which ridicule Anne and Marie joined. Marie had appointed Richelieu, in the former days of his favour, lord-steward for life of her household; and had presented him with the Hôtel du Petit Luxembourg, a mansion joining her own palace, as his official residence. This office she had commanded him to resign; also, possession of le Petit Luxembourg, which was then inhabited by the Cardinal's niece, Madame de Combalet. Richelieu audaciously disregarded the mandate, alleging that the office of lord-steward was permanent: as for the Petit Luxembourg, Queen Marie had promised him an indemnity of 30,000 livres, if, at the command of the King, or from any other motive, she was compelled to resume her gift; which otherwise, was to be considered a donation given and accepted for life. Marie appealed to the King, and offered to pay the indemnity; but Louis decided that the hôtel belonged to his minister, and that the Queen could not thus arbitrarily annul an appointment.* Thus thwarted, Marie injudiciously sought support from Monsieur, who entered into the quarrel with acrimony—so much so, that meeting the minister one day in public, he again passed him without salutation, or any notice whatever. Meantime, the friends of Queen Marie held almost open communication with M. de Soissons, and other exiled princes. State secrets oozed out in a mysterious manner at the courts of Madrid, London, and Nancy. Couriers were continually passing to and from those countries bearing dispatches for the Queen-mother, for Queen Anne, or for Monsieur, the contents of which were never disclosed. The clandestine visits of Anne to her community at the Val de Grâce became more frequent than ever: and the Cardinal obtained information that she constantly there granted interviews to M. de Mirabel and Madame de Fargis, who had had the audacity to visit Paris in disguise ; and to one Croft,† who acted as the

* " Louis déclara que le Petit Luxembourg demeureroit à Richelieu. Il fallut encore que la Reine Marie dévorât encore le chagrin d'apprendre qu'on faisoit des changements dans son palais au gré du Cardinal et de sa nièce, qu'on y bâtissoit des bains, et qu'on y touchoit même à la maîtresse muraille du Grand Palais."—Galerie des Personnages Illustres de la Cour de France.

† Sir Herbert Croft, who, espousing the faith of Rome, became a lay-brother of the Benedictines of Douay, 1607. Croft died April, 1632, leaving four sons and three daughters, born in wedlock previous to his

agent of the English government, and to whom Queen Anne was accused of betraying any state secrets she might become possessed of, relating to the Huguenot subjects of the realm. There can be little doubt that Anne, in her anger at the coercion to which she was subjected, did impart much information to the envoys of foreign states. Dazzled by the promise of future power and consideration, guaranteed to her by her ambitious mother-in-law, and by Monsieur, she eagerly entered into their miserable plots to overthrow Richelieu. Matters were brought to a crisis by a rude refusal on the part of the President le Jay to pay a pecuniary mandate of considerable amount drawn on the treasury by Queen Marie; also, by the independent act of the Cardinal, who bestowed the government of the Pays d'Aunis with La Rochelle, without previously consulting M. d'Orleans, which was a breach, as Monsieur alleged, of their late treaty of amity. Monsieur, consequently, waited on his Eminence one morning, attended by a numerous suite—all having previously been concerted with the Queens:—" Your Eminence will doubtless feel surprise at my visit," began Monsieur, in a tone which Richelieu shrank not from calling insolent, in his account of the interview to the

profession. Croft, and Montague were heart and soul devoted to the interests of Anne of Austria.

King. "As long as I believed that you were inclined faithfully to serve my interests, I was willing to remain your friend; now, as I perceive that you fail to perform that which you promised, and have, therefore, broken faith with me, I am here to withdraw my promise to aid and to patronise you." * The great minister inclined before the young Prince, and, with an air of deep respect, "begged to be informed in what manner he had failed to give satisfaction to his royal Highness?"   "Monsieur, you have failed in all your engagements relative to the Duke of Lorraine: you have also done all in your power to throw discredit, and to attribute loss of influence, to Queen Marie your benefactress, and to myself." "Monseigneur," replied Richelieu, "have not I promised to consider the claims of M. de Lorraine, when the said prince shall invite me so to do by his envoys? As for yourself, your highness, receiving all, and more than you demand, can have no just cause of complaint." Monsieur replied that further argument was unnecessary; upon which his Eminence made profound obeisance. The Duke next observed that he was intending to retire to Orleans, where, in case of need, he should "know how to defend himself." This notification was also received by the Cardinal with low reverence; and his Highness

---

* Journal de Richelieu—Retraite de Monsieur.

then departed, making signs to his cavaliers to close round him, so that Richelieu might be prevented from conducting him to his coach. Monsieur then repaired to the Luxembourg to hold final conference with the Queen-mother on the order and method of the seditious risings they contemplated in the provinces. As her quota towards the fund requisite to organise the demonstrations, Marie gave 200,000 francs, and jewels to a large amount. She, also, delivered to Monsieur the diamonds which had belonged to his late wife; * and which, by the King's command, had been entrusted to her guardianship for her infant grand-daughter Mademoiselle, whose nursery was in the adjacent palace of the Tuileries. Monsieur was also informed, by another " exalted personage," that the Spanish Government had paid in a large sum to his credit in the bank at Brussels, to be applied to purposes heretofore agreed upon. The exhortations, and commendations of his mother, and sister-in-law raised the duke's opinion of his prowess and power;

* Journal du Cardinal de Richelieu.   The Duke had an interview with the Princess de Conty, which lasted three hours.   The same evening these illustrious ladies, Mesdames de Conty, de Mouay, and the Duchess d'Ornano, conversing together, betrayed their suspicion of the flight of Monsieur, which Richelieu states, that they could only have learned from Queen Anne.   " Je gage que Monsieur n'aura pas le cœur de publier qu'il est sorty à cause du traitement qu'on fait à la Reyne sa mère," said Madame d'Ornano.   " Si fera, que je croy," replied Madame de Conty.   " Il le fera," continued the princess ; " j'en suis asseurée ; et je vous dis que la Reyne savoit bien sa sortie."   This conversation Richelieu remembered.

and persuaded him that their great enemy must disappear before his first hostile manifesto. Letters were then signed and despatched to the exiled Princes, to the Duke de Montmorency, to the chieftains of Rohan, and to the Duke de Bouillon; whose possession of the independent principality and fortress of Sédan rendered him an important ally in any seditious rising. Monsieur next wrote to the King his brother, assurances of personal zeal, and devoted loyalty; this missive he despatched by his equerry Chaudebonne, as he entered his coach to quit Paris; for Gaston wisely deemed his liberty in danger, if, after the warlike notification he had made in the morning at the Palais Cardinal, he spent another night in Paris. The same night Marie feigned to be overwhelmed with consternation. On learning the flight from Paris of M. d'Orleans, she despatched a gentleman of her household, named Villiers, to the King, to explain her dismay at "this ill-advised step of her misguided son;" the shock of which had caused her almost to faint * on learning that Monsieur had actually quitted the capital. From the lips of his minister, however, and by the unerring pages of the Cardinal's famous Diary, Louis had been initiated, step by step, in the intrigue; and had

---

* "Que peu s'en étoit fallu qu'elle ne fust évanouie quand Monsieur luy avoit mandé qu'il s'en alloit de la cour."

been brought round to the opinion, that his mother was ready to sacrifice himself and his realm, in the pursuit of her revenge, and ambition. The following morning Louis visited the Queen-mother at the Luxembourg; and a scene of mutual reproach and violence ensued, during which Marie was compelled to acknowledge that she had given the Montpensier diamonds to her son, for purposes which she pretended to ignore. She nevertheless betrayed her influence over Monsieur at this crisis, by offering to effect his return to Paris, provided that the King granted him *carte blanche* respecting his marriage either with Marie de Gonzague, or with the Princess Marguerite of Lorraine; and gave him the investiture of the fortresses and governments of l'Isle de France, Soissons, Coussi, Charny, Laon, and Montpellier. Louis absolutely refused; adding, "that he doubted not Monsieur would soon be brought to reason and to obedience." His Majesty then requested the Queen to retire for an interval from court, as his government was unhappily so distasteful; and suggested, that her dower castle of Moulins would be an appropriate residence. Louis moreover, commanded her to withdraw her support from the exiled Princes; and to remain absolutely neutral in the pending contest excited by her agents. The King then took his leave, before her

Majesty had recovered from the first effects of her surprise, and fury on hearing such propositions. The next day Marie sent her confessor, le Père Souffran,* to decline obeying the commands of her son, "as her proposed sojourn at Moulins was only a subtle snare of the Cardinal to entice her from Paris, that her person might be seized, and her liberty endangered."† A council was therefore summoned, when it was decided to give her Majesty the alternative of signing a document, in which she engaged herself by a solemn promise not to undertake, abet, or encourage risings in the realm; and to withdraw protection, friendship, and communication from all persons exiled by the King for political offences. Marie returned the document, accompanied by a written refusal; as she said, "experience had proved to her that the opponents of M. de Richelieu were considered as the foes of the King; and that she was not disposed to sacrifice her friends, and dependents to the evil wrath of the said minister." A second council was then assembled, at which Richelieu spoke, after he had been commanded expressly so to do by Louis. With the eloquence, and precision in facts for which he was renowned, Richelieu obeyed. He represented

---

* Jean Souffran, Jesuit, confessor to Marie de' Medici and to Louis XIII. He followed the queen in her exile, and died at Flushing in 1641.

† Mém. Recondite.—Mém. du Cardinal de Richelieu.—Notice des Editeurs. MSS., Bibl. Imp., Lettres de Marie de' Medici.—F. Colbert.

" that the Emperor, the Kings of Spain and England, and the Dukes of Savoy and Lorraine, jealous of the glory of Louis, and unable to mar the prosperity of France by open warfare, sought to effect their object by troubling the kingdom by secret intrigue, and seduction—that considerable sums had been subscribed for that purpose by Spain and England; while a contingent of troops had been promised by Germany. " Sire, the Duke of Lorraine, and his kindred of Guise, have dared to brave your authority, and that of our venerated Parliament. The malcontents are supported by the approval of her Majesty your consort, and by Queen Marie—a fact incredible almost, and unparalleled in the annals of history. Monsieur, therefore, will never make submission while he is supported by the Queen-mother; and as long as this Princess remains at court she is formidable, inasmuch as the power of procuring the dismissal of your minister is attributed to her. In the midst of such intrigues and insubordination, order becomes impossible—sedition will increase; and on your first indisposition, Sire, the Queen-mother will render herself master of your person, and state. Your faithful servants cannot defend you—happy, indeed, will they be if they can shield themselves from the vengeance of two Princesses, whose anger we know to be implacable."

Richelieu then proposed the arrest of Marie de' Medici—"a decree which it would be advisable to execute with every forbearance, and honour possible, but with every precaution, and resolution; as, if the affair be attempted and fail, the condition of the realm will be worse than before." Every metaphor of deprecation, regret, and condolence is abundantly employed by the skilful minister in this oration; which, nevertheless, terminates by exhorting his Majesty "to be brave and politic; and to remember that an able surgeon, when severing a diseased limb, is careless of the amount of blood which he sheds." Should Louis, nevertheless, in his wisdom, judge it expedient to tolerate the present order of affairs, Richelieu emphatically demanded release from the toil, and perils of office. All the members of the council present applauded this harangue. Louis lay back thoughtfully in his chair, with a face expressive of blank consternation; and in reply to the entreaties of the lords present, promised to advise privately with his minister, and to take a definite resolution. When news of these troubles reached England, Charles I. blamed the blind violence, and obstinacy of Marie de' Medici. "The Queen your mother is in the wrong," said King Charles, to his consort Henrietta Maria. "The Cardinal de Richelieu has rendered glorious services to the King, his master. These intrigues remind one of an accusation levelled by the Roman people against Scipio, who listened calmly, and then exclaimed — 'I remember only, fellow-citizens, that on this day I defeated the Carthaginian army. Romans! let us repair to the Capitol, and return thanks to the Gods.' If I had been, therefore, in the place of the Cardinal, I should have contented myself with observing to your brother — 'Sire, within two years La Rochelle has fallen; thirty-five Huguenot towns have capitulated; Casale has been twice relieved; Savoy, and the half of Piedmont have been conquered. Sire, these successes, the result of my care and labour, are the guarantees which I offer to you for my ability, my loyalty, and my fidelity.' Where, then, Madame, would have appeared in the face of these great triumphs, the paltry complaints of Queen Marie?"[*]

To accomplish the purpose meditated by the Cardinal great address was required. The King shrunk from violent measures[†] against his mother; and again sought to move her generous forbearance. Finding persuasion fail, Louis ordered a departure of the court for Compiègne, at the suggestion of Riche-

---

[*] Galerie des Personnages Illustres de la Cour de France, t. 4.

[†] "Le roy parlant du conseil qu'il prit pour ce regard dit à tout le monde, que la nécessité de ses affaires ne lui pouvoit permettre d'en prendre d'autre."

lieu; who comforted his Majesty by inspiring a hope that the Queen-mother might be more accessible when away from Paris—if, indeed, Marie consented to leave the Luxembourg, which she had vowed never again to venture.

The young Queen received a command which she dared not disobey, to repair to Compiègne attended by Madame de Senécé, by Madame de la Flotte, and by Marie de Hautefort, whom the Cardinal, by every species of *cajolerie*, was trying to win over to his interests. The court arrived at Compiègne about the 17th of February. The King was joined *en route* at Senlis by Marie de' Medici; who, remembering the result of the abandonment of her son on the memorable Journée des Dupes, now hastened with her accustomed precipitation, to help her enemy in consummating the *coup d'état* which he had plotted. A prudent, and politic princess would still have extricated herself from the dilemma; and have converted the visible abasement into which she had fallen into a triumph of magnanimity. Marie de' Medici, however, headstrong and short-sighted, attempted to subdue her enemy by sullen pertinacity. Richelieu still hesitated to offer final defiance to his late benefactress; while the King, with tears drawn forth by his own lugubrious forebodings, besought his minister to try once more

to move the compassion, and clemency of the
Queen. In obedience to this order, Richelieu entered
the chapel of the old castle of St. Germain on the
Sunday following; and, meeting Queen Marie as
she was leaving the altar after receiving the Holy
Sacrament, he fell at her feet, and conjured her to
forgive him his transgressions.* Marie haughtily
retreated; when the Cardinal, rising, approached the
altar whereon the Sacred Elements were exposed,
and, taking the cup in his hand, made a solemn vow
that in nothing had he willingly, or maliciously
offended her Majesty; but that he still continued in
the mind to serve her, as his best benefactress, and
mistress. The Queen eyed the Cardinal for a few
minutes in silence, and a softer expression stole over
her face; she, however, finally turned away, and
without vouchsafing a word, quitted the chapel.
When Louis was informed of the failure of this
attempt at conciliation, he rose with sudden impulse,
and signified his assent to the measures proposed
by Richelieu.

A rumour, meantime, had been spread by the adherents of Queen Marie, that her Majesty intended to
leave Compiègne speedily, " as it was not her inten-

* Mém. du Cardinal de Richelieu.—Leti, Teatro Gallico.—" La Reine-
mère," writes Bassompierre, " fut encore sollicitée par le Roy de s'accom-
moder avec le Cardinal. Mais comme elle est très entière et opiniâtre,
et que la plaie était encore récente, elle n'y put être portée."

tion to share the deliberations of the council; nor longer to sanction by her presence the infamous mandates of M. de Richelieu." Louis therefore signed the requisite mandates necessary for the detention of the Queen-mother; and the arrest of her most zealous adherents. It was determined, moreover, that same night to execute the project; by leaving Marie at Compiègne under the charge and *sureveillance* of the Marshal d'Estrées and his regiment of guards, then on duty in, and about the palace. The design was well considered, feasible, and avoided violence, or show of disrespect to the unhappy Princess. D'Estrées was one of the most polished of the courtiers; a nobleman of wit, refined manners, and *savoir-faire*. He unhesitatingly undertook the office pressed upon him: he promised to Richelieu unwearied vigilance and fidelity; and assured the King that no effort on his part should be wanting, to reconcile the Queen to her position; and to induce her to make overtures likely to prove satisfactory to his Majesty and the realm. One by one the gentlemen in attendance on the King were summoned, and instructed to meet their royal master at midnight in the Capuchin monastery of Compiègne, under an injunction of strict secrecy.

Anne, of Austria, meantime, retired at her usual hour, unsuspicious that any event of moment impended.   Louis had too little faith in her loyalty and discretion to impart his design; neither, it is to be feared, was he greatly concerned at the fright likely to be inflicted, by the sudden revelation of so startling an event.   Anne had passed the evening in the apartments of Marie de' Medici, and had returned therefrom much depressed.   In the middle of the night the Queen and her ladies, Mesdames de Senécé and de la Flotte, were aroused by a loud knocking at the door of the antechamber.   The blows were repeated with greater energy, and voices were heard without.   Anne opened her curtains in affright, and called Madame de Senécé, who directed Mademoiselle Filandre, a *femme de chambre*, to inquire who the intruders were, and their business.[*]   "It is the King, the King!" exclaimed Anne, fearfully; "open to his Majesty!"   The sound of male voices, and the ring of arms now reached the ears of the eager listeners.   Daylight just glimmered; and all the Queen's ladies and women, pale with fright, crowded round their royal mistress.   "A thousand fearful thoughts then agitated the mind of the Queen," relates Madame de Motteville.   "She had every reason to distrust the King her husband; and, as she confided to me, she believed that some dreadful event was about to happen to her—the least that she

* Mém. de Motteville, t. 1.

expected being, that she was to be banished from the realm. Looking upon the next few minutes as the supreme moments of her fate, the Queen prepared herself for the emergency, and summoned all her courage. She had a firm mind, and a resolute will; and I doubt not, judging from what her Majesty told me when relating these particulars, that the first shock being over, she would have received, with the utmost resignation and patience, the fate Heaven had destined her to endure." The Queen's suspense was at length relieved by the return of Mademoiselle Filandre, with the intelligence that Monseigneur, the Lord Keeper Châteauneuf, desired to speak to her Majesty on behalf of the King. Anne rose from her bed; and putting on the *robe de chambre* presented by Madame de Senécé, who afterwards described herself as " plus morte que vive," ordered M. de Châteauneuf to be admitted. Châteauneuf bowed before his young mistress as she tremblingly advanced with flushed cheeks, and in utter disarray. " Madame," said he, " I have to make known to your Majesty the orders which I have received from the lips of the King our master. To insure the welfare of this realm, his Majesty finds himself compelled to leave his mother at Compiègne, under the *surveillance* of the Marshal d'Estrées. It is therefore his Majesty's command, that you attempt not an interview with her said Majesty, the Queen-mother; but that you immediately hasten to the church of the Capuchin convent, where his Majesty expects you." * Château-neuf then withdrew, before the emotion of the Queen permitted her to reply. The lord-keeper, however, managed to whisper an injunction into the ear of the Marquise de Senécé to hasten the preparations of her young mistress, unless she wished to see her involved in the same disgrace as her mother-in-law. Anne soon recovered her accustomed coolness and decision; and, with many anathemas on the Cardinal's audacity and tyranny, she refused to leave the palace without a parting interview with Marie de' Medici. Time was elapsing; and the king's orders had been precise that Anne should not see the Queen-mother, but hasten to join him in the church of the Capuchins. Madame de Senécé, knowing the wayward perverseness of her mistress, and anxious to save her from a direct act of disobedience in a juncture of such importance, proposed that Mademoiselle Filandre should be despatched on a journey of discovery to the Queen's apartments; from whence she should bring a message from Marie, in case her Majesty still remained ignorant of the *coup d'état,* expressing a desire to see Queen Anne.

* Mém. de Motteville.—Le Vassor, Hist. de Louis XIII. Journal de Richelieu.

The apartments of the Queen-mother were silent and undisturbed. Filandre made her way to the bed of Caterina Selvaggio, chief tirewoman, and whispered an agitated entreaty that Queen Marie would send to request an interview with her daughter-in-law, as her Majesty had something to impart, and dared not leave her apartments unsummoned. This *ruse* succeeded: Marie, ever on the alert, sent Caterina to summon Queen Anne, under pretext that she had had an agitating dream, and found herself indisposed. Anne flew to the apartments of Marie, followed by Madame de Senécé, carrying a portion of her mistress's attire.* Marie was sitting up in bed, clasping her knees, with a face of deepest woe. Anne threw herself in the arms of the unhappy princess, sobbing forth the words, " Oh ! ma mère, ma mère—I am to leave you—I have not an instant to explain—the King expects me at the Capuchin church !" " Ma fille, am I to die ?—am I a prisoner ? Speak ! The King, does he desert me ? What is to become of me ? " Anne then signed to Madame de Senécé to retire out of hearing; and while she finished dressing, she recounted all that had befallen her, with the order signified by Château-

* " La Reine prit seulement une robe de chambre, et toute en chemise passa chez la Reine sa belle-mère, qu'elle trouva dans son lit assise sur son séant. Elle tenoit les genoux embrassés, ne sachant que deviner de ce mystère."—Motteville, t. 1.

neuf. With many tears the princesses then embraced, and separated.*

King Louis received his consort in the choir of the Capuchin church. His Majesty was attended by the Cardinal minister, by Châteauneuf, by the abbot of the Capuchins, and by a swarm of courtiers, many of whom had been roused from their beds to join the King, and scarcely yet comprehended their position. Two ladies also were present—Madame de la Flotte and her lovely grand-daughter. The King briefly recapitulated his reason for the arrest of the Queen his mother. "Madame," continued his Majesty, addressing his consort, "the indiscretions of Madame de Fargis having caused her removal from your service, I present to you in her stead Madame de la Flotte Hauterive; and for second *dame d'atours*, Mademoiselle Marie de Hautefort. For both these ladies I request your favour." †   Anne had hitherto steadily declined to permit any lady to fulfil the functions of the exiled Madame de Fargis ; ‡ she was, however, now compelled to put the best face on the matter, as the King was evidently in no humour to be trifled with. "*Elle les reçut toutes deux faisant la meilleure mine du*

Motteville, t. 1 ; MS. Beth. B. Imp., Fontanieu.

† Motteville, t. 1.—Victor Cousin, Vie de Madame de Hautefort.

‡ Madame de Senécé was first *dame du palais* to Queen Anne.

monde," relates Madame de Motteville. Anne, however, still clung to her de Fargis, who, like herself, was an adherent of the Queen-mother of Spain, and of the French malcontents; and she viewed her new ladies, especially Mademoiselle de Hautefort, not only as her rival in the King's favour, but as an enemy, and a spy in the pay of the Cardinal.

Marie de Hautefort was the daughter of Charles, Marquis de Hautefort, and of Renée du Belley. At this period she had accomplished her eighteenth year. Her beauty was less dazzling than that of Madame de Chevreuse, but of a nobler type. The expression of her features was serious and thoughtful: she was pious, ambitious, sedate in manner, and reserved to a surprising degree for a damsel of her age, so early introduced at the court of France. When Mademoiselle de Hautefort spoke, she did so advisedly: her language was well chosen, and perfectly expressed her ideas. The poor but illustrious family from which Marie sprang, had little to bestow on a younger daughter of their race, and she had been destined for the cloister. Louis, however, had now resolved that Mademoiselle de Hautefort should be drafted into the household of the young Queen; as he found indescribable consolation in her repose of manner, decorous discourse, and sweet smiles. Marie, on her part, professed respectful devotion for Louis Treize; and exalted him into a hero, whose domestic misfortunes inspired profound sympathy. The two, however, had never met in private; for their interviews were holden in a small cabinet adjacent to the saloon in which Marie de' Medici received the court. The King, with a *triste* expression on his sallow, pensive face, sat and sighed by the object of his admiration; who, serenely gracious, entertained him with the *on-dits* of conventual gossip; or related her early reminiscences of rural life, in which his Majesty seemed to take deep interest.

The King and Queen, after their salutations in the grey twilight of this February morning, commanded mass to be said before they quitted the chapel. Louis seized the opportunity to indicate that a fresh influence had dawned over the court. The maids of the Queen, according to custom, sat and knelt on the ground during mass, the ladies of honour having alone the privilege of cushions and stools. The King, observing this, rose, and taking the velvet cushion of his own *prie-Dieu*, sent it to Mademoiselle de Haute-fort with a gracious gesture. Marie blushed, for she felt that the eyes of all persons present were watching her. She, in her turn, looked anxiously at Queen Anne, who signed to her to take the cushion. Marie obeyed, but modestly laid it by her; and, when mass was concluded, she rose, and, with a deep obeisance, returned the cushion to the King.*   Louis continued his journey with the court to Senlis. There, many victims were sacrificed to the hate, and to the fears of Richelieu; arrests, perhaps rendered necessary by the catastrophe of Marie's detention at Compiègne. An hour after his arrival in Senlis, M. Vaultier, Marie's obnoxious physician and friend, was on his way to the Bastille under escort. *Lettres de cachet* were despatched by M. de la Ville-aux-Clercs to the Princess de Conty, Marguerite de Lorraine-Guise, the intimate companion of the Queens, and the wife of Bassompierre; which exiled her to the castle of Eu, permitting her only six hours to set out from Paris.   On the 24th of February, Bassompierre, the brilliant and popular trifler, was arrested, ostensibly as a partizan of Marie de' Medici; but, as it was surmised, to avenge the counsel which he had given at Lyons in 1630, to imprison Richelieu for life.   It was also debated in council to arrest the Duke d'Epernon, and the Marshal de Crequi.   The Duchesses d'Elbœuf, de Rohan, d'Ornano likewise received an order to retire from Paris.   All things seemed now at the feet of the victorious minister: he possessed the ear of the King; and directed at will the resources, and alliances of the realm.   The enemies which remained to be overthrown, Richelieu prepared

* Cousin, Vie de Madame de Hautefort. p. 10.

to do battle against, in the full conviction of eventual triumph.

Queen Marie was at first paralysed by grief and amazement at her detention. For hours, it is recorded, she wept with passionate excitement,* and threatened the authors of her disgrace with future retribution. From the hour of her arrest Richelieu never intended to promote her reconciliation with Louis; and from Paris, and the court she was for ever to be exiled, so long as the Cardinal retained power. Nevertheless, Richelieu deemed it politic to temporise—the conscience, and the filial feelings of King Louis might prompt him to annul the act accomplished after so many relentings and doubts. It is certain that Marie was urged, nay implored, to leave Compiègne, and take up her abode at Moulins, unfettered by restrictions of any kind, except her parole, not to leave the town without the permission of her son. The letters addressed to his mother by Louis, in this sorrowful crisis of their history, are forbearing and modest. His first letter, after their separation, written at the beginning of the following month of March, contains the following passage : †—" The continual excuses which it has

Bassompierre states, " Que les larmes de la Reine-mère ne couloient pas, mais se dardoient hors de ses yeux."

† MS. Bibl. Imp. Fontanieu, 262, p. 126. Madame de Guercheville

pleased you to assign against taking up your abode in your house at Moulins render it necessary for me again to remind you how requisite it is for the welfare of my realm, that you should yield to the entreaties that I have aforetime made, and make again. You would be there accommodated more at your pleasure and mine, as you would not be surrounded with unpleasant facts as at Compiègne. Neither, Madame, is it true that the plague is raging at Moulins, nor that your house there is out of repair; nevertheless, as I have told you before, you can, if you choose, stay at Nevers. I am writing on the subject to the Marshal d'Estrées; you will, therefore, if it pleases you, give credit to anything which he may impart to you in my name." In answer to this letter, Queen Marie writes to inform her son, that indisposition has hitherto prevented her from setting out to Moulins: she then reproaches him bitterly for his abandonment of her; avers that she has been always a good and conscientious mother; and that the reward which she now reaps for countless privations, and devoted zeal for the interests of his Majesty and the realm, is, that she is sacrificed to the vengeance of her bitter foe! Finally, her Majesty asserts that her health is not in condition to

remained as lady-in-waiting on the Queen. She had also her favourites, Caterina Selvaggio, and M. Fabroni and his wife.

undertake so long a journey; that her nerves are shaken; and that she may as well meet death, if such be her son's will, at Compiègne, as in a lone castle, badly drained, where she would be in the power of M. le Premier, who coveted her life, and was ready to sanction any unhallowed act of violence.* Driven thus into a corner by her enemy the Cardinal, Marie de' Medici had not the tact to dissimulate her resentment and *dépit;* her protests against the outrage to which she had been subjected, resounded throughout the realm, and at the courts of London, Madrid, and Brussels. The Queen drew up a violent diatribe against the Cardinal, which she forwarded to the Parliament of Paris. The members, however, prudently transmitted the document to the King with its seals unbroken. The Marquis de Mirabel meantime, instigated by Anne of Austria, asked audience of King Louis on behalf of his Catholic Majesty, Don Philip IV., to intercede for the Queen-mother; and to request permission to visit her Majesty at Compiègne. Louis wrathfully refused permission. " Sire, apparently, then, her Majesty is a prisoner under

* MS. Bibl. Imp. Fontanieu, 262, p. 131. MS. Dupuy, Bibl. Imp., 49. The King sent the secretary of state, Ville-aux-Cleres, to inform his mother, " Qu'elle avait liberté de sortir, et de se promener lorsque le temps le voudroit permettre." Also, that M. Vaultier, her physician, should return to her when she had obeyed the command of the King to retire to Moulins.—Aubéry, Mém. pour servir à l'Histoire du Card. de Richelieu. Lettre de Ville-aux-Cleres.

arrest?" "Monseigneur, nobody but ignorant people, or people perversely malignant, will so assert," answered the King, impatiently. "I find it, however, strange that the King of Spain should interfere; foreign princes have no right to intervene in such matters. Remember, M. l'Ambassadeur, that when the ambassador of Charles IX. asked permission to see Queen Elizabeth de Valois, a daughter of France, he could not obtain his desire. I will not recur, Monsieur, to the sequel of that unhappy history; suffice for the present, that you have no reason to take amiss my decision in this matter!" "The King spoke thus," relates the Cardinal in his Journal, "because the Queen his mother, had boasted to his Majesty, that the Spanish ambassador was privy to all her intrigues for the ruin of the Cardinal." *

Louis continued his correspondence with his mother from Dijon, where he had arrived at the head of a *corps d'armée* in pursuit of Monsieur; who, on receiving the intelligence of his mother's arrest, proclaimed a levy of troops over all the lands of his appanage, and fled to Nancy, after publishing a

* Journal du Cardinal de Richelieu. "L'ambassadeur tesmoigna au Roi, et ensuite à tant d'autres personnes, le déplaisir qu'il avait de ce refus, et qu'il était sur le point d'en faire une plainte publique au Nonce, et aux autres ambassadeurs, mais il s'était retenu par les persuasions de son secrétaire."

hostile manifesto against Richelieu.   His Majesty wrote thus from Dijon : —

LOUIS XIII. TO QUEEN MARIE DE' MEDICI.*

"MADAME,—I have no occasion to enter into explanations with you relative to the reason and just causes, which have compelled me to separate myself from you for an interval, for nobody understands such better than yourself; also, the efforts I have made to save both yourself and me from such annoyance. You are aware that remaining at my court, offended and discontented as you have for some time declared yourself to be, prevented me from providing remedy to put down the intrigues which there abound; and, failing to subdue which, my realm and my person are in danger. Nevertheless, all this need not prevent me from feeling and testifying for you, the respect and the friendship which you can expect from a good son; although my duty to my subjects, and to my crown is esteemed by me as my first earthly calling. Having always received from me numberless proofs of regard, I feel astonished that you should imagine that I am capable of conceiving against you violent resolutions : believe me, Madame, that such thoughts have never entered my head, nor have they been

* MS. Bibl. Imp. Fontanieu, 262, p. 131.

concerted by any of my servants. For what end,
or aim, you persist in impressing upon the world
that your ruin is resolved I cannot imagine, when all
the evil which you have hitherto received is separation
from myself—a fact, which you have yourself brought
about, by opposing and alienating all persons who
please me, and are likely to serve me, and my realm.
I hear, also, with extreme displeasure, that you are
still delaying your departure from Compiègne. If
indisposition is the cause of your delay, I shall experience a double annoyance; but I do not hear that
your illness is serious enough to prevent you from
travelling. I request you, therefore, to set out; for
your departure is important to my crown, and will
check the rumours which you have spread, that I have
made you a prisoner. At Moulins, moreover, you will
have no person near you likely to offend you, or to
curtail in any way your freedom. I doubt not,
therefore, Madame, that you will promptly comply
with my desire; the which accomplished, you shall
always receive the truest tokens of regard and honour
from, Madame,

> "Your majesty's humble, and obedient son,
>
> "LOUIS."

Marie replied in tones of indignant reproach; she
denies that she had ever troubled the realm, and

asserts that M. le Cardinal never desired reconciliation, and was not sincere in his overtures to be restored to her good graces. "Do me the favour, if it pleases you, to believe that it is out of my power to comply with your Majesty's commands to leave this place, and to journey towards Moulins. I beg you to reflect, that having received the treatment which I have, I possess good cause for the apprehensions which smite me, and which prevent me from repairing to Moulins; from which place I might be seized and put in a boat on the Rhône, and so, against my will, be transported on board your Majesty's galleys, which are assembling (at Marseilles) for Italy. Italy, it is true, is the land of my birth; but as I brought from thence into France all the wealth which appertained to me, there remains for me, even in my own country, neither honour, riches, nor refuge, except by the favour of distant relatives, who have never seen me; and who would have great right to decline to receive me in their dominions, seeing that my own son could not tolerate me, nor suffer me to end my days within his potent realm." * The unhappy princess continues thus throughout a long letter of three pages; and her despair everywhere transpires, as the promptings of her own vindictive temper convinced her that Richelieu would never permit her reconciliation with

* Marie de' Medici à Louis XIII.; Bibl. Imp., MS. Font., 262, p. 135.

the King; or share his power with one whom he had so mortally offended.* The hopes of the Queen for liberty and revenge, centred in her second son, the heir-presumptive. Monsieur had safely arrived in Lorraine, pursued by the victorious arms of his brother to the very walls of Nancy. Richelieu, nevertheless, found it requisite to dissimulate in order to achieve his final purpose; which was, to drive Marie de' Medici to a voluntary flight from the realm, by practising on her rash and impulsive temper; and on her dread of his craft and enmity.† In this design he found a ready ally in Père Joseph, who had managed to render himself agreeable to the Queen, and was not suspected by her. The King had evidently misgivings, and perhaps relentings, in

---

* "The Queen pertinaciously demanded that her physician, Vaultier, should return to her. The King promised that he should meet her at Moulins. Meantime, however, Marie was informed of his committal to the Bastille. The King consented that two of the Queen's women should return to the Luxembourg, to pack up her wardrobe and rich effects. Also that Calignon, her secretary, might visit, and arrange her papers."

† The King seems animated by the most perfect good faith throughout his correspondence during Marie's detention at Compiègne. His Majesty appeared willing to make any concession, short of permitting the Queen-mother to return to Paris. Finding that Marie's objections to Moulins were not to be overcome, he offered her the choice of the castle of Angers, or of any other château in that government. He proposed that she should occupy the castle of Blois; he offered to dismiss her guards, and to provide that everywhere the Queen should be treated as "souveraine dame, mère, et reine." Louis wished his mother to quit Compiègne, to contradict the reports that he had arrested and confined her to that palace. Marie, with her usual obstinacy, protested that nothing should induce her to leave Compiègne, except to rejoin his Majesty in Paris. "Elle a envoyé quérir des soyes pour travailler à des ouvrages, à présent que les jours sont grands," wrote d'Estrées to the secretary, Ville-aux-Clercs.

favour of his mother; nor was it probable that Louis could ever be induced to sign against her a decree of exile, or of imprisonment in a state fortress. The Cardinal perceived that the very tenure of his power depended on the dissensions of the royal family—on the absence of his haughty and intriguing patroness; in the humiliation of Queen Anne of Austria; the disgrace of M. d'Orléans; the banishment of the Princes of the blood royal, and the discontent of such formidable vassals of the crown, as Bouillon, Guise, Rohan, Epernon, and others. Le Père Joseph, therefore, wrote to Marie, offering his good offices to reconcile her with the minister, and sent his missive by a humble Capuchin brother. In that clever satire, "Le Catolicon Français," which professes to reveal the mental craft of the statesmen of this period, Richelieu is made thus to argue :—"Whilst I diverted that good lady (Marie de' Medici) by divers journeyings to and from Compiègne, I built up and cemented, by Père Joseph, the old suspicions that I had infused on both sides; telling the King that Monsieur was the elder born in his mother's affection; and to the Queen, that her son, who piqued himself on his powers of dissimulation, meant to snare, entrap, and hold her captive." Marie de' Medici, meantime, had been herself busily weaving an intrigue by which she hoped to break her bonds, and taste the delights of revenge. Marie de Beuil, Countess de Moret, once a mistress of Henri Quatre, had espoused the son of the Marquis de Vardes, governor of the neighbouring fortress of La Capelle, and resided with her husband in that stronghold. The countess found means to communicate secretly with the Queen, and offered to receive her in La Capelle, provided she could escape from Compiègne. Marie eagerly embraced the overture; taking the precaution, however, to write to the Archduchess Isabel, asking for temporary refuge at Brussels, in case any accident, after leaving Compiègne, should frustrate her design. The Queen, therefore, escaped the *surveillance* of her jailors, at ten o'clock on the night of July 10th, attended only by La Mazure, lieutenant of her body-guard.* Her fears had been strongly excited during the preceding day by the report of d'Estrées, that the Marshal Schomberg was on his way to Compiègne, at the head of 1200 horse, to convey her to Marseilles; where she was to be put on board a ship bound for Leghorn. There is no doubt that the subtle Richelieu, aware of the Queen's intrigues with Madame de Vardes, employed gentle pressure to urge her departure from Compiègne; and had taken care to remove

---

* Information faite par M. de Nesmond, Maître des Requêtes, sur la sortie de la Reine-mère de Compiègne.—Aubéry, Mém. pour servir à l'Hist. du Card. de Richelieu.

all obstacles.   At the end of the street of Compiègne,
the Queen found a coach and six, provided by Madame
de Fresney, niece of the Bishop of Léon, who took her
uncle's equipage without his knowledge or assent—a
freedom which nearly cost the bishop his see.*   The
Queen passed the river Aisne at Choisy ; relays
of horses awaited her along the road; and the venture appeared to prosper beyond her most sanguine hopes.   Madame de Vardes, however, failed to
meet her Majesty at the appointed place—a league
from La Capelle.   After an interval of suspense, a
messenger appeared, who announced that the old
Marquis de Vardes, had suddenly entered La
Capelle; and, after arresting his son for his traitorous correspondence with the Queen-mother, had
sent Madame de Vardes and the ladies privy to
the plot to deliver up the fortress, under strong
escort to Paris, to await the stern pleasure of the
Cardinal.   Richelieu received daily advices from
Compiègne, all of which he jotted down in his
Journal.   Aware, therefore, of the design of the
Queen to entrench herself in La Capelle, he had
given notice to the Marquis de Vardes † to circum-

* Ibid. The bishop was tried for high treason ; suspended from his
episcopal functions ; and was restored only after the decease of the
cardinal.—Urquefort, L'Ambassadeur et ses Fonctions, livre 1, p. 112.
† René Dubec, premier Marquis de Vardes. The marquis married
Hélène d'O. His son, René II. du nom, espoused Jacqueline de Beuil,

vent the project by his own opportune arrival. The unfortunate Marie, therefore, not daring to return to Compiègne, took the road, with the utmost precipitation, to the town of Avesne, where she was received with ostentatious honour by the Marquis de Crèvecœur. A messenger was despatched to Brussels to inform the Infanta Doña Isabel of the Queen's arrival. The Prince d'Epinay, governor of the province of Hainault, received commands to attend her Majesty to Mons; where the Infanta repaired for an interview. Marie, again fatally swayed by her resentments, suffered herself to be escorted by the Spanish ambassador, the Marquis de Aytona, whom she subsequently deputed to compliment, and thank Doña Isabel. The frantic anger of Louis XIII., against his mother, needed no further impetus after her imprudence had been expatiated upon in council, by the Cardinal de Richelieu. In reply to the letter despatched by Marie, the King wrote :—" Madame, my cousin the Cardinal de Richelieu gives me daily numerous proofs of devotion, fidelity, affection, and sincerity. He pays a religious deference to my commands: and the faithful care he gives to the welfare of my realm, and my own person vouch for

Countess de Moret ; and their eldest son, the third Marquis de Varde, Count de Moret, was the celebrated cavalier of Louis XIV., captain of the Swiss and body guards.

his truth. You will therefore permit me, Madame, to observe, that the act which you have just committed, and the intrigues in which you participate, have enlightened me as to your past intentions, and put me on my guard against future attempts. The respect, Madame, which I ought to bear you prevents me from adding more to this epistle." *

Some officious person at this season remarked to Anne of Austria, that, at least, M. le Cardinal showed her more indulgence, and respect than he had vouchsafed to Queen Marie. Anne assumed her most icy manner, and replied, with scornful gesture, "There can and shall be no comparison between the Queen-mother, and myself: her rank is not such as mine: she has not the influence and support which I possess, and which I have the right to expect." †

The triumphant Richelieu consummated his victory by the issue of a proclamation of outlawry against all the followers of the Duc d'Orleans. The names of the proscribed traitors were the Count de Moret, natural brother of the King; the Dukes de Bellegarde, d'Elbœuf, de Rohan; the Presidents le Coigneux and de Payen, and M. de Puylaurent, le P. Chanteloube, ‡ confessor to Marie de' Medici;

Lettre de Louis XIII. à Marie de' Medici.—Bibl. Imp. MS. Font. 264.
† Journal de Richelieu.
‡ Le Père Chanteloube was banished, or rather fled, to Brussels, to

and Mousignot, private secretary to Monsieur.
When this edict was sent to the Parliament to be
registered, the members modified the decree against
the adherents of the heir presumptive, by entering
on the register what was called *un arrêt de par-
tage;* which placed on record the names of the
members protesting against the decree. The King
therefore commanded the attendance of the High
Court in the great gallery of the Louvre. Louis
commanded the registers to be laid before him;
and with his own hand he tore therefrom the leaf
upon which the act had been inscribed under protest. The King then caused a decree of the privy
council to be inserted, which prohibited any debate
in the Chambers upon matters relating to state affairs
 topics, which appertained only to the ministers,
and sworn counsellors of the crown.

Judicial proceedings were next instituted against
the Countess de Fargis, who was supposed to be
lingering in the neighbourhood of Paris in disguise.
Such was the terror inspired by the late proceedings
of the King and his minister, that the friends of
Anne of Austria failed in their allegiance to her

avoid arrest for an alleged connivance in a plot to carry off Madame de
Combalet. "Afin de mettre le cardinal à la raison, quand elle auroit
ce qu'il aimoit tant. Mademoiselle de Rambouillet étoit avec elle ; elle
alloit voir Madame de Rambouillet." The plot was real—one of Marie
de' Medici's insane expedients to annoy the cardinal.

service, and caprice.   The Abbess of the Val de Grâce,* stirred by a significant hint from the Palais Cardinal, that seditiously inclined sisterhoods had been dissolved, and their members draughted into more loyal communities, hastened to send information to the Cardinal that two suspicious personages, thought to be Croft and Montagu, had asked at the gate of the convent to speak with her Majesty; moreover, that a letter had been delivered into the hands of the Queen by an unknown person, as her Majesty entered the nunnery upon her first visit after the return of the court from Compiègne.   The personages mentioned in the letters of de Fargis, taken from M. Senelle, were arrested, and subjected to severe inter-rogatories.   Amongst these persons were the Marquis de Crequi, and the Count de Cramail, M. Senelle, and Mademoiselle du Tillet.   This last lady deposed that she had twice forwarded letters from the accused to M. de Cramail; also, that two days after the return of the court from Compiègne, Anne had sent for her to take charge of a letter which her Majesty desired secretly to forward to de Fargis, but that the Queen had decided finally to send it by a special messenger.   "I feel no surprise that Madame de

---

* M. de St. Etienne married Marie de Tremblay, sister of Father Joseph. The Abbess of the Val de Grâce was a sister of M. de St. Etienne, and therefore honoured with marks of gracious notice by the famous Capuchin.

Fargis has been dismissed from the Queen's service; the mystery is, what influence could ever induce M. le Cardinal to sanction the nomination of *une femme si décriée* to the first office in her Majesty's household!" * was the malicious comment of Mademoiselle du Tillet; in allusion to the notorious intrigues which once subsisted between de Fargis, Cramail, Richelieu, and the disgraced Lord-Keeper de Marillac. As the countess never surrendered to take her trial in obedience to the citation of the criminal court sitting at the Arsenal, judgment was allowed to go by default. The award of the court declared la Dame de Fargis d'Angennes guilty of high treason, and sentenced her to decapitation; which decree was performed on an effigy of the countess in the Place du Carrefour de St. Paul, November 8th, 1631. M. Senelle, upon whom the letters of the countess were found, was condemned to the galleys for life; Vaultier, to perpetual imprisonment in the Bastille.† The Marshal de Marillac, generalissimo of the Italian army, towards whom Richelieu bore inveterate hate, was arrested and put upon his trial upon frivolous charges of malversation during the construction of the citadel of Verdun, by which he had derived illicit profit: and of mal-administration

* Journal du Cardinal de Richelieu.—Amsterdam, 1664.
† Ibid.

of the King's moneys forwarded for the payment of
the army under his command. The true crime of
Marillac was, his offer at the memorable secret conference at Lyons, during the King's illness, to slay
the obnoxious Cardinal minister with his own hand.
The Lord-Keeper Châteauneuf presided at the trial,
which took place, against all precedent, in the private mansion of Richelieu, at Ruel. On the 8th
of May, sentence of decapitation was pronounced
upon Marillac; the crime of this old, and faithful
servant of Henri Quatre being his devoted attachment to the widow of his late master; and the power
which his probity, virtue, and affability enabled him
to exercise over the army under his command. " A
page ought not to be flogged for the misdeeds for
which I am arraigned! For forty years I have
served two great kings: all that they can accuse me
of, are trifling inaccuracies in accounts for lime,
straw, hay, wood, and stone!" The following day
the head of Marillac fell.* So great was the horror
and irritation of Queen Marie when she heard of this
murder, that she is said to have made a solemn vow
that if ever she returned to France, and regained
her lost power, the head of Richelieu should be

* Vie du Maréchal de Marillac. Bayle, Dict. Tallemant des Réaux.
Bassompierre. Mém. du Sieur de Pontis; the which, contain a full
detail of the trial and execution of the unfortunate marshal, as De Pontis
was the officer charged with the guard of Marillac after his arrest.

severed, without form or process, on the spot upon which the virtuous, and good marshal suffered. The ex-Lord-Keeper brother of Marillac, survived his brother only four months: he died at Châteaudun, crippled from the dampness, and unhealthiness of his prison; and overwhelmed with grief at the ruin of his house.

Richelieu, meantime, despatched letters and missives in every direction, to express his dismay at the arrest, and flight of Marie de' Medici; towards whom he positively avers that no harm, or disgrace was intended, except a temporary exile to her dower castle of Moulins.

In one of these epistles addressed to the Cardinal de la Valette, Richelieu thus expresses his regrets:— "It is with the most incredible and smarting regret that I announce to you the resolve which his Majesty found himself obliged to take at Compiègne, to request the Queen his mother, to retire for a time to Moulins. I would wish, at the price of my blood, and at the forfeiture of my life, to have rendered this separation unnecessary, although, please God, its duration will be brief. If it had pleased Almighty God to have granted my prayers, my last moment would have preceded this alienation; for which I can never be consoled, seeing a Queen whom I have so long revered, and served, reduced to this condition.

But the sway of evil and termagant spirits had too long dominated over the court. During the war in Italy, they did all they could to produce a failure of that campaign; since which Monsieur has fled from court. The King, on many occasions, entreated the Queen his mother, to open her eyes upon these woes and to arrest their progress, but her Majesty was not pleased to comply; nor would she enter the council chamber, saying that she did not wish her name to be used as an authority for the indispensable measures there resolved. The King, finding her inexorable in this resolution, wisely decided that if she declined to permit her influence to be used in support of his government, her presence in Paris was highly adverse to the welfare of his realm—as declaring herself malcontent, and remaining at court, gave to many personages boldness and freedom to proclaim themselves so likewise."* A few days later, the Cardinal wrote to the Commander de la Porte, uncle of M. de St. Simon, to announce the departure of Marie from Compiègne. In this letter he says—" Believe me, there is nothing in the world which we would not have done to persuade the Queen to renounce her alliance with Monsieur, and with the realm of Spain. We offered to confide to her the government of Anjou, and to confirm her

* Aubéry, Mém. pour l'Hist. du Cardinal de Richelieu, t. 5.

Majesty's sway over other places already conferred ;
but she steadily refused all honourable terms, and
requisite precautions, which we proposed."*   "The
Queen," said Richelieu, "treated in the same manner
persons, who brought her an atrocious calumny, or a
pure truth. She kept the secret of all, and received
true friends, and false ones with the same cordiality.
Everyone, therefore, fearlessly palmed upon her bad
coin mingled with good. I lost my hold on the
Queen-mother," continues he, "by not putting down
evil cabals when they first cropped out. To save
one's self one must seize the initiative. It is better,
in such circumstances, to do much rather than little ;
provided precaution goes only the length of exiling
from court all personages, who, being able to perpe-
trate evil, inspire suspicions by imprudent, or malignant conduct and censure."†

Having thus punished his late opponents, exiled
the Queen-mother, and suspended a threatening
scourge over the head of his sovereign's wife,
Richelieu next offered admonition to his royal
master. Imbued with a thorough persuasion of his

----

* Aubéry, Mém. pour l'Hist. du Cardinal de Richelieu, t. 5.

† Mémoire donné au Roy par le Cardinal de Richelieu après que la
Reyne-mère l'eut éloigné de sa maison, touchant les cabales dans la cour.
Aubéry, t. 5, p. 266. "Il ne faut pas croire, Sire, qu'on puisse avoir des
preuves mathématiques des conspirations et des cabales ; elles ne se
connoissent ainsi que par l'événement, lorsqu'elles ne sont plus capables
de remède," writes the politic minister.

own administrative capacity, and the weakness of the King, Richelieu caused the following maxims to be laid before Louis by the Capuchin Joseph; in which, article by article, he prescribed the manner in which he chose to wield the arbitrary power he had usurped :—

1.

A great Prince ought to have a council of state to advise with on the affairs of his realm.

2.

It is necessary for a King to have a prime minister; and this prime minister must have three qualities, to whit,—to possess no other interest than that of his Prince; to be able, and faithful; and to be a member of Holy Church.

3.

A Prince ought to love his prime minister with perfect affection.

4.

A Prince ought never to dismiss, or degrade his prime minister.

5.

A Prince ought to confide implicitly in his prime minister.

6.

A Prince ought always to grant free, and constant access to his presence to his prime minister.

7.

A Prince ought to invest his prime minister with sovereign authority over the people of the realm.

8.

A Prince ought to heap honours, and riches on his prime minister.

9.

A Prince ought to regard his prime minister as his richest treasure.

10.

A Prince ought to put no faith in reports and accusations against his prime minister: he ought not to take pleasure in such slander: but, on the contrary, rigorously punish him by whom his minister is falsely accused.

11.

A Prince ought to make plenary revelation to his prime minister of all slanders, and accusations hurled against the said minister; even when the King may have solemnly promised secrecy.

12.

A Prince ought not only to love his realm, but his prime minister also; after them, his kindred, and relatives.

13.

A Prince ought to forestal calamity by wise provision.

14.

A Prince is not to be blamed for using just severity in governing his realm.

15.

A Prince ought carefully to prevent his kingdom from being governed by women, and favourites.

The audacity of these fifteen maxims wrung a grim smile from Louis XIII. He, however, carefully put the paper by, in the presence of the wily Capuchin; and desired the reverend father to assure himself that he had perfect faith in the fidelity, ability, and resource of M. le Cardinal.

CHAPTER VI.

1631—1637.

AFTER the return of Anne of Austria from Compiègne, her restless spirit subsided. Everywhere the policy and the will of Richelieu were dominant: alliance with him conferred power, and opposition to his fiats, disgrace and ignominy. The palace swarmed with his spies; and, even in the retirement of her bedchamber, Anne knew that the Cardinal's wary eye tracked her actions, and analysed her motives. But one fact foiled the will of the Cardinal—and that was her own indomitable hate and enmity. Had the Queen joined her interests to those of Richelieu,—had she smiled on the minister, and have declared herself favourable to his policy and to his power,—the aspect of Anne's daily life would probably have been transformed from a lot of obscurity and persecution, to the most brilliant and powerful position ever occupied by a queen-consort of France. The proposition had been more than once made to her by the Cardinal through Mesdames de Chevreuse, and de Fargis.*   Often, Richelieu was heard to lament the division subsisting between himself and Queen Anne, and to laud rapturously her beauty, wit, and sagacity; while he pathetically deplored that these rare gifts should be employed in plots against the government, in upholding rebel vassals of the crown, and, above all, in supporting M. d'Orleans in his criminal attempts to inflict upon France the curse of civil war, and foreign invasion. The hidden motives of this disloyalty, and indifference to the interests and glory of her adopted country, the Cardinal discerned in the uncertainty of the King's life; and in the hope which ever animated the childless Queen that, on the death of Louis XIII., she might a second time ascend the throne as the consort of the brother, and successor of her husband. Actuated by this wicked foresight, Anne, Richelieu averred, and with much apparent truth, sacrificed her conjugal and queenly duty; and made no effort to conciliate

---

* "Le Cardinal lui fit dire par Madame de Fargis, dame d'atours, que si elle vouloit, il la tireroit bientôt de la misère dans laquelle elle vivoit. La reine alors, qui ne croyoit point que ce fut lui qui la fit maltraiter, pensa d'abord que ce fut par compassion qu'il lui offrit son assistance, souffrit qu'il lui écrivit et lui fit même réponse; car elle ne s'imaginoit point que ce commerce produisit autre chose qu'une simple galanterie."
—Tallemant.

her husband, or to efface from his suspicious mind
the impression cast thereon by the revelations consequent on the trial of Chalais. No relations could
be colder than those subsisting between Louis and
his consort during the winter, and the spring of the
years 1631-2. The King avoided his wife in
private; while in public, ceremonious etiquette
divided them. Anne never set foot within the
King's apartments: all her communications with
his Majesty passed through the hands of Richelieu, and were generally imparted to the minister
by the Spanish ambassador, or by Madame de
Senécé. When Louis visited his palaces of Compiègne, Fontainebleau, Versailles, or Vincennes, notice was given to her Majesty, who made preparation
to follow the King; or, accepting the alternative
generally offered, she retired to St. Germain, and
lived there in strict privacy. Anne now received a
liberal allowance for her privy purse : at this period,
the sum amounted to ten thousand pounds yearly,
which she disposed of at will; and upon which no
demand was made for expenses connected with her
household.

With the people of Paris Anne was popular;
there was a fascination in her smile and manner
which made the Parisians greet her with enthusiasm;
besides, they half resented her shabby equipages,

and the absence of pompous *appareil*, and of the attendants, which had formed the escort of the queens her predecessors. The Queen was never attended by more than three ladies ; and the edict, given after the trial of Chalais, suspended the functions of the noblemen of her household, excepting when the royal pair made a joint progress. The people, therefore, cheered their young Queen on her dreary progresses to the convents of Val de Grâce, and the Carmelites of the Rue St. Jacques, despite her well-known mutinous defiance of the will of her liege lord Louis XIII. and the law of his minister. The Queen was, nevertheless, compelled to dissimulate her discontent : utter isolation might lead to her banishment from the capital, could Louis be persuaded that her presence had little influence on the assembling at the Louvre of the few great personages in the good graces of the Cardinal, who composed the court. She had, therefore, summoned Mirabel to the Val de Grâce,—who obeyed her behests at the risk of being arrested, conducted to the frontier, and dismissed the realm,—to request him to wait upon Richelieu, and hint, in the name of his Catholic Majesty, that " the latter regretted his Eminence did not frequent the *lever*, or the saloon of Queen Anne his sister, as such intimacy could not fail to be productive of happy results, and might give M. le Cardinal opportunity for friendly counsel."* Richelieu thanked the ambassador for his obliging discourse; but gave no intimation as to whether he purposed to act in accord thereto. Probably the Cardinal preferred to trust to the good offices of Madame de Chevreuse to bring about a better understanding between the Queen and himself; rather than to venture alone into her Majesty's presence. The approaching return of Marie de Rohan to court excited in the bosom of the powerful minister, hopes which were never realised. He professed profound admiration for the clever and witty duchess; he wished for her friendly alliance; and, if the scandalous chronicles of this reign are to be believed, he desired of her something more in addition. Marie, wearied of her enforced sojourn at Dampierre, and anxious to share the power of her friend Châteauneuf, befooled the Cardinal by professions of admiration; and by promises of converting Anne of Austria from his foe, to a devoted ally. The adoration which King Louis began to lavish on Mademoiselle de Hautefort, any comment upon which his Majesty fiercely resented, began to inflict uneasiness on the minister. Anne had already thrown the glamour of her fascinations

* Journal de Richelieu. "L'ambassadeur m'a dit qui j'y devois aller librement quand le roy y étoit, ou n'y étoit pas, luy dire un mot de ce qu'elle devoit faire, tantôt la divertir de ce qu'on jugeroit à propos; que je luy ferois plaisir d'en user ainsi."

over her young *dame d'atours,* and showed no jealousy of her influence with the King; while Marie de Hautefort bravely informed Richelieu, "that she loved and revered her royal mistress; and could not blame her Majesty if, when surrounded by neglect and persecutions, she had recourse to the sympathy and aid of her brother King Philip." One of the most remarkable faculties possessed by the Queen was the power of commanding the affectionate attachment of her principal ladies; those who most disapproved of her intrigues, when they entered her service, never afterwards betrayed her to the minister. The gentle manners of the Queen, her apparent helplessness, her affectionate condescension, the interest she showed in the personal affairs of her friends, and the tearful softness of her blue eyes, were powerful weapons against the ascendency of the Cardinal, within the precincts of the palace.

Meantime, the sombre and imperious admiration of Louis XIII. filled the mind of Marie de Hautefort with foreboding. Amongst the beautiful women of the era of Louis XIII., Marie de Hautefort stands prominent, as one of the most noble, heroic, and virtuous. Firm in her principles, and devoted in her friendship and duty to the Queen her mistress, Marie seems to have confided to Anne her misgivings. Endowed with a heart worthy of a queen, or of a heroine, Marie at first beheld with complacency the homage of her King; and accepted with elation the assiduities of Richelieu. For her sake, and to obtain the coveted interview, Louis daily repaired, twice and thrice, to the apartments of the Queen, where Mademoiselle de Hautefort was often summoned from a conference with her Majesty to become the recipient of the sighs, and plaints of the King. Anne comforted and reassured her friend; the King professed sentiments purely Platonic; he wanted, he said, the solace of friendship, and confidential intercourse; he liked to cavil at his minister; above all, he desired faithful, exclusive attachment. Marie, inspired with genuine compassion for the dreariness of a life of emotions so repressed, accepted; with the secret sanction of the Queen, the office of comforter. Anne gloried in the hope that in this *liaison* she descried the future germ of her enemy's downfall. The King's bashful shyness in his intercourse with Marie, allayed the most prudish suspicion. It is related, that one day Louis abruptly entered the Queen's closet, when Anne was sitting *tête-à-tête* with her *dame d'atours;* who, with heightened colour, was reading to her Majesty a note, which, on the entrance of the King, she hastily folded. A dark shadow gloomed over the King's brow; and he peremptorily demanded to see the letter so hastily hidden. Treason to his realm might afford a daily pastime to Anne of Austria; while treason against his attachment might give delight to Marie de Hautefort—for Louis had been informed by his minister of the admiration professed by the Duc de Liancour, and the young Prince de Marsillac,* for the lovely young *dame d'atours*. By some historians, the letter is said to have been written by Richelieu, and that it contained offers of a reciprocal friendly alliance; others, state that the epistle congratulated Mademoiselle de Hautefort on her favour, and ended by a demand for protection from some cringing courtier. True to herself, however, Marie refused to gratify the curiosity of the King; and to end the debate she hid the note in her bosom.† Anne, meantime, looked on with mocking derision; especially when she beheld the confusion of the King, and his hesitation to draw the note from its hiding-place. Her Majesty, however, presently seized the hands of Mademoiselle de Hautefort, and laughingly exhorted the King "to take the note while she thus held its owner captive." Louis

---

* Heir of La Rochefoucauld, and afterwards the celebrated duke of that name, author of "The Maxims."

† Monglat states that Mademoiselle de Hautefort exclaimed, "Prenez-la (la lettre) tant que vous voudrez à cette heure!"—Cousin, Vie de Madame de Hautefort.

blushed, stammered, advanced, and retreated; and at length, taking up from the hearth a small pair of silver tongs, he tried to possess himself of the note, which was visible beneath the transparent lace which covered Marie's bosom. The peals of laughter which this extraordinary device drew from the Queen; and the blushing confusion, and deprecatory looks of Marie, fairly drove Louis from the apartment.* The ladies then hastened to destroy the letter, just in time to forestal a formal summons for its surrender, by the under secretary of state, Machault. "Mademoiselle de Hautefort is of tall stature and fine figure; her eyes are blue, large, open, and full of vivacity; her nose is aquiline; her mouth small and rosy; while her smile displays teeth, white and even as pearls. Two little dimples give a grace to the lovely mouth and cheeks. The colour of her hair is *blond cendré*, of which she has an abundance, falling in ringlets around a beautiful and stately throat. In her aspect there is altogether so much dignity, gentleness, and grace, that it excites sentiments of tenderness, awe, and esteem." Such is the description given of the charms of the young

---

* "Le roi prit de pincettes d'argent qui étaient auprès du feu pour essayer s'il pouvait avoir ce billet avec les pincettes : mais elle l'avait mis trop avant, et ainsi la reine la laissa aller, après s'être bien divertie de la peur de Madame de Hautefort, et de celle du roi."—Vie de Madame de Hautefort.—Cousin, quoted from la Vie MS.

dame d'atours by a contemporary.*   The heavy assiduities of Louis were often felt as insupportable restraints by one so gifted and charming; who beheld
all the cavaliers of the court vanquished by her fascinations; but, nevertheless, withheld from offering personal homage, daunted by their dread of exciting the
resentment of the sovereign.   Madame de la Flotte,
however, did not fail to remind her granddaughter
that the homage of Louis XIII. had enabled her
adorers to discern many a captivating grace hitherto
undiscovered, when Marie was the humble *fille
d'honneur* of the exiled Queen-mother.   When the
Louvre rang with the praises of Mademoiselle de
Hautefort,† and the courtiers celebrated the charms
of—

> Hautefort la merveille '
>   Réveille
> Tous les sens de Louis,
> Quand sa bouche vermeille
> Lui fait voir un souris !

the Cardinal deemed it time to provide an antidote,
which he summoned in the form of the Duchess de
Chevreuse; and in the promotion to a more distinguished position in the royal household of another
fair young maid of honour, Louise Angélique Motier
de la Fayette.   Richelieu felt that if the Duchess was

---

* Vie de Madame de Hautefort.—Cousin, quoted from la Vie MS.
† Mademoiselle de Hautefort was known at court by the *sobriquet* of
" Sainte Hautefort."

on his side, he had nothing to fear from the probable combination of the Queen and La Hautefort. He relied on the sagacity of Marie de Rohan* to resume her old ascendency over the heart of Anne of Austria ; and to drive into obscurity the presumptive girl who had dared to aspire to royal favour, and to the confidence of the Queen. After five years of exile, Madame de Chevreuse, therefore, re-appeared permanently, as she hoped, on the scene of her ancient triumphs, much to the dismay of her husband ; who, during her enforced residence at Dampierre, had been revelling in luxurious ease, troubling himself seldom with the wishes, or the fate of his consort. Madame de Chevreuse, as the widow and sole heiress of the late Constable de Luynes, had brought her second husband immense wealth in jewels, lands, and rich effects. The Duc de Chevreuse was recklessly extravagant : being in want of a coach, he was once known to command fifteen to be built that he might select the most comfortable. His donations to dissolute companions were immense. The Duke, nevertheless, knew how to uphold his dignity as became a scion

* When the Queen Marie de' Medici heard of the return to Paris of Madame de Chevreuse, she exclaimed, " Hé bien, elle retourne après cinq ans de banissement ; et avoir été en divers lieux. Le cardinal ne sauroit avoir pensé, n'y faire la moindre action que je ne sache à quoi elle tend."—Aubéry, Mém. pour l'Hist. du Card. de Richelieu, t. 2.

of Lorraine Guise, and greatly disapproved of his wife's proceedings. The return of the Duchess, therefore, was an event which he deprecated—the more especially, as, under the cloak of her new favour with Richelieu, and the Lord-Keeper Châteauneuf, Madame de Chevreuse commenced a suit against her husband for profligate expenditure during her absence, and demanded a *séparation de corps et de biens*, which she easily obtained. Monsieur de Chevreuse, therefore, retired from the Hôtel Luynes ; while the Duchess complacently established herself alone in that splendid mansion, and prepared for the career before her. Anne received her old friend with open arms ; and this cordiality ought to have aroused Richelieu to examine the sincerity of the professions of the Duchess. Madame de Chevreuse became a daily visitor at the Louvre ; though Louis refused to reinstate her in her old apartments within the palace, and evidently regarded her presence as an unwelcome intrusion. The court, nevertheless, during the next few months, was joyous and gallant. Richelieu and his master required the splendour and excitement of a few brilliant festivals to neutralize, in degree, the gloom everywhere prevalent, and to divert public attention from politics, and from the discontent manifested in the provinces at the exile of the Queen-mother, and of the heir presumptive.

"The court was very agreeable at this period," recounts Mademoiselle :* " the attachment of the King to Madame de Hautefort contributed greatly to our pleasure, as his Majesty tried to find her daily diversion. Hunting was the greatest of the King's recreations; and we often accompanied his Majesty. Mesdames de Hautefort and St. Louis, d'Escars and de Beaumont attended me. We were attired in our respective colours, and rode palfreys richly accoutred. To shade our complexion from the sun, we all wore hats ornamented with a great quantity of drooping plumes. The hunt always was made to take the direction of some great house, where we found a sumptuous collation prepared. When we returned the King usually entered my coach, sitting between me, and Madame de Hautefort. When his Majesty was in good humour, he conversed very agreeably. At this period he permitted us to speak of the Cardinal de Richelieu; and as a sign that he was not displeased at our comments, he joined in our conversation. As soon as we returned to the Louvre, we repaired to the saloon of the Queen, where I took pleasure in waiting upon her Majesty whilst she supped, her maidens handing the dishes. Three times a week we had the diversion of music,

* La Grande Mademoiselle Anne Louise d'Orléans, daughter of Monsieur and of Marie, Duchesse de Montpensier.—Mém., t. i.

and the King's musicians attended. The airs played and sung were generally composed by the King: he also wrote the words of the songs, which had always Madame de Hautefort for their theme. The humour of the King, at this period, was so gallant, that at the country collations which he gave us, he sometimes declined to take his place at table, but waited upon the ladies; though we were aware that this civility had but one object. He took his repast after we had finished, but pretended not to pay more attention to Madame de Hautefort than to any one of us, so anxious was his Majesty to conceal his gallant devoirs. Nevertheless, if any dispute happened between them, all our diversions were immediately suspended; and if the King came, during this interval, into the Queen's saloon, he spoke to no one, neither did any person dare to address his Majesty. He retired into a corner, and there sat, yawned, and slept. The King's melancholy aspect chilled everybody; and during this interval, between the quarrel and reconciliation, he consoled himself by putting down on paper all that he had said to Madame de Hautefort, with her replies; and so true is this fact, that after his Majesty's death copious minutes were found amongst his private papers detailing at length all the quarrels he had had with his mistresses; to the eternal praise of whom, be it avowed, as also to his Majesty's honour, he never loved any but the most virtuous, and discreet of women." Louis had the greatest horror of profligate *liaisons:* and though alienated from the Queen, he was rigidly faithful to her. "Mademoiselle de Hautefort told me," writes Madame de Motteville, "that the decorum of the King was such that he seldom talked to her on any subjects but about his dogs, his birds, and hunting. I have seen her, with all her wisdom and virtue, relate with derision the fright the King was in when with her alone; and that at such periods he scarcely dared approach near enough to discourse with her." On occasions, however, when the King and Mademoiselle de Hautefort were alone, Marie spoke earnestly respecting the Queen, and besought the King to become reconciled to her; and the subject of their frequent disputes, to which Mademoiselle alludes, was the zeal which Marie displayed for the cause of her royal mistress. Louis confided his suspicions, and stated his conviction that Anne was the accomplice of Chalais; and that he owed his life, and crown to the vigilance of Richelieu. "The Queen hates me,— she intrigues against my realm—she is Spanish at heart—she is perpetually plotting against my happiness." This conviction nothing could ever shake. "Madame," continued Louis; "mark my words—you love and support an ungrateful woman. Wait, and

see how one day she will repay your services!"
Marie de Hautefort, like many others, believed fervently in the Queen, with her sweet smiles, and gentle seductions.   Anne was mistress of the arts of persuasion; and the disgraces which followed her persistent petty treasons seemed the more to endear her to her adherents.   Perhaps her power lay in the unpopularity of the King.   The penalties, moreover, with which her deviations were visited, lay open to the comment and pity of the court; while the cause of this severity was often concealed by the express command of Louis, who shrank from the publication of his domestic miseries.   Anne persuaded her friends that her clandestine correspondences with Spain were innocent; and that her stolen conferences with the Spanish ambassador, and with Gerbier, Montague, and Croft, Catholic agents of Queen Henrietta of England, were legitimate.   She was persecuted,—her Majesty, therefore, appealed to the sympathy of her brother King Philip, and to that of Marie de' Medici, and of Monsieur, and disregarded the tyrannical orders of the minister, to be silent and submit.   The word of Anne of Austria, as Richelieu often observed, could not be depended upon.   Her Majesty, it was true, rarely perjured herself; but her modes of evasion, and equivocation were so diverse and ingenious, that she

seldom avowed what she wished to conceal, even under the most rigid examination; or promised exactly that which she knew she had no intention to fulfil.   If Anne could have accepted her lot, and her uncongenial consort with resignation, her court might have been brilliant and joyous, despite the absence of the great personages disgraced by the policy of the minister.   Beautiful women, such as the Duchesses de Montbazon,* de Chevreuse, and the Princess de Guémené,† adorned the court circle; the wit of the Marquise de Sablé, and of the Prince de Marsillac, of Madame de Rambouillet, and of the Princesses Marie, and Anne de Gonzague-Nevers, gave *verve* and animation; the rich heiress of the elder branch of Rohan, the granddaughter of Sully, was a prize sufficient to excite a *piquant* emulation amongst the younger courtiers; while the charms of Anne's maidens, Hautefort, and la Fayette, and de Chemérault, and the grace and repartee of Ma-

* Marie de Vertus dite de Bretagne, daughter of Claude de Bretagne, Count de Vertus, and of Catherine Fouquet. She married, in 1628, Hercules de Rohan, Duke de Montbazon, father of the Duchess de Chevreuse. Marie was quite a child when she married the Duke, who took her from a convent, where she was destined to make profession. The Duke de Montbazon, therefore, always called her " *Ma religieuse*." Madame de Montbazon was one of the most beautiful women of the court, and one of the most *intrigante*, and masculine in mind. She died in 1657, aged 45.

† Anne de Rohan, wife of M. de Guémené, eldest son of the Duke de Montbazon, and brother of Madame de Chevreuse.

demoiselle de Vendôme, all might have contributed
to the renown of the court.   Moreover, there stood
in close proximity to the throne Marguerite de Montmorency, Princesse de Condé, in the bright zenith
of her charms, and still encircled by the halo of
the mad passion of Henri le Grand.   Besides her,
was her daughter Anne Geneviève de Bourbon, lovely
like her mother, of strong intellect, apt at political
intrigue, in the which she had been nurtured ; but
shrinking at this very period from sharing the grand
ancestral home, name, and mature years of the
Duc de Longueville.   By Madame de Condé was
her son—after M. d'Orléans, heir of the crown
—afterwards known as the great Condé, whose
powerful arm first shook, and then established the
throne of the future Louis Quatorze.   The eagle eye
of Richelieu had marked this noble heir of the
Condés ; and with unfaltering faith in his own
fortunes and ability, he had resolved on the first
fortunate contingency—some opportunity, when the
dark jealousy of Louis Treize had been roused
against the princes of his blood—to unite the young
Duc d'Enghein with his niece, Claire Clémence
de Maillé-Brézé.   Mademoiselle de Brézé was one of
the playfellows of Mademoiselle in her nursery at
the Tuileries : she was excessively *petite* in stature,
and wore high-heeled shoes, which entailed upon

her many a fall while dancing the *leste courante*
with the merry princess, who seems to have amused
herself heartily with the terrors of the timid child.
One day Mademoiselle ordered a ballet to be performed in honour of the return of her father Monsieur, to Paris, in which she and her maidens
performed.   During a scene of the ballet, a number
of caged birds were liberated; and a linnet, after
flying about the apartment, nestled into one of the
deep plaits of the ruff worn by Mademoiselle de
Brézé, who screamed with fright, and fainted as the
bird fluttered about her neck.   It was to propitiate
Madame de Condé that Richelieu caused that won-
drous doll's house to be constructed, the first that had
ever been seen in France, at a cost of 2000 crowns,
and presented it to Mademoiselle de Bourbon.*   The
trusty friend and equerry of Anne of Austria, de
Rochechouart, Chevalier de Jars, had also received a
pardon, and a recall from his banishment in England,
where he had remained ever since the memorable
embassy of the Duke of Buckingham to Paris; having
been convicted of carrying to London certain missives addressed to the ambassador by his royal

---

* "Où il y avait six poupées, une femme en couches, une nourrice,
quasi au naturel, un enfant, une garde, une sage-femme, et la grand'-
maman. Mesdemoiselles de Rambouillet et de Bouteville jouaient avec
elle, déshabillaient et couchaient tous les jours ces poupées, etc."—Tallemant, Hist. du Card. de Richelieu.

mistress. The Christmas of 1631 passed away in this negative state of tranquillity, when, with the public declaration of the marriage of Monsieur with Marguerite,* sister of the Duke of Lorraine, occurred the rising, in Languedoc, on behalf of Monsieur and of his mother the exiled Queen ; and the news that Spain was preparing to invade France at the summons of the heir presumptive. The gallant Duc de Montmorency, seduced by the promises and entreaties of Monsieur; and misled by his statements of the forces he could muster in support of his revolt, promised to receive the duke in Languedoc; and to place the fortresses and towns therein, in the possession of the rebel forces. The Duke pledged himself to Montmorency to enter France at the head of 2000 men—levies with he purposed to raise in the Netherlands, with funds placed at his disposal by the Queen his mother, who had disposed of her jewels for this purpose ; and by the aid of the treasury of Spain. Moreover, the Duke of Lorraine had engaged to join their army with a reinforcement of 1500 men ; while a powerful body of Spanish troops was to appear on the frontiers of Savoy, to aid in the overthrow of the usurping minister, and thus

* Marguerite de Lorraine Vaudemont, daughter of François, Count de Vaudemont, and of Françoise de Salms. Her father was the brother of Henri, Duc de Lorraine, and father of Duke Charles IV., Duke of Lorraine in right of his wife Nicole.

to achieve the salvation of France, the reunion of the royal family, and the liberation of the King. Unhappily, some private sources of discontent rendered Montmorency an easy dupe to the sophistry of Monsieur.* He allied himself with the Duke; promised to take up arms in his cause; and to open to him a high road through his government of Languedoc. Having agreed to the convention, Montmorency effectually closed against himself the avenues of mercy in the breast of the suspicious Louis, by sending the Count de Grammont to assure the King of his fidelity; and that the rumours current of his alliance with Monsieur were unfounded. Three days afterwards, Monsieur made his appearance at Lodève, at the head of an undisciplined band, half Walloon, half Spanish, officered by a few French adventurers and malcontents, ready to throw for the same lot as Monsieur. With such an army of adventurers, the Duke hesitated not to endanger the lives of cavaliers like Montmorency, Elbœuf, Moret, and M. de la

---

* Montmorency had asked for the sword of Constable, and for the government of the citadel of Montpellier, which were refused to his solicitations: "On n'avait garde de rendre le Duc plus puissant en Languedoc." The Duke had a trifling quarrel with the Duke de Chevreuse which had incurred the resentment and bad offices of Madame de Chevreuse.—Vie du Duc de Montmorency—Galerie des Personnages Illustres. The Duke proposed to the States of the province to vote a supply for the King's service, which he intended to divert to the purposes of the revolt, as Montmorency himself allows in a letter to Monsieur : "On saisira les secours d'argent qu'ils doivent accorder au Roi pour le service de Monsieur."—Mém. du Duc de Montmorency : Paris, 1665.

Valette, the husband of his half-sister, Gabrielle de Bourbon; and, to make the risk still more fatal, he entered France three days before the period agreed upon, and while Montmorency was at Lunel. All true patriots throughout the realm, much as they deprecated Richelieu's harsh treatment of the mother, brother, and wife of his sovereign, rose to repulse the invaders. Marshal Schomberg was dispatched with an army to bar Monsieur's advance on Orléans, and to offer battle to the rebels; while the Marshal de la Force entered Languedoc by the Pont St. Esprit, at the head of a second division. The marriage of Monsieur with Marguerite de Lorraine was solemnly declared null and void, by a mandate of the privy council, and by edict of the Parliament; while Louis himself, accompanied by Queen Anne, departed for the scene of conflict.

Before the arrival of his Majesty, the fight of Castelnaudari had put down the rebellion, by the capture of Mortmorency on the battle-field; and by the total rout of the rebels by the troops under Schomberg. Monsieur fled from the field, without making effort to retrieve the fortune of the day, or to save the lives of the brave men deluded to their ruin by his representations. The Duke sought refuge in Beziers, himself secure from the punishment due to his rebellion, by his position as heir-presumptive.

A great example of royal justice, nevertheless, was
needed : and it was decreed that the brave and
chivalrous Montmorency should suffer the death of a
traitor on the scaffold, as a wholesome warning to
the Duc de Bouillon, to Soissons, and other seditious
subjects at large. Monsieur, therefore, was informed
that pardon for his late enterprise might be obtained,
on condition, that he abandoned Montmorency, and
other noble captives taken at Castelnaudari, to the
penalty they had incurred ; and promised, for the
future, "*to love*, and to support the Cardinal-minister." All this Gaston promised with alacrity : his
craven spirit cowered beneath the threats of Louis
and his minister, who were now on their way to
Toulouse, followed by the Princesse de Condé, who
journeyed thither to intercede for her gallant brother.
On the 27th of October, Montmorency was brought,
under escort, by the Marshal de Brézé, to Toulouse ;
and a commission was constituted, headed by the
Lord-Keeper Châteauneuf, to try him for treason.
On the morrow the Duke appeared before his judges.
On the 30th of October, 1632, sentence was pro-
nounced ; and during the afternoon of the same day,
Montmorency expiated his crime on the scaffold.
Incredible exertions had been made to save his life.
Monsieur sent special messengers three times to im-
plore his pardon. Madame de Condé knelt at the

fect of the Cardinal imploring his mercy, having been refused admittance to his Majesty's presence. The Dukes d'Epernon and de Chevreuse, the Cardinal de la Valette* and the Papal Nuncio Spada, implored that the doom of death might be averted. Louis gloomily replied to all supplications—"The fate of M. de Montmorency remains with the Parliament of Toulouse, his judge!" In former years, the Duke had subscribed himself the devoted admirer and servant of Anne of Austria; and now, in Montmorency's great extremity, the Duc d'Epernon requested audience of her Majesty to implore her intercession. Anne turned very pale: she hesitated, but at length promised to speak to M. le Cardinal. Around the arm of the Duke, when the sleeve of his habit was cut on the field of battle, to enable the surgeons to dress his wounds, a bracelet was found, containing the portrait of the Queen. The Marshal de Brézé, the officer to whom Montmorency surrendered, took the bracelet, which he sent to his kinsman, Richelieu. "The King," says Anquetil, "who was before disposed to show mercy

* Brother of the first Duc d'Epernon, a prelate whose theological attainments were far inferior to his military acquirements. For details of the trial and execution of Montmorency, see Vie du Duc de Montmorency. Paris, 1665 ; Galerie des Personnages Illustres de la Cour de Louis XIII., t. 1 ; Mém. de Bassompierre, de Pontis, Tallemant ; Aubéry, Hist. du Cardinal de Richelieu ; Père Griffet, Continuation de l'Histoire du Père Daniel ; Le Vassor, Hist. de Louis XIII. ; Madame de Motteville, Mém., t. 1.

to the Duke, became inflexibly resolved on his death,
when he was informed by his minister that a portrait
had been taken from the person of the Duke, the
original of which respect forbade him to name; but
a portrait, nevertheless, which deeply interested the
King."* Whether Anne was aware of this circumstance cannot be ascertained: she, nevertheless,
ventured to appeal to Richelieu, who, in his conduct
to the Queen mingled a certain gallantry, even in
his fiercest repulses; and when she condescended to
petition, it had often prevailed. Perhaps the thought
of the brave hearts, and noble reputations, wrecked
by her levity, may have inspired Anne with courage
on this occasion. The Duke de Bellegarde owed the
disfavour which had terminated in exile to her
smiles; Buckingham had perished by the hand of
an assassin, when arming in her behalf—and, as
some believed, by her secret command, for the invasion of her adopted country; Montmorency was
about to perish on a scaffold; the Duc d'Orléans, betrayed in the first instance, by her beauty and alleged
regard, into treasonable conspiracy against the state,

* Anquetil. Le Père Griffet, who states that Richelieu revealed the
circumstance to the King, with the intention of increasing the wrath of
his Majesty. "Le Duc de Montmorency," writes Madame Motteville,
"étoit très assidu auprès d'Anne d'Autriche ; il fit même le passionné,
et il pourrait être arrivé qu'il se fut paré de son portrait par une galanterie espagnole, assez à la mode dans ce temps."

remained a perpetual dishonour to the crown to which his birth rendered him heir-presumptive, and lived an alien from France. Upon Mesdames de Vernet, de Chevreuse, de Fargis, ruin had fallen for their faithful devotion to Anne of Austria; while exile, death, and imprisonment had been, besides, the fate of numerous less-known agents in her intrigues. Anne, therefore, took courage, and resolved to make an attempt to save the life of Montmorency. Moreover, the Queen often asserted that she possessed power over the inclinations of the Cardinal-minister; and that her supplications, when she condescended to make such, would prevail over the most important state interests. This assertion, which was frequently made by Anne, is not devoid of probability. Richelieu's anger at her underhand proceedings seems ever prompted by secret *dépit;* while the vexatious persecutions· by the which he avenged himself, appeared rather to bespeak mortification, and an irritable impatience at not being able to command submission and confidence. Richelieu listened to Anne's pleadings for the life of Montmorency, in silence and tears. *"Je plains M. de Montmorency; mais il ne peut éviter la mort, ou une prison perpétuelle,"* said he. Her Majesty then asked the Cardinal whether intercession with the King would avail, as she was resolved to

petition le Roi Monsigneur. "Madame," replied
Richelieu, significantly, " it is quite possible that
your prayers will make a great impression on the
mind of the King your consort : they might even
induce him to grant your petition ; nevertheless,
Madame, I should recommend your silence, for the
violence which his Majesty might lay on his own
wishes, and resolves, would be likely to bring about
a return of the serious illness under which the King
laboured at Lyons.   You understand, Madame!" *
Anne comprehended that she had received a tacit
interdiction ; and that, if she scorned his prohibition,
the Cardinal intended to warn the King that her
entreaties to him to revoke his resolves had been
taken in defiance of the apprehensions expressed
by Richelieu concerning the royal health—the in-
ference thereby to be deduced being, that Anne
cared more for the rescue of Montmorency than for
the health of her consort. Louis suffered many
relentings, and much mental emotion, before he
suffered the strong hand of Richelieu to guide his
own, for the signature of the Duke's death-warrant.
Strict justice, doubtless, clamoured for the head of
Montmorency ; but Monsieur ought not to have
escaped retribution for invading France at the head

Anquetil ; Motteville ; le P. Griffet ; Galerie des Personnages
Illustres de la Cour de Louis XIII.

of a foreign force, levied by funds provided by
Queen Marie, and increased by contributions from
the Spanish exchequer.*   If Monsieur had possessed
military talent, or even common sagacity and punctu-
ality, a frightful civil war might have ravaged the
kingdom.   This formidable invasion had been neutra-
lised only by the childish impatience of Monsieur, who
arrived at Lodève three days earlier than the time
fixed for the outbreak of hostilities.   "As a private
individual," said the King, "I would fain save M. de
Montmorency; but I should not act as a king if I
suffered my people to be invaded, and myself to be
defied by rebels.   I may not exercise compassion:
my duty is stern, but it is inexorable." †

The death of the Marshal de Montmorency was
first resolved in a private council, at which were
present only the King, the Cardinal, his shadow
the Capuchin Joseph, and Châteauneuf, lord-keeper.
The crime of Montmorency was the more unpar-
donable, inasmuch as M. d'Orléans had been received in Languedoc with, and by the tacit consent
of, the States of the province, on the demand of the

---

* "Bullion vint à bout de faire abandonner Montmorency par Monsieur, en lui persuadant qu'il falloit absolument une victime à la justice
du Roi ; et qu'on le laissoit le maitre de sacrifier Puylaurents ou le Duc
de Montmorency, et que c'étoit pour lui de voir s'il vouloit conserver le
Duc, ou Puylaurents."

† Vie du Duc de Montmorency.

Marshal,—an aggravation of his treason which merited direst expiation. The matter was afterwards laid before the privy council. Richelieu opened the debate by demanding that Justice should be permitted to take her course; that a commission should be empannelled to try M. de Montmorency; and that the sentence of the judges should be confirmed. No person present dared to plead in defiance of the opinion of the Cardinal.* The blood of Montmorency haunted, ever afterwards, the unfortunate King. Madame la Princesse left no pause of forgetfulness to any personage who had promoted the catastrophe of her brother's overthrow. Her enmity to the Duke of Orleans, who so dishonourably abandoned Montmorency to his fate, never relaxed. The Lord-Keeper Châteauneuf, the presiding judge at the trial of the Marshal, ere long felt the effect of the vengeance of the Condé family; which refused to be propitiated by the gift of a great part of the confiscated possessions of Montmorency, including Chantilly, Econen, Marlou, and other magnificent domains.† The mental and personal gifts of the Duc de Montmorency, so highly lauded by most contemporary historians, are more soberly

* Vie du Père Joseph Leclerc de Tremblay, Capucin, Instituteur de l'Ordre des Filles de Calvaire.

† The château of Dammartin was given to the Duchesse de Ventadour, half-sister of the unhappy Duke.

discussed by Tallemant des Réaux, the Brantôme of
the seventeenth century. "The last Duc de Montmorency," writes Tallemant,* " became master of his
revenues at the age of nineteen. Although his eyes
squinted somewhat, the Duke was a handsome man.
He was an adept in the use and practice of the most
refined and agreeable gestures, and spoke rather
by his arms, than with his tongue. He sometimes
commenced a compliment, and was obliged to stop
half way ; so that often, it was as much as one
could do not to laugh. He did not talk nonsense,
but he had little wit, and no readiness of diction.
He was brave, rich, gallant, liberal, a good dancer, a
graceful rider; a hospitable host to men of wit and
learning, many of whom he engaged in his service,
and who furnished him with verses, and sentiments.
He gave away to the poor: he was beloved by all
the world, and adored by his own people. He was
very generous. One day the Duke overheard a
gentleman exclaim, ' If I could find any person
who would lend me 20,000 crowns for two years,
my fortune would be made!' Montmorency lent
the sum. At the expiration of the two years, the
gentleman honourably offered the money. ' Go,
monsieur,' said the Duke; ' by keeping your word
you have sufficiently repaid me. I present to you

* Historiette de M. de Montmorency, t. 3 ; Tallemant des Réaux.

this sum with all my heart.' During his passion for Madame de Sablé, the Duke one day sent her deeds, making donation of an estate worth 40,000 livres annually; which, however, the Marquise declined to accept. Montmorency fell desperately in love with Queen Anne of Austria; but Buckingham and his English lords counteracted that passion."

The executions over, consequent on the defeat of Castelnaudari, and the awards announced, Louis departed for Versailles, sick and dismal in mind and body, and anxious to revert to confidential discussions with Mademoiselle de Hautefort. Monsieur was permitted to repair to Orléans, gratified by the assurances given him by the Capuchin Joseph, "that his Majesty pardoned his treason; but could on no account acknowledge the legality of his marriage with Marguerite de Lorraine." The Duke's penitence was always very evanescent, and his fears of Richelieu acute: he, therefore, speedily again took occasion to retire to Brussels, on the plea that, after the execution of the Duc de Montmorency, his honour forbade him to remain a placid spectator of the "perfidious perfidies" of M. le Cardinal de Richelieu, which tended to the ruin of the kingdom, and of the royal dynasty. Louis, on his departure from Toulouse, left Queen Anne in the safe custody of his minister; who conducted her, attended by the Duchess de Chevreuse and the Marquise de Senécé, to Bordeaux. Much against her will, the Queen had been compelled to accompany her consort to the scene of warfare in the West; but the risk had been considered too great to suffer Anne to remain alone in the capital, while the kingdom was menaced by a Spanish invasion both in Languedoc and Picardy. The ambassador Mirabel, it was true, was withdrawn from Paris, in consequence of the close alliance now subsisting between France, the Protestant princes of Germany, and Sweden, to cripple the imperial power of Ferdinand II.; and to promote the downfall of Spanish predominance in the councils of Europe. Anne, nevertheless, was strongly suspected of making communications to her brother through one Gerbier, an attaché of the English embassy. Moreover, it had been ascertained that she had sent for Señor Navas, Spanish *chargé d'affaires*, then resident in Paris, who was introduced, at dusk hour, into an apartment of the Salles des Bains, at the Louvre. The Queen addressed Navas as she passed out, attended by Madame de Chevreuse, on her way to the *grands appartements*, and said only, though significantly, the words— "Take care of yourselves; I know that there is a traitor amongst you, who betrays to M. le Cardinal all that passes." This intimation was given just before the rising in the South, and excited much suspicion. Richelieu, from that moment, watched Madame de Chevreuse, Châteauneuf, and others, who, under colour of devotion to his interests, might be carrying on a double game. Châteauneuf was always present when the minister communicated to Louis the *cancans*, as well as the more important facts gleaned by his secret police. Anne, therefore, in consequence of these reports, had not been suffered to seek her accustomed refuge at St. Germain during the King's progress to the South. In answer to some inquiries made by Richelieu, Madame de Chevreuse, nevertheless, had boldly replied that, "having asked her Majesty whether she might assure the King that her correspondence and conduct were such as his Majesty approved, Queen Anne had frankly replied in the affirmative. The Duchess, therefore, informs M. le Cardinal that she believes the Queen has no relations with Spain, with Monsieur, with the Queen-mother, or with any person."*

After his return to Paris, Richelieu set himself to elucidate the mystery which tormented him ; and, by the aid of his trained spies, to investigate more closely the life of Madame de Chevreuse. During the sojourn of Anne and her court at Bordeaux, the Cardinal had been severely indisposed, from the

* Journal du Cardinal de Richelieu.

fatigue and agitation of the late trials—so much so, that for some hours his case was thought desperate. The Queen, however, had not thought proper to suspend her evening reception; and the Cardinal was informed that the beautiful Duchess and her friend Châteauneuf had danced together merrily; and had even been overheard to make sundry uncomplimentary allusions to the sick minister. Such levity seemed ill to accord with the expressions of devotion proffered by Madame de Chevreuse; or with the gratitude so fluently professed by M. de Châteauneuf for his elevation to the high office of Lord-Keeper of the Great Seal of France. The King retired to St. Germain after giving his minister a splendid welcome back to Paris, where he brooded over his regrets for the death of Montmorency; and nursed his returning indignation against the Queen, upon whom he mentally resented every fresh aggression on France, made by her Spanish kindred. The Queen, again established amid the solitudes of the Louvre, summoned her little knot of intimates. These personages were Mesdames de Chevreuse, de Senécé,* de Montbazon, de Hautefort, de la Fayette, Madame de la Flotte, the Princess de Condé, the

* Marie Catherine de la Rochefoucauld, Countess de Rendan, widow of Henri de Beauffremont Marquis de Senécé, governor of Auxonne, and ambassador at Madrid during three years of the regency.

Lord-Keeper Châteauneuf, the Chevalier de Jars, the
Count de Biron, Montagu, and many personages of
inferior rank, who in former reigns would not have
been admitted to *les petites entrées* of the Queen of
France.   A precious document,* found by M. Victor
Cousin in the archives of the French Foreign Office
—that rich mine of historical wealth now unfortunately closed to the public—recounts the surgings of
the great Cardinal's wrath against his suspected foe,
Châteauneuf, as daily he added one fact to another;
until, exasperated by such ingratitude, Richelieu ordered his arrest, February, 1633, and the seizure
of the papers, and effects of the unhappy Lord-
Keeper.   The true cause of this arrest was occasioned by the mad jealousy of Richelieu, who found
that he had been deceived and flouted by the beautiful woman, whose professions of love and fidelity
had disarmed his suspicion.   Madame de Chevreuse had all along been the ally, and, it must
be added, the mistress of Châteauneuf, over whom
she exercised such sway, that the political secrets of
the Cardinal, of necessity confided to the Lord-
Keeper, had been betrayed to the Duchess, and by
her confided to Anne of Austria.   Far, therefore,

---

* Cousin.   Mém. de M. le Cardinal de Richelieu contre M. de Châteauneuf.— Archives des Affaires Etrangères ; France, t. ci. ; douze pages de
la main de Charpentier, un des secrétaires de Richelieu.

from having performed the conditions of her recall from exile, the Duchess had fomented, and had been the soul of every hostile intrigue—"indeed, the world seemed too small to hold this intriguing and turbulent pair." "Châteauneuf," writes the Cardinal in his Memoir, "mingled in all the cabals of the court; particularly he took part with our factious ladies, the principal of whom was the Duchess of Chevreuse, whose conduct and evil spirit had often displeased the King, as she never failed to join the cabals raised against his crown; but more than this, she appeared always as a dangerous leader of parties." Richelieu commences the recital of his private grievances against Châteauneuf from a very early period. "During the predominance of the Marquis d'Ancre, le Sieur de Châteauneuf was on bad terms with the Cardinal de Richelieu. When the Cardinal believed himself to be dismissed ('Journée des Dupes'), the said Sieur de Châteauneuf did all he could against him." In this curious document, the names of the persons mentioned are indicated by ciphers: number 9 stood for Madame de Chevreuse. Richelieu accuses Châteauneuf of gross perfidy; of being on the side of Monsieur and the Queen-mother, while taking office under his ministry; of betraying state secrets to Madame de Chevreuse, and even to Queen Anne; of keeping up a private and traitorous correspondence

with England, of which the Cardinal had been
warned by Weston, the English Ambassador in Paris;
who declared that the Lord-Keeper constantly corresponded with Queen Henrietta Maria, and gave
pernicious advice to her Majesty upon religious
questions;[*] that her Britannic Majesty had been
heard several times to express disgust at the
policy of the Cardinal, in supporting the Protestant
princes of Germany against the Emperor; adding,
" that M. le Garde des Sceaux did not share in such
councils; but that he was her especial friend and
servant, and that France would be much better
governed after the death of M. le Cardinal."
Richelieu also accuses Châteauneuf of duplicity in
the affair of M. de Montmorency; stating, that the
Lord-Keeper told M. de Chaudebonne, the confidential
agent of Monsieur and others, that he had desired
to save the life of the Duke, and had vainly made
intercession—when, on the contrary, M. le Garde des
Sceaux had been the first to propose the execution

* Châteauneuf did not stand alone in this misdemeanour.   The king,
writing to his sister Queen Henrietta Maria, advises her to have the new-
born Prince of Wales baptised privately by her Roman Catholic chaplain,
which, if she consented to do, Louis XIII. promises to stand sponsor to the
child. " Vous savez, ma sœur, que le seul moyen de vous donner con-
tentement, que la reyne ma mère, et moi nous tenions sur les fonts de
baptême le prince mon neveu, c'est qu'il soit baptisé à la catholique : à quoi
vous pouvez beaucoup contribuer, puisque cela se peut faire par votre
aumônier dans votre oratoire, le roy mon frère pouvant alors dire que
vous l'avez fait sans son sceu, et consentement."—Lettre de Louis XIII. à
la Reyne d'Angleterre.—Aubéry, Hist. du Card. de Richelieu, t. 5. p. 575.

of the said Duke, and had told the Cardinal that he would never consent to so pernicious a use of the royal clemency; that he had moreover, proposed that execution should be done by mandate of the council; and had angrily deprecated the resolve taken to try M. de Montmorency before a regularly constituted court; that Châteauneuf had betrayed to Madame de Chevreuse the fact of the marriage of Monsieur with Marguerite de Lorraine, when it greatly imported to the royal service that the accomplishment of such should be held secret. Châteauneuf had also tried to discredit the Cardinal de Richelieu with the Jesuit Order. He was also in frequent correspondence with the exiled rebels—with Monsieur and Queen Marie—all in defiance of his oath of fidelity to the King, and of the duties, and responsibilities of his office. This paper the Cardinal drew up for his own special use, and it does not seem to have been produced against the Lord-Keeper. On the 25th of February, 1633, Châteauneuf was arrested at St. Germain-en-Laye, on leaving the palace after an audience of the King, and conducted under a strong escort to his château at Ruffec, in Limousin. The day following, his house in Paris was searched by the under secretaries of state, Bouthillier, Bullion, and Chavigny, who seized his papers, which filled several large coffers, and conveyed them to

the abode of M. de Bullion.   On the 29th of
February, the papers were sorted, and analysed, and
forwarded to Richelieu, who discovered what he
suspected—a large packet of letters addressed to
Châteauneuf by the Duchess de Chevreuse, partly
written in cipher; the key to which, however, was
found in an ebony cabinet which had been also
conveyed from the house of the Lord-Keeper, on the
supposition that important papers were concealed in
its secret recesses.   Amongst the spoil captured
were fifty-two letters from Madame de Chevreuse;
thirty-one from Montagu, which treated of foreign
alliances and conspiracies, for the overthrow of
Richelieu's power; twenty-nine letters from the
Chevalier du Jars, who seems to have acted as a
busy agent of M. d'Orléans in France during the
late risings, and as his royal highness's servant in
every mischievous intrigue for the subversion of
the government; thirty-one letters from the Queen
of Great Britain; and one paper of verses—all
which were immediately placed in a portfolio, and
forwarded unopened to King Louis, at St. Germain.
Numbers of letters, also, were found from Lord
Holland, M. de Puylaurens favourite-in-chief of
Monsieur, from the Duke de Vendôme, and the Count
de Biron—all bitter opponents of the Cardinal.[*]

* Procès-Verbal de la Visite des Papiers de M. de Châteauneuf, faite

The correspondence of Madame de Chevreuse with the Lord-Keeper was the booty which Richelieu panted to peruse, and to gain possession of which he had instituted these summary proceedings. The rage and mortification of Richelieu are not to be described, when he discovered by this correspondence that the woman whom he admired, and whom he had restored to her former proud position, was faithless ; and pitilessly ridiculed his weakness to his fortunate rival. What was worse, the Cardinal saw himself designated in their correspondence under a *sobriquet* too insulting and indecent to find place in these pages. "28* (Madame de Chevreuse) saw 22 (the cardinal) to-day, when with 24 (the queen). He paid 24 all the compliments imaginable before 28, to whom he affected to speak coldly and indifferently; but she treated him in her accustomed manner, and feigned not to perceive his humour. In reply to a jest hazarded by the Cardinal, Madame de Chevreuse rallied him, even to the point of speaking slightingly of his power. The Cardinal seemed astonished rather than angry, and changed his tone to one of civility and great courtesy. I know not whether it was, that

par MM. Bouthillier et de Bullion; copie communiquée par M. le Duc de Luynes; Cousin, Vie de Madame de Chevreuse, p. 212.

  * The names in the correspondence between Madame de Chevreuse and Châteauneuf were indicated by ciphers : 22 stood for Richelieu ; 24, the queen ; 28, Madame de Chevreuse, who always alludes to herself in the third person.

he did not wish to show anger in the presence of the Queen, or whether he did not desire to quarrel with Madame de Chevreuse. I am to see the Cardinal to-morrow at two o'clock. Be assured, that Madame de Chevreuse will have left this world when she ceases to belong to you."* In another letter, Richelieu stumbled on the following observations :—" I (Madame de Chevreuse) have no news lately from the Cardinal. If he is as glad not to hear of me as I am not to hear from him, he is now highly content, and I delivered from a persecution from which time, and my own good wit may free me. The tyranny of the Cardinal momentarily increases. He storms and raves because 28 (Madame de Chevreuse) does not call upon him. Twice I have written to him compliments of which he is unworthy—a thing I should never have done but for M. de Chevreuse, who tells me that is the way to buy peace. The favour of the King has raised his presumption to a pitch which cannot be surpassed. He thinks to daunt me ; and would fain persuade himself that there is nothing that I would not do to appease him, although I prefer to perish rather than to make submission. The pride of the Cardinal is intolerable to me. He said

---

* Cousin, Vie de Madame de Chevreuse. These letters are also quoted by le P. Griffet, Hist. du Règne de Louis XIII.; Continuation de l'Hist. de France du Père Daniel.

recently to my husband that my humour was unbearable to a sensitive person like himself; and that he had resolved to render me in future no especial attention, as I was not capable of conferring either friendship, or confidence.   I confide this only to you. Do not apprise M. de Chevreuse that you know this. He has quarrelled with me ; being intimidated by the insolence of the said Cardinal. and because I would not endure such obloquy.   I have that opinion of your courage and affection, that I wish you to know everything that concerns me.   I so entirely trust you, that I deem my interests as safe in your hands as in my own.   Love me with fidelity ; and believe that, despite of persecution, I will ever show myself worthy thereof."   Again the duchess wrote :—" To-night the Cardinal sent me a letter by express. to implore me to grant him two things : the first was, not to speak to M. de Biron ; and the second, never to admit you (M. de Châteauneuf).   My resolve to demonstrate my affection for M. de Châteauneuf is stronger than any consideration for the Cardinal.   I have therefore excused myself to the said Cardinal on the plea, that my affairs with M. de Chevreuse compel me to see M. de Châteauneuf."   The duchess sends. with this letter, a valuable diamond to her lover ; she exhorts him to be firm as the precious gem she sends him ; and to shine. like its lustrous

rays, a light amid darkness. Again she writes, in
the third person : "I believe that M. de Châteauneuf is absolutely devoted to Madame de Chevreuse.
Madame de Chevreuse promises eternal fidelity to
M. de Châteauneuf. If all the world turn against
M. de Châteauneuf, Madame de Chevreuse will love
and esteem him worthily. If he loves her as he
states, Madame de Chevreuse will satisfy him, for all
the powers of earth cannot make her change her
resolve. She swears to you that this is fact, and
commands you to believe it, and to love faithfully."
The duchess kept this vow. To the day of his death
she was faithful in her attachment to the Lord-Keeper
through weal and woe ; refusing to participate in any
future triumphs after the death of their enemy,
Richelieu, unless shared by him. Châteauneuf had
passed his 50th year : he was plain in person,
without courtly grace, or wit. Amid all her aberrations, Madame de Chevreuse never abjured her one
great redeeming attribute—fidelity. Bitter must
have been Richelieu's reflections as he perused this
correspondence, and probably pictured the mocking
lip, and wicked merriment of the beautiful syren
whom he feared ; and whom, because he so feared, he
wished to bend to his toils. "The Cardinal's mad
vagaries are wonderful!" continues the impracticable
duchess. "He sent for Madame de Chevreuse, and

made strange complaints. He declared that she was perpetually sparring with him in the presence of Lord Jermyn, in order that the said lord might return to his country, and recount how little respect she bore him. He said he knew that Madame de Chevreuse and M. de Châteauneuf understand each other; and that she also receives M. de Biron, though all the world knows that the said Biron is in love with her—a proceeding M. le Cardinal is resolved no longer to tolerate. Madame de Chevreuse is in better health, and more resolved than ever to esteem M. de Châteauneuf, as she has promised him." " Châteauneuf," writes Tallemant, " *éloit un homme tout confit en galanterie.* I have seen him ride on horseback by the Queen's coach, on the side occupied by Madame de Chevreuse, attired in a splendid satin robe, and displaying his horsemanship. The Cardinal was devoured with jealousy, especially as it was suspected that the Garde des Sceaux was also an admirer of the Queen." The thunder of the minister's wrath soon fell on these unhappy triflers. The very nature of the correspondence seized in the dwelling of M. de Châteauneuf precluded his public arraignment for treason. The King's sister, Henrietta Maria, was compromised: and Richelieu shrank from public ridicule, such as would have befallen him on the publication of the letters of Madame de

Chevreuse; and from the unsparing revelations likely to fall from the lips of the duchess, if put upon her trial by the side of Châteauneuf. Orders were despatched to remove the ex-Lord-Keeper to the citadel of Angoulême; where he was subjected to severe incarceration and privations, for what the Cardinal called "*un mauvais procédé*," and totally debarred from communication with the world. Having thus avenged himself on his faithless friend, Richelieu proceeded next to exile the Duchess de Chevreuse, with all startling formalities. In the dead of the night, an officer of the royal guard, followed by a troop, entered the court-yard of the superb dwelling of the duchess. An instant interview was demanded *de par le roi*. Madame de Chevreuse appeared and was presented with a *lettre de cachet*, which exiled her to Dampierre, where she was to remain under *surveillance*. Five hours only were allowed her to make preparation for departure from the capital. Escorted by a guard of soldiers, Madame de Chevreuse reached her destination, before the Queen heard of her exile.

The minor personages, meanwhile—those within the reach of the minister's vengeance—paid the penalty of their patron's misdemeanour. Arrests were made on all sides : a fear came over the people

* Cousin, Vie de Madame de Chevreuse : Motteville, t. c.

of Paris that another dire conspiracy had transpired. The Chevalier du Jars was arrested, thrown into the Bastille, tried before the infamous Judge Laffémas, popularly called *le bourreau du Cardinal*, tortured, condemned to decapitation for holding intelligence with Monsieur, and for treasonable collusion with the enemies of the realm. On the scaffold with his head on the block, the unfortunate man, waiting for the headsman's swift blow, was informed that the King's gracious clemency had commuted his punishment into incarceration for life in the Bastille.* The Chevalier fainted away; and suffered ever afterwards from partial paralysis of the limbs. The brother of the Garde des Sceaux, the Marquis de Hauterive, escaped, in disguise, to the coast, put off from France in a fishing smack, and was landed in Holland, after undergoing extraordinary perils and privations. The Count de Leuville, the young son of Hauterive, was seized, and conveyed to the Bastille by command of Richelieu; while every relative, however distant, of the ex-Keeper of the Seals was banished from the capital. The *dépit amoureux* of the Cardinal could scarcely avenge itself more rigorously; especially after Queen Anne received commands, from the lips of her royal consort, to cease all correspondence with the

* Cousin. Vie de Madame de Chevreuse: Motteville, t. c.

exiled duchess, on pain of incurring his signal displeasure.

Anne, deeming that she had been treated with very little deference in the matter; and that some communication was due to her dignity before her chief lady of honour was summarily deposed and exiled, listened to her husband's prohibition with that icy composure which Louis said, " was always a sure indication that the Queen intended to follow her own pleasure." It was now the Queen's habit, when in Paris, to retire during a part of every day to the Val-de-Grâce. In the oratory stood a box, in which Anne placed any correspondence she wished to despatch secretly; and in which she found the letters sent to her privately under cover to the abbess, or that had been boldly left for her at the gate. The *tourière* was the Queen's devoted servant, and received all letters, which she gave to the abbess; who at the same time confided to her any which had been written by the Queen, and left at the convent to be despatched. Letters from the King of Spain, from the Empress Marguerite her sister, from the Infant Don Ferdinando, from Queen Henrietta Maria, from the Queen-mother, and from Monsieur, thus came to Anne privately, and unknown to the King. At this period the energies of France were almost spent in maintaining the national honour. War was raging

in Germany, and every political betrayal might cause
events of momentous import ; and French soldiers
were meeting on the field of battle the combined
hosts of Spain, and the Empire.   From the Val-de-
Grâce Anne, therefore, communicated with the
Duchess de Chevreuse ; and for some weeks they
interchanged a secret, but active correspondence.
Madame de Chevreuse, furious against the Cardinal,
was ready to sacrifice anything for vengeance. Dampierre, the place of her exile, was then a dreary, and
half-furnished château.*   M. de Chevreuse cherished
a great distaste for the place ; which, during the
reign of Henri Quatre, had likewise been his prison,
to avenge the audacity of his homage to the favourite, the Marquise de Verneuil.   Richelieu had
managed to infuse an additional sting in his punishment, by sending the duchess to her husband's castle
of Dampierre ; from whom, when in the plenitude of
her power and pride, she had obtained a separation.
Correspondence at length failed to satisfy the Queen
and her friend : they determined to meet, in de-

* Dampierre became subsequently one of the most magnificent seats
in France. It was restored by the grandson of Madame de Chevreuse,
son of her son by the Constable de Luynes, upon whom the peerage of her
second husband was confirmed. The Duke de Chevreuse and De Luynes
married the eldest daughter of the famous Colbert, who was a wealthy
heiress. Madame de Chevreuse had three daughters by her second
husband ; Anne Marie de Lorraine, abbess of Pont-aux-Dame ; Henriette, abbess of Jouarre ; and Mademoiselle de Chevreuse, celebrated
for her beauty, and the admiration of the coadjutor De Retz.

fiance of the minister, and his mandates. One day therefore, Marie disguised herself in the coarse garb of a peasant woman, and, stealing from the castle on foot, actually arrived at the Val-de-Grâce at vesper hour. Anne was in her oratory ; and the two friends fell into each other's arms to weep, and lament their persecution, and to devise fresh snares to entrap their common enemy. "Madame de Chevreuse," writes Tallemant, " was exiled to Dampierre, from whence she came to visit the Queen. in the disguise of a dirty vagrant, at the hour we call *entre chien et loup.*" This meeting occurred twice, according to the statement which. at a subsequent period. the Queen was compelled to make on oath. Other chroniclers, however, relate that the clandestine interviews between Anne and her friend were frequent : and were, for an interval. enjoyed with impunity.

The audacious defiance of his command. nevertheless, at length came to the knowledge of the Cardinal. and was by him communicated to King Louis. A few hours later a coach, escorted by a company of musketeers, drove into the court-yard of the castle of Dampierre, and Madame de Chevreuse was directed to enter the vehicle. In vain Marie expostulated, and petitioned for delay ; she was compelled to submit; and, on being shown the instructions given to the commanding officer of the escort, even to congratulate herself on the leniency with which she was treated. The Constable de Luynes had bequeathed the domain, and château de Milly to his widow. The castle was a few miles from Tours, and stood in the midst of a vast forest. Before the high altar of its chapel was the tomb of the late Constable. To this lonesome abode Richelieu now consigned the duchess; one waiting-woman only was permitted to share her captivity; her actions were subjected to strict *surveillance ;* and all pecuniary expenses incurred by the inmates of the château were to be defrayed, and regulated by the Duc de Chevreuse! In vain Marie, frantic with impotent rage, defied, and even threatened, her foe: so vigilantly was the *surveillance* maintained by the officer on guard that, for an interval, the restless *intrigante* was thoroughly caged.

King Louis XIII., during these events, gave the Cardinal no less cause for dissatisfaction. His Majesty's platonic friendship with De Hautefort prospered not : if the latter spoke to any cavalier of the court, if she smiled while Louis felt sad, if she yawned with irrepressible *ennui* during their evening's discourse, sombre suspicion enveloped the King's mind, and petulant repinings ensued. "This young lady," relates Tallemant, "wishing to marry and secure a position, suffered the King's attentions impatiently.

She was very handsome; but during eight days the King agreed well with her, and during a subsequent eight days he quarrelled with her." Louis vainly tried to detach Mademoiselle de Hautefort from her duty and affection for the Queen, whom Marie resolutely supported. He forbade her to accompany her mistress to the Carmelites, or to the Val-de-Grâce; but as this injunction was never officially communicated, Marie chose to treat the King's wishes with disregard. She likewise showed herself impenetrable to the overtures of the Cardinal, and frequently spoke in derisive terms of his designs; while she dared to amuse his Majesty by the repetition of the scandals current in Paris, respecting certain private incidents in the life of the great minister. A cabal in the household was therefore formed, under the auspices of Richelieu, to dethrone a personage so self-willed and disinterested; and to attempt to enlist the royal sympathies for Louise de la Fayette, another of her Majesty's maidens, who, in addition to a pretty face, was an accomplished singer. Accordingly, the Duc de St. Simon, the Bishop of Limoges, uncle of Mademoiselle de la Fayette, the Duke d'Halluyn,* Madame de Senécé, and

* Charles de Schomberg, Duc d'Halluyn, Pair et Marechal de France, Marquis d'Epinay, and Comte de Nanteuil. This nobleman eventually married Mademoiselle de Hautefort, September 24, 1646. The duke died 1656.

Mesdemoiselles d'Aiches, de Vieux-Pont, and de Polignac, and M. Sanguin, *maître d'hôtel* to the King, and to whom Louis showed much friendly regard, united in lauding the perfections of la Fayette. St. Simon, and the Cardinal feigned anger and vexation at the impertinent independence displayed by la Hautefort; and confidentially advised the King to punish her, by appearing to transfer the honour of his notice to la Fayette.* The King approved, and promised to follow the counsel of his friends. The same evening la Fayette was desired by the Cardinal, to take her harp and to sing a song, composed and set to music by his Majesty. The delight and astonishment of the King were extreme; the beautiful voice of la Fayette had never before charmed the court-circle, during his dreary, and decorous flirtation with la Hautefort. From that evening Louis devoted himself to la Fayette. The timid blushing girl, brimful of sentiment and reverence, proved to be a more congenial companion than the stately, and imperturbable la Hautefort; who had condescended to listen to the royal plaints, but who by no means deemed it requisite to sympathise therein. Louise Angelique Motier de la Fayette was the only daughter of Jean de la Fayette, Seigneur de Hautefeuille, and of Marguerite de

Mém. de la Porte. Petitot. t. 59.

Bourbon Busset,* who was descended from an illegitimate branch of Bourbon Montpensier. Her great-grandmother, Suzanne de Bourbon Busset, Madame de Miossin, was the faithful friend of Queen Jeanne d'Albret, and the governess of Henri Quatre. In family influence, therefore, Mademoiselle de la Fayette surpassed Mademoiselle de Hautefort. Her uncle was the Bishop of Limoges, a prelate well known at the court. She was also cousin-german to the Marquise de Senécé, lady-in-waiting to the Queen; and second cousin of the famous Capuchin Joseph de Tremblay. The governess of the Queen's maids, Mademoiselle de Polignac, was also a near relative. With such connections at court—persons placed, all of them, in influential positions—it has been a subject of wonder that the sagacity of Richelieu did not rather induce him to withdraw from the notice of his royal master a lady so powerfully supported. Mademoiselle de la Fayette is described as possessed of many personal attractions : she was a brunette, with shining eyes ; rather *embonpoint* in figure, without much dignity of carriage ; shy, and sedate in manner and speech : given to sentiment, poetry, and meditation ; and preferring

---

* Daughter of César de Bourbon, Count de Busset, and of Louise de Montmorillon. The branch of Bourbon Busset descended from the turbulent Louis, Archbishop of Liège, who died in 1482, son of Charles I., Duke of Bourbon, and of Agnes of Burgundy.

a secluded life, to courtly gaieties. She had also
been destined from her early youth to a cloister:
her father was poor and proud, and despairing of
finding for his daughter an alliance suitable to her
birth, he had encouraged the longings of the pensive
girl for seclusion.   In her seventeenth year, Louise
was presented to the Queen by Madame de Senécé,
and enrolled amongst Anne's maids of honour.   It
is supposed, that the determination of Louise, sooner
or later to embrace a religious life, inspired her
with that indifference to censure, and disregard of
worldly interest which distinguished her career.
Her regard for the King soon deepened into the
purest, and most enthusiastic attachment: she entered into Louis's fears and heart-quakings at the
power of his minister ; she soothed and encouraged
him, while maintaining inviolable silence on all that
he confided to her ear; she interested herself, as far
as might be, in his pastimes ; and, above all, she
sympathised in his resentment against Anne of
Austria; and, to please the King, confined herself to
the merest routine of duty in her relations with her
royal mistress.   The interviews between Louis and
la Fayette were generally holden in the little cabinet, opening from the Queen's state reception-room :
there the pair met to weep and confer.   The utmost
decorum prevailed during these meetings: not a

wanton thought, it is said, ever troubled the serenity
of the King, or brought a blush to the fair cheek
of his *confidente*. "*Le Roi Louis XIII.*," said the
sarcastic Christina, Queen of Sweden, "*n'aime que
l'espèce en femmes—il est entouré de dames d'une
sagesse, et continence reconnues !*" As for Louis, la
Fayette was the idol before whom he offered heart-
felt adoration—"*Angélique était sa joie et sa couronne !*" If a thought, however, arose that might
sully her purity, the King, it is stated, summoned
his confessor, and expiated such unholy desire by
penance. He seems to have devoutly believed that
Providence had set the seal of election on the brow
of Louise; and that eventually a cloister would shield
her from his love, and from the world's perils.
Meantime, it was his duty to respect and watch
vigilantly that no alloy of illicit love might mar the
merit of such a sacrifice. Notwithstanding the repute which Louis le Chaste had obtained, there were
found persons who disbelieved in such self-denial;
and urged the King to console himself for the indifference, and misconduct of Anne of Austria, by
following the example of his father. These counsels
at length made impression on the King; and yielding to the temptation, he one day abruptly proposed
to Mademoiselle de la Fayette an establishment at
Versailles, and the rank of a duchess. With horror

and misgiving la Fayette listened to the King's solicitation; and so edifying, it is recorded, were her admonitions, that Louis consented to a temporary suspension of their daily interviews to expiate his error. "It was to la Fayette that the King confided his chagrins relative to the Cardinal de Richelieu," relates Madame de Motteville. "That girl had an upright heart; and though she was aware that this confidence would probably be fatal to her interests, she kept the King's secret, and confirmed him in his aversion to the minister; for she perceived that he was dishonoured by his compliance with the will of the Cardinal. The said Cardinal did all in his power to gain her over to his side, as he did to all persons possessing influence with the King; but la Fayette showed more courage than those courtiers who had the mean cowardice to carry to the Cardinal an exact account of what the King said to them. A woman showed a firmer and more noble spirit; but la Fayette had courage to defy the turns of fortune, by her resolution eventually to enter a cloister. The King, therefore, discovering that she was trustworthy, virtuous, and beautiful—esteemed and loved her; and I know that he entertained thoughts of her far above the usual feelings of men. The same prudence which induced this generous woman to refuse alliance with the Cardinal de Richelieu, prompted

her to live on tolerable terms with the Queen. An
attachment so perfect could not fail to give content-
ment to the King, and displeasure to the Queen ;
who, however, was now accustomed to the misfortune
of not being beloved by the King, her husband. La
Fayette confessed her attachment to the King ; and
as they loved, each as the other desired, their bliss
ought to have insured the happiness of their lives."
Richelieu, however, saw further into human nature
than good prosing Madame de Motteville: he perceived that he had every evil to dread from the
supremacy of la Fayette. The King, it was true,
naïvely betrayed the impressions inspired by the
observations of his mistress to his minister, avow-
ing them to be such ; but he maintained their propriety, and justness with characteristic obstinacy.
The moment, therefore, that la Fayette ceased to
resist, and to rebuke the inclinations of the King,
her ascendency would be omnipotent : and from Versailles she might dictate the edict of his dismissal
from power. As yet, Mademoiselle de la Fayette
had abstained from interfering in political matters.
" *La Fayette ne fait ni bien, ni mal,*" was the
report hitherto given by Chavigny to the Cardinal
de la Valette, and others, of the doings in the palace.
In vain Richelieu tried to neutralise la Fayette's
favour by the same artifice which had succeeded for

the downfall of Mademoiselle de Hautefort.   Louis
would not look at another of Anne's maidens ; and
listened in gloomy silence to Richelieu's laudation of
any one amongst the fair bevy.   The sole avenue,
therefore, likely to lead to the overthrow of Mademoiselle de la Fayette's influence, was to foment
the religious scruples of the pair ; and to daunt the
proud heart of Louise with imaginary dangers, even
by inspiring her with a secret conviction that her life
was in danger, and therefore, that a cloister was her
only refuge.   The system of spies, of warning inti-
mations, and the bribery by which the Cardinal inaugurated and maintained his power, rendered possible
a conflict such as he now offered to la Fayette.   The
popular confessor to the ladies, and courtiers of the
Louvre was le Père Jean Baptiste Carré, Superior of
the order of the Dominicans of France ; an ecclesiastic devoted to Richelieu, whom he worshipped, and
obeyed with servile zeal.   This personage, who was
considered a light in his Order—being a man distinguished by learning, eloquence, ecclesiastical power,
and religious zeal—took yearly a solemn oath of obedience * to the Cardinal minister, whom he regarded

* The words of this oath were, " Ego Frater Joannes Baptista Carré,
ordinis Prædicatorum, vestri Novitiatus Generalis Prioris, voveo et pro-
metto obedientiam tibi, Domino Eminentissimo Armando Cardinali Duci
de Richelieu, usque ad mortem."—Archives des Affaires Étrangères,
France, t. 78 ; Cousin, Vie de Madame de Hautefort.

as the incarnation of human power, wisdom, and
benevolence.   Carré addressed to his patron long
memorials on public affairs, written with consummate
skill; he transmitted notes describing the condition
of public feeling towards the minister at home and
abroad, gathered from the reports of the foreign
monks of his order; he placed all members of the
Dominican community in France at the disposal of
Richelieu; while his judicious counsels, and fervent
zeal aided the minister in many a dark hour of
uncertainty, and doubt.   This ecclesiastic, therefore,
was confessor to the court; and by him much service
might be achieved.   The post of confessor to the
King and Queen was a privilege bestowed by Henri
Quatre on the Jesuits; and at this period, the
commencement of the year 1636. was, fortunately
for the designs of Richelieu, vacant, by the dismissal
of le P. Souffran, who had followed the fortunes of
Queen Marie.

Richelieu, by the advice of his own confessor,
counselled Louis to confer that office upon Nicholas
Caussin, a Jesuit father, who had obtained high
repute for probity, and virtue; and who was the
author of a book of religious meditations, called " La
Cour Sainte," very much admired by pious persons.
Intimation of his promotion was given to Caussin,
who was desired by his Eminence to wait upon the

King on the morning of the Feast of the Annunciation, as it was his Majesty's purpose to confess, before receiving the Holy Eucharist; but, previously, he was instructed to visit the Cardinal at Ruel. This mandate was conveyed to the Jesuit monastery by a young page greatly favoured by the Cardinal, the young Marquis de Cinq-Mars, second son of the Marshal d'Effiat. Caussin repaired to Ruel on the 23rd of March, 1636, and was at once admitted to private audience with the minister. With *suave* indifference Richelieu greeted the reverend father; and, after repeating the flattering intimation, that the King contemplated bestowing upon him the much coveted post of confessor in ordinary, provided that his Majesty received satisfaction from his ministrations on the morrow, proceeded to inform Caussin, "that the King was a noble prince, without vice whatever; and that his virtue, being a benediction to the realm, it was necessary to encourage such holy inclinations. It was true that, unfortunately, his Majesty had lately appeared much attached to one of the Queen's ladies, although he suspected nothing wrong; nevertheless, as a great affection between persons of opposite sexes was dangerous, it would be prudent to check such partialities." * The tone of the Cardinal was careless, but his manner

* Le Père Griffet, Hist. du Règne de Louis XIII., t. 3.

significant. Caussin, therefore, departed initiated
in the line of action expected from him, but by
no means disposed to implicit submission. The following day, Caussin met his royal penitent, whose
confession fully enlightened him on the nature of his
liaison with Mademoiselle de la Fayette. The King
declared himself " more than content " with his new
spiritual director, and signed, on the same day, his
letters of office. Caussin being, a few days subsequently at St. Germain—for the king's confessor
had apartments assigned him in all the royal palaces
—M. de Noyers, chief secretary of the war depart-
ment, and Richelieu's confidential friend. paid him a
visit at midnight ; and said, " that he had been
directed by M. le Cardinal to apprise him that the
young lady, whom his Eminence had mentioned to
the reverend father. contemplated leaving the court,
to embrace a religious life ; and that M. le Cardinal
desired he should examine her vocation, and induce
her as soon as possible to carry such design into
execution." De Noyers enforced profound secrecy
respecting his visit ; but exhorted Caussin to carry
out the views of his Eminence, whose patriotic and
disinterested counsels conferred prosperity on the
realm.* It was subsequently represented to Caussin
that Queen Anne beheld the ascendency of la

* Griffet, t. 3.

Fayette with extreme displeasure, and disbelieved in the innocence of such *liaison* with her royal consort; and that the King of Spain, who was devoted to his sister, was not likely to be conciliated by the establishment of a *maîtresse en titre* at the Louvre. It was true that Anne did not show the same toleration towards la Fayette as she had manifested towards Mademoiselle de Hautefort; who still remained her confidential friend, and often shared with her royal mistress the questionable vigils at the Val-de-Grâce. De Hautefort hated Richelieu; disapproved the conduct of the King towards his wife; and did all in her power to reconcile the one, and to overthrow the other. La Fayette was the enemy of Richelieu only so far as such enmity pleased the King; who needed a *confidente* to whom he might exhale his jealousy, and occasional exasperation against his minister. She sympathised with and admired the King; and felt no regard for Anne of Austria, whose intrigues she declined to share. Her crime in Richelieu's eyes was her independence, and her true regard for Louis; which made him apprehend that one day the restraints interposed by virtue, and piety, might be cast aside for ever, and that France would adore in Louise Angélique de la Fayette, a second Gabrielle d'Estrées. Caussin, the director of the royal conscience, was, meantime, disinclined to follow the dictation of Richelieu. His Order was jealous of the Dominican communities and of their Superior, Carré ; and resented the fact that Richelieu had not chosen a Jesuit monk for his own confessor. The Jesuits, moreover, strongly protested against the foreign policy of France. The alliance between France, Gustavus Adolphus King of Sweden, the deposed Elector Palatine, and the German Protestant Princes, was abhorrent to their principles. and hostile to their interests. They sympathised with the exiled Queen-mother, and desired her recall ; they approved of the marriage of M. d'Orléans, and blamed the minister for his persecution of the heir-presumptive. The enmity displayed by Richelieu towards le P. Chanteloube, at one time confessor to Queen Marie de' Medici, who had taken refuge in Brussels to escape the Bastille. added another item to the list of grievances against the Cardinal. In Mademoiselle de la Fayette, therefore, Caussin and his Order descried the antidote to the heretical policy of France ; and a source by which peace with Spain, and the Empire might be achieved. The Queen's household was a very focus of intrigue ; every person appertaining thereto adhered to one of the factions of the Queen, the Cardinal, or la Fayette. Mademoiselle de Polignac, governess of the maids, the Duc de St.

Simon, Madame de la Flotte, *dame d'atours*, Mademoiselle de Chémerault, Mademoiselle de Filandre, head-dresser to her Majesty, Sanguin, chief *maître d'hôtel*, and others, were the hidden spies of Richelieu, who held in his pay even the very scullions of the royal kitchen.

The Queen herself was hostile to la Fayette, and desired her exile from court; though, since the marriage of Monsieur, a marked change had come over her Majesty, who seemed now to be less the opponent of Richelieu personally, but rather disaffected, on account of his warlike designs upon her brother, Don Philip of Spain. Madame de Senécé, and the Bishop of Limoges, befriended la Fayette, and did all in their power to induce her to relinquish her monastic resolves, and to accept the position of state and influence opening to her. The King was in the habit of sending his written communications to Mademoiselle de la Fayette by one Boiszenval, his first *valet de chambre*. This Boiszenval had been raised from the subordinate service of a *valet de garde robe* by the favour of Louise; who had obtained for him promotion, in the hope of securing one faithful attendant not seduced by the benefits of M. le Ministre. Richelieu, however, soon contrived to lure Boiszenval from his allegiance to a lady, whom the Cardinal assured him was on the eve of withdrawing from

the world ; and whose favour could be but temporarily exerted in his behalf.   Partly intimidated by
the half-uttered threat of the minister, and partly
prompted by self-interested motives, Boiszenval sold
himself to the Cardinal.   Whenever, therefore, he
was intrusted with a note by the King to carry to
la Fayette, Boiszenval took it straight to Richelieu ;
who first perused, and then, by the aid of his experts
in imitating handwriting, caused the letters to be
copied again, altering any profession, or statement
therein which displeased him.*   The same method
he pursued with regard to verbal messages interchanged between the lovers, which the Cardinal suppressed altogether, or moulded to suit his purpose.
For some little time this duplicity succeeded; until
one day Boiszenval, with unparalleled insolence, said
to Mademoiselle de la Fayette, on presenting her
with a billet from the King, "If you are sincere,
Madame, in your design to become a nun, do so
without delay : this probation is too tantalising to
his Majesty!"   Such words naturally roused suspicion ; and, upon comparing notes, the King and
la Fayette discovered how they had been deceived.
A few days subsequently Louis suddenly addressed

* Siri, Mémoire Recondite, t. 4 ; L'Espion, Turc. t. 4 (written by one
Paolo Marana) ; Dreux du Radier, t. 6 ; Vie de Mademoiselle de la
Fayette.

Boiszenval, who was performing his functions at the *lever* of his Majesty, when the royal chamber was crowded with courtiers. "Boiszenval," said the King, "I have discovered that you are a consummate traitor. I therefore dismiss you. Go! Never presume to present yourself in my presence again."[*] Boiszenval retired: his patron, the Cardinal, dared not interfere; or, perhaps deemed it more politic not to interpose when Louis was roused into so unusual an exercise of decision. Meantime Caussin took every opportunity to ingratiate himself with Mademoiselle de la Fayette; and one day, when the Queen was leaving the chapel at St. Germain, she approached him timidly, saying, "Reverend Father, I wish, if possible, to speak with you." Caussin excused himself from an immediate interview, and fixed four o'clock in the afternoon for the conference. During the interval he saw the King, and asked his Majesty's permission to confer with a lady of the household, whose name he pretended not to know. "Ah!" said his Majesty, "it was la Fayette. She wishes to consult you on the design she has long entertained of going into a nunnery. Yes; I consent to the conference." Caussin, therefore, held a long consultation with Mademoiselle

---

[*] Siri, t. 8; Dreux du Radier, t 6; Le Père Griffet, t. 3; Hist. de Louis XIII.

de la Fayette, in the presence of Mademoiselle de Polignac, who having been secretly bribed by Richelieu, took notes of the conference which ensued. La Fayette then said, that she was resolved to enter a nunnery; that God called her to that vocation; that she prayed the reverend father to dispose the mind of the King to permit her retreat; that she was miserable, and had scruples on her *liaison* with the King; and was wearied with the envy and hate of malignant personages. Caussin, thereupon, represented the privations and hardships of a nun; and asked the pertinent question, "whether she had a true call, and was not lured thereto by worldly chagrin, and by the representations of interested personages?" La Fayette replied with tears, "that in her early youth a religious life had been her election; that she wished now to enter as a novice the Convent of La Visitation des Filles de Ste Marie; that she should quit the world without bitterness, or regret; and that she requested the reverend father to broach the subject to the King, which was the object of the interview which she had requested." * Caussin, therefore, honestly performed the task imposed upon him. Louis heard him in gloomy despair. "Although," replied his Majesty, "I regret and deplore her decision, yet I dare not hinder

* Griffet, t. 3.

her vocation. Nevertheless, tell her to wait until my departure to join my army. Meantime, consult Madame de Senécé on the subject—I leave all to her."

Madame de Senécé, when appealed to by Caussin, as the King doubtless anticipated, absolutely refused her assent to the project; and insisted that letters should be despatched to the father and mother of la Fayette, Monsieur and Madame de Hautefeuille, who alone, she averred, could grant the desired permission. The answer was many months in arriving: the jealous agonies of the Cardinal became intense; and he bitterly reproached Caussin for his lukewarm zeal. "I feared to render myself obnoxious, and so to defeat my purpose, by a show of too much zeal," answered the discreet Jesuit. Richelieu turned away with a wrathful gesture; and forthwith charged le Père Carré to examine and report on the condition of la Fayette's mind, and to insinuate himself, if possible, into her confidence.[*] The subterfuge failed: Louise made one confession to Carré, and then refused to open her mind further to the stern Dominican; who, if he failed, in obtaining her confidence, at any rate served the Cardinal's purpose by maintaining, through other ladies of the palace, his penitents, the most rigid *surveillance* over her

* Le Père Griffet, t. 3 ; Mém. de Motteville, t. 1.

conduct. The curious letters of Carré addressed to the Cardinal still exist in the French Foreign Office —every little incident, every insignificant remark, every vacillation of mind relating to the poor girl whom it was Richelieu's purpose to coerce, were there recorded. Carré, at the beginning of the year 1636, writes to his patron :*—"I address your Eminence, in much depression, on account of the danger which besets the vocation of Mademoiselle de la Fayette. M. de Limoges, Madame de Senécé, and M. le Chevalier de la Fayette, uncle of the said lady, came to call upon me this morning between the hours of nine, and ten o'clock. All three attacked me furiously—M. de Limoges † by angry argument and abuse, Madame de Senécé by bitter reproaches, and M. le Chevalier by atrocious insinuations—all because they said that I had plotted, and negotiated the retreat of their niece into a convent. They asked me why I so acted, and why I had not consulted them ? I replied that my conscience forbade me to take counsel of persons interested, as they were, in the result ; upon which they poured more abuse on my head, and gave me a formal interdiction, as they said, on behalf of the Queen not to meddle

* Cousin, Vie de Madame de Hautefort, Appendix sur Mademoiselle de la Fayette ; Archives des Affaires Étrangères, France, t. 78, fol. 63.

† "L'oncle espérait pour moins obtenir un chapeau par le moyen de la petite."

with the conscience of a lady of her household;
and forbade me, on their own responsibility, to interfere with their niece. So behold me, Monseigneur,
in despair, at being quite powerless to forward the
good work, unless your Eminence assists me!" Carré
goes on to relate that he had called upon the abbess
of Ste Marie, who promised to receive the young
postulant, upon the responsibility of Carré alone.
In the evening, Carré accidentally exchanged a few
words with la Fayette, and exhorted her to retire
without further parley, and to address letters of
farewell from the convent to the King, to the Cardinal, and to her own relatives ; also, if she so desired, to the Queen. Mademoiselle de la Fayette
then remarked, " that was unnecessary, as the Queen
would rejoice at her retreat." The following month,
la petite was still at court, and threw fresh alarm
into the mind of Richelieu's zealous agent—who
was regarded as the most holy, and devoted of men
—by stopping the reverend father, whom she encountered in the apartment of Madame de la
Flotte, to inform him, " that her relatives, and the
King forbade her retreat ; and threatened, if she
entered a convent, to take her thence by edict of
Parliament, as being under age." "I replied,"
writes Carré, " that she need be under no apprehen-
sion, for that your Eminence would protect her.

I then asked her what her own wishes were? She replied, in a labyrinth of words, ' that in a few years she might feel better assured of her vocation.' I said, that two supreme reasons induced me earnestly to desire her immediate retreat : the first was, the salvation of her soul ; the second, the welfare of Christendom, by the conclusion of peace, which good work, the reverend General of our order commanded me to forward ; but that it was not probable that the King of Spain would consent to lay down arms, while he knew that our holy and good King loved any other woman except his wife, sister of his Catholic Majesty, although he might be aware of the purity, and innocency of such attachment. It was my opinion, therefore. that all conscientious persons should contribute toward so merciful an object." * Another day Carré writes to the Cardinal to inform him that Mademoiselle Thomassin† told him that la Fayette was suffering from agonies of indecision ; that she feared the King's passion, and shuddered at the thought of involving his Majesty in mortal sin ; that she dreaded the resentment of the Cardinal ; and even feared that some personal catastrophe would befall her—indeed,

* Archives des Affaires Étrangères, France, t. 78, fol. 124.
† Mademoiselle Thomassin was a dresser in the service of Anne of Austria.

every little vexatious incident was now interpreted
by *la petite* as a sign of Divine wrath at her
indecision ;—" for instance, this morning la Fayette
came into my apartment," said Thomassin, " and
said that God drew her towards a religious life, by
inflicting upon her countless little mortifications : she
then showed me a little pimple which had appeared
on her right cheek during the night, ' a sign,' she said,
' that God is displeased at my delay.' " *   Richelieu
caused it to be intimated to la Fayette that she
should become a benefactress to any convent she
might select, by presenting the community with
30,000 francs.   Never was there a more zealous ex-
ponent than Carré of the minister's wishes: the more
difficult the enterprise, the more important did it appear to Richelieu to separate Louis from his mistress.

Caussin, meantime, prompted by the wishes of the
King, if not by his direct commands, did all in his
power to induce la Fayette to delay the commencement
of her noviciate.   He represented to her, in glowing
language, the hardships to which she was desirous to
submit.   Even when she had taken her final resolution to abandon the thorny path of intrigue, and of
a vain wrestling with the inexorable mind which ruled
France, Caussin's earnest counsel followed her :—

* Archives des Affaires Étrangères, France, t. 78, fol. 150, quoted from
M. Cousin, Appendix, Vie de Madame de Hautefort.

"What! will you quit the court, a King who esteems you, and brilliant prospects, to take the veil, and bury yourself between four walls! There are only too many unhappy women, who have thrown themselves into convents without due reflection; and will you, Madame, increase the number? You do not know what it is to relinquish your judgment, to abandon your will, and to live by, and at the dictation of strangers, who will not permit you to dispose of a pin without their sanction! You have been as a bird of paradise at court, fed with amber and cinnamon; you have heard nothing but praise. compliments. and adulation. Greatly amazed, therefore, will you feel, when a heavy cross is laid on your shoulders, and you are hurried up the steep path to Calvary. If you were an old woman, desirous to give your last days to penitent repentance, no one would feel surprised at your resolve; but for a young girl of seventeen years old, good and innocent, to fly from a King to entomb herself in a prison, surpasses belief! The conversation of the King. has it ever offended you, and evoked scruples? Are you not pure as when you first attracted his regard? You know his Majesty too well to feel apprehensive that he will ever ask from you anything which the law of God forbids you to grant. I advise you, therefore, stay with the King, and do all the good you can through him, as God has been pleased to endow you with such power over his Majesty's mind."* Distracted thus by opposite counsels, Mademoiselle de la Fayette fell ill under the conflict: grave scruples of conscience tormented her; but though she pitied and admired Louis XIII., she had no confidence in his faithful support. She knew that the King could hide nothing from his minister; and that their most secret confidences he often disclosed, especially, if she had in any respect assailed the policy, or the character of Richelieu. It was a point of honour and habit with the King to repeat to Richelieu every inimical speech. La Fayette could never be sure that the King would not denounce, and then retire with her to weep and bewail Richelieu's tyranny! "Louis XIII.," said le Père Caussin, "refrains from expressing all he feels: he does not all that he wills, and wills not all that he can!" But with support so precarious, la Fayette might well shrink from continuing to brave the hostility of the minister, against which not one of the King's near kindred could prevail.

In the early part of May, 1637, Mademoiselle de la Fayette, therefore, took her final resolve. One morning, when the court was at St. Germain, she presented herself before the King, and asked his

* Mém. de Richelieu. t. x.

permission to make an excursion to Paris to see the
abbess of the Visitandines, of the Rue St. Antoine.
Louis wept, but consented ; laying, however, strict
commands that she should return to St. Germain by
a given hour. Accompanied by Madame de Senécé,
Mademoiselle de la Fayette had an interview with
the abbess, who agreed to receive her as a novice, at
any moment. No further opposition was encountered
from Madame de Senécé, who had been silenced by a
threat conveyed to her by Carré.* "that if she sought
again to dissuade Mademoiselle de la Fayette from
the resolve which it had taken so long to render
active, her own exile from court would ensue." The
evident displeasure, and impatience of Queen Anne,
moreover, had due weight with her lady of honour;
and so la Fayette was sacrificed to expediency, and
to the will of the Cardinal. To the reluctant Caussin
was intrusted the mission of obtaining the final assent
of King Louis. "It is true," said the King, "that she
is very dear to me. God help me! but if a religious
life is her vocation, let her depart! I consent."
The same evening. la Fayette appeared for the last
time in the royal circle. Louis drew her apart,
and conversed for some time. everybody present

* Louis XIII. had no very elevated opinion of the capacity of the
zealous Dominican. "Le bon Père Carré." said his Majesty one day,
"est un de ces saints qu'on gagne aisément dès qu'on a bien doré une
chapelle."

remarking on the extreme pallor of the King. In the presence of the court, she then thanked the King for his permission, which enabled her to "fulfil the dearest wish of her life." "Go, Madame," replied Louis, scarcely master of his emotion. "God calls you: it is not for man to oppose His will. My authority would have sufficed to assure your continued residence here, for I could have forbidden every abbess in the realm to receive you ! Nevertheless, I appreciate the excellency and privilege of so holy a life; and, in my last hour, God forbid that my conscience should be burdened with the thought that I had deprived you of so precious a vocation !" Louise then said farewell to her royal mistress— "*qui ne la pouvait aimer.*" Anne coldly smiled.* "The only bitterness of departure," exclaimed Louise afterwards, "is the joy and triumph of my enemies !" La Fayette then retired to the apartment of the Countess de Fleix, daughter of Madame de Senéce. A fit of hysterical weeping relieved her overstrained feelings, during which the coach of the King drew up under the archway of the quadrangle ; for Louis, in bitter affliction, insisted on leaving St. Germain for a retirement, of some days, at Versailles. "Alas, alas ! I shall never see him

* Mém. de Motteville : Griffet, Règne de Louis XIII. ; Dreux du Radier, t. 6.

again !" exclaimed Mademoiselle de la Fayette, as she watched the departure, by torchlight, of the *cortège*. At dawn, Louise, attended by Madame de Senécé, and by three of the Queen's maidens, departed for the Convent of the Visitation, Rue St. Antoine ; and was received, with great honour and parade, by the abbess, who was a Séguier, and niece of the new Lord-Keeper of the Seals, and of the Bishop of Meaux.*

The King, meantime, on his arrival at Versailles, took to his bed, and refused, during two days, to grant audiences. On the third day, it was suggested by M. de St. Simon, "that his Majesty need not longer deprive himself of the pleasure of seeing Mademoiselle de la Fayette, as all the convents opened their portals to the King of France." Louis rose eagerly, and with his own hand wrote to the abbess of the Visitandines, that he should visit the convent on the morrow, to have an interview with Mademoiselle de la Fayette. On the arrival of his Majesty, he encountered, to his surprise, M. de Noyers, the confidential friend of the minister. The King sharply enquired his business ; and was informed that M. de Noyers had been commissioned to confer with the abbess on the payment of the dowry of the novice. Louis was then solaced by the sight of la

* Mém. de Motteville ; Grillet, Règne de Louis XIII. ; Dreux du Radier, t. 6.

Fayette, with whom he conversed for three hours in the convent *parloir*, while his suite waited without the gate. "He was so moved by the description given him by la Fayette of the joys and peace of the monastic state, that his Majesty afterwards confessed to le Père Caussin, that but for his duty to his realm, he would willingly follow her example." This interview was followed by many more during the next two months, before the departure of the King for his camp in Picardy. "*La cabale de Mademoiselle de la Fayette subsiste toujours!*" was the mournful comment of Chavigny to the Cardinal de la Valette, generalissimo of the army in Italy. From her retreat Louise dared to speak openly to the King on politics; and pathetically deplored "those great crimes," as she termed them, of his reign—the exile of the Queen-mother; and the alliance of France with the Protestants of Germany, against the orthodox, and Catholic monarchs of Austria, and Spain. She described Richelieu as a man, unscrupulous and relentless in his hatred, unmeasured in his ambition, and who, sooner or later, must, from motives of self-interest, and the lust of power, separate his lot from that of the childless King, and join the faction of the heir-presumptive. She made touching allusion to the fragility of the health of the King, which at any moment might fail; and she implored him to listen

to the enlightened counsel of le Père Caussin, his
spiritual director, and a personage also of great
political *savoir*. In the privacy of the confessional,
Louis was assailed by the same entreaties. The
sombre, and even menacing aspect of the King,
meanwhile, greatly disturbed the Cardinal : he
therefore summoned Caussin ; and asked, upon what
the interviews between the King and la Fayette
turned, as every one was surprised to see a great
King interest himself in the fate, and caprices of an
insignificant little girl ? Caussin skilfully dissembled ;
but said that the King was disquieted by reports,
that his Eminence intended to cause Mademoiselle
de la Fayette to be carried off secretly, and immured
in a dismal house—an offshoot of the Visitandines
of Paris, situated in the wilds of Auvergne. " Ah,
Monsieur," continued Caussin, " cease to trouble
yourself about this *petite demoiselle*. What can you
fear ? Mademoiselle de la Fayette is only a child."
" *Doucement, mon père*," retorted Richelieu, ironically ;
" you are simple, if not evil-minded, I perceive!
Let me enlighten you, and expose the malice of the
world. Know that this child, as you term her, has
been near overthrowing all.* Let her take the veil

* Cousin, Vie de Madame de Hautefort, Bibl. Imp. Val. 73, 74, MS.
" Le Cardinal m'a dit que quand le Roi eut été trois jours sans voir la
Fayette il seroit guéri, que je ne pouvais ignorer ce que disoit St.
Jérôme, qu'il falloit passer sur le corps de son père, pour courir à

and occupy herself with her breviary. The King
complains that she has entered a nunnery : it is
her own fault. Have you not often told me that she
complained of his Majesty's eccentric, and unequal
temper ; and that the fear of sudden disgrace made
her take the resolve to profess ? " Richelieu then,
according to the relation of Caussin himself, proposed a strict alliance, averring that all other con-
fessors of the King had lived in confidential intercourse with him, and that, if Caussin would support
on all occasions his policy, he might command any
favour for himself, for his order, or for his kinsmen.
The wily Jesuit made cautious reply to these overtures ; but the cold indifference of Caussin's manner
convinced his Eminence that his sophistry had then
failed to gain so important an ally, as the director of
the conscience of King Louis.

l'etendard de la croix. Je lui aurois pu dire," adds Caussin, "que le Saint-
Esprit ne se prend pas à coups de canon ; mais je lui dis seulement
que si j'eusse pressé davantage, j'aurois tout gâté."

 END OF VOL. I.

www.ingramcontent.com/pod-product-compliance
Lightning Source LLC
Chambersburg PA
CBHW032014120726
47902CB00013B/916